Praise for beloved romance author Betty Neels

"Neels is especially good at painting her scenes with choice words, and this adds to the charm of the story."
—USATODAY.com's *Happy Ever After* blog on *Tulips for Augusta*

"Betty Neels surpasses herself with an excellent storyline, a hearty conflict and pleasing characters."
—*RT Book Reviews* on *The Right Kind of Girl*

"Once again Betty Neels delights readers with a sweet tale in which love conquers all."
—*RT Book Reviews* on *Fate Takes a Hand*

"One of the first Harlequin authors I remember reading. I was completely enthralled by the exotic locales… Her books will always be some of my favorites to re-read."
—*Goodreads* on *A Valentine for Daisy*

"I just love Betty Neels!… If you like a good old-fashioned romance…you can't go wrong with this author."
—*Goodreads* on *Caroline's Waterloo*

Romance readers around the world were sad to note the passing of **Betty Neels** in June 2001. Her career spanned thirty years, and she continued to write into her ninetieth year. To her millions of fans, Betty epitomized the romance writer, and yet she began writing almost by accident. She had retired from nursing, but her inquiring mind still sought stimulation. Her new career was born when she heard a lady in her local library bemoaning the lack of good romance novels. Betty's first book, *Sister Peters in Amsterdam*, was published in 1969, and she eventually completed 134 books. Her novels offer a reassuring warmth that was very much a part of her own personality. She was a wonderful writer, and she is greatly missed. Her spirit and genuine talent live on in all her stories.

BETTY NEELS

Always and Forever
& An Independent Woman

HARLEQUIN® SPECIAL RELEASE

ISBN-13: 978-1-335-00785-8

Always and Forever & An Independent Woman

Copyright © 2019 by Harlequin Books S.A.

The publisher acknowledges the copyright holder of the individual works as follows:

Always and Forever
Copyright © 2001 by Betty Neels

An Independent Woman
Copyright © 2001 by Betty Neels

Recycling programs for this product may not exist in your area.

This edition published by arrangement with Harlequin Books S.A.

For questions and comments about the quality of this book, please contact us at CustomerService@Harlequin.com.

® and TM are trademarks of Harlequin Enterprises Limited or its corporate affiliates. Trademarks indicated with ® are registered in the United States Patent and Trademark Office, the Canadian Intellectual Property Office and in other countries.

Printed in U.S.A.

www.Harlequin.com

CONTENTS

ALWAYS AND FOREVER   7

AN INDEPENDENT WOMAN   205

ALWAYS AND FOREVER

Chapter 1

There was going to be a storm; the blue sky of a summer evening was slowly being swallowed by black clouds, heavy with rain and thunder, flashing warning signals of flickering lightning over the peaceful Dorset countryside, casting gloom over the village. The girl gathering a line of washing from the small orchard behind the house standing on the village outskirts paused to study the sky before lugging the washing basket through the open door at the back of the house.

She was a small girl, nicely plump, with a face which, while not pretty, was redeemed by fine brown eyes. Her pale brown hair was gathered in an untidy bunch on the top of her head and she was wearing a cotton dress which had seen better days.

She put the basket down, closed the door and went

in search of candles and matches, then put two old-fashioned oil lamps on the wooden table. If the storm was bad there would be a power cut before the evening was far advanced.

This done to her satisfaction, she poked up the elderly Aga, set a kettle to boil and turned her attention to the elderly dog and battle-scarred old tomcat, waiting patiently for their suppers.

She got their food, talking while she did so because the eerie quiet before the storm broke was a little unnerving, and then made tea and sat down to drink it as the first heavy drops of rain began to fall.

With the rain came a sudden wind which sent her round the house shutting windows against the deluge. Back in the kitchen, she addressed the dog.

'Well, there won't be anyone coming now,' she told him, and gave a small shriek as lightning flashed and thunder drowned out any other sound. She sat down at the table and he came and sat beside her, and, after a moment, the cat got onto her lap.

The wind died down as suddenly as it had arisen but the storm was almost overhead. It had become very dark and the almost continuous flashes made it seem even darker. Presently the light over the table began to flicker; she prudently lit a candle before it went out.

She got up then, lighted the lamps and took one into the hall before sitting down again. There was nothing to do but to wait until the storm had passed.

The lull was shattered by a peal on the doorbell, so unexpected that she sat for a moment, not quite believing it. But a second prolonged peal sent her to the door, lamp in hand.

A man stood in the porch. She held the lamp high in order to get a good look at him; he was a very large man, towering over her.

'I saw your sign. Can you put us up for the night? I don't care to drive further in this weather.'

He had a quiet voice and he looked genuine. 'Who's we?' she asked.

'My mother and myself.'

She slipped the chain off the door. 'Come in.' She peered round him. 'Is that your car?'

'Yes—is there a garage?'

'Go round the side of the house; there's a barn—the door's open. There's plenty of room there.'

He nodded and turned back to the car to open its door and help his mother out. Ushering them into the hall, the girl said, 'Come back in through the kitchen door; I'll leave it unlocked. It's across the yard from the barn.'

He nodded again, a man of few words, she supposed, and he went outside. She turned to look at her second guest. The woman was tall, good-looking, in her late fifties, she supposed, and dressed with understated elegance.

'Would you like to see your room? And would you like a meal? It's a bit late to cook dinner but you could have an omelette or scrambled eggs and bacon with tea or coffee?'

The older woman put out a hand. 'Mrs Fforde—spelt with two ffs, I'm afraid. My son's a doctor; he was driving me to the other side of Glastonbury, taking a short-cut, but driving had become impossible. Your sign was like something from heaven.' She had to raise her voice against the heavenly din.

The girl offered a hand. 'Amabel Parsons. I'm sorry you had such a horrid journey.'

'I hate storms, don't you? You're not alone in the house?'

'Well, yes, I am, but I have Cyril—that's my dog—and Oscar the cat.' Amabel hesitated. 'Would you like to come into the sitting room until Dr Fforde comes? Then you can decide if you would like something to eat. I'm afraid you will have to go to bed by candlelight…'

She led the way down the hall and into a small room, comfortably furnished with easy chairs and a small round table. There were shelves of books on either side of the fireplace and a large window across which Amabel drew the curtains before setting the lamp on the table.

'I'll unlock the kitchen door,' she said and hurried back to the kitchen just in time to admit the doctor.

He was carrying two cases. 'Shall I take these up?'

'Yes, please. I'll ask Mrs Fforde if she would like to go to her room now. I asked if you would like anything to eat…'

'Most emphatically yes. That's if it's not putting you to too much trouble. Anything will do—sandwiches…'

'Omelettes, scrambled eggs, bacon and eggs? I did explain to Mrs Fforde that it's too late to cook a full meal.'

He smiled down at her. 'I'm sure Mother is longing

for a cup of tea, and omelettes sound fine.' He glanced round him. 'You're not alone?'

'Yes,' said Amabel. 'I'll take you upstairs.'

She gave them the two rooms at the front of the house and pointed out the bathroom. 'Plenty of hot water,' she added, before going back to the kitchen.

When they came downstairs presently she had the table laid in the small room and offered them omelettes, cooked to perfection, toast and butter and a large pot of tea. This had kept her busy, but it had also kept her mind off the storm, still raging above their heads. It rumbled away finally in the small hours, but by the time she had cleared up the supper things and prepared the breakfast table, she was too tired to notice.

She was up early, but so was Dr Fforde. He accepted the tea she offered him before he wandered out of the door into the yard and the orchard beyond, accompanied by Cyril. He presently strolled back to stand in the doorway and watch her getting their breakfast.

Amabel, conscious of his steady gaze, said briskly, 'Would Mrs Fforde like breakfast in bed? It's no extra trouble.'

'I believe she would like that very much. I'll have mine with you here.'

'Oh, you can't do that.' She was taken aback. 'I mean, your breakfast is laid in the sitting room. I'll bring it to you whenever you're ready.'

'I dislike eating alone. If you put everything for Mother on a tray I'll carry it up.'

He was friendly in a casual way, but she guessed that he was a man who disliked arguing. She got a tray ready, and when he came downstairs again and sat down at the kitchen table she put a plate of bacon, eggs and mushrooms in front of him, adding toast and marmalade before pouring the tea.

'Come and sit down and eat your breakfast and tell me why you live here alone,' he invited. He sounded so like an elder brother or a kind uncle that she did so, watching him demolish his breakfast with evident enjoyment before loading a slice of toast with butter and marmalade.

She had poured herself a cup of tea, but whatever he said she wasn't going to eat her breakfast with him...

He passed her the slice of toast. 'Eat that up and tell me why you live alone.'

'Well, really!' began Amabel and then, meeting his kindly look, added, 'It's only for a month or so. My mother's gone to Canada,' she told him. 'My married sister lives there and she's just had a baby. It was such a good opportunity for her to go. You see, in the summer we get quite a lot of people coming just for bed and breakfast, like you, so I'm not really alone. It's different in the winter, of course.'

He asked, 'You don't mind being here by yourself? What of the days—and nights—when no one wants bed and breakfast?'

She said defiantly, 'I have Cyril, and Oscar's splendid company. Besides, there's the phone.'

'And your nearest neighbour?' he asked idly.

'Old Mrs Drew, round the bend in the lane going to the village. Also, it's only half a mile to the village.' She still sounded defiant.

He passed his cup for more tea. Despite her brave words he suspected that she wasn't as self-assured as she would have him believe. A plain girl, he considered, but nice eyes, nice voice and apparently not much interest in clothes; the denim skirt and cotton blouse were crisp and spotless, but could hardly be called fashionable. He glanced at her hands, which were small and well shaped, bearing signs of housework.

He said, 'A lovely morning after the storm. That's a pleasant orchard you have beyond the yard. And a splendid view…'

'Yes, it's splendid all the year round.'

'Do you get cut off in the winter?'

'Yes, sometimes. Would you like more tea?'

'No, thank you. I'll see if my mother is getting ready to leave.' He smiled at her. 'That was a delicious meal.' But not, he reflected, a very friendly one. Amabel Parsons had given him the strong impression that she wished him out of the house.

Within the hour he and his mother had gone, driving away in the dark blue Rolls-Royce. Amabel stood in the open doorway, watching it disappear round the bend in the lane. It had been providential, she told herself, that they should have stopped at the house at the height of the storm; they had kept her busy and she hadn't had the time to be frightened. They had been no trouble— and she needed the money.

It would be nice, she thought wistfully, to have someone like Dr Fforde as a friend. Sitting at breakfast with him, she'd had an urgent desire to talk to him, tell him how lonely she was, and sometimes a bit scared, how

tired she was of making up beds and getting breakfast
for a succession of strangers, keeping the place going
until her mother returned, and all the while keeping
up the façade of an independent and competent young
woman perfectly able to manage on her own.

That was necessary, otherwise well-meaning people
in the village would have made it their business to dis-
suade her mother from her trip and even suggest that
Amabel should shut up the house and go and stay with
a great-aunt she hardly knew, who lived in Yorkshire
and who certainly wouldn't want her.

Amabel went back into the house, collected up the
bedlinen and made up the beds again; hopefully there
would be more guests later in the day...

She readied the rooms, inspected the contents of the
fridge and the deep freeze, hung out the washing and
made herself a sandwich before going into the orchard
with Cyril and Oscar. They sat, the three of them, on
an old wooden bench, nicely secluded from the lane but
near enough to hear if anyone called.

Which they did, just as she was on the point of going
indoors for her tea.

The man on the doorstep turned round impatiently
as she reached him.

'I rang twice. I want bed and breakfast for my wife,
son and daughter.'

Amabel turned to look at the car. There was a young
man in the driver's seat, and a middle-aged woman and
a girl sitting in the back.

'Three rooms? Certainly. But I must tell you that

there is only one bathroom, although there are hand-basins in the rooms.'

He said rudely, 'I suppose that's all we can expect in this part of the world. We took a wrong turning and landed ourselves here, at the back of beyond. What do you charge? And we do get a decent breakfast?'

Amabel told him, 'Yes.' As her mother frequently reminded her, it took all sorts to make the world.

The three people in the car got out: a bossy woman, the girl pretty but sulky, and the young man looking at her in a way she didn't like…

They inspected their rooms with loud-voiced comments about old-fashioned furniture and no more than one bathroom—and that laughably old-fashioned. And they wanted tea: sandwiches and scones and cake. 'And plenty of jam,' the young man shouted after her as she left the room.

After tea they wanted to know where the TV was.

'I haven't got a television.'

They didn't believe her. 'Everyone has a TV set,' complained the girl. 'Whatever are we going to do this evening?'

'The village is half a mile down the lane,' said Amabel. 'There's a pub there, and you can get a meal, if you wish.'

'Better than hanging around here.'

It was a relief to see them climb back into the car and drive off presently. She laid the table for their breakfast and put everything ready in the kitchen before getting herself some supper. It was a fine light evening, so she strolled into the orchard and sat down on the bench.

Dr Fforde and his mother would be at Glastonbury, she
supposed, staying with family or friends. He would be
married, of course, to a pretty girl with lovely clothes—
there would be a small boy and a smaller girl, and they
would live in a large and comfortable house; he was
successful, for he drove a Rolls-Royce…

Conscious that she was feeling sad, as well as wasting her time, she went back indoors and made out the
bill; there might not be time in the morning.

She was up early the next morning; breakfast was
to be ready by eight o'clock, she had been told on the
previous evening—a decision she'd welcomed with relief. Breakfast was eaten, the bill paid—but only after
double-checking everything on it and some scathing
comments about the lack of modern amenities.

Amabel waited politely at the door until they had
driven away then went to put the money in the old tea
caddy on the kitchen dresser. It added substantially to
the contents but it had been hard earned!

The rooms, as she'd expected, had been left in a dis-
graceful state. She flung open the window, stripped
beds and set about turning them back to their usual pristine appearance. It was still early, and it was a splendid
morning, so she filled the washing machine and started
on the breakfast dishes.

By midday everything was just as it should be. She
made sandwiches and took them and a mug of coffee
out to the orchard with Cyril and Oscar for company,
and sat down to read the letter from her mother the postman had brought. Everything was splendid, she wrote.
The baby was thriving and she had decided to stay an-

other few weeks, if Amabel could manage for a little longer—*For I don't suppose I'll be able to visit here for a year or two, unless something turns up.*

Which was true enough, and it made sense too. Her mother had taken out a loan so that she could go to Canada, and even though it was a small one it would have to be paid off before she went again.

Amabel put the letter in her pocket, divided the rest of her sandwich between Cyril and Oscar and went back into the house. There was always the chance that someone would come around teatime and ask for a meal, so she would make a cake and a batch of scones.

It was as well that she did; she had just taken them out of the Aga when the doorbell rang and two elderly ladies enquired if she would give them bed and breakfast.

They had come in an old Morris, and, while wellspoken and tidily dressed, she judged them to be not too free with their money. But they looked nice and she had a kind heart.

'If you would share a twin-bedded room?' she suggested. 'The charge is the same for two people as one.' She told them how much and added, 'Two breakfasts, of course, and if you would like tea?'

They glanced at each other. 'Thank you. Would you serve us a light supper later?'

'Certainly. If you would fetch your cases? The car can go into the barn at the side of the house.'

Amabel gave them a good tea, and while they went for a short walk, she got supper—salmon fish cakes, of tinned salmon, of course, potatoes whipped to a satiny smoothness, and peas from the garden. She popped an egg custard into the oven by way of afters and was rewarded by their genteel thanks.

She ate her own supper in the kitchen, took them a pot of tea and wished them goodnight. In the morning she gave them boiled eggs, toast and marmalade and a pot of coffee, and all with a generous hand.

She hadn't made much money, but it had been nice to see their elderly faces light up. And they had left her a tip, discreetly put on one of the bedside tables. As for the bedroom, they had left it so neat it was hard to see that anyone had been in it.

She added the money to the tea caddy and decided that tomorrow she would go to the village and pay it into the post office account, stock up on groceries and get meat from the butcher's van which called twice a week at the village.

It was a lovely morning again, and her spirits rose despite her disappointment at her mother's delayed return home. She wasn't doing too badly with bed and breakfast, and she was adding steadily to their savings. There were the winter months to think of, of course, but she might be able to get a part-time job once her mother was home.

She went into the garden to pick peas, singing cheerfully and slightly off key.

Nobody came that day, and the following day only a solitary woman on a walking holiday came in the early evening; she went straight to bed after a pot of tea and left the next morning after an early breakfast.

After she had gone, Amabel discovered that she had taken the towels with her.

Two disappointing days, reflected Amabel. I wonder what will happen tomorrow?

She was up early again, for there was no point in lying in bed when it was daylight soon after five o'clock. She breakfasted, tidied the house, did a pile of ironing before the day got too hot, and then wandered out to the bench in the orchard. It was far too early for any likely person to want a room, and she would hear if a car stopped in the lane.

But of course one didn't hear a Rolls-Royce, for it made almost no sound.

Dr Fforde got out and stood looking at the house. It was a pleasant place, somewhat in need of small repairs and a lick of paint, but its small windows shone and the brass knocker on its solid front door was burnished to a dazzling brightness. He trod round the side of the house, past the barn, and saw Amabel sitting between Cyril and Oscar. Since she was a girl who couldn't abide being idle, she was shelling peas.

He stood watching her for a moment, wondering why he had wanted to see her again. True, she had interested him, so small, plain and pot valiant, and so obviously terrified of the storm—and very much at the mercy of undesirable characters who might choose to call. Surely she had an aunt or cousin who could come and stay with her?

It was none of his business, of course, but it had seemed a good idea to call and see her since he was on his way to Glastonbury.

He stepped onto the rough gravel of the yard so that she looked up.

She got to her feet, and her smile left him in no doubt that she was glad to see him.

He said easily, 'Good morning. I'm on my way to Glastonbury. Have you quite recovered from the storm?'

'Oh, yes.' She added honestly, 'But I was frightened, you know. I was so very glad when you and your mother came.'

She collected up the colander of peas and came towards him. 'Would you like a cup of coffee?'

'Yes, please.' He followed her into the kitchen and sat down at the table and thought how restful she was; she had seemed glad to see him, but she had probably learned to give a welcoming smile to anyone who knocked on the door. Certainly she had displayed no fuss at seeing him.

He said on an impulse, 'Will you have lunch with me? There's a pub—the Old Boot in Underthorn—fifteen minutes' drive from here. I don't suppose you get any callers before the middle of the afternoon?'

She poured the coffee and fetched a tin of biscuits.

'But you're on your way to Glastonbury…'

'Yes, but not expected until teatime. And it's such a splendid day.' When she hesitated he said, 'We could take Cyril with us.'

She said then, 'Thank you; I should like that. But I must be back soon after two o'clock; it's Saturday…'

They went back to the orchard presently, and sat on the bench while Amabel finished shelling the peas. Oscar had got onto the doctor's knee and Cyril had sprawled under his feet. They talked idly about nothing much and Amabel, quite at her ease, now answered his carefully put questions without realising just how much she was telling him until she stopped in mid-sentence, aware that her tongue was running away with her. He saw that at once and began to talk about something else.

They drove to the Old Boot Inn just before noon and found a table on the rough grass at its back. There was a small river, overshadowed by trees, and since it was early there was no one else there. They ate home-made pork pies with salad, and drank iced lemonade which the landlord's wife made herself. Cyril sat at their feet with a bowl of water and a biscuit.

The landlord, looking at them from the bar window, observed to his wife, 'Look happy, don't they?'

And they were, all three of them, although the doctor hadn't identified his feeling as happiness, merely pleasant content at the glorious morning and the undemanding company.

He drove Amabel back presently and, rather to her surprise, parked the car in the yard behind the house, got out, took the door key from her and unlocked the back door.

Oscar came to meet them and he stooped to stroke him. 'May I sit in the orchard for a little while?' he asked. 'I seldom get the chance to sit quietly in such peaceful surroundings.'

Amabel stopped herself just in time from saying, 'You poor man,' and said instead, 'Of course you may, for as long as you like. Would you like a cup of tea, or an apple?'

So he sat on the bench chewing an apple, with Oscar on his knee, aware that his reason for sitting there was to cast an eye over any likely guests in the hope that before he went a respectable middle-aged pair would have decided to stay.

He was to have his wish. Before very long a middle-aged pair did turn up, with mother-in-law, wishing to stay for two nights. It was absurd, he told himself, that he should feel concern. Amabel was a perfectly capable young woman, and able to look after herself; besides, she had a telephone.

He went to the open kitchen door and found her there, getting tea.

'I must be off,' he told her. 'Don't stop what you're doing. I enjoyed my morning.'

She was cutting a large cake into neat slices. 'So did I. Thank you for my lunch.' She smiled at him. 'Go carefully, Dr Fforde.'

She carried the tea tray into the drawing room and went back to the kitchen. They were three nice people—polite, and anxious not to be too much trouble. 'An evening meal?' they had asked diffidently, and had accepted her offer of jacket potatoes and salad, fruit tart and coffee with pleased smiles. They would go for a short walk presently, the man told her, and when would she like to serve their supper?

When they had gone she made the tart, put the potatoes in the oven and went to the vegetable patch by the orchard to get a lettuce and radishes. There was no hurry, so she sat down on the bench and thought about the day.

She had been surprised to see the doctor again. She had been pleased too. She had thought about him, but she hadn't expected to see him again; when she had looked up and seen him standing there it had been like seeing an old friend.

'Nonsense,' said Amabel loudly. 'He came this morning because he wanted a cup of coffee.' What about taking you out to lunch? asked a persistent voice at the back of her mind.

'He's probably a man who doesn't like to eat alone.'

And, having settled the matter, she went back to the kitchen.

The three guests intended to spend Sunday touring around the countryside. They would return at tea time and could they have supper? They added that they would want to leave early the next morning, which left Amabel with almost all day free to do as she wanted.

There was no need for her to stay at the house; she didn't intend to let the third room if anyone called. She would go to church and then spend a quiet afternoon with the Sunday paper.

She liked going to church, for she met friends and acquaintances and could have a chat, and at the same time assure anyone who asked that her mother would be coming home soon and that she herself was perfectly content on her own. She was aware that some of the older members of the congregation didn't approve of her mother's trip and thought that at the very least some friend or cousin should have moved in with Amabel.

It was something she and her mother had discussed at some length, until her mother had burst into tears, declaring that she wouldn't be able to go to Canada. Amabel had said at once that she would much rather be on her own, so her mother had gone, and Amabel had written her a letter each week, giving light-hearted and slightly optimistic accounts of the bed and breakfast business.

Her mother had been gone for a month now; she had phoned when she had arrived and since then had written regularly, although she still hadn't said when she would be returning.

Amabel, considering the matter while Mr Huggett, the church warden, read the first lesson, thought that her mother's next letter would certainly contain news of her return. Not for the world would she admit, even to herself, that she didn't much care for living on her own. She was, in fact, uneasy at night, even though the house was locked and securely bolted.

She kept a stout walking stick which had belonged to her father by the front door, and a rolling pin handy in the kitchen, and there was always the phone; she had only to lift it and dial 999!

Leaving the church presently, and shaking hands with the vicar, she told him cheerfully that her mother would be home very soon.

'You are quite happy living there alone, Amabel? You have friends to visit you, I expect?'

'Oh, yes,' she assured him. 'And there's so much to keep me busy. The garden and the bed and breakfast people keep me occupied.'

He said with vague kindness, 'Nice people, I hope, my dear?'

'I'm careful who I take,' she assured him.

It was seldom that any guests came on a Monday; Amabel cleaned the house, made up beds and checked the fridge, made herself a sandwich and went to the orchard to eat it. It was a pleasant day, cool and breezy, just right for gardening.

She went to bed quite early, tired with the digging, watering and weeding. Before she went to sleep she allowed her thoughts to dwell on Dr Fforde. He seemed like an old friend, but she knew nothing about him. Was he married? Where did he live? Was he a GP, or working at a hospital? He dressed well and drove a Rolls-Royce, and he had family or friends somewhere on the other side of Glastonbury. She rolled over in bed and closed her eyes. It was none of her business anyway...

The fine weather held and a steady trickle of tourists knocked on the door. The tea caddy was filling up nicely again; her mother would be delighted. The week slid imperceptibly into the next one, and at the end of it there was a letter from her mother. The postman arrived with it at the same time as a party of four—two couples sharing a car on a brief tour—so that Amabel had to put it in her pocket until they had been shown their rooms and had sat down to tea.

She went into the kitchen, got her own tea and sat down to read it.

It was a long letter, and she read it through to the end—and then read it again. She had gone pale, and drank her cooling tea with the air of someone unaware of what they were doing, but presently she picked up the letter and read it for the third time.

Her mother wasn't coming home. At least not for several months. She had met someone and they were to be married shortly.

I know you will understand. And you'll like him. He's a market gardener, and we plan to set up a garden centre from the house. There's plenty of room and he will build a large glasshouse at the bottom of the orchard. Only he must sell his own market garden first, which may take some months.

It will mean that we shan't need to do bed and breakfast any more, although I hope you'll keep on with it until we get back. You're doing so well. I know that the tourist season is quickly over but we hope to be back before Christmas.

The rest of the letter was a detailed description of her husband-to-be and news too, of her sister and the baby.
You're such a sensible girl, her mother concluded, *and I'm sure you're enjoying your independence. Probably when we get back you will want to start a career on your own.*

Amabel was surprised, she told herself, but there was no reason for her to feel as though the bottom had dropped out of her world; she was perfectly content to stay at home until her mother and stepfather should return, and it was perfectly natural for her mother to suppose that she would like to make a career for herself.

Amabel drank the rest of the tea, now stewed and cold. She would have plenty of time to decide what kind of career she would like to have.

That evening, her guests in their rooms, she sat down with pen and paper and assessed her accomplishments. She could cook—not quite cordon bleu, perhaps, but to a high standard—she could housekeep, change plugs, cope with basic plumbing. She could tend a garden… Her pen faltered. There was nothing else.

She had her A levels, but circumstances had never allowed her to make use of them. She would have to train for something and she would have to make up her mind what that should be before her mother came home. But training cost money, and she wasn't sure if there would be any. She could get a job and save enough to train…

She sat up suddenly, struck by a sudden thought. Waitresses needed no training, and there would be tips. In one of the larger towns, of course. Taunton or Yeovil? Or what about one of the great estates run by the National Trust? They had shops and tearooms and house guides. The more she thought about it, the better she liked it.

She went to bed with her decision made. Now it was just a question of waiting until her mother and her stepfather came home.

Chapter 2

It was almost a week later when she had the next letter, but before that her mother had phoned. She was so happy, she'd said excitedly; they planned to marry in October—Amabel didn't mind staying at home until they returned? Probably in November?

'It's only a few months, Amabel, and just as soon as we're home Keith says you must tell us what you want to do and we'll help you do it. He's so kind and generous. Of course if he sells his business quickly we shall come home as soon as we can arrange it.'

Amabel had heard her mother's happy little laugh. 'I've written you a long letter about the wedding. Joyce and Tom are giving a small reception for us, and I've planned such a pretty outfit—it's all in the letter...'

The long letter when it arrived was bursting with excitement and happiness.

You have no idea how delightful it is not to have to worry about the future, to have someone to look after me—you too, of course. Have you decided what you want to do when we get home? You must be so excited at the idea of being independent; you have had such a dull life since you left school...

But a contented one, reflected Amabel. Helping to turn their bed and breakfast business into a success, knowing that she was wanted, feeling that she and her mother were making something of their lives. And now she must start all over again.

It would be nice to wallow in self-pity, but there were two people at the door asking if she could put them up for the night...

Because she was tired she slept all night, although the moment she woke thoughts came tumbling into her head which were better ignored, so she got up earlier than usual and went outside in her dressing gown with a mug of tea and Cyril and Oscar for company.

It was pleasant sitting on the bench in the orchard in the early-morning sun, and in its cheerful light it was impossible to be gloomy. It would be nice, though, to be able to talk to someone about her future...

Dr Fforde's large, calm person came into her mind's eye; he would have listened and told her what she should do. She wondered what he was doing...

* * *

Dr Fforde was sitting on the table in the kitchen of his house, the end one in a short terrace of Regency houses in a narrow street tucked away behind Wimpole Street in London. He was wearing a tee shirt and elderly trousers and badly needed a shave; he had the appearance of a ruffian—a handsome ruffian. There was a half-eaten apple on the table beside him and he was taking great bites from a thick slice of bread and butter. He had been called out just after two o'clock that morning to operate on a patient with a perforated duodenal ulcer; there had been complications which had kept him from his bed and now he was on his way to shower and get ready for his day.

He finished his bread and butter, bent to fondle the sleek head of the black Labrador sitting beside him, and went to the door. It opened as he reached it. The youngish man who came in was already dressed, immaculate in a black alpaca jacket and striped trousers. He had a sharp-nosed foxy face, and dark hair brushed to a satin smoothness.

He stood aside for the doctor and wished him a severe good morning.

'Out again, sir?' His eye fell on the apple core. 'You had only to call me. I'd have got you a nice hot drink and a sandwich...'

The doctor clapped him on the shoulder. 'I know you would, Bates. I'll be down in half an hour for one of your special breakfasts. I disturbed Tiger; would you let him out into the garden?'

He went up the graceful little staircase to his room,

his head already filled with thoughts of the day ahead of him. Amabel certainly had no place in them.

Half an hour later he was eating the splendid breakfast Bates had carried through to the small sitting room at the back of the house. Its French windows opened onto a small patio and a garden beyond where Tiger was meandering round. Presently he came to sit by his master, to crunch bacon rinds and then accompany him on a brisk walk through the still quiet streets before the doctor got into his car and drove the short distance to the hospital.

Amabel saw her two guests on their way, got the room ready for the next occupants and then on a sudden impulse went to the village and bought the regional weekly paper at the post office. Old Mr Truscott, who ran it and knew everyone's business, took his time giving her her change.

'Didn't know you were interested in the *Gazette*, nothing much in it but births, marriages and deaths.' He fixed her with a beady eye. 'And adverts, of course. Now if anyone was looking for a job it's a paper I'd recommend.'

Amabel said brightly, 'I dare say it's widely read, Mr Truscott. While I'm here I'd better have some more air mail letters.'

'Your ma's not coming home yet, then? Been gone a long time, I reckon.'

'She's staying a week or two longer; she might not get the chance to visit my sister again for a year or two. It's a long way to go for just a couple of weeks.'

Over her lunch she studied the jobs page. There were heartening columns of vacancies for waitresses: the basic wage was fairly low, but if she worked full-time she could manage very well… And Stourhead, the famous National Trust estate, wanted shop assistants, help in the tearooms and suitable applicants for full-time work in the ticket office. And none of them were wanted until the end of September.

It seemed too good to be true, but all the same she cut the ad out and put it with the bed and breakfast money in the tea caddy.

A week went by, and then another. Summer was almost over. The evenings were getting shorter, and, while the mornings were light still, there was the ghost of a nip in the air. There had been more letters from Canada from her mother and future stepfather, and her sister, and during the third week her mother had telephoned; they were married already—now it was just a question of selling Keith's business.

'We hadn't intended to marry so soon but there was no reason why we shouldn't, and of course I've moved in with him,' she said. 'So if he can sell his business soon we shall be home before long. We have such plans…!'

There weren't as many people knocking on the door now; Amabel cleaned and polished the house, picked the last of the soft fruit to put in the freezer and cast an eye over the contents of the cupboards.

With a prudent eye to her future she inspected her wardrobe—a meagre collection of garments, bought with an eye to their long-lasting qualities, in good taste but which did nothing to enhance her appearance.

Only a handful of people came during the week, and no one at all on Saturday. She felt low-spirited—owing to the damp and gloomy weather, she told herself—and even a brisk walk with Cyril didn't make her feel any better. It was still only early afternoon and she sat down in the kitchen, with Oscar on her lap, disinclined to do anything.

She would make herself a pot of tea, write to her mother, have an early supper and go to bed. Soon it would be the beginning of another week; if the weather was better there might be a satisfying number of tourists—and besides, there were plenty of jobs to do in the garden. So she wrote her letter, very bright and cheerful, skimming over the lack of guests, making much of the splendid apple crop and how successful the soft fruit had been. That done, she went on sitting at the kitchen table, telling herself that she would make the tea.

Instead of that she sat, a small sad figure, contemplating a future which held problems. Amabel wasn't a girl given to self-pity, and she couldn't remember the last time she had cried, but she cried now, quietly and without fuss, a damp Oscar on her lap, Cyril's head pressed against her legs. She made no attempt to stop; there was no one there to see, and now that the rain was coming down in earnest no one would want to stop for the night.

Dr Fforde had a free weekend, but he wasn't particularly enjoying it. He had lunched on Saturday with friends, amongst whom had been Miriam Potter-Stokes, an elegant young widow who was appearing more and more frequently in his circle of friends. He felt vaguely sorry for her, admired her for the apparently brave face she was showing to the world, and what had been a casual friendship now bid fair to become something more serious—on her part at least.

He had found himself agreeing to drive her down to Henley after lunch, and once there had been forced by good manners to stay at her friend's home for tea. On the way back to London she had suggested that they might have dinner together.

He had pleaded a prior engagement and gone back to his home feeling that his day had been wasted. She was an amusing companion, pretty and well dressed, but he had wondered once or twice what she was really like. Certainly he enjoyed her company from time to time, but that was all...

He took Tiger for a long walk on Sunday morning and after lunch got into his car. It was no day for a drive into the country, and Bates looked his disapproval.

'Not going to Glastonbury in this weather, I hope, sir?' he observed.

'No, no. Just a drive. Leave something cold for my supper, will you?'

Bates looked offended. When had he ever forgotten to leave everything ready before he left the house?

'As always, sir,' he said reprovingly.

It wasn't until he was driving west through the quiet city streets that Dr Fforde admitted to himself that he knew where he was going. Watching the carefully nurtured beauty of Miriam Potter-Stokes had reminded him of Amabel. He had supposed, in some amusement, because the difference in the two of them was so marked. It would be interesting to see her again. Her mother would be back home by now, and he doubted if there were many people wanting bed and breakfast now that summer had slipped into a wet autumn.

He enjoyed driving, and the roads, once he was clear of the suburbs, were almost empty. Tiger was an undemanding companion, and the countryside was restful after the bustle of London streets.

The house, when he reached it, looked forlorn; there were no open windows, no signs of life. He got out of the car with Tiger and walked round the side of the house; he found the back door open.

Amabel looked up as he paused at the door. He thought that she looked like a small bedraggled brown hen. He said, 'Hello, may we come in?' and bent to fondle the two dogs, giving her time to wipe her wet cheeks with the back of her hand. 'Tiger's quite safe with Cyril, and he likes cats.'

Amabel stood up, found a handkerchief and blew her nose. She said in a social kind of voice, 'Do come in. Isn't it an awful day? I expect you're on your way to Glastonbury. Would you like a cup of tea? I was just going to make one.'

'Thank you, that would be nice.' He had come into the kitchen now, reaching up to tickle a belligerent Oscar under the chin. 'I'm sorry Tiger's frightened your cat. I don't suppose there are many people about on a day like this—and your mother isn't back yet?'

She said in a bleak little voice, 'No...' and then to her shame and horror burst into floods of tears.

Dr Fforde sat her down in the chair again. He said comfortably, 'I'll make the tea and you shall tell me all about it. Have a good cry; you'll feel better. Is there any cake?'

Amabel said in a small wailing voice, 'But I've been crying and I don't feel any better.' She gave a hiccough before adding, 'And now I've started again.' She took the large white handkerchief he offered her. 'The cake's in a tin in the cupboard in the corner.'

He put the tea things on the table and cut the cake, found biscuits for the dogs and spooned cat food onto a saucer for Oscar, who was still on top of a cupboard. Then he sat down opposite Amabel and put a cup of tea before her.

'Drink some of that and then tell me why you are crying. Don't leave anything out, for I'm merely a ship which is passing in the night, so you can say what you like and it will be forgotten—rather like having a bag of rubbish and finding an empty dustbin...'

She smiled then. 'You make it sound so—so normal...' She sipped her tea. 'I'm sorry I'm behaving so badly.'

He cut the cake and gave her a piece, before saying matter-of-factly, 'Is your mother's absence the reason? Is she ill?'

'Ill? No, no. She's married someone in Canada...'

It was such a relief to talk to someone about it. It all came tumbling out: a hotch-potch of market gardens, plans for coming back and the need for her to be independent as soon as possible.

He listened quietly, refilling their cups, his eyes on her blotched face, and when she had at last finished her muddled story, he said, 'And now you have told me you feel better about it, don't you? It has all been bottled up inside you, hasn't it? Going round inside your head like butter in a churn. It has been a great shock to you, and shocks should be shared. I won't offer you advice, but I will suggest that you do nothing—make no plans, ignore your future—until your mother is home. I think that you may well find that you have been included in their plans and that you need no worries about your future. I can see that you might like to become independent, but don't rush into it. You're young enough to stay at home while they settle in, and that will give you time to decide what you want to do.'

When she nodded, he added, 'Now, go and put your hair up and wash your face. We're going to Castle Cary for supper.'

She gaped at him. 'I can't possibly...'

'Fifteen minutes should be time enough.'

She did her best with her face, and piled her hair neatly, then got into a jersey dress, which was an off the peg model, but of a pleasing shade of cranberry-red, stuck her feet into her best shoes and went back into the kitchen. Her winter coat was out of date and shabby, and for once she blessed the rain, for it meant that she could wear her mac.

Their stomachs nicely filled, Cyril and Oscar were

already half asleep, and Tiger was standing by his master, eager to be off.

'I've locked everything up,' observed the doctor, and ushered Amabel out of the kitchen, turned the key in the lock and put it in his pocket, and urged her into the car. He hadn't appeared to look at her at all, but all the same he saw that she had done her best with her appearance. And the restaurant he had in mind had shaded rose lamps on its tables, if he remembered aright...

There weren't many people there on a wet Sunday evening, but the place was welcoming, and the rosy shades were kind to Amabel's still faintly blotchy face. Moreover, the food was good. He watched the pink come back into her cheeks as they ate their mushrooms in garlic sauce, local trout and a salad fit for the Queen. And the puddings were satisfyingly shrouded in thick clotted cream...

The doctor kept up a gentle stream of undemanding talk, and Amabel, soothed by it, was unaware of time passing until she caught sight of the clock.

She said in a shocked voice, 'It's almost nine. You will be so late at Glastonbury...'

'I'm going back to town,' he told her easily, but he made no effort to keep her, driving her back without more ado, seeing her safely into the house and driving off again with a friendly if casual goodbye.

The house, when he had gone, was empty—and too quiet. Amabel settled Cyril and Oscar for the night and went to bed.

It had been a lovely evening, and it had been such a relief to talk to someone about her worries, but now she had the uneasy feeling that she had made a fool of herself, crying and pouring out her problems like a hysterical woman. Because he was a doctor, and was used to dealing with awkward patients, he had listened to her, given her a splendid meal and offered sensible suggestions as to her future. Probably he dealt with dozens like her...

She woke to a bright morning, and around noon a party of four knocked on the door and asked for rooms for the night, so Amabel was kept busy. By the end of the day she was tired enough to fall into bed and sleep at once.

There was no one for the next few days but there was plenty for her to do. The long summer days were over, and a cold wet autumn was predicted.

She collected the windfalls from the orchard, picked the last of the beans for the freezer, saw to beetroots, carrots and winter cabbage and dug the rest of the potatoes. She went to the rickety old greenhouse to pick tomatoes. She supposed that when her stepfather came he would build a new one; she and her mother had made do with it, and the quite large plot they used for vegetables grew just enough to keep them supplied throughout the year, but he was bound to make improvements.

It took her most of the week to get the garden in some sort of order, and at the weekend a party of six stayed for two nights, so on Monday morning she walked to the villager to stock up on groceries, post a letter to her mother and, on an impulse, bought the local paper again.

Back home, studying the jobs page, she saw with

regret that the likely offers of work were no longer in it. There would be others, she told herself stoutly, and she must remember what Dr Fforde had told her—not to rush into anything. She must be patient; her mother had said that they hoped to be home before Christmas, but that was still weeks away, and even so he had advised her to do nothing hastily...

It was two days later, while she was putting away sheets and pillowcases in the landing cupboard, when she heard Cyril barking. He sounded excited, and she hurried downstairs; she had left the front door unlocked and someone might have walked in...

Her mother was standing in the hall, and there was a tall thickset man beside her. She was laughing and stooping to pat Cyril, then she looked up and saw Amabel.

'Darling, aren't we a lovely surprise? Keith sold the business, so there was no reason why we shouldn't come back here.'

She embraced Amabel, and Amabel, hugging her back, said, 'Oh, Mother—how lovely to see you.'

She looked at the man and smiled—and knew immediately that she didn't like him and that he didn't like her. But she held out a hand and said, 'How nice to meet you. It's all very exciting, isn't it?'

Cyril had pushed his nose into Keith's hand and she saw his impatient hand push it away. Her heart sank.

Her mother was talking and laughing, looking into the rooms, exclaiming how delightful everything looked. 'And there's Oscar.' She turned to her husband.

'Our cat, Keith. I know you don't like cats, but he's one of the family.'

He made some non-committal remark and went to fetch the luggage. Mrs Parsons, now Mrs Graham, ran upstairs to her room, and Amabel went to the kitchen to get tea. Cyril and Oscar went with her and arranged themselves tidily in a corner of the kitchen, aware that this man with the heavy tread didn't like them.

They had tea in the sitting room and the talk was of Canada and their journey and their plans to establish a market garden.

'No more bed and breakfast,' said Mrs Graham. 'Keith wants to get the place going as soon as possible. If we can get a glasshouse up quickly we could pick up some of the Christmas trade.'

'Where will you put it?' asked Amabel. 'There's plenty of ground beyond the orchard.'

Keith had been out to look around before tea, and now he observed, 'I'll get that ploughed and dug over for spring crops, and I'll put the glasshouse in the orchard. There's no money in apples, and some of the trees look past it. We'll finish picking and then get rid of them. There's plenty of ground there—fine for peas and beans.'

He glanced at Amabel. 'Your mother tells me you're pretty handy around the house and garden. The two of us ought to be able to manage to get something started—I'll hire a man with a rotavator who'll do the rough digging; the lighter jobs you'll be able to manage.'

Amabel didn't say anything. For one thing she was too surprised and shocked; for another, it was early days to be making such sweeping plans. And what about her mother's suggestion that she might like to train for something? If her stepfather might be certain of his plans, but why was he so sure that she would agree to them? And she didn't agree with them. The orchard had always been there, long before she was born. It still produced a good crop of apples and in the spring it was so beautiful with the blossom...

She glanced at her mother, who looked happy and content and was nodding admiringly at her new husband.

It was later, as she was getting the supper that he came into the kitchen.

'Have to get rid of that cat,' he told her briskly. 'Can't abide them, and the dog's getting on a bit, isn't he? Animals don't go well with market gardens. Not to my reckoning, anyway.'

'Oscar is no trouble at all,' said Amabel, and tried hard to sound friendly. 'And Cyril is a good guard dog; he never lets anyone near the house.'

She had spoken quietly, but he looked at her face and said quickly, 'Oh, well, no hurry about them. It'll take a month or two to get things going how I want them.'

He in his turn essayed friendliness. 'We'll make a success of it, too. Your mother can manage the house and you can work full-time in the garden. We might even take on casual labour after a bit—give you time to spend with your young friends.'

He sounded as though he was conferring a favour upon her, and her dislike deepened, but she mustn't allow it to show. He was a man who liked his own way and intended to have it. Probably he was a good husband to her mother, but he wasn't going to be a good stepfather...

Nothing much happened for a few days; there was a good deal of unpacking to do, letters to write and trips to the bank. Quite a substantial sum of money had been transferred from Canada and Mr Graham lost no time in making enquiries about local labour. He also went up to London to meet men who had been recommended as likely to give him financial backing, should he require it.

In the meantime Amabel helped her mother around the house, and tried to discover if her mother had meant her to have training of some sort and then changed her mind at her husband's insistence.

Mrs Graham was a loving parent, but easily dominated by anyone with a stronger will than her own. What was the hurry? she wanted to know. A few more months at home were neither here nor there, and she would be such a help to Keith.

'He's such a marvellous man, Amabel, he's bound to make a success of whatever he does.'

Amabel said cautiously, 'It's a pity he doesn't like Cyril and Oscar...'

Her mother laughed. 'Oh, darling, he would never be unkind to them.'

Perhaps not unkind, but as the weeks slipped by it was apparent that they were no longer to be regarded as pets around the house. Cyril spent a good deal of time outside, roaming the orchard, puzzled as to why the kitchen door was so often shut. As for Oscar, he only came in for his meals, looking carefully around to make sure that there was no one about.

Amabel did what she could, but her days were full, and it was obvious that Mr Graham was a man who rode roughshod over anyone who stood in his way. For the sake of her mother's happiness Amabel held her tongue; there was no denying that he was devoted to her mother, and she to him, but there was equally no denying that he found Amabel, Cyril and Oscar superfluous to his life.

It wasn't until she came upon him hitting Cyril and then turning on an unwary Oscar and kicking him aside that Amabel knew that she would have to do something about it.

She scooped up a trembling Oscar and bent to put an arm round Cyril's elderly neck. 'How dare you? Whatever have they done to you? They're my friends and I love them,' she added heatedly, 'and they have lived here all their lives.'

Her stepfather stared at her. 'Well, they won't live here much longer if I have my way. I'm the boss here. I don't like animals around the place so you'd best make up your mind to that.'

He walked off without another word and Amabel, watching his retreating back, knew that she had to do something—and quickly.

She went out to the orchard—there were piles of bricks and bags of cement already heaped near the bench, ready to start building the glasshouse—and with Oscar on her lap and Cyril pressed against her she reviewed and discarded several plans, most of them too far-fetched to be of any use. Finally she had the nucleus of a sensible idea. But first she must have some money, and secondly the right opportunity...

As though a kindly providence approved of her efforts, she was able to have both. That very evening her stepfather declared that he would have to go to London in the morning. A useful acquaintance had phoned to say that he would meet him and introduce him to a wholesaler who would consider doing business with him once he was established. He would go to London early in the morning, and since he had a long day ahead of him he went to bed early.

Presently, alone with her mother, Amabel seized what seemed to be a golden opportunity.

'I wondered if I might have some money for clothes, Mother. I haven't bought anything since you went away...'

'Of course, love. I should have thought of that myself. And you did so well with the bed and breakfast business. Is there any money in the tea caddy? If there is take whatever you want from it. I'll ask Keith to make you an allowance; he's so generous...'

'No, don't do that, Mother. He has enough to think about without bothering him about that; there'll be enough in the tea caddy. Don't bother him.' She looked across at her mother. 'You're very happy with him, aren't you, Mother?'

'Oh, yes, Amabel. I never told you, but I hated living here, just the two of us, making ends meet, no man around the place. When I went to your sister's I realised what I was missing. And I've been thinking that perhaps it would be a good idea if you started some sort of training…'

Amabel agreed quietly, reflecting that her mother wouldn't miss her…

Her mother went to bed presently, and Amabel made Oscar and Cyril comfortable for the night and counted the money in the tea caddy. There was more than enough for her plan.

She went to her room and, quiet as a mouse, got her holdall out of the wardrobe and packed it, including undies and a jersey skirt and a couple of woollies; autumn would soon turn to winter…

She thought over her plan when she was in bed; there seemed no way of improving upon it, so she closed her eyes and went to sleep.

She got up early, to prepare breakfast for her stepfather, having first of all made sure that Oscar and Cyril weren't in the kitchen. Once he had driven away she got her own breakfast, fed both animals and got dressed. Her mother came down, and over her coffee suggested that she might get the postman to give her a lift to Castle Cary.

'I've time to dress before he comes, and I can get my hair done. You'll be all right, love?'

It's as though I'm meant to be leaving, reflected Amabel. And when her mother was ready, and waiting for the postman, reminded her to take a key with her—'For I might go for a walk.'

Amabel had washed the breakfast dishes, tidied the house, and made the beds by the time her mother got into the post van, and if she gave her mother a sudden warm hug and kiss Mrs Graham didn't notice.

Half an hour later Amabel, with Oscar in his basket, Cyril on a lead, and encumbered by her holdall and a shoulder bag, was getting into the taxi she had requested. She had written to her mother explaining that it was high time she became independent and that she would write, but that she was not to worry. *You will both make a great success of the market garden and it will be easier for you both if Oscar, Cyril and myself aren't getting under your feet,* she had ended.

The taxi took them to Gillingham where—fortune still smiling—they got on the London train and, once there, took a taxi to Victoria bus station. By now Amabel realised her plans, so simple in theory, were fraught with possible disaster. But she had cooked her goose. She bought a ticket to York, had a cup of tea, got water for Cyril and put milk in her saucer for Oscar and then climbed into the long-distance bus.

It was half empty, and the driver was friendly. Amabel perched on a seat with Cyril at her feet and Oscar in his basket on her lap. She was a bit cramped, but at least they were still altogether...

It was three o'clock in the afternoon by now, and it was a hundred and ninety-three miles to York, where they would arrive at about half past eight. The end of the journey was in sight, and it only remained for Great-Aunt Thisbe to offer them a roof over their heads. A moot point since she was unaware of them coming...

'I should have phoned her,' muttered Amabel, 'but there was so much to think about in such a hurry.'

It was only now that the holes in her hare-brained scheme began to show, but it was too late to worry about it. She still had a little money, she was young, she could work and, most important of all, Oscar and Cyril were still alive...

Amabel, a sensible level-headed girl, had thrown her bonnet over the windmill with a vengeance.

She went straight to the nearest phone box at the bus station in York; she was too tired and light-headed from her impetuous journey to worry about Great-Aunt Thisbe's reaction.

When she heard that lady's firm, unhurried voice she said without preamble, 'It's me—Amabel, Aunt Thisbe. I'm at the bus station in York.'

She had done her best to keep her voice quiet and steady, but it held a squeak of panic. Supposing Aunt Thisbe put down the phone...

Miss Parsons did no such thing. When she had been told of her dead nephew's wife's remarriage she had disapproved, strongly but silently. Such an upheaval: a strange man taking over from her nephew's loved memory, and what about Amabel? She hadn't seen the girl for some years—what of her? Had her mother considered her?

She said now, 'Go and sit down on the nearest seat, Amabel. I'll be with you in half an hour.'

'I've got Oscar and Cyril with me.'

'You are all welcome,' said Aunt Thisbe, and rang off.

Much heartened by these words, Amabel found a bench and, with a patient Cyril crouching beside her and Oscar eyeing her miserably from the little window in his basket, sat down to wait.

Half an hour, when you're not very happy, can seem a very long time, but Amabel forgot that when she saw Great-Aunt Thisbe walking briskly towards her, clad in a coat and skirt which hadn't altered in style for the last few decades, her white hair crowned by what could best be described as a sensible hat. There was a youngish man with her, short and sturdy with weather-beaten features.

Great-Aunt Thisbe kissed Amabel briskly. 'I am so glad you have come to visit me, my dear. Now we will go home and you shall tell me all about it. This is Josh, my right hand. He'll take your luggage to the car and drive us home.'

Amabel had got to her feet. She couldn't think of anything to say that wouldn't need a long explanation, so she held out a hand for Josh to shake, picked up Oscar's basket and Cyril's lead and walked obediently out into the street and got into the back of the car while Aunt Thisbe settled herself beside Josh.

It was dark now, and the road was almost empty of traffic. There was nothing to see from the car's window but Amabel remembered Bolton Percy was where her aunt lived, a medieval village some fifteen miles from York and tucked away from the main roads. It must be ten years since she was last here, she reflected; she had been sixteen and her father had died a few months earlier...

The village, when they reached it, was in darkness, but her aunt's house, standing a little apart from the row of brick and plaster cottages near the church, welcomed them with lighted windows.

Josh got out and helped her with the animals and she followed him up the path to the front door, which Great-Aunt Thisbe had opened.

'Welcome to my home, child,' she said. 'And yours for as long as you need it.'

Chapter 3

The next hour or two were a blur to Amabel; her coat was taken from her and she was sat in a chair in Aunt Thisbe's kitchen, bidden to sit there, drink the tea she was given and say nothing—something she was only too glad to do while Josh and her aunt dealt with Cyril and Oscar. In fact, quite worn out, she dozed off, to wake and find Oscar curled up on her lap, washing himself, and Cyril's head pressed against her knee.

Great-Aunt Thisbe spoke before she could utter a word.

'Stay there for a few minutes. Your room's ready, but you must have something to eat first.'

'Aunt Thisbe—' began Amabel.

'Later, child. Supper and a good night's sleep first. Do you want your mother to know you are here?'

'No, no. I'll explain…'

'Tomorrow.' Great-Aunt Thisbe, still wearing her hat, put a bowl of fragrant stew into Amabel's hands. 'Now eat your supper.'

Presently Amabel was ushered upstairs to a small room with a sloping ceiling and a lattice window. She didn't remember getting undressed, nor did she feel surprised to find both Oscar and Cyril with her. It had been a day like no other and she was beyond surprise or questioning; it seemed quite right that Cyril and Oscar should share her bed. They were still all together, she thought with satisfaction. It was like waking up after a particularly nasty nightmare.

When she woke in the morning she lay for a moment, staring up at the unfamiliar ceiling, but in seconds memory came flooding back and she sat up in bed, hampered by Cyril's weight on her feet and Oscar curled up near him. In the light of early morning yesterday's journey was something unbelievably foolhardy—and she would have to explain to Great-Aunt Thisbe.

The sooner the better.

She got up, went quietly to the bathroom, dressed and the three of them crept downstairs.

The house wasn't large, but it was solidly built, and had been added to over the years, and its small garden had a high stone wall. Amabel opened the stout door and went outside. Oscar and Cyril, old and wise enough to know what was wanted of them, followed her cautiously.

It was a fine morning but there was a nip in the air, and the three of them went back indoors just as Great-Aunt Thisbe came into the kitchen.

Her good morning was brisk and kind. 'You slept well? Good. Now, my dear, there's porridge on the Aga; I dare say these two will eat it. Josh will bring suitable food when he comes presently. And you and I will have a cup of tea before I get our breakfast.'

'I must explain...'

'Of course. But over a cup of tea.'

So presently Amabel sat opposite her aunt at the kitchen table, drank her tea and gave her a carefully accurate account of her journey. 'Now I've thought about it, I can see how silly I was. I didn't stop to think, you see—only that I had to get away because my—my stepfather was going to kill...' She faltered. 'And he doesn't like me.'

'Your mother? She is happy with him?'

'Yes—yes, she is, and he is very good to her. They don't need me. I shouldn't have come here, only I had to think of something quickly. I'm so grateful to you, Aunt Thisbe, for letting me stay last night. I wondered if you would let me leave Oscar and Cyril here today, while I go into York and find work. I'm not trained, but there's always work in hotels and people's houses.'

The sound which issued from Miss Parsons' lips would have been called a snort from a lesser mortal.

'Your father was my brother, child. You will make this your home as long as you wish to stay. As to work— it will be a godsend to me to have someone young about the place. I'm well served by Josh and Mrs Josh, who cleans the place for me, but I could do with company, and in a week or two you can decide what you want to do.

'York is a big city; there are museums, historical

houses, a wealth of interest to the visitor in Roman remains—all of which employ guides, curators, helpers of all kinds. There should be choice enough when it comes to looking for a job. The only qualifications needed are intelligence, the Queen's English and a pleasant voice and appearance. Now go and get dressed, and after breakfast you shall telephone your mother.'

'They will want me to go back—they don't want me, but he expects me to work for him in the garden.'

'You are under no obligation to your stepfather, Amabel, and your mother is welcome to come and visit you at any time. You are not afraid of your stepfather?'

'No—but I'm afraid of what he would do to Oscar and Cyril. And I don't like him.'

The phone conversation with her mother wasn't entirely satisfactory—Mrs Graham, at first relieved and glad to hear from Amabel, began to complain bitterly at what she described as Amabel's ingratitude.

'Keith will have to hire help,' she pointed out. 'He's very vexed about it, and really, Amabel, you have shown us a lack of consideration, going off like that. Of course we shall always be glad to see you, but don't expect any financial help—you've chosen to stand on your own two feet. Still, you're a sensible girl, and I've no doubt that you will find work—I don't suppose Aunt Thisbe will want you to stay for more than a week or two.' There was a pause. 'And you've got Oscar and Cyril with you?'

'Yes, Mother.'

'They'll hamper you when you look for work. Really, it would have been better if Keith had had them put down.'

'Mother! They have lived with us for years. They don't deserve to die.'

'Oh, well, but they're neither of them young. Will you phone again?'

Amabel said that she would and put down the phone. Despite Great-Aunt Thisbe's sensible words, she viewed the future with something like panic.

Her aunt took one look at her face, and said, 'Will you walk down to the shop and get me one or two things, child? Take Cyril with you—Oscar will be all right here—and we will have coffee when you get back.'

It was only a few minutes' walk to the stores in the centre of the village, and although it was drizzling and windy it was nice to be out of doors. It was a small village, but the church was magnificent and the narrow main street was lined with small solid houses and crowned at its end by a large brick and plaster pub.

Amabel did her shopping, surprised to discover that the stern-looking lady who served her knew who she was.

'Come to visit your auntie? She'll be glad of a bit of company for a week or two. A good thing she's spending the winter with that friend of hers in Italy...'

Two or three weeks, decided Amabel, walking back, should be enough time to find some kind of work and a place to live. Aunt Thisbe had told her that she was welcome to stay as long as she wanted to, but if she did that would mean her aunt would put off her holiday. Which would never do... She would probably mention it in a day or two—especially if Amabel lost no time in looking for work.

But a few days went by, and although Amabel reiterated her intention of finding work as soon as possible her aunt made no mention of her holiday; indeed she insisted that Amabel did nothing about it.

'You need a week or two to settle down,' she pointed out, 'and I won't hear of you leaving until you have decided what you want to do. It won't hurt you to spend the winter here.'

Which gave Amabel the chance to ask, 'But you may have made plans...'

Aunt Thisbe put down her knitting. 'And what plans would I be making at my age, child? Now, let us say no more for the moment. Tell me about your mother's wedding?'

So Amabel, with Oscar on her lap and Cyril sitting between them, told all she knew, and presently they fell to talking about her father, still remembered with love by both of them.

Dr Fforde, immersed in his work though he was, nevertheless found his thoughts wandering, rather to his surprise, towards Amabel. It was some two weeks after she had left home that he decided to go and see her again. By now her mother and stepfather would be back and she would have settled down with them and be perfectly happy, all her doubts and fears forgotten.

He told himself that was his reason for going: to reassure himself that, knowing her to be happy again, he could dismiss her from his mind.

It was mid-afternoon when he got there, and as he parked the car he saw signs of activity at the back of the house. Instead of knocking on the front door he walked round the side of the house to the back. Most of the orchard had disappeared, and there was a large concrete foundation where the trees had been. Beyond the orchard the ground had been ploughed up; the bench had gone, and the fruit bushes. Only the view beyond was still beautiful.

He went to the kitchen door and knocked.

Amabel's mother stood in the doorway, and before she could speak he said, 'I came to see Amabel.' He held out a hand. 'Dr Fforde.'

Mrs Graham shook hands. She said doubtfully, 'Oh, did you meet her when she was doing bed and breakfasts? She's not here; she's left.'

She held the door wide. 'Come in. My husband will be back very shortly. Would you like a cup of tea?'

'Thank you.' He looked around him. 'There was a dog…'

'She's taken him with her—and the cat. My husband won't have animals around the place. He's starting up a market garden. The silly girl didn't like the idea of them being put down—left us in the lurch too; she was going to work for Keith, help with the place once we get started—we arc having a big greenhouse built.'

'Yes, there was an orchard there.'

He accepted his tea and, when she sat down, took a chair opposite her.

'Where has Amabel gone?' The question was put so casually that Mrs Graham answered at once.

'Yorkshire, of all places—and heaven knows how she got there. My first husband's sister lives near York—a

small village called Bolton Percy. Amabel went there—
well, there wasn't anywhere else she could have gone
without a job. We did wonder where she was, but she
phoned when she got there... Here's my husband.'

The two men shook hands, exchanged a few minutes'
conversation, then Dr Fforde got up to go.

He had expected his visit to Amabel's home to reassure him as to her future; it had done nothing of the
sort. Her mother might be fond of her but obviously this
overbearing man she had married would discourage her
from keeping close ties with Amabel—he had made no
attempt to disguise his dislike of her.

Driving himself back home, the doctor reflected that
Amabel had been wise to leave. It seemed a bit drastic
to go as far away as Yorkshire, but if she had family
there they would have arranged her journey. He reminded himself that he had no need to concern himself about her; she had obviously dealt with her own
future in a sensible manner. After all, she had seemed
a sensible girl...

Bates greeted him with the news that Mrs Potter-
Stokes had telephoned. 'Enquiring if you would take
her to an art exhibition tomorrow evening which she
had already mentioned.'

And why not? reflected Dr Fforde. He no longer
needed to worry about Amabel. The art exhibition
turned out to be very avant-garde, and Dr Fforde, es-
corting Miriam Potter-Stokes, listening to her rather
vapid remarks, trying to make sense of the childish
daubs acclaimed as genius, allowed his thoughts to wander. It was time he took a few days off, he decided. He

would clear his desk of urgent cases and leave London for a while. He enjoyed driving and the roads were less busy now.

So when Miriam suggested that he might like to spend the weekend at her parents' home, he declined firmly, saying, 'I really can't spare the time, and I shall be out of London for a few days.'

'You poor man; you work far too hard. You need a wife to make sure that you don't do too much.'

She smiled up at him and then wished that she hadn't said that. Oliver had made some rejoinder dictated by good manners, but he had glanced at her with indifference from cold blue eyes. She must be careful, she reflected; she had set her heart on him for a husband…

Dr Fforde left London a week later. He had allowed himself three days: ample time to drive to York, seek out the village where Amabel was living and make sure that she was happy with this aunt and that she had some definite plans for her future. Although why he should concern himself with that he didn't go into too deeply.

A silly impetuous girl, he told himself, not meaning a word of it.

He left after an early breakfast, taking Tiger with him, sitting erect and watchful beside him, sliding through the morning traffic until at last he reached the M1. After a while he stopped at a service station, allowed Tiger a short run, drank a cup of coffee and drove on until, mindful of Tiger's heavy sighs, he stopped in a village north of Chesterfield.

The pub was almost empty and Tiger, his urgent needs dealt with, was made welcome, with a bowl of water and biscuits, while the doctor sat down before a plate of beef sandwiches, home-made pickles and half a pint of real ale.

Much refreshed, they got back into the car presently, their journey nearing its end. The doctor, a man who, having looked at the map before he started a journey, never needed to look at it again, turned off the motorway and made his way through country roads until he was rewarded by the sight of Bolton Percy's main street.

He stopped before the village stores and went in. The village was a small one; Amabel's whereabouts would be known…

As well as the severe-looking lady behind the counter there were several customers, none of whom appeared to be shopping with any urgency. They all turned to look at him as he went in, and even the severe-looking lady smiled at his pleasant greeting.

An elderly woman at the counter spoke up. 'Wanting to know the way? I'm in no hurry. Mrs Bluett—' she indicated the severe lady '—she'll help you.'

Dr Fforde smiled his thanks. 'I'm looking for a Miss Amabel Parsons.'

He was eyed with even greater interest.

'Staying with her aunt—Miss Parsons up at the End House. End of this street; house stands on its own beyond the row of cottages. You can't miss it. They'll be home.' She glanced at the clock. 'They sit down to high tea around six o'clock, but drink a cup around half past three. Expecting you, is she?'

'No…' Mrs Bluett looked at him so fiercely that he felt obliged to add, 'We have known each other for some time.' She smiled then, and he took his leave, followed by interested looks.

Stopping once more a hundred yards or so down the street, he got out of the car slowly and stood just for a moment looking at the house. It was red brick and plaster, solid and welcoming with its lighted windows. He crossed the pavement, walked up the short path to the front door and knocked.

Miss Parsons opened it. She stood looking at him with a severity which might have daunted a lesser man.

'I have come to see Amabel,' observed the doctor mildly. He held out a hand. 'Fforde—Oliver Fforde. Her mother gave me this address.'

Miss Parsons took his hand and shook it. 'Thisbe Parsons. Amabel's aunt. She has spoken of you.' She looked round his great shoulder. 'Your car? It will be safe there. And a dog?'

She took another good luck at him and liked what she saw. 'We're just about to have a cup of tea. Do bring the dog in—he's not aggressive? Amabel's Cyril is here…'

'They are already acquainted.' He smiled. 'Thank you.'

He let Tiger out of the car and the pair of them followed her into the narrow hallway.

Miss Parsons marched ahead of them, opened a door and led the way into the room, long and low, with windows at each end and an old-fashioned fireplace at its centre. The furniture was old-fashioned too, beautifully kept and largely covered by photos in silver frames and small china ornaments, some of them valuable, and a

Always and Forever

quantity of pot plants. It was a very pleasant room, lived in and loved and very welcoming.

The doctor, treading carefully between an occasional table and a Victorian spoon-back chair, watched Amabel get to her feet and heaved a sigh of relief at the pleased surprise on her face.

He said, carefully casual, 'Amabel...' and shook her hand, smiling down at her face. 'I called at your home and your mother gave me this address. I have to be in York for a day or two and it seemed a good idea to renew our acquaintance.'

She stared up into his kind face. 'I've left home...'

'So your stepfather told me. You are looking very well.'

'Oh, I am. Aunt Thisbe is so good to me, and Cyril and Oscar are happy.'

Miss Parsons lifted the teapot. 'Sit down and have your tea and tell me what brings you to York, Dr Fforde. It's a long way from London—you live there, I presume?'

The doctor had aunts of his own, so he sat down, drank his tea meekly and answered her questions without telling her a great deal. Tiger was sitting beside him, a model of canine obedience, while Cyril settled near him. Oscar, of course, had settled himself on top of the bookcase. Presently the talk became general, and he made no effort to ask Amabel how she came to be so far from her home. She would tell him in her own good time, and he had two days before he needed to return to London.

Miss Parsons said briskly, 'We have high tea at six

o'clock. We hope you will join us. Unless you have some commitments in York?'

'Not until tomorrow morning. I should very much like to accept.'

'In that case you and Amabel had better take the dogs for a run while I see to a meal.'

It was dark by now, and chilly. Amabel got into her mac, put Cyril's lead on and led the way out of the house, telling him, 'We can go to the top of the village and come back along the back lane.'

The doctor took her arm and, with a dog at either side of them, they set off. 'Tell me what happened,' he suggested.

His gentle voice would have persuaded the most unwilling to confide in him and Amabel, her arm tucked under his, was only too willing. Aunt Thisbe was a dear, loving and kind under her brusque manner, but she hadn't been there; Dr Fforde had, so there was no need to explain about Cyril and Oscar or her stepfather...

She said slowly, 'I did try, really I did—to like him and stay at home until they'd settled in and I could suggest that I might train for something. But he didn't like me, although he expected me to work for him, and he hated Cyril and Oscar.'

She took a breath and began again, not leaving anything out, trying to keep to the facts and not colouring them with her feelings.

When she had finished the doctor said firmly, 'You did quite right. It was rather hazardous of you to undertake the long journey here, but it was a risk worth taking.'

They were making their way back to the house, and although it was too dark to see he sensed that she was crying. He reminded himself that he had adopted the role of advisor and impersonal friend. That had been his intention and still was. Moreover, her aunt had offered her a home. He resisted a desire to take her in his arms and kiss her, something which, while giving him satisfaction would possibly complicate matters. Instead he said cheerfully, 'Will you spend the afternoon with me tomorrow? We might drive to the coast.'

Amabel swallowed tears. 'That would be very nice,' she told him. 'Thank you.' And, anxious to match his casual friendliness, she added, 'I don't know this part of the world, do you?'

For the rest of the way back they discussed Yorkshire and its beauties.

Aunt Thisbe was old-fashioned; the younger generation might like their dinner in the evening, but she had remained faithful to high tea. The table was elegantly laid, the teapot at one end, a covered dish of buttered eggs at the other, with racks of toast, a dish of butter and a home-made pâté. There was jam too, and a pot of honey, and sandwiches, and in the centre of the table a cakestand bearing scones, fruitcake, oatcakes and small cakes from the local baker, known as fancies.

The doctor, a large and hungry man, found everything to his satisfaction and made a good meal, something which endeared him to Aunt Thisbe's heart, so that when he suggested he might take Amabel for a drive the following day she said at once that it was a splendid idea. Here was a man very much to her liking; it was a pity that it was obvious that his interest in Amabel was only one of impersonal kindness. The girl had been glad to see him, and heaven knew the child needed friends. A pity that he was only in York for a few days and lived so far away...

He washed the dishes and Amabel dried them after their meal. Aunt Thisbe, sitting in the drawing room, could hear them talking and laughing in the kitchen. Something would have to be done, thought the old lady. Amabel needed young friends, a chance to go out and enjoy herself; life would be dull for her during the winter. A job must be found for her where she would meet other people.

Aunt Thisbe felt sharp regret at the thought of the holiday she would have to forego: something which Amabel was never to be told about.

Dr Fforde went presently, making his goodbyes with beautiful manners, promising to be back the following afternoon. Driving to York with Tiger beside him, he spoke his thoughts aloud. 'Well, we can put our minds at rest, can we not, Tiger? She will make a new life for herself with this delightful aunt, probably find a pleasant job and meet a suitable young man and marry him.' He added, 'Most satisfactory.' So why did he feel so dissatisfied about it?

He drove to a hotel close to the Minster—a Regency townhouse, quiet and elegant, and with the unobtrusive service which its guests took for granted. Tiger, accommodated in the corner of his master's room, settled down for the night, leaving his master to go down to the bar for a nightcap and a study of the city.

The pair of them explored its streets after their break-fast. It was a fine day, and the doctor intended to drive to the coast that afternoon, but exploring the city would give him the opportunity of getting to know it. After all, it would probably be in York where Amabel would find a job.

He lunched in an ancient pub, where Tiger was wel-comed with water and biscuits, and then went back to the hotel, got into his car and drove to Bolton Percy.

Amabel had spent the morning doing the small chores Aunt Thisbe allowed her to do, attending to Os-car's needs and taking Cyril for a walk, but there was still time to worry about what she should wear for her outing. Her wardrobe was so scanty that it was really a waste of time to worry about it.

It would have to be the pleated skirt and the short coat she had travelled in; they would pass muster for driving around the country, and Dr Fforde never looked at her as though he actually saw her. It had been lovely to see him again, like meeting an old friend—one who listened without interrupting and offered suggestions, never advice, in the friendliest impersonal manner of a good doctor. He was a doctor, of course, she reminded herself.

He came punctually, spent ten minutes talking to Miss Parsons, suggested that Cyril might like to share the back seat with Tiger, popped Amabel into the car and took the road to the coast.

Flamborough stood high on cliffs above the North Sea, and down at sea level boats sheltered in the har-bour. Dr Fforde parked the car, put the dogs on their

leads and walked Amabel briskly towards the penin-
sula. It was breezy, but the air was exhilarating, and
they seemed to be the only people around.

When they stopped to look out to sea, Amabel said
happily, 'Oh, this is marvellous; so grand and beautiful—fancy living here and waking up each morning
and seeing the sea.'

They walked a long way, and as they turned to go
back Dr Fforde said, carefully casual, 'Do you want to
talk about your plans, Amabel? Perhaps your aunt has
already suggested something? Or do you plan to stay
with her indefinitely?'

'I wanted to ask you about that. There's a problem.
You won't mind if I tell you about it, and perhaps you
could give me some advice. You see I was told quite
unwittingly, by Mrs Bluett who owns the village shop,
that Aunt Thisbe had plans to spend the winter in Italy
with a friend. I haven't liked to ask her, and she hasn't
said anything, but I can't allow her to lose a lovely holiday like that because I'm here. After all, she didn't
expect me, but she's so kind and she might feel that
she should stay here so that I've got a home, if you see
what I mean.'

They were standing facing each other, and she stared
up into his face. 'You can see that I must get a job very
quickly, but I'm not sure how to set about it. I mean,
should I answer advertisements in the paper or visit
an agency? There's not much I can do, and it has to be
somewhere Cyril and Oscar can come too.'

He said slowly, 'Well, first you must convince your
aunt that you want a job—and better not say that you

know of her holiday. Go to York, put your name down at any agencies you can find…' He paused, frowning. 'What can you do, Amabel?'

'Nothing, really,' she said cheerfully. 'Housework, cooking—or I expect I could be a waitress or work in a shop. They're not the sort of jobs people want, are they? And they aren't well paid. But if I could get a start somewhere, and also somewhere to live…'

'Do you suppose your aunt would allow you to live at her house while she was away?'

'Perhaps. But how would I get to work? The bus service is only twice weekly, and there is nowhere in the village where I could work.' She added fiercely, 'I must be independent.'

He took her arm and they walked on. 'Of course. Now, I can't promise anything, Amabel, but I know a lot of people and I might hear of something. Do you mind where you go?'

'No, as long as I can have Cyril and Oscar with me.'

'There is no question of your returning home?'

'None whatever. I'm being a nuisance to everyone, aren't I?'

He agreed silently to that, but he didn't say so. She was determined to be independent, and for some reason which he didn't understand he wanted to help her.

He asked, 'Have you some money? Enough to pay the rent and so on?'

'Yes, thank you. Mother let me have the money in the tea caddy, and there is still some left.'

He decided it wasn't worth while asking about the tea caddy. 'Good. Now we are going to the village; I noticed a pub as we came through it—the Royal Dog and Duck. If it is open they might give us tea.'

They had a splendid meal in the snug behind the bar: a great pot of tea, scones and butter, cream and jam, great wedges of fruitcake and, in case that wasn't enough, a dish of buttered toast. Tiger and Cyril, sitting under the table, provided with water and any tidbits which came their way, were tired after their walk, and dozed quietly.

He drove back presently through the dusk of late autumn, taking side roads through charming villages—Burton Agnes, with its haunted manor and Norman church, through Lund, with its once-upon-a-time cockpit, on to Bishop Burton, with its village pond and little black and white cottages, and finally along country roads to Bolton Percy.

The doctor stayed only as long as good manners dictated, although he asked if he might call to wish them goodbye the following morning.

'Come for coffee?' invited Miss Parsons.

The stiff breeze from yesterday had turned into a gale in the morning, and he made that his excuse for not staying long over his coffee. When Amabel had opened the door to him he had handed her a list of agencies in York, and now he wanted to be gone; he had done what he could for her. She had a home, this aunt who was obviously fond of her, and she was young and healthy and sensible, even if she had no looks to speak of. He had no further reason to be concerned about her.

All the same, driving down the M1, he was finding it difficult to forget her. She had bidden him goodbye in a quiet voice, her small hand in his, wished him a safe journey and thanked him. 'It's been very nice knowing you,' she had told him.

It had been nice knowing her, he conceded, and it was a pity that their paths were unlikely to cross in the future.

That evening Amabel broached the subject of her future to her aunt. She was careful not to mention Aunt Thisbe's holiday in Italy, pointing out with enthusiasm her great wish to become independent.

'I'll never be grateful enough to you,' she assured her aunt, 'for giving me a home—and I love being here with you. But I must get started somewhere, mustn't I? I know I shall like York, and there must be any number of jobs for someone like me—I mean, unskilled labour. And I won't stop at that. You do understand, don't you, Aunt?'

'Yes, of course I do, child. You must go to York and see what there is there for you. Only you must promise me that if you fall on hard times you will come here.' She hesitated, then, 'And if I am not here, go to Josh and Mrs Josh.'

'I promise, Aunt Thisbe. There's a bus to York tomorrow morning, isn't there? Shall I go and have a look round—spy out the land…?'

'Josh has to take the car in tomorrow morning; you shall go with him. The bus leaves York in the afternoon around four o'clock, but if you miss it phone here and Josh will fetch you.'

It was a disappointing day. Amabel went from one

agency to the next, and was entered on their books, but there were no jobs which would suit her; she wasn't a trained lady's maid, or a cashier as needed at a café, she had neither the training nor the experience to work at a crèche, nor was she suitable as a saleslady at any of the large stores—lack of experience. But how did one get experience unless one had a chance to learn in the first place?

She presented a brave face when she got back to her aunt's house in the late afternoon. After all, this was only the first day, and her name was down on several agencies' books.

Back in London, Dr Fforde immersed himself in his work, assuring Bates that he had had a most enjoyable break.

'So why is he so gloomy?' Bates enquired of Tiger. 'Too much work. He needs a bit of the bright lights— needs to get out and about a bit.'

So it pleased Bates when his master told him that he would be going out one evening. Taking Mrs Potter-Stokes to the theatre, and supper afterwards.

It should have been a delightful evening; Miriam was a charming companion, beautifully dressed, aware of how very attractive she was, sure of herself, and amusing him with anecdotes of their mutual friends, asking intelligent questions about his work. But she was aware that she hadn't got his full attention. Over supper she exerted herself to gain his interest, and asked him prettily if he had enjoyed his few days off. 'Where did you go?' she added.

'York…'

'York?' She seized on that. 'My dear Oliver, I wish I'd known; you could have called on a great friend of mine—Dolores Trent. She has one of those shops in the Shambles—you know, sells dried flowers and pots and expensive glass. But she's hopeless at it—so impractical, breaking things and getting all the money wrong. I had a letter from her only a few days ago—she thinks she had better get someone to help her.'

She glanced at the doctor and saw with satisfaction that he was smiling at her. 'How amusing. Is she as attractive as you, Miriam?'

Miriam smiled a little triumphant smile, the evening was a success after all.

Which was what the doctor was thinking…

Chapter 4

When Amabel came back from walking Cyril the next morning she was met at the door by her aunt.

'A pity. You have just missed a phone call from your nice Dr Fforde. He has heard of a job quite by chance from a friend and thought you might be interested. A lady who owns a shop in the Shambles in York—an arty-crafty place, I gather; she needs someone to help her. He told me her name—Dolores Trent—but he doesn't know the address. You might like to walk through the Shambles and see if you can find her shop. Most thoughtful of him to think of you.'

Josh drove her in after lunch. She was, her aunt had decreed, to spend as long as she wanted in York and phone when she was ready to return; Josh would fetch her.

She walked through the city, found the Shambles

and started to walk its length. It was a narrow cobbled street, lined by old houses which overhung the lane, almost all of which were now shops: expensive shops, she saw at once, selling the kind of things people on holiday would take back home to display or give as presents to someone who needed to be impressed.

She walked down one side, looking at the names over the doors and windows, pausing once or twice to study some beautiful garment in a boutique or look at a display of jewellery. She reached the end and started back on the other side, and halfway down she found what she was looking for. It was a small shop, tucked between a bookshop and a mouthwatering patisserie, its small window displaying crystal vases, great baskets of dried silk flowers, delicate china and eye-catching pottery. Hung discreetly in one corner was a small card with 'Shop Assistant Required' written on it.

Amabel opened the door and went inside.

She supposed that the lady who came to meet her through the bead curtain at the back of the shop was Dolores Trent; she so exactly fitted her shop. Miss Trent was a tall person, slightly overweight, swathed in silky garments and wearing a good deal of jewellery, and she brought with her a cloud of some exotic perfume.

'You wish to browse?' she asked in a casual manner. 'Do feel free…'

'The card in the window?' said Amabel. 'You want an assistant. Would I do?'

Dolores Trent looked her over carefully. A dull little creature, she decided, but quite pleasant to look at, and she definitely didn't want some young glamorous girl who might distract customers from buying.

She said sharply, 'You live here? Have you references? Have you any experience?'

'I live with my aunt at Bolton Percy, and I can get references. I've no experience in working in a shop, but I'm used to people. I ran a bed and breakfast house...'

Miss Trent laughed. 'At least you sound honest. If you come here to work, how will you get here? Bolton Percy's a bit rural, isn't it?'

'Yes. I hope to find somewhere to live here.'

Several thoughts passed with quick succession through Dolores Trent's head. There was that empty room behind the shop, beyond the tiny kitchenette and the cloakroom; it could be furnished with odds and ends from the attic at home. The girl could live there, and since she would have rent-free accommodation there would be no need to pay her the wages she would be entitled to...

Miss Trent, mean by nature, liked the idea.

'I might consider you, if your references are satisfactory. Your hours would be from nine o'clock till five, free on Sundays. I'd expect you to keep the shop clean and dusted, unpack goods when they arrive, arrange shelves, serve the customers and deal with the cash. You'd do any errands, and look after the shop when I'm not here. You say you want to live here? There's a large room behind the shop, with windows and a door opening onto a tiny yard. Basic furniture and bedding. There's a kitchenette and a cloakroom which you can use. Of course you do understand that if I let you live here I won't be able to pay you the usual wages?'

She named a sum which Amabel knew was not much more than half what she should have expected. On the other hand, here was shelter and security and independence.

'I have a dog and a cat. Would you object to them?'

'Not if they stay out of sight. A dog would be quite a good idea; it's quiet here at night. You're not nervous?'

'No. Might I see the room?'

It was a pleasant surprise, quite large and airy, with two windows and a small door opening onto a tiny square of neglected grass. But there were high walls surrounding it; Cyril and Oscar would be safe there.

Dolores Trent watched Amabel's face. The girl needed the job and somewhere to live, so she wasn't likely to leave at a moment's notice if she found the work too hard or the hours too long. Especially with a dog and a cat...

She said, 'Provided your references are okay, you can come on a month's trial. You'll be paid weekly. After the month it will be a week's notice on either side.' As they went back to the shop she said, 'I'll phone you when I've checked the references.'

Amabel, waiting for Josh to fetch her in answer to her phone call, was full of hope. It would be a start: somewhere to live, a chance to gain the experience which was so necessary if she wanted to get a better job. She would have the chance to look around her, make friends, perhaps find a room where Cyril and Oscar would be welcome, and find work which was better paid. But that would be later, she conceded. In the meantime she was grateful to Dr Fforde for his help. It was a pity she couldn't see him and tell him how grateful she was. But he had disappeared back into his world, somewhere in London, and London was vast…

Convincing Aunt Thisbe that the offer of work from Miss Trent was exactly what she had hoped for was no easy task. Aunt Thisbe had said no word of her holiday, only reiterating her advice that Amabel should spend the next few weeks with her, wait until after Christmas before looking for work…

It was only after Amabel had painted a somewhat over-blown picture of her work at Miss Trent's shop, the advantages of getting one foot in the door of future prospects, and her wish to become independent, that Miss Parsons agreed reluctantly that it might be the chance of a lifetime. There was the added advantage that, once in York, the chance of finding an even better job was much greater than if Amabel stayed at Bolton Percy.

So Amabel sent off her references and within a day or so the job was hers, if she chose to take it. Amabel showed her aunt the letter and it was then that Aunt Thisbe said, 'I shall be sorry to see you go, child. You must spend your Sundays here, of course, and any free time you have.' She hesitated. 'If I am away then you must go to Josh and Mrs Josh, who will look after you. Josh will have a key, and you must treat the house as your home. If you need the car you have only to ask…'

'Will you be away for long?' asked Amabel.

'Well, dear, I have been invited to spend a few weeks

with an old friend who has an apartment in Italy. I hadn't made up my mind whether to go, but since you have this job and are determined to be independent...'

'Oh, Aunt Thisbe, how lovely for you—and hasn't everything worked out well? I'll be fine in York and I'll love to come here, if Mrs Josh won't mind. When are you going?'

'You are to start work next Monday? I shall probably go during that week.'

'I thought I'd ask Miss Trent if I could move in on Sunday...'

'A good idea. Josh can drive you there and make sure that everything is all right. Presumably the shop will be empty?'

'I suppose so. I'd have all day to settle in, and if it's quiet Cyril and Oscar won't find it so strange. They're very adaptable.'

So everything was settled. Miss Trent had no objection to Amabel moving in on Sunday. The key would be next door at the patisserie, which was open on Sundays, and the room had been furnished; she could go in and out as she wished and she was to be ready to open the shop at nine o'clock on Monday morning. Miss Trent sounded friendly enough, if a trifle impatient.

Amabel packed her case and Miss Parsons, with brisk efficiency, filled a large box with food: tins of soup, cheese, eggs, butter, bread, biscuits, tea and coffee and plastic bottles of milk and, tucked away out of sight, a small radio. Amabel, for all her brave face, would be lonely.

Aunt Thisbe decided that she would put off her holiday until the following week; Amabel would spend Sunday with her and she would see for herself if she could go away with a clear conscience... She would miss Amabel, but the young shouldn't be held back.

She would have liked to have seen the room where Amabel was to live, but she sensed that Amabel didn't want that—at least not until she had transformed it into a place of which her aunt would approve. And there were one or two things she must tell Josh—that nice Dr Fforde might return. It wasn't very likely, but Aunt Thisbe believed that one should never overlook a chance.

Saying goodbye to Aunt Thisbe wasn't easy. Amabel had been happy living with her; she had a real affection for the rather dour old lady, and knew that the affection was reciprocated, but she felt in her bones that she was doing the right thing. Her aunt's life had been disrupted by her sudden arrival and that must not be made permanent. She got into the car beside Josh and turned to smile and wave; she would be back on Sunday, but this was the real parting.

There were few people about on an early Sunday morning: tourists strolling along the Shambles, peering into shop windows, church goers. Josh parked the car away from the city centre and they walked, Amabel with the cat basket and Cyril on his lead, Josh burdened with her case and the box of food.

They knew about her at the patisserie; she fetched the key and opened the shop door, led the way through the shop and opened the door to her new home.

Miss Trent had said that she would furnish it, and

indeed there was a divan bed against one wall, a small table by the window with an upright chair, a shabby easy chair by the small electric fire and a worn rug on the wooden floor. There was a pile of bedding and a box of cutlery, and a small table lamp with an ugly plastic shade.

Josh put the box down on the table without saying a word, and Amabel said, too brightly, 'Of course it will look quite different once I've arranged things and put up the curtains.'

Josh said, 'Yes, miss,' in a wooden voice. 'Miss Parsons said we were to go next door and have a cup of coffee. I'll help you sort out your things.'

'I'd love some coffee, but after that you don't need to bother, Josh. I've all the rest of the day to get things how I want. And I must take Cyril for a walk later. There's that park by St Mary Abbot's Church, and then I must take a look round the shop.'

They had their coffee and Josh went away, promising to return on the Sunday morning, bidding her to be sure and phone if she needed him or her aunt. She sensed that he didn't approve of her bid for independence and made haste to assure him that everything was fine...

In her room presently, with the door open and Cyril and Oscar going cautiously around the neglected patch of grass, Amabel paused in her bedmaking to reflect that Miss Trent was certainly a trusting kind of person. 'You would have thought,' said Amabel to Oscar, peering round the open door to make sure that she was there, 'that she would have wanted to make sure that I had come. I might have stolen whatever I fancied from the shop.'

Well, it was nice to be trusted; it augered well for the future…

Dolores Trent had in fact gone to Harrogate for the weekend, with only the briefest of thoughts about Amabel. The girl would find her own way around. It had been tiresome enough finding someone to help out in the shop. Really, she didn't know why she kept the place on. It had been fun when she had first had it, but she hadn't realised all the bookwork there would be, and the tiresome ordering and unpacking…

If this girl needed a job as badly as she had hinted, then she could take over the uninteresting parts and leave Dolores to do the selling. It might even be possible to take more time for herself; the shop was a great hindrance to her social life…

Amabel arranged the odds and ends of furniture to their best advantage, switched on the fire, settled her two companions before it and unpacked the box of food. Aunt Thisbe had been generous and practical. There were tins of soup and a tin opener with them, tins of food for Oscar and Cyril, and there was a fruitcake— one of Mrs Josh's. She stowed them away, together with the other stores, in an empty cupboard she found in the tiny kitchenette.

She also found a saucepan, a kettle, some mugs and plates and a tin of biscuits. Presumably Miss Trent made herself elevenses each morning. Amabel opened a tin of soup and put the saucepan on the gas ring, then went to poke her nose into the tiny cloakroom next to the kitchenette. There was a small geyser over the washbasin; at least there would be plenty of hot water.

She made a list while she ate her soup. A cheap rug for the floor, a pretty lampshade, a couple of cushions, a vase—for she must have flowers—and a couple of hooks so that she could hang her few clothes. There was no cupboard, nowhere to put her undies. She added an orange box to the list, with a question mark behind it. She had no idea when she would have the chance to go shopping. She supposed that the shop would close for the usual half-day during the week, though Miss Trent hadn't mentioned that.

She made Oscar comfortable in his basket, switched off the fire, got Cyril's lead and her coat and left the shop, locking the door carefully behind her. It was mid-afternoon by now, and there was no one about. She walked briskly through the streets to St Mary's, where there was a park, and thought there would be time each morning to take Cyril for a quick run before the shop opened. They could go again after the shop closed. There was the grass for him and Oscar during the day; she could leave the door open...

And there were Sundays to look forward to...

On the way back she wondered about Dr Fforde; she tried not to think about him too often, for that was a waste of time. He had come into her life but now he had gone again. She would always be grateful to him, of course, but she was sensible enough to see that he had no place in it.

When she reached the shop she saw that the patisserie was closing its doors, and presently, when she went to look, the shop lights had been turned out. It seemed very quiet and dark outside, but there were lights here and there above the shops. She took heart from the sight of them.

After she had had her tea she went into the shop, turned on the lights and went slowly from shelf to shelf, not touching but noting their order. She looked to see where the wrapping paper, string and labels were kept, for she felt sure Miss Trent would expect her to know that. She wasn't going to be much use for a few days, but there were some things she would be expected to discover for herself.

She had her supper then, let Oscar and Cyril out for the last time, and got ready for bed. Doing the best she could with a basin of hot water in the cloakroom, she pondered the question of baths—or even showers. The girl at the patisserie had been friendly; she might be able to help. Amabel got into her bed, closely followed by her two companions, and fell instantly asleep.

She was up early—and that was another thing, an alarm clock, she thought as she dressed—opened the door onto the grass patch and then left the shop with Cyril. The streets were empty, save for postmen and milkmen, but there were signs of life when she returned after Cyril's run in the park. The shops were still closed, but curtains were being drawn above them and there was a delicious smell of baking bread from the patisserie.

Amabel made her bed, tidied the room, fed the animals and sat down to her own breakfast—a boiled egg, bread and butter and a pot of tea. Tomorrow, she promised herself, she would buy a newspaper when she went out with Cyril, and, since the patisserie opened at half past eight, she could get croissants or rolls for her lunch.

She tidied away her meal, bade the animals be good and shut and locked the door to the shop. They could go outside if they wanted, and the sun was shining...

She was waiting in the shop when Miss Trent arrived. Beyond a nod she didn't reply to Amabel's good morning, but took off her coat, took out a small mirror and inspected her face.

'I don't always get here as early as this,' she said finally. 'Open the shop if I'm not here, and if I'm not here at lunchtime just close the shop for half an hour and get yourself something. Have you had a look round? Yes? Then put the "Open" sign on the door. There's a feather duster under the counter; dust off the window display then unpack that box under the shelves. Be careful, they are china figures. Arrange them on the bottom shelf and mark the price. That will be on the invoice inside the box.'

She put away the mirror and unlocked the drawer in the counter. 'What was your name?' When Amabel reminded her, she said, 'Yes, well, I shall call you Amabel—and you'd better call me Dolores. There probably won't be any customers until ten o'clock. I'm going next door for a cup of coffee. You can have yours when I get back.'

Which was half an hour later, by which time Amabel had dealt with the china figures, praying silently that there would be no customers.

'You can have fifteen minutes,' said Dolores. 'There's

coffee and milk in the kitchenette; take it into your room if you want to.'

Cyril and Oscar were glad to have her company, even if only for a few minutes, and it made a pleasant break in the morning.

There were people in the shop by now, picking things up and putting them down again, taking their time choosing what they would buy. Dolores sat behind the counter, paying little attention to them and leaving Amabel to wrap up their purchases. Only occasionally she would advise a customer in a languid manner.

At one o'clock she told Amabel to close the door and lock it.

'Open up again in half an hour if I'm not back,' she said. 'Did I tell you that I close on Wednesday for a half-day? I shall probably go a bit earlier, but you can shut the shop and then do what you like.'

Amabel, while glad to hear about the half-day, thought that her employer seemed rather unbusinesslike. She closed the shop and made herself a sandwich before going to sit on the patch of grass with Oscar and Cyril for company.

She was glad when it was one o'clock on Wednesday; standing about in the shop was surprisingly tiring and, although Dolores was kind in a vague way, she expected Amabel to stay after the shop shut so that she could unpack any new goods or rearrange the windows. Dolores herself did very little, beyond sitting behind the counter holding long conversations over the phone. Only when a customer showed signs of serious buying did she exert herself.

She was good at persuading someone to buy the more expensive glass and china, laughing and chatting in an animated way until the sale was completed, then made no effort to tell Amabel how to go on, seeming content to let her find things out for herself. Amabel supposed that she must make a living from the shop, although it was obvious that she had very little interest in it.

It was a temptation to phone Aunt Thisbe and ask if Josh would fetch her for her half-day, but there were things she wished to do. Shopping for food and material for a window curtain, a new lampshade, flowers... Next week, when she had been paid, she would find a cheerful bedspread for the bed and a cloth for the table.

She did her shopping and took Cyril for a walk, and then spent the rest of her day rearranging her room, sitting by the electric fire eating crumpets for her tea and reading the magazine Dolores had left behind the counter.

Not very exciting, reflected Amabel, but it was early days, and there was Sunday to look forward to. She wrote a letter to her mother, read the magazine from end to end and allowed her thoughts to wander to Dr Fforde.

Sunday came at last, bringing Josh and the prospect of a lovely day and the reality of a warm welcome from Aunt Thisbe.

Warm as well as practical. Amabel was despatched to the bathroom to lie in a pine-scented bath—'For that is something you must miss,' said Miss Parsons. 'Come down when you are ready and we will have coffee and you shall tell me everything.'

Amabel, pink from her bath, settled before the fire

in her aunt's drawing room with Oscar and Cyril beside her, and gave a detailed account of her week. She made it light-hearted.

'It's delightful working in such a pleasant place,' she pointed out. 'There are some lovely things in the shop, and Miss Trent—she likes to be called Dolores—is very kind and easygoing.'

'You are able to cook proper meals?'

'Yes, and I do—and the room looks so nice now that I have cushions and flowers.'

'You are happy there, Amabel? Really happy? You have enough free time and she pays you well?'

'Yes, Aunt. York is such a lovely city, and the people in the other shops in the Shambles are so friendly...'

Which was rather an exaggeration, but Aunt Thisbe must be convinced that there was no reason why she shouldn't go to Italy...

She would go during the following week, Miss Parsons told Amabel, and Amabel was to continue to spend her Sundays at End House; Josh would see to everything...

Amabel, back in her room with another box of food and a duvet her aunt had declared she didn't want, was content that she had convinced the old lady that she was perfectly happy; they would write to each other, and when Aunt Thisbe came back in the New Year they would review the future.

A week or two went by. Amabel bought a winter coat, a pretty cover for the duvet, a basket for Cyril and a cheap rug. She also saved some money—but not much.

After the first two weeks Dolores spent less and less

time at the shop. She would pop in at opening time and then go and have her hair done, or go shopping or meet friends for coffee. Amabel found it odd, but there weren't many customers. Trade would pick up again at Christmas, Dolores told her.

Amabel, aware that she was being underpaid and overworked, was nonetheless glad to have her days filled. The few hours she spent in her room once the shop was closed were lonely enough. Later, she promised herself, once she felt secure in her job, she would join a club or go to night school. In the meantime she read and knitted and wrote cheerful letters home.

And when she wasn't doing that she thought about Dr Fforde. Such a waste of time, she told herself. But there again, did that matter? It was pleasant to remember… She wondered what he was doing and wished she knew more about him. Wondered too if he ever thought of her…

To be truthful, he thought of her very seldom; he led a busy life and time was never quite his own. He had driven to Glastonbury once or twice to see his mother, and since the road took him past Amabel's home he had slowed the car to note the work being carried out there. He had thought briefly of calling to see Mrs Graham, but decided against it. There was no point now that Amabel was in York and happy. He hoped that she had settled down by now. Perhaps when he had time to spare he would drive up and go to see her…

He was seeing a good deal of Miriam, and friends were beginning to invite them together to dinner par-

ties. He often spent evenings with her at the theatre
when he would much rather have been at home, but she
was amusing, and clever enough to appear to have a
sincere interest in his work. Hardly aware of it, he was
being drawn into her future plans...

It wasn't until one evening, returning home after a
long day at the hospital to be met by Bates with a message from Miriam—she—and he—were to join a party
of theatregoers that evening, he was to call for her at
seven-thirty and after the theatre he would take her out
to supper—that he realised what was happening.

He stood for a moment without speaking, fighting
down sudden anger, but when he spoke there was nothing of it in his voice.

'Phone Mrs Potter-Stokes, please, and tell her that I
am unable to go out this evening.' He smiled suddenly
as an idea drowned the anger. 'And, Bates, tell her that
I shall be going away.'

There was no expression on Bates's foxy face, but he
felt a deep satisfaction. He didn't like Mrs Potter-Stokes
and, unlike the doctor, had known for some time that
she was set on becoming Mrs Fforde. His 'Very good,
Doctor,' was the model of discretion.

As for Dr Fforde, he ate a splendid supper and spent
the rest of the evening going through his diary to see
how soon he could get away for a couple of days. He
would go first to Miss Parsons' house, for Amabel
might have chosen to ignore the chance of working in
a shop in York. In any case her aunt would know where
she was. It would be interesting to meet again...

Almost a week later he set off for York, Tiger beside him. It was a sullen morning, but once he was clear of the endless suburbs the motorway was fairly clear and the Rolls ate up the miles. He stopped for a snack lunch and Tiger's need for a quick trot, and four hours after he had left his home he stopped before Miss Parsons' house.

Of course no one answered his knock, and after a moment he walked down the narrow path beside the house to the garden at the back. It appeared to be empty, but as he stood there Josh came out of the shed by the bottom hedge. He put down the spade he was carrying and walked up the path to meet him.

'Seeking Miss Amabel, are you? House is shut up. Miss Parsons is off to foreign parts for the winter and Miss Amabel's got herself a job in York—comes here of a Sunday; that's her day off.'

He studied the doctor's face. 'You'll want to know where she's working. A fancy shop in the Shambles. Lives in a room at the back with those two animals of hers. Brings them here of a Sunday, spends the day at End House, opens the windows and such, airs the place, has a bath and does her washing and has her dinner with us. Very independent young lady, anxious not to be a nuisance. Says everything is fine at her job but she doesn't look quite the thing, somehow...'

Dr Fforde frowned. 'She got on well with her aunt? They seemed the best of friends...'

'And so they are. I'm not knowing, mind, but I fancy Miss Amabel took herself off so's Miss Parsons didn't have to alter her plans about her holiday.'

'I think you may be right. I'll go and see her, make sure everything is as it should be.'

'You do that, sir. Me and the missus aren't quite easy. But not knowing anyone to talk to about it…'

'I'm here for a day or two, so I'll come and see you again if I may?'

'You're welcome, sir. You and your dog.' Josh bent to stroke Tiger. 'Miss Amabel does know to come here if needful.'

'I'm glad she has a good friend in you, Josh.'

Dr Fforde got back into his car. It was mid afternoon and drizzling; he was hungry, and he must book in at the hotel where he had stayed before, but before doing so he must see Amabel.

She was on her hands and knees at the back of the shop, unpacking dozens of miniature Father Christmases intended for the Christmas market. Dolores was at the hairdresser and would return only in time to lock the till, tell her to close the shop and lock up.

She was tired and grubby, and there hadn't been time to make tea. Dolores expected everything to be cleared away before she got back. At least there had been no customers for a while, but Amabel was becoming increasingly worried at the amount of work Dolores expected her to do. It had been fine for the first few weeks, but Dolores's interest was dwindling. She was in the shop less, and dealing with the customers and sorting out the stock was becoming increasingly difficult. To talk to her about it was risky; she might so easily give Amabel a week's notice, and although she might find work easily enough there were Oscar and Cyril to consider...

She unwrapped the last of the little figures and looked up as someone came into the shop.

Dr Fforde stood in the doorway looking at her. His instant impression was that she wasn't happy, but then she smiled, her whole face alight with pleasure.

He said easily, 'Josh told me where you were. He also told me that Miss Parsons is away.' He glanced round him. 'You live here? Surely you don't run the place on your own?'

She had got to her feet, dusting off her hands, brushing down her skirt.

'No. Dolores—that is, Miss Trent—is at the hairdresser. Are you just passing through?'

'I'm here for a couple of days. When do you close this shop?'

'Five o'clock. But I tidy up after that.'

'Will you spend the evening with me?'

She had bent to stroke Tiger's head. 'I'd like that, thank you. Only I have to see to Oscar and Cyril, and take Cyril for a walk, so I won't be ready until about six o'clock.'

'I'll be here soon after five...'

Dolores came in then, assuming her charming manner at the sight of a customer. 'Have you found something you like? Do take a look round.'

She smiled at him, wondering where he came from; if he was on his own she might suggest showing him what was worth seeing in the city—the patisserie wasn't closed yet...

'I came to see Amabel,' he told her. 'We have known each other for some time, and since I am here for a day or two...'

'You're old friends?' Dolores asked artlessly. 'I expect you know York well? You don't live here?'

'No, but I have been here before. We met some time ago, in the West Country.'

Still artless, Dolores said, 'Oh, I thought you might be from London—I've friends there.' An idea—an unlikely idea—had entered her head. 'But I don't suppose you would know them. I came up here after my divorce, and it was an old schoolfriend—Miriam Potter-Stokes—who persuaded me to do something instead of sitting aimlessly around...'

She knew her wild guess had been successful when he said quietly, 'Yes, I know Miriam. I must tell her how successful you are.'

'Do, please. I must be off. Amabel, close at five o'clock. There'll be a delivery of those candlesticks before nine o'clock tomorrow morning, so be sure to be ready for it.' She gave the doctor a smiling nod. 'Nice to have met you. I hope you enjoy your stay here.'

She wasted no time when she reached her home, but poured herself a drink and picked up the phone.

'Miriam, listen and don't interrupt. Do you know where this Oliver of yours is? You don't? He's a big man, handsome, rather a slow voice, with a black dog? He's in my shop. On the best of terms with Amabel, the girl who works for me. It seems they've known each other for some time.' She gave a spiteful little laugh. 'Don't be too sure that Oliver is yours, Miriam.'

She listened to Miriam's outraged voice, smiling to herself. Miriam was an old schoolfriend, but it wouldn't hurt her to be taken down a peg. Dolores said soothingly, 'Don't get so upset, darling. He's here for a few days; I'll keep an eye on things and let you know if there's anything for you to worry about. Most unlikely, I should think. She's a small dull creature and she wears the most appalling clothes. I'll give you a ring tomorrow some time.'

When Dolores had gone the doctor said, 'Where do you live, Amabel? Surely not here?'

'Oh, but I do. I have a room behind the shop.'

'You shall show it to me when I come back.' He glanced at his watch. 'In half an hour.'

She said uncertainly, 'Well…'

'You're glad to see me, Amabel?'

She said without hesitating, 'Oh, yes, I am.'

'Then don't dither,' he said.

He came closer, and, looking down into her face, took her hands in his. 'There is a Nigerian proverb which says, "Hold a true friend with both your hands,"' he said. He smiled and added gently, 'I'm your true friend, Amabel.'

Chapter 5

Closing the shop, tidying up, feeding Oscar and Cyril, doing her face and hair, Amabel was conscious of a warm glow deep inside her person. She had a friend, a real friend. She was going to spend the evening with him and they would talk. There was so much she wanted to talk about…

He had said that he would be back at half past five, so at that time she shut her room door and went back into the shop to let him in, stooping to pat Tiger. 'I still have to take Cyril for a walk,' she told him as she led the way to her room.

He stood in the middle of it, looking round him, absently fondling Cyril. He didn't allow his thoughts to show on his face, but remarked placidly, 'Having access to space for Oscar and Cyril is an advantage, isn't it? They're happy here with you?'

'Well, yes. It's not ideal, but I'm lucky to have found it. And I have you to thank for that. I couldn't thank you before because I didn't know where you lived.'

'A lucky chance. Can we leave Oscar for a few hours?'

'Yes, he knows I take Cyril out in the evening. I'll get my coat.'

She was longing for a cup of tea; the afternoon had been long and she hadn't had the chance to make one. She was hungry too. He had told her that they were true friends, but she didn't know him well enough to suggest going to a café, and besides, Cyril needed his run.

They set off, talking of nothing much at first, but presently, walking briskly through the park, she began to answer his carefully put questions with equally careful answers.

They had been walking steadily for half an hour when he stopped and caught her by the arm. 'Tea,' he said. 'Have you had your tea? What a thoughtless fool I am.'

She said quickly, 'Oh, it doesn't matter, really it doesn't,' and added, 'It was such a lovely surprise when you came into the shop.'

He turned her round smartly. 'There must be somewhere we can get a pot of tea.'

So she got her tea, sitting at a very small table in a chintzy teashop where shoppers on their way home were still lingering. Since she was hungry, and the doctor seemed hungry too, she tucked into hot buttered toast, hot mince pies and a slice of the delicious walnut cake he insisted that she have.

'I thought we'd have dinner at my hotel,' he told her. 'But if you're not too tired we might take a walk through the streets. York is such a splendid place, and I'd like to know more of it.'

'Oh, so would I. But about going to the hotel for dinner—I think it would be better if I didn't. I mean, there's Cyril, and I'm not—that is—I didn't stop to change my dress.'

'The hotel people are very helpful about dogs. They'll both be allowed to stay in my room while we dine. And you look very nice as you are, Amabel.'

He sounded so matter-of-fact that her doubts melted away, and presently they continued with their walk.

None of the museums or historical buildings was open, but they wouldn't have visited them anyway; they walked the streets—Lendal Street, Davey Gate, Parliament Street and Coppergate, to stare up at Clifford's Tower, then back through Coppergate and Fosse Gate and Pavement and so to the Shambles again, this time from the opposite end to Dolores's shop. They lingered for a while so that she could show him the little medieval church where she sometimes went, before going on to the Minster, which they agreed would need leisurely hours of viewing in the daylight.

The hotel was close by, and while Amabel went away to leave her coat and do the best she could with her face and hair the doctor went with the dogs. He was waiting for her when she got back to the lounge.

'We deserve a drink,' he told her, 'and I hope you are as hungry as I am.'

It wasn't a large hotel, but it had all the unobtrusive perfection of service and comfort. They dined in a softly lit restaurant, served by deft waiters. The *maître d'* had ushered them to one of the best tables, and no one so much as glanced at Amabel's dowdy dress.

They dined on tiny cheese soufflés followed by roast beef, Yorkshire pudding, light as a feather, crisp baked potatoes and baby sprouts, as gently suggested by the doctor. Amabel looked as though a good meal wouldn't do her any harm, and she certainly enjoyed every mouthful—even managing a morsel of the lemon mousse which followed.

Her enjoyment was unselfconscious, and the glass of claret he ordered gave her face a pretty flush as well as loosening her tongue. They talked with the ease of two people who knew each other well—something which Amabel, thinking about it later, found rather surprising—and presently, after a leisurely coffee, the doctor went to fetch the dogs and Amabel her coat and they walked back to the shop.

The clocks were striking eleven as they reached the shop door. He took the key from her, opened the door and handed her Cyril's lead.

'Tomorrow is Wednesday—you have a half-day?' When she nodded he said, 'Good. Could you be ready by half past one? We'll take the dogs to the sea, shall we? Don't bother with lunch; we'll go next door and have coffee and a roll.'

She beamed up at him. 'Oh, that would be lovely.

Dolores almost always goes about twelve o'clock on Wednesdays, so I can close punctually, then there'll only be Oscar to see to.' She added anxiously, 'I don't need to dress up?'

'No, no. Wear that coat, and a scarf for your head; it may be chilly by the sea.'

She offered a hand. 'Thank you for a lovely evening: I have enjoyed it.'

'So have I.' He sounded friendly, and as though he meant it—which of course he did. 'I'll wait until you're inside and locked up. Goodnight, Amabel.'

She went through the shop and turned to lift a hand to him as she opened the door to her room and switched on the light. After a moment he went back to his hotel. He would have to return to London tomorrow, but he could leave late and travel through the early part of the night so that they could have dinner together again.

'Am I being a fool?' he enquired of Tiger, whose gruff rumble could have been either yes or no…

It was halfway through the busy morning when Dolores asked casually, 'Did you have a pleasant evening with your friend, Amabel?'

Amabel warmed to her friendly tone. 'Oh, yes, thank you. We went for a walk through the city and had dinner at his hotel. And this afternoon we're going to the sea.'

'I dare say you found plenty to talk about?'

'Yes, yes, we did. His visit was quite unexpected. I really didn't expect to see him again…'

'Does he come this way often? It's quite a long journey from London.'

'Well, yes. He came just before I started work here—my mother told him where I was and he looked me up.'

She had answered readily enough, but Dolores was prudent enough not to ask any more questions. She said casually, 'You must wrap up; it will be cold by the sea. And you can go as soon as he comes for you; I've some work I want to do in the shop.'

She's nicer than I thought, reflected Amabel, going back to her careful polishing of a row of silver photo frames.

Sure enough, when the doctor's large person came striding towards the shop, Dolores said, 'Off you go, Amabel. He can spend ten minutes in the shop while you get ready.'

While Amabel fed Oscar, got Cyril's lead and got into her coat, tidied her hair and made sure that she had everything in her handbag, Dolores invited the doctor to look round him. 'We're showing our Christmas stock,' she told him. 'It's always a busy time, but we close for four days over the holiday. Amabel will be able to go to her aunt's house. She's away at present, Amabel told me, but I'm sure she'll be back by then.' She gave him a sly glance. 'I dare say you'll manage to get a few days off?'

'Yes, I dare say.'

'Well, if you see Miriam give her my love, won't you? Are you staying here long?'

'I'm going back tonight. But I intend to return before Christmas.'

Amabel came then, with Cyril on his lead. She looked so happy that just for a moment Dolores had a quite unusual pang of remorse. But it was only a pang, and the moment they had gone she picked up the phone.

'Miriam—I promised to ring you. Your Oliver has just left the shop with Amabel. He's driving her to the sea and spending the rest of the day with her. What is more, he told me that he intends returning to York before Christmas. You had better find yourself another man, darling!'

She listened to Miriam raging for a few minutes. 'I shouldn't waste your breath getting into a temper. If you want him as badly as all that then you must think of something. When you have, let me know if I can help.'

Miriam thought of something at once. When Dolores heard it she said, 'Oh, no, I can't do that.' For all her mischief-making she wasn't deliberately unkind. 'The girl works very well, and I can't just sack her at a moment's notice.'

'Of course you can; she's well able to find another job—plenty of work around before Christmas. When he comes tell Oliver she's found a better job and you don't know where it is. Tell him you'll let him know if you hear anything of her; he won't be able to stay away from his work for more than a couple of days at a time. The girl won't come to any harm, and out of sight is out of mind...'

Miriam, most unusually for her burst into tears, and Dolores gave in; after all, she and Miriam were very old friends...

The doctor and his little party had to walk to where he had parked the car, and on the way he marshalled them into a small pub in a quiet street to lunch upon a sustaining soup, hot crusty bread and a pot of coffee— for, as he explained, they couldn't walk on empty stomachs. That done, he drove out of the city, north through the Yorkshire Moors, until he reached Staithes, a fishing village between two headlands.

He parked the car, tucked Amabel's hand under his arm and marched her off into the teeth of a strong wind, the dogs trotting happily on either side of them. They didn't talk; the wind made that difficult and really there was no need. They were quite satisfied with each other's company without the need of words.

The sea was rough, grey under a grey sky, and once away from the village there was no one about. Presently they turned round, and back in the village explored its streets. The houses were a mixture of cottages and handsome Georgian houses, churches and shops. They lingered at the antiques shops and the doctor bought a pretty little plate Amabel admired before they walked on beside the Beck and finally turned back to have tea at the Cod and Lobster pub.

It was a splendid tea; Amabel, her cheeks pink, her hair all over the place and glowing with the exercise, ate the hot buttered parkin, the toast and home-made jam and the fruit cake with a splendid appetite.

She was happy—the shop, her miserable little room, her loneliness and lack of friends didn't matter. Here she was, deeply content, with someone who had said that he was her friend.

They didn't talk about themselves or their lives; there

were so many other things to discuss. The time flew by and they got up to go reluctantly.

Tiger and Cyril, nicely replete with the morsels they had been offered from time to time, climbed into the car, went to sleep and didn't wake until they were back in York. The doctor parked the car at his hotel, led the dogs away to his room and left Amabel to tidy herself. It was no easy task, and she hardly felt at her best, but it was still early evening and the restaurant was almost empty.

They dined off chicken *à la king* and lemon tart which was swimming in cream, and the doctor talked comfortably of this and that. Amabel wished that the evening would go on for ever.

It didn't of course. It was not quite nine o'clock when they left the hotel to walk back to the shop. The girl who worked in the patisserie was still there, getting ready to leave. She waved as they passed and then stood watching them. She liked Amabel, who seemed to lead a very dull and lonely life, and now this handsome giant of a man had turned up...

The doctor took the key from Amabel, opened the shop door and then gave it back to her.

'Thank you for a lovely afternoon—Oliver. I feel full of fresh air and lovely food.'

He smiled down at her earnest face. 'Good. We must do it again, some time.' When she looked uncertain, he added, 'I'm going back to London tonight, Amabel. But I'll be back.'

He opened the door and pushed her inside, but not before he had given her a quick kiss. The girl in the patis-

serie saw that, and smiled. Amabel didn't smile, but she
glowed from the top of her head to the soles of her feet.

He had said that he would come back…

Dolores was in a friendly mood in the morning; she
wanted to know where Amabel had gone, if she had
had a good dinner, and was her friend coming to see
her again?

Amabel, surprised at the friendliness, saw no reason
to be secretive. She gave a cheerful account of her afternoon, and when Dolores observed casually, 'I dare
say he'll be back again?' Amabel assured her readily
enough that he would.

Any niggardly doubts Dolores might have had about
Miriam's scheme were doused by the girl in the patisserie who served her coffee.

'Nice to see Amabel with a man,' she observed chattily. 'Quite gone on her, I shouldn't doubt. Kissed her
goodbye and all. Stood outside the shop for ages, making sure she was safely inside. He'll be back, mark my
words! Funny, isn't it? She's such a plain little thing,
too…'

This was something Miriam had to know, so Dolores sent Amabel to the post office to collect a parcel
and picked up the phone.

She had expected rage, perhaps tears from Miriam,
but not silence. After a moment she said, 'Miriam?'

Miriam was thinking fast; the girl must be got rid of,
and quickly. Any doubts Dolores had about that must
be quashed at once. She said in a small broken voice,
'Dolores, you must help me. I'm sure it's just a passing

infatuation—only a few days ago we spent the evening together.' That there wasn't an atom of truth in that didn't worry her; she had to keep Dolores's sympathy.

She managed a sob. 'If he goes back to see her and she's gone he can't do anything about it. I know he's got commitments at the hospital he can't miss.' Another convincing lie. 'Please tell him that she's got another job but you don't know where? Or that she's got a boy-friend? Better still tell him that she said she would join her aunt in Italy. He wouldn't worry about her then. In fact that's what she will probably do...'

'That cat and dog of hers—' began Dolores.

'Didn't you tell me that there was a kind of handy-man who does odd jobs for the aunt? They'll go to him.'

Put like that, it sounded a reasonable solution. 'You think she might do that?' Dolores was still doubtful, but too lazy to worry about it. She said, 'All right, I'll sack her—but not for a day or two. There's more Christmas stock to be unpacked and I can't do that on my own.'

Miriam gave a convincing sob. 'I'll never be able to thank you enough. I'm longing to see Oliver again; I'm sure everything will be all right once he's back here and I can be with him.'

Which was unduly optimistic of her. Oliver, once back home, made no attempt to contact her. When she phoned his house it was to be told by a wooden-voiced Bates that the doctor was unavailable.

In desperation she went to his consulting rooms, where she told his receptionist that he was expecting her when he had seen his last patient, and when presently he came into the waiting room from his consulting room she went to meet him.

'Oliver—I know I shouldn't be here. Don't blame your receptionist; I said you expected me. Only it is such a long time since we saw each other.'

She lifted her faced to his, aware that she was at her most attractive. 'Have I done something to annoy you? You are never at home when I phone; that man of yours says you're not available.' She put a hand on his sleeve and smiled the sad little smile she had practised before her mirror.

'I've been busy—am still. I'm sorry I haven't been free to see you, but I think you must cross me off your list, Miriam.' He smiled at her. 'I'm sure there are half a dozen men waiting for the chance to take you out.'

'But they aren't you, Oliver.' She laughed lightly. 'I don't mean to give you up, Oliver.' She realised her mistake when she saw the lift of his eyebrows, and added quickly, 'You are a perfect companion for an evening out, you know.'

She wished him a light-hearted goodbye then, adding, 'But you'll be at the Sawyers' dinner party, won't you? I'll see you then.'

'Yes, of course.' His goodbye was friendly, but she was aware that only good manners prevented him from showing impatience.

The sooner Dolores got rid of that girl the better, thought Miriam savagely. Once she was out of the way she would set about the serious business of capturing Oliver.

But Dolores had done nothing about sacking Amabel. For one thing she was too useful at this busy time of the year, and for another Dolores's indolence prevented her from making decisions. She was going to have to do something about it, because she had said she would, but later.

Then an ill-tempered and agitated phone call from Miriam put an end to indecision. A friend of Miriam's had mentioned casually that it was a pity that Oliver would be away for her small daughter's—his goddaughter's—birthday party. He'd be gone for several days, he had told her. The birthday was in three days' time…

'You must do something quickly—you promised.' Miriam managed to sound desperately unhappy, although what she really felt was rage. But it wouldn't do to lose Dolores's sympathy. She gave a sob. 'Oh, my dear, I'm so unhappy.'

And Dolores, her decision made for her, promised. 'The minute I get to the shop in the morning.'

Amabel was already hard at work, unwrapping Christmas tree fairies, shaking out their gauze wings and silky skirts, arranging them on a small glass shelf. She wished Dolores good morning, the last of the fairies in her hand.

Dolores didn't bother with good morning. She disliked unpleasantness if it involved herself, and the quicker it was dealt with the better.

'I'm giving you notice,' she said, relieved to find that once she had said it it wasn't so difficult. 'There's not enough work for you, and besides, I need the room at the back. You can go this evening, as soon as you've packed up. Leave your bits and pieces; someone can collect them. You'll get your wages, of course.'

Amabel put the last fairy down very carefully on the shelf. Then she said in a small shocked voice, 'What have I done wrong?'

Dolores picked up a vase and inspected it carefully. 'Nothing. I've just told you; I want the room and I've no further use for you in the shop.' She looked away from Amabel. 'You can go back to your aunt, and if you want work there'll be plenty of casual jobs before Christmas.'

Amabel didn't speak. Of what use? Dolores had made herself plain enough; to tell her that her aunt was still away, and that she had had a card from Josh that morning saying that he and Mrs Josh would be away for the next ten days and would she please not go and visit them as usual next Sunday, would be useless.

Dolores said sharply, 'And it's no use saying anything. My mind's made up. I don't want to hear another word.'

She went to the patisserie then, to have her coffee, and when she came back told Amabel that she could have an hour off to start her packing.

Amabel got out her case and began to pack it, explaining to Cyril and Oscar as she did so. She had no idea where she would go; she had enough money to pay for a bed and breakfast place, but would they take kindly to the animals? There wouldn't be much time to find somewhere once she left the shop at five o'clock. She stripped the bed, packed what food she had in a box and went back to the shop.

When five o'clock came Dolores was still in the shop.

She gave Amabel a week's wages, told her that she could give her name for a reference if she needed to, and went back to sit behind the counter.

'Don't hang about,' she said. 'I want to get home.'

But Amabel wasn't going to hurry. She fed Oscar and Cyril and had a wash, made a cup of tea and a sandwich, for she wasn't sure where the next meal would come from, and then, neatly dressed in her new winter coat, with Cyril on his lead, Oscar in his basket and carrying her case, she left the shop.

She didn't say anything. Good evening would have been a mockery; the evening was anything but good. She closed the shop door behind her, picked up her case, waved to the girl in the patisserie, and started off at a brisk pace, past the still lighted shops.

She didn't know York well, but she knew that she wasn't likely to find anywhere cheap in and around the main streets. If she could manage until Josh and his wife got back…

She reached the narrow side streets and presently saw a café on a street corner. It was a shabby place, but it had a sign in its window saying 'Rooms to Let'. She went inside and went to the counter, where a girl lounged reading a magazine.

The place was almost empty; it smelled of fried food and wasn't too clean, but to Amabel it was the answer to her prayers.

The girl was friendly enough. Yes, there was a room, and she could have it, but she didn't know about the dog and cat. She went away to ask and came back to say that there was a room on the ground floor where the animals could stay with her, but only at night; during the day she would have to take them with her. 'And since we're doing you a favour we'll have to charge more.'

A lot more. But at least it was a roof over their heads. It was a shabby roof, and a small ill-furnished room, but there was a wash handbasin and a window opening onto a window box which had been covered by wire netting, and that solved Oscar's problems.

Amabel handed over the money, left her case, locked the door and went out again, intent on finding a cafeteria. Presently, feeling all the better for a meal, still accompanied by Oscar in his basket and Cyril, she bought a take away meat pie and milk, carrying them to her room.

Oscar, let out of his basket at last, made a beeline for the window box, and then settled down to eat the meat in the pie while Cyril wolfed the crust, washing it down with the milk before climbing onto the bed.

Amabel washed in tepid water, cleaned her teeth, got into her nightie and then into bed. She was tired, too tired to think rationally, so she closed her eyes and went to sleep.

She was up early, asked for tea and toast from the girl at the counter and took Cyril out for five minutes. Since she didn't dare to leave Oscar he went too, grumbling in his basket.

Assuring the girl they would be back in the evening, she locked the door and set off into the cold bright morning.

It was apparent by midday that a job which would admit Cyril and Oscar was going to be hard to find.

Amabel bought a carton of milk and a ham roll and found a quiet corner by St Mary's, where she fed Oscar and Cyril from the tin she had in her shoulder bag before letting a timid Oscar out to explore the flowerbeds. With a cat's good sense he stayed close to her, and soon got back into his basket and settled down again. He was a wise beast and he was aware that they were, the three of them, going through a sticky patch…

The afternoon was as disappointing as the morning, and the café, when Amabel got back to it, looked uninviting. But it spelled security of a sort, and tomorrow was another day.

Which turned out to be most unfortunately, just like the previous one. The following morning, when Amabel went to her frugal breakfast in the café, the girl at the counter leaned across to say, 'Can't put you up any longer. Got a regular booked the room for a week.'

Amabel chewed toast in a dry mouth. 'But there's another room I can rent?'

'Not with them animals. Be out by ten o'clock, will you? So's I can get the bed changed.'

'But just for a few nights?'

'Not a hope. The boss turned a blind eye for a couple of nights but that's it. Tried the Salvation Army, have you? There's beds there, but you'd have to find somewhere for that dog and cat.'

It was another fine morning, but cold. Amabel found a sheltered seat in the park and sat down to think. She discarded the idea of going home. She had escaped once; it might not be as easy again, and nothing was going to make her abandon Cyril and Oscar.

It was a question of waiting for eight days before Josh and his wife returned, and, however careful she was, there wasn't enough money in her purse to buy them bed and board for that time. She would try the Salvation Army—after five o'clock the girl had said—and hope that they would allow Cyril and Oscar to stay with her.

She had bought a local paper, so now she scanned the vacancies in the jobs columns. She ticked off the most promising, and set off to find the first of them. It was a tiresome business, for her suitcase was quite heavy and Oscar's basket got in the way. Each time she was rejected. Not unkindly, but with an indifference which hurt.

It was after four o'clock when she finally gave up and started on her way to the Salvation Army shelter. She had to pass the end of the Shambles to reach it, and on an impulse she turned aside and went through the half-open door of the little church she had sometimes visited. It was quiet inside and there was no one there. It was cold too, and dimly lighted, but there was peace there...

Amabel sat down in one of the old-fashioned high-backed pews, put Oscar's basket beside her, and, with her case on the other side and Cyril at her feet, allowed the tranquillity of the little church to soothe her.

She said aloud, 'Things are never as bad as they seem,' and Cyril thumped his tail in agreement. Presently, tired from all the walking, he went to sleep. So did Oscar, but Amabel sat without moving, trying to make plans in her tired head which, despite her efforts, was full of thoughts of Oliver. If he were there, she thought dreamily, he would know exactly what to do...

* * *

The doctor had reached York shortly after lunch, booked a room at the hotel and, with the faithful Tiger loping beside him, made his way to Dolores's shop. She was sitting behind the counter, reading, but she looked up as he went in and got to her feet. She had known that sooner or later he would come, but she still felt a momentary panic at the sight of him. Which was silly of her; he stood there in the doorway, large and placid, and his quiet greeting was reassuring.

'I've come to see Amabel,' he told her. 'Will you allow her to have an hour or two off? Or perhaps the rest of the afternoon? I can't stay in York long…'

'She's not here…'

'Oh, not ill, I hope?'

'She's gone. I didn't need her any more.' There was no expression on his face, but she took a step backwards. 'She's got an aunt to go to.'

'When was this? She had a week's notice, presumably?'

Dolores picked up a vase on the counter and put it down again. She said again, 'There's this aunt…'

'You sent her packing at a moment's notice?' The doctor's voice was quiet, but she shivered at the sound of it. 'She took the cat and dog with her?'

'Of course she did.'

'Did you know that her aunt was away from home?'

Dolores shrugged. 'She did mention it.' She would have to tell him something to make him see that it was useless looking for the girl. 'Amabel said something about going to stay with friends of her mother—somewhere near...' She paused for a moment, conjuring up names out of the back of her head. 'I think she said Nottingham—a Mrs Skinner...'

She heaved a sigh of relief; she had done that rather well.

He stood looking at her, his face inscrutable, his eyes cold. 'I don't believe you. And if any harm comes to Amabel I shall hold you responsible.'

He left the shop, closing the door quietly behind him, and Dolores flew to the kitchenette and reached for the bottle of whisky she kept hidden away there. Which meant that she missed seeing the girl at the patisserie go to the door and call to the doctor.

'Hi—you looking for Amabel? Poor kid got the sack at a moment's notice—told she wasn't wanted by that Dolores, I suppose...'

'You spoke to her?'

'Didn't have a chance. Had me hands full of customers. She waved though—had her case and that dog and cat, going heaven knows where. Haven't seen hair nor hide of her since...'

'How long ago?'

'Two days?'

'Dolores said that she had gone away to friends.'

The girl sniffed. 'Don't you believe it—that woman will tell you anything she thinks you want to hear.'

'Yes. You think Amabel is still in York? I'm going to drive to her aunt's house now; there's a man, Josh...'

'I've seen 'im once or twice of a Sunday—brings her back here—she goes there on her free day.'

The doctor thanked her. 'Probably she is there—and thank you. I'll let you know if I find her.'

'You do that—I liked her.'

She watched him go. He was a man to satisfy any girl's dreams, not to mention the money. That was a cashmere coat, and a silk tie costing as much as one of her dresses...

Of course there was no one at Miss Parsons' house, and no response from Josh's cottage when he knocked. He was equally unsuccessful at the village shop—Josh was away, he was told, and there had been no sign of Amabel.

The doctor drove back to York, parked the car once more at the hotel and set off with Tiger to scour the city. He was worried, desperately concerned as to Amabel's whereabouts. He forced himself to think calmly as he systematically combed the streets of the inner city.

He didn't believe for one moment that Amabel had left York, and he thought it unlikely that she would have had enough money to get her home. And to go home was the most unlikely thing she would do. She was here, still in York. It was just a question of finding her...

He stopped at several of the smaller shops to ask if anyone had seen her and was told in one of them—a shabby little café—that there had been a girl with a dog. She had bought a roll and had coffee two days ago. A slender clue, but enough to take the doctor through the streets once more.

It was as he reached the lower end of the Shambles for the second time that his eye lighted on the little church close by. He remembered then that Amabel had told him that she had gone there from time to time. He went through its open door and stood just inside, aware of the quiet and the cold, and he saw Amabel, a small vague figure in the distance.

He heaved a great sigh and went quietly to where she was sitting. 'Hello, Amabel,' he said in a calm voice, 'I thought I might find you here.'

She turned her head slowly as Cyril got to his feet, wagging his tail and whining with pleasure. 'Oliver—Oliver, is it really you?'

She stopped because she was crying, and he went and sat down beside her and put a great arm around her shoulders. He sat quietly and let her weep, and when her sobs became sniffs offered a handkerchief.

'So sorry,' said Amabel. 'You were a surprise—at least, I was thinking about you, and there you were.'

He was relieved to hear that her voice, while still watery, was quite steady.

'Are you staying in York?' she asked politely. 'It's nice to see you again. But don't let me keep you.'

The doctor choked back a laugh. Even in dire circumstances, Amabel, he felt sure, would always be polite. He said gently, 'Amabel, I went to the shop and that woman—Dolores—told me what she had done. I've spent hours looking for you, but we aren't going to talk about it now. We are going to the hotel, and after a meal and a good night's sleep we will talk.'

'No,' said Amabel quite forcibly. 'I won't. What I mean is, thank you, but no. Tomorrow…'

He had Oscar's basket, and her case. Now he said, 'One day at a time, Amabel.'

Chapter 6

Several hours later Amabel, fed and bathed and in bed, with Cyril curled up on the floor and Oscar stretched out on her feet, tried to sort out the evening so that it made sense. As it was, it had been a fairy tale dream. In no other way could she account for the last few hours.

How had Oliver been able to conjure a private sitting room out of thin air? A tray of tea, food for Oscar and Cyril? Her case had been unpacked and its contents whisked away to be washed and pressed, she was in a bedroom with a balcony where Oscar could feel free, had had a delicious meal and a glass of wine, and Oliver urging her to eat and drink and not ask questions but to go to bed since they must leave early in the morning.

She had obeyed sleepily, thanked him for her supper and said goodnight, then spent ages in the bath. And it had all seemed perfectly normal—just as a dream was always normal. In the morning she must find a way of leaving, but now she would just close her eyes...

She opened them to thin sunshine through the drawn curtains and a cheerful girl with a tray of tea.

'Dr Fforde asks that you dress quickly and meet him in the sitting room in twenty minutes—and I'm to take the dog with me so that he can have a run with the doctor's dog.'

Amabel drank her tea, put Oscar on the balcony and went into the sitting room. She showered and dressed with all speed, anxious not to keep Oliver waiting, so her hair didn't look its best and her make-up was perfunctory, but she looked rested and ready for anything.

The doctor was at a window, looking out onto the street below. He turned round as she went in and studied her. 'That's better. You slept well?'

'Yes. Oh, yes, I did. It was like heaven.' She bent to stroke Cyril's head. 'Thank you for taking him out. And thank you for letting me stay here. It's like a dream.'

Breakfast was brought in then, and when they had sat down at the table she said, 'I expect you are in a hurry. The maid asked me to be quick. I'm very grateful, Oliver, for your kindness.' She added, 'There are several jobs I shall go and see about this morning.'

The doctor loaded toast with marmalade. 'Amabel, we are friends, so let us not talk nonsense to each other. You are a brave girl, but enough is enough. In half an hour or so we are leaving York. I have written to Josh so that he will know what has happened when he comes

back home, and we will let Miss Parsons know as soon
as possible.'

'Know what?'

'Where you will be and what you will be doing.'

'I'm not going home.'

'No, no, of course not. I am hoping that you will
agree to do something for me. I have a great-aunt re-
covering from a slight stroke. Her one wish is to return
to her home, but my mother hasn't been able to find
someone who will live with her for a time. No nursing
is needed, but a willingness to talk and be talked to,
join in any small amusement she may fancy, help her to
make life enjoyable. She is old, in her eighties, but she
loves her garden and her home. She has a housekeeper
and a housemaid who have both been with her for years.
And don't think that I'm asking you to do this because
you happen to be between jobs...'

Which sounded so much better, reflected Amabel,
than being out of work, or even destitute. He was asking for her help and she owed him a great deal. Besides,
he was her friend, and friends help each other when
they were needed.

She said, 'If your great-aunt would like me to be with
her, then I'll go to her. But what about Cyril and Oscar?'

'She has a house in the country; she likes animals
and they will be welcome there. I should point out that
she is a very old lady and liable to have another stroke,
so the prospect for you is not a permanent one.'

Amabel drank the last of her coffee. 'Well, I expect
for someone like me, with no special skills, it would be

hard to find permanent work. But I must write to Aunt Thisbe and tell her.'

'Better still, if you have her phone number you can ring her up.'

'May I? When we get to wherever we are going?'

He crossed the room to the telephone on a side table. 'You have the number with you?' He held out a hand and she handed him the grubby slip of paper she had carried everywhere with her. He got the receptionist and waited for her to get the number, then handed Amabel the phone.

Aunt Thisbe's voice was loud and clear, demanding to know who it was.

'It's me. Amabel. There's nothing wrong, but I must tell you—that is, I must explain—'

The phone was taken from her. 'Miss Parsons? Oliver Fforde. Perhaps I can set your mind at rest. Amabel is with me and quite safe. She will explain everything to you, but I promise you that you have no need to worry about her.' He handed the phone back. 'I'll take the dogs for a quick walk—tell Miss Parsons that you will phone again this evening.'

Aunt Thisbe's firm voice begging her to take her time and tell her what had happened collected Amabel's wits for her. She gave a fairly coherent account of what had been happening. 'And Oliver has told me that he has a job waiting for me with an old aunt and has asked me to take it. And I've said I would because I should like to repay his kindness.'

'A sensible decision, child. An opportunity to express your thanks and at the same time give you a chance to decide what you intend to do. I heard Oliver saying that you will phone again this evening. This has changed things, of course. I was thinking of returning for Christmas, so that you would have somewhere to come over the holiday period, but now that there is no need of that and so I shall stay here for another few weeks. But remember, Amabel, if you need me I will return at once. I am very relieved that Oliver has come to your aid. A good man, Amabel, and one to be trusted.'

Amabel put down the phone as Oliver returned. He said briskly, 'I've put the dogs in the car. If you will get your coat, we'll be off.'

He shovelled Oscar into his basket. 'I must be back at the hospital by three o'clock, so I'll drop you off on the way.' He added impatiently, 'I'll explain as we go.'

Since it was obvious to her that he had no intention of saying anything more until it suited him, Amabel did as she was told.

Consumed by curiosity, and a feeling of uncertainty about her future, Amabel had to wait until they were travelling fast down the M1 before the doctor had anything to say other than enquiries as to her comfort.

'We are going to Aldbury in Hertfordshire. It's a small village a few miles from Berkhamsted. My mother is there, arranging for my aunt's return, and she will explain everything to you—time off, salary and so on—and stay overnight to see you settled in. She is very relieved that you have agreed to take the job and you will be very welcomed, both by her and by Mrs Twitchett, the housekeeper, and Nelly.'

Amabel said, 'Your great-aunt might not like me.'

'There is nothing about you to dislike, Amabel.'

A remark which did nothing for her ego. She had never had delusions about herself, but now she felt a nonentity...

The doctor glanced at her as he spoke, at her unassuming profile as she looked steadily ahead. She looked completely unfazed, accepting the way in which he had bulldozed her into an unknown future. He had had no chance to do otherwise; there had been no time, and to have left her there alone in York would have been unthinkable. He said, 'I've rushed you, haven't I? But sometimes one has to take a chance!'

Amabel smiled. 'A lucky chance for me. I'm so grateful, and I'll do my best with your great-aunt. Would you tell me her name?'

'Lady Haleford. Eighty-seven years old, widowed for ten years. No children. Loves her garden, birds, the country and animals. She likes to play cards and cheats. Since her stroke she has become fretful and forgetful and at times rather peevish.' He added, 'No young society, I'm afraid.'

'Well, I have never gone out much, so that doesn't matter.'

When he could spare the time, he reflected, he would take her out. Dinner and dancing, a theatre or concert. He didn't feel sorry for her, Amabel wasn't a girl one could pity, but she deserved some fun and he liked her. He was even, he had to admit, becoming a little fond of her in a brotherly sort of way. He wanted to see her safely embarked on the life she wanted so that she would

have the chance to meet people of her own age, marry…
He frowned. Time enough for that…

They travelled on in silence, comfortable in each
other's company, and after a while he asked, 'Do you
want to stop? There's a quiet pub about ten miles ahead;
we can let the dogs out there.'

The pub stood back from the road and the car park
was almost empty. 'Go on inside,' the doctor told her.
'I'll see to the dogs and make sure Oscar's all right. We
can't stay long.'

As long as it's long enough to find the Ladies'
thought Amabel, wasting no time.

They had beef sandwiches and coffee, saw to the
dogs and got back into the car. Oscar, snoozing in his
basket, was hardly disturbed. Life for him had had its
ups and downs lately, but now he was snug and safe and
Amabel's voice reassured him.

Travelling in a Rolls-Royce was very pleasant, reflected Amabel, warm and comfortable and sliding past
everything else on the road. And Oliver drove with relaxed skill. She supposed that he was a man who wasn't
easily put out.

When he turned off the motorway he said, 'Not long
now,' and sure enough, a few miles past Berkhamsted, he took a side turning and then a narrow lane
and slowed as they reached Aldbury. It was a charming village, having its origin in Saxon times. There
was a village green, a duck pond and a pub close by,
and standing a little apart was the church, and beyond
the village there was a pleasing vista of parkland and
woods. Amabel, staring round her, knew that she would

like living here, and hoped that it might be in one of the brick and timber cottages they were passing.

The doctor drove to the far side of the pond and stopped before a house standing on its own. Its front door opened directly onto the pavement—and it was brick and timber, as the others. It had a thatched roof, just as those did, but it was considerably larger and yet looked just as cosy.

He got out and opened Amabel's door. 'Come in and meet my mother again,' he invited. 'I'll come for the dogs and Oscar in a moment.'

The house door had been opened and a short stout woman stood there, smiling. She said comfortably, 'So here you are, Master Oliver, and the young lady...'

'Miss Amabel Parsons. Amabel, this is Mrs Twitchett.'

He bent to kiss her cheek and Amabel offered a hand, aware that as it was being shaken she was being studied closely. She hoped that Mrs Twitchett's smiling nod was a good sign.

The hall was wide with a wood floor, handsomely carpeted, but Amabel had no time to look around her for a door was thrust open and Mrs Fforde came to meet them.

The doctor bent to kiss her. 'No need to introduce you,' he said cheerfully. 'I'll leave you for a moment and see to the dogs and Oscar.'

'Yes, dear. Can you stay?'

'Ten minutes. I've a clinic in a couple of hours.'

'Coffee? It'll be here when you've seen to the dogs. What about the cat?'

'Oscar is a much-travelled beast; he'll present no problems and the garden is walled.'

He went away and Mrs Fforde took Amabel's arm. 'Come and sit down for a moment. Mrs Twitchett will bring the coffee; I'm sure you must need it. I don't suppose Oliver stopped much on the way?'

'Once—we had coffee and sandwiches.'

'But it's quite a drive, even at his speed. Take off your coat and come and sit down.'

'My husband's aunt, Lady Haleford, is old and frail. I expect Oliver has told you that. The stroke has left her in need of a good deal of assistance. Nothing that requires nursing, you understand, just someone to be there. I hope you won't find it too arduous, for you are young and elderly people can be so trying! She is a charming old lady, though, and despite the fact that she can be forgetful she is otherwise mentally alert. I do hope that Oliver made that clear to you?'

Mrs Fforde looked so anxious that Amabel said at once, 'Yes, he did. I'll do my best to keep Lady Haleford happy, indeed I will.'

'You don't mind a country life? I'm afraid you won't have much freedom.'

'Mrs Fforde, I am so grateful to have a job where Cyril and Oscar can be with me—and I love the country.'

'You will want to let your mother know where you are?' asked Mrs Fforde gently. 'Presently, when you are settled in, phone her. I shall be staying here overnight and will fetch Lady Haleford in the morning.'

The doctor joined them then, and Mrs Twitchett followed him in with a tray of coffee, Tiger and Cyril sidling in behind her.

'Oscar is in the kitchen,' he observed. 'What a sensible animal he is. Mrs Twitchett and Nelly have already fallen for his charms.' He smiled at Amabel and turned to his mother. 'You'll go home tomorrow? I'll try and get down next weekend. You will discuss everything with Amabel before you go? Good.' He drank his coffee and bent to kiss her cheek. 'I'll phone you…'

He laid a hand on Amabel's shoulder. 'I hope you will be happy with my aunt, Amabel. If there are any problems, don't hesitate to tell my mother.'

'All right—but I don't expect any. And thank you, Oliver.'

He was going again out of her life, and this time it was probably for the last time. He had come to her aid, rescued her with speed and a lack of fuss, set her back on her feet once more and was now perfectly justified in forgetting all about her. She offered her hand and her smile lighted up her face. 'Goodbye, Oliver.'

He didn't reply, only patted her shoulder and a moment later he was gone.

'We will go upstairs,' said Mrs Fforde briskly. 'I'll show you your room, and then we will go over the rest of the house so that you will feel quite at home before Lady Haleford arrives. We should be back in time for lunch and I'll leave soon after that. You're sure you can manage?'

'Yes,' said Amabel gravely. 'I'm sure, Mrs Fforde.' It might not be easy at first, but she owed Oliver so much…

They went up the staircase, with its worn oak treads, to the landing above, with several doors on either side and a passage leading to the back of the house.

'I've put you next to my aunt's room,' said Mrs Fforde. 'There's a bathroom between—hers. Yours is on the other side of your room. I hope you won't have to get up in the night, but if you are close by it will make that easier.'

She opened a door and they went in together. It was a large room, with a small balcony overlooking the side of the house, and most comfortably furnished. It was pretty chintz curtains matching the bedspread, thick carpeting and a dear little easy chair beside a small table close to the window. The small dressing table had a stool before it and there was a pink-shaded lamp on the bedside table.

Mrs Fforde led the way across the room and opened a door. 'This is your bathroom—rather small, I'm afraid...'

Amabel thought of the washbasin behind the shop. 'It's perfect,' she said.

'And here's the door to my aunt's bathroom...' They went through it, and on into Lady Haleford's room at the front of the house. It was magnificently furnished, its windows draped in damask, the four-poster bed hung with the same damask, the massive dressing table loaded with silver-backed brushes and mirror, little cut-glass bottles and trinkets.

'Has Lady Haleford always lived here?'

'Yes—at least since her husband died. They lived in the manor house before that, of course, but when her son inherited he moved there with his wife and children and she came here. That was ten years ago. She has often told me that she prefers this house to the manor. For one thing the garden here is beautiful and the rooms aren't too large. And, being in the village, she can still see her friends without having to go too far. Until she had her stroke she drove herself, but of course that won't be possible now. Do you drive?'

'Yes,' said Amabel. 'But I'm not used to driving in large towns.'

'It would be driving Lady Haleford to church and back, and perhaps to call on local friends.'

'I could manage that,' said Amabel.

They went round the house in a leisurely manner. It was, she considered, rather large for one old lady and her two staff, but it was comfortable, rather old-fashioned, and it felt like home. Downstairs, beside the drawing room, there was a dining room, the morning room and a small sitting room—all immaculate. The kind of rooms, reflected Amabel, in which one could sit all day.

The last room they went into was the kitchen, as old-fashioned as the rest of the house. Something smelled delicious as they went in, and Mrs Twitchett turned from the Aga to warn them that dinner would be on the table in half an hour. Nelly was doing something at the table, and sitting before the Aga, for all the world as though they had lived there for ever, were Cyril and Oscar, pleased to see her but making no effort to rouse themselves.

'Happen they're tired out,' said Mrs Twitchett. 'They've eaten their fill and given no trouble.'

Amabel stooped to pat them. 'You really don't mind them being here?'

'Glad to have them. Nelly dotes on them. They'll always be welcome in here.'

Amabel had a sudden urge to burst into tears, a foolishness she supposed, but the relief to have a kind home for her two companions was great. They deserved peace and quiet after the last few months…

She smiled uncertainly at Mrs Twitchett and said thank you, then followed Mrs Fforde out of the kitchen.

Over dinner she was told her duties—not onerous but, as Mrs Fforde pointed out, probably boring and tiring. She was to take her free time when and where she could, and if it wasn't possible to have a day off each week she was to have two half-days. She might have to get up at night occasionally, and, as Mrs Fforde pointed out, the job at times might be demanding. But the wages she suggested were twice as much as Dolores had paid her. Living quietly, thought Amabel, I shall be able to save almost all of them. With a little money behind her she would have a chance to train for a career which would give her future security.

The next morning, buoyed up by high hopes, she waited for Mrs Fforde's return with Lady Haleford. All the same she was nervous.

It was a pity that she couldn't know that the doctor, sitting at his desk in his consulting rooms, had spared a moment to think of her as he studied his next patient's notes. He hoped that she would be happy with his greataunt; the whole thing had been hurriedly arranged and even now she might be regretting it. But something had had to be done to help her.

He stood up to greet his patient and dismissed her from his thoughts.

Mrs Fforde's elderly Rover stopped in front of the door and Amabel went into the hall, standing discreetly at a distance from Mrs Twitchett and Nelly, waiting at the door. She and Cyril had been out early that morning for a walk through the country lanes; now he stood quietly beside her, and Oscar had perched himself close by, anxious not to be overlooked.

Lady Haleford was small and thin, and walked with a stick and the support of Mrs Fforde's arm, but although she walked slowly and hesitantly there was nothing invalidish about her.

She returned Mrs Twitchett's and Nelly's greetings in a brisk manner and asked at once, 'Well, where's this girl Oliver has found to look after me?'

Mrs Fforde guided her into the drawing room and sat her in a high-backed chair. 'Here, waiting for you.' She said over her shoulder, 'Amabel, come and meet Lady Haleford.'

Amabel put a cautionary finger on Cyril's head and went to stand before the old lady.

'How do you do, Lady Haleford?'

Lady Haleford studied her at some length. She had dark eyes, very bright in her wrinkled face, a small beaky nose and a mouth which, because of her stroke, drooped sideways.

'A plain girl,' she observed to no one in particular.

'But looks are only skin-deep, so they say. Nice eyes and pretty hair, though, and young…' She added peevishly, 'Too young. Old people are boring to the young. You'll be gone within a week. I'm peevish and I forget things and I wake in the night.'

Amabel said gently, 'I shall be happy here, Lady Haleford. I hope you will let me stay and keep you company. This is such a lovely old house, you must be glad to be home again, you will get well again now that you are home.'

Lady Haleford said, 'Pooh,' and then added, 'I suppose I shall have to put up with you.'

'Only for as long as you want to, Lady Haleford,' said Amabel briskly.

'Well, at least you've a tongue in your head,' said the old lady. 'Where's my lunch?'

Her eye fell on Cyril. 'And what's this? The dog Oliver told me about? And there's a cat?'

'Yes. They are both elderly and well-behaved, and I promise you they won't disturb you.'

Lady Haleford said tartly, 'I like animals. Come here, dog.'

Cyril advanced obediently, not much liking to be called dog when he had a perfectly good name. But he stood politely while the old lady looked him over and then patted his head.

Mrs Fforde went home after lunch, leaving Amabel to cope with the rest of the day. Oliver had advised her to let Amabel find her own feet. 'She's quite capable of dealing with any hiccoughs,' he had pointed out, 'and the sooner they get to know each other the better.'

A remark which hadn't prevented him from thinking that perhaps he had made a mistake pitching Amabel into a job she might dislike. She was an independent girl, determined to make a good future for herself; she had only accepted the job with his great-aunt because she had to have a roof over her head and money in her pocket. But he had done his best, he reflected and need waste no more time thinking about her.

But as he had decided not to think any more about Amabel, so Miriam was equally determined to think about him. Dolores had phoned her and told her of his visit. 'I told him that she had left York—I invented an aunt somewhere or other, a friend of her mother's...' She didn't mention that he hadn't believed her. 'He went away and I didn't see him again. Is he back in London? Have you seen him?'

'No, not yet, but I know he's back. I rang his consulting rooms and said I wanted an appointment. He's been back for days. He can't have wasted much time in looking for her. You've been an angel, Dolores, and so clever to fob him off.'

'Anything for a friend, darling. I'll keep my eyes and ears open just in case she's still around.' She giggled. 'Good hunting!'

As far as she was concerned she didn't intend to do any more about it, although she did once ask idly if anyone had seen Amabel or her visitor when she had her coffee in the patisserie. But the girl behind the counter didn't like Dolores; she had treated Amabel shabbily and she had no need to know that that nice man had gone back one evening and told her that Amabel and her companions were safe with him.

Miriam had phoned Oliver's house several times to be told by Bates that his master was not home.

'He's gone away again?' she'd asked sharply.

'No. No, miss. I assume that he's very busy at the hospital.'

He told the doctor when he returned in the evening. 'Mrs Potter-Stokes, sir, has been ringing up on several occasions. I took it upon myself to say that you were at the hospital. She didn't wish to leave a message.' He lowered his eyes. 'I should have told you sooner, sir, but you have been away from home a good deal.'

'Quite right, Bates. If she should phone again, will you tell her that I'm very busy at the moment? Put it nicely.'

Bates murmured assent, concealing satisfaction; he disliked Mrs Potter-Stokes.

It was entirely by chance that Miriam met a friend of her mother's one morning. A pleasant lady who enjoyed a gossip.

'My dear, I don't seem to have seen you lately. You and Oliver Fforde are usually together...' She frowned. 'He is coming to dinner on Thursday, but someone or other told me that you were away.'

'Away? No, I shall be at home for the next few weeks.' Miriam contrived to look wistful. 'Oliver and I have been trying to meet for days—he's so busy; you would never believe how difficult it is to snatch an hour or two together.'

Her companion, a woman without guile and not expecting it in others, said at once, 'My dear Miriam, you must come to dinner. At least you can sit with each other and have a little time together. I'll get another man to make up the numbers.'

Miriam laid a hand on her arm. 'Oh, how kind of you; if only we can see each other for a while we can arrange to meet.'

Miriam went home well satisfied, so sure of her charm and looks that she was positive that Oliver, seeing her again, would resume their friendship and forget that silly girl.

But she was to be disappointed. He greeted her with his usual friendly smile, listened to her entertaining chatter, and with his usual beautiful manners evaded her questions as to where he had been. It was vexing that despite all her efforts he was still no more than one of her many friends.

At the end of the evening he drove her home, but he didn't accept her invitation to go in for a drink.

'I must be up early,' he told her, and wished her a pleasantly cool goodnight.

Miriam went angrily to her bed. She could find no fault in his manner towards her, but she had lost whatever hold she'd thought she had on him. Which made her all the more determined to do something about it. She had always had everything she wanted since she was a small girl, and now she wanted Oliver.

It was several days later that, an unwilling fourth at one of her mother's bridge parties, she heard someone remark, 'Such a pity he cannot spare the time to join us; he's going away for the weekend...'

The speaker turned to Miriam. 'I expect you knew that already, my dear?'

Miriam stopped herself just in time from trumping her partner's ace.

'Yes, yes, I do. He's very fond of his mother...'

'She lives at such a pleasant place. He's going to see an old aunt as well.' She laughed. 'Not a very exciting weekend for him. You won't be with him, Miriam?' The speaker glanced at her slyly.

'No, I'd already promised to visit an old school-friend.'

Miriam thought about that later. There was no reason why Oliver shouldn't visit an old aunt; there was no reason why she should feel uneasy about it. But she did.

She waited for a day or two and then phoned him, keeping her voice deliberately light and understanding. There was rather a good film on; how about them going to see it together at the weekend?

'I'll be away,' he told her.

'Oh, well, another time. Visiting your mother?'

'Yes. It will be nice to get out of London for a couple of days.'

He was as pleasant and friendly as he always had been, but she knew that she was making no headway with him. There was someone else—surely not that girl still?

She gave the matter a good deal of thought, and finally telephoned Mrs Fforde's home; if she was home, she would hang up, say 'wrong number', or make some

excuse, but if she was lucky enough to find her out and
the housekeeper, a garrulous woman, answered, she
might learn something...

She was in luck, and the housekeeper, told that this
was an old friend of the doctor's, was quite ready to
offer the information that he would be staying for the
weekend and leaving early on Sunday to visit Lady
Haleford.

'Ah, yes,' said Miriam encouragingly, 'his great-aunt.
Such a charming old lady.'

The housekeeper went on, 'Back home after a stroke,
madam told me. But they've got someone to live with
her—a young lady, but very competent.'

'I must give Lady Haleford a ring. Will you let me
have her number?'

It was an easy matter to phone and, under the pretext
of getting a wrong number, discover that Lady Haleford
lived at Aldbury. It would be wise to wait until after
Oliver had been there, but then she would find some
reason for calling on the old lady and see for herself
what it was about this girl that held Oliver's interest.

Satisfied that she had coped well with what she considered a threat to her future, Miriam relaxed.

Amabel, aware that fate was treating her kindly, set
about being as nearly a perfect companion as possible.
No easy task, for Lady Haleford was difficult. Not only
was she old, she was accustomed to living her life as
she wished—an impossibility after her stroke—so that
for the first few days nothing was right, although she

tolerated Cyril and Oscar, declaring that no one else understood her.

For several days Amabel was to be thoroughly dispirited; she had done nothing right, said nothing right, remained silent when she should have spoken, spoken when she was meant to be silent. It was disheartening, but she liked the old lady and guessed that underneath the peevishness and ill-temper there was a frightened old lady lurking.

There had been no chance to establish any kind of routine. She had had no free time other than brief walks round the garden with Cyril. But Mrs Twitchett and Nelly had done all they could to help her, and she told herself that things would improve.

She had coaxed Lady Haleford one afternoon, swathed in shawls, to sit in the drawing room, and had set up a card table beside her, intent on getting her to play two-handed whist. Her doctor had been that morning, pronounced himself satisfied with her progress and suggested that she might begin to take an interest in life once more.

He was a hearty man, middle-aged and clearly an old friend. He had taken no notice of Lady Haleford's peevishness, told her how lucky she was to have someone so young and cheerful to be with her and had gone away, urging Amabel at the same time to get out into the fresh air.

'Nothing like a good walk when you're young,' he had observed, and Mabel, pining for just that, had agreed with him silently.

Lady Haleford went to sleep over her cards and Amabel sat quietly, waiting for her to rouse herself again. And while she sat, she thought. Her job wasn't easy, she had no freedom and almost no leisure, but on the other hand she had a roof—a comfortable one—over her head, Oscar and Cyril had insinuated themselves into the household and become household pets, and she would be able to save money. Besides, she liked Lady Haleford, she loved the old house and the garden, and she had so much to be thankful for she didn't know where to begin.

With the doctor, she supposed, who had made it all possible. If only she knew where he lived she could write and tell him how grateful she was...

The drawing room door opened soundlessly and he walked in.

Amabel gaped at him, her mouth open. Then she shut it and put a finger to it. 'She's asleep,' she whispered unnecessarily, and felt a warm wave of delight and content at the sight of him.

He dropped a kiss on her cheek, having crossed the room and sat down.

'I've come to tea,' he told her, 'and if my aunt will invite me, I'll stay for supper.'

He sounded matter-of-fact, as though dropping in for tea was something he did often, and he was careful to hide his pleasure at seeing Amabel again. Still plain, but good food was producing some gentle curves and there were no longer shadows under her eyes.

Beautiful eyes, thought the doctor, and smiled, feeling content in her company.

Chapter 7

Lady Haleford gave a small snort and woke up.

'Oliver—how delightful. You'll stay for tea? Amabel, go and tell Mrs Twitchett. You know Amabel, of course?'

'I saw her as I came in, and yes, I know Amabel. How do you find life now that you are back home, Aunt?'

The old lady said fretfully, 'I get tired and I forget things. But it is good to be home again. Amabel is a good girl and not impatient. Some of the nurses were impatient. You could feel them seething under their calm faces and I can sympathise with them.'

'You sleep well?'

'I suppose so. The nights are long, but Amabel makes tea and we sit and gossip.' She added in an anxious voice, 'I shall get better, Oliver?'

He said gently, 'You will improve slowly, but getting well after illness is sometimes harder than being ill.'

'Yes, it is. How I hate that wheelchair and that horrible thing to help me walk. I won't use it, you know. Amabel gives me an arm...'

The old lady closed her eyes and nodded off for a moment, before adding, 'It was clever of you to find her, Oliver. She's a plain girl, isn't she? Dresses in such dull clothes too, but her voice is pleasant and she's gentle.' She spoke as though Amabel wasn't there, sitting close to her. 'You made a good choice, Oliver.'

The doctor didn't look at Amabel. 'Yes, indeed I did, Aunt.'

Nelly came in with the tea tray then, and he began a casual conversation about his mother and his work and the people they knew, giving Amabel time to get over her discomfort. She was too sensible to be upset by Lady Haleford's remarks, but he guessed that she felt embarrassed...

Tea over, Lady Haleford declared that she would take a nap. 'You'll stay for dinner?' she wanted to know. 'I see you very seldom.' She sounded peevish.

'Yes, I'll stay with pleasure,' he told her. 'While you doze Amabel and I will take the dogs for a quick run.'

'And I shall have a glass of sherry before we dine,' said the old lady defiantly.

'Why not? We'll be back in half an hour or so. Come along, Amabel.'

Amabel got up. 'Is there anything you want before we go, Lady Haleford?' she asked.

'Yes, fetch Oscar to keep me company.'

Oscar, that astute cat, knew on which side his bread was buttered, for he settled down primly on the old lady's lap and went to sleep.

It was cold outside, but there was a bright moon in a starry sky. The doctor took Amabel's arm and walked her briskly through the village, past the church and along a lane out of the village. They each held a dog lead and the beasts trotted beside them, glad of the unexpected walk.

'Well,' said the doctor, 'how do you find your job? Have you settled in? My aunt can be difficult, and now, after her stroke, I expect she is often querulous.'

'Yes, but so should I be. Wouldn't you? And I'm very happy here. It's not hard work, and you know everyone is so kind.'

'But you have to get up during the night?'

'Well, now and then.' She didn't tell him that Lady Haleford woke up during the early hours most nights and demanded company. Fearful of further probing questions, she asked, 'Have you been busy? You haven't needed to go to York again?'

'No, that is a matter happily dealt with. You hear from your mother and Miss Parsons?'

'Yes, Aunt Thisbe is coming home at the end of January, and my mother seems very happy. The market garden is planted and they have plenty of help.' She faltered for a moment. 'Mother said not to go home and see her yet, Mr Graham is still rather—well, I think he'd rather that I didn't visit them…'

'You would like to see your mother?' he asked gently.

'Yes, but if she thinks it is best for me to stay away then I will. Perhaps later...'

'And what do you intend to do later?'

They turned for home and he tucked her hand under his arm.

'Well, I shall be able to save a lot of money. It's all computers these days, isn't it? So I'll take a course in them and get a good job and somewhere to live.' She added anxiously, 'Your aunt does want me to stay for a while?'

'Oh, most certainly. I've talked to her doctor and he thinks that she needs six weeks or two months living as she does at present, and probably longer.'

They had reached the house again.

'You have very little freedom,' he told her.

She said soberly, 'I'm content.'

They had supper early, for Lady Haleford became easily tired, and as soon as the meal was finished the doctor got up to go.

'You'll come again?' demanded his aunt. 'I like visitors, and next time you will tell me about yourself. Haven't you found a girl to marry yet? You are thirty-four, Oliver. You've enough money and a splendid home and the work you love; now you need a wife.'

He bent to kiss her. 'You shall be the first to know when I find her.' And to Amabel he said, 'No, don't get up. Mrs Twitchett will see me out.' He put a hand on Amabel's shoulder as he passed her chair, and with Tiger at his heels was gone.

His visit had aroused the old lady; she had no wish to go to bed, she said pettishly. And it was a pity that

Oliver could visit her so seldom. She observed, 'He is a busy man, and I dare say has many friends. But he needs to settle down. There are plenty of nice girls for him to choose from, and there is that Miriam...' She was rambling a bit. 'The Potter-Stokes widow—been angling for him for an age. If he's not careful she'll have him.' She closed her eyes. 'Not a nice young woman...'

Lady Haleford dozed for a while so Amabel thought about Oliver and the prospect of him marrying. She found the idea depressing, although it was the obvious thing for a man in his position to do. Anyway, it was none of her business.

A week went by, almost unnoticed in the gentle routine of the old house. Lady Haleford improved a little, but not much. Some days her testiness was enough to cast a blight over the entire household, so that Mrs Twitchett burnt the soup and Nelly dropped plates and Amabel had to listen to a diatribe of her many faults. Only Cyril and Oscar weathered the storm and her fierce little rages, sitting by her chair and allowing her peevish words to fly over their heads.

But there were days when she was placid, wanting to talk, play at cards, and walk slowly round the house, carefully hitched up under Amabel's arm.

Her doctor came, assured her that she was making steady progress, warned Amabel to humour her as much as possible and went away again.

Since humouring her meant getting up in the small hours to read to the old lady, or simply to talk until she drowsed off to a light sleep, Amabel had very little time for herself. At least each morning she took Cyril for a walk while Lady Haleford rested in her bed after breakfast before getting up, and she looked forward to her half-hour's freedom each day, even when it was cold and wet.

On this particular morning it was colder and wetter than it had been for several days, and Amabel, trudging back down the village street with Cyril beside her, looked rather as though she had fallen into a ditch and been pulled out backwards. Her head down against the wind and rain, she didn't see the elegant little sports car outside Lady Haleford's gate until she was beside it.

Even then she would have opened the door and gone inside if the woman in the car hadn't wound down the window and said in an anxious voice, 'Excuse me— if you could spare a moment? Is this Lady Haleford's house? My mother is a friend of hers and asked me to look her up as I was coming this way. But it's too early to call. Could I leave a message with someone?'

She smiled charmingly while at the same time studying Amabel's person. This must be the girl, reflected Miriam. Plain as a pikestaff and looks like a drowned rat. I can't believe that Oliver is in the least bit interested in her. Dolores has been tricking me... She spent a moment thinking of how she would repay her for that, then said aloud, at her most charming, 'Are you her granddaughter or niece? Perhaps you could tell her?'

'I'm Lady Haleford's companion,' said Amabel, and saw how cold the lovely blue eyes were. 'But I'll give her a message if you like. Would you like to come back later, or come and wait indoors? She has been ill and doesn't get up early.'

'I'll call on my way back,' said Miriam. She smiled sweetly. 'I'm sorry you're so wet standing there; I am thoughtless. But perhaps you don't mind the country in winter. I don't like this part of England. I've been in York for a while, and after that this village looks so forlorn.'

'It's very nice here,' said Amabel. 'But York is lovely; I was there recently.'

Her face ringed by strands of wet hair, she broke into a smile she couldn't suppress at the remembrance of the doctor.

Miriam said sharply, 'You have happy memories of it?'

Amabel, lost in a momentary dream, didn't notice the sharpness. 'Yes.'

'Well, I won't keep you.' Miriam smiled and made an effort to sound friendly. 'I'll call again.'

She drove away and Amabel went indoors. She spent the next ten minutes drying herself and Cyril and then went to tidy herself before going to Lady Haleford's room.

The old lady was in a placid mood, not wanting to talk much and apt to doze off from time to time. It wasn't until she was dressed and downstairs in her normal chair by the drawing room fire that she asked, 'Well, what have you been doing with yourself, Amabel?'

Glad of something to talk about, Amabel told her of her morning's encounter. 'And I'm so sorry but she didn't tell me her name, and I forgot to ask, but she said that she'll be back.'

Lady Haleford said worriedly, 'I do have trouble remembering people… What was she like? Dark? Fair? Pretty?'

'Fair and beautiful, very large blue eyes. She was driving a little red car.'

Lady Haleford closed her eyes. 'Well, she'll be back. I don't feel like visitors today, Amabel, so if she does call make my apologies—and ask her name.'

But of course Miriam didn't go back, and after a few days they forgot about her.

Miriam found it just impossible to believe that Oliver could possibly have any interest in such a dull plain girl, but all the same it was a matter which needed to be dealt with. She had begun to take it for granted that he would take her to the theatre, out to dine, to visit picture galleries, and even when he had refused on account of his work she had been so sure of him…

Her vanity prevented her from realising that he had merely been fulfilling social obligations, that he had no real interest in her.

She would have to change her tactics. She stopped phoning him with suggestions that they should go to the theatre or dine out, but she took care to be there at a mutual friend's house if he were to be there, too. Since Christmas was approaching, there were dinner parties and social gatherings enough.

Not that he was always to be found at them. Oliver had many friends, but his social life depended very much on his work so that, much to Miriam's annoyance, she only saw him from time to time, and when they did meet he was his usual friendly self, but that was all. Her pretty face and charm, her lovely clothes and witty talk were wasted on him.

When they had met at a friend's dinner party, and she'd asked casually what he intended to do for Christmas, he'd told her pleasantly that he was far too busy to make plans.

'Well, you mustn't miss our dinner party,' she'd told him. 'Mother will send you an invitation.'

The days passed peacefully enough at Aldbury. Lady Haleford had her ups and downs—indeed it seemed to Amabel that she was slowly losing ground. Although perhaps the dark days of the winter made the old lady loath to leave her bed. Since her doctor came regularly, and assured Amabel that things were taking their course, she spent a good many hours sitting in Lady Haleford's room, reading to her or playing two-handed patience.

All the same she was glad when Mrs Fforde phoned to say that she would be coming to spend a day or two. 'And I'm bringing two of my grandchildren with me—Katie and James. We will stay for a couple of days before I take them to London to do the Christmas shopping. Lady Haleford is very fond of them and it may please her to see them. Will you ask Mrs Twitchett to come to the phone, Amabel? I leave it to you to tell my aunt that we shall be coming.'

It was a piece of news which pleased the old lady mightily. 'Two nice children,' she told Amabel. 'They must be twelve years old—twins, you know. Their mother is Oliver's sister.' She closed her eyes for a moment and presently added, 'He has two sisters; they're both married, younger than he.'

They came two days later; Katie was thin and fair, with big blue eyes and a long plait of pale hair and James was the taller of the two, quiet and serious. Mrs Fforde greeted Amabel briskly.

'Amabel—how nice to see you again. You're rather pale—I dare say that you don't get out enough. Here are Katie and James. Why not take them into the garden for a while and I will visit Lady Haleford? Only put on something warm.' Her eyes lighted on Cyril, standing unexpectedly between the children.

'They are happy, your cat and dog?'

'Yes, very happy.'

'And you, Amabel?'

'I'm happy too, Mrs Fforde.'

Oscar, wishing for a share of the attention, went into the garden too, and, although it was cold, it was a clear day with no wind. They walked along its paths while the children told Amabel at some length about their shopping trip to London.

'We spend Christmas at Granny's,' they explained. 'Our aunt and uncle and cousins will be there, and Uncle Oliver. We have a lovely time and Christmas is always the same each year. Will you go home for Christmas, Amabel?'

'Oh, I expect so,' said Amabel, and before they could ask any more questions added, 'Christmas is such fun, isn't it?'

They stayed for two days, and Amabel was sorry to see them go, but even such a brief visit had tired Lady

Haleford, and they quickly slipped back into the placid pattern of their days.

Now that Christmas was near Amabel couldn't help wishing that she might enjoy some of the festivities, so it was a delightful surprise when Lady Haleford, rather more alert than she had been, told her that she wanted her to go to Berkhamstead and do some Christmas shopping. 'Sit down,' she commanded, 'and get a pen and some paper and write down my list.'

The list took several days to complete, for Lady Haleford tended to doze off a good deal, but finally Amabel caught the village bus, her ears ringing with advice and instructions from Mrs Twitchett, the list in her purse and a wad of banknotes tucked away safely.

It was really rather exciting, and shopping for presents was fun even if it was for someone else. It was a long list, for Lady Haleford's family was a large one: books, jigsaw puzzles, games for the younger members, apricots in brandy, a special blend of coffee, Stilton cheese in jars, a case of wine, boxes of candied fruits, and mouthwatering chocolates for the older ones.

Amabel, prowling round the small grocer's shop which seemed to stock every luxury imaginable, had enjoyed every minute of her shopping. She had stopped only briefly for a sandwich and coffee, and now, with an hour to spare before the bus left, she did a little shopping for herself.

High time too, she thought, stocking up on soap and toiletries, stockings and a thick sweater, shampoos and toothpaste. And then presents: patience cards for Lady Haleford, a scarf for Mrs Twitchett, a necklace for Nelly, a new collar for Cyril and a catnip mouse for Oscar. It was hard to find a present for her mother; she chose a blouse, in pink silk, and, since she couldn't ignore him, a book token for her stepfather.

At the very last minute she saw a dress, silvery grey in some soft material—the kind of dress, she told herself, which would be useful for an occasion, and after all it was Christmas… She bought it and, laden with parcels, went back to Aldbury.

The old lady, refreshed by a nap, wanted to see everything. Amabel drank a much needed cup of tea in the kitchen and spent the next hour or so carefully unwrapping parcels and wrapping them up again. Tomorrow, said Lady Haleford, Amabel must go into the village shop and get coloured wrapping paper and labels and write appropriate names on them.

The village shop was a treasure store of Christmas goods. Amabel spent a happy half-hour choosing suitably festive paper and bore it back for the old lady's approval. Later, kneeling on the floor under Lady Haleford's eyes, she was glad of her experience in Dolores's shop, for the gifts were all shapes and sizes. Frequently it was necessary to unwrap something and repack it because Lady Haleford had dozed off and got muddled…

The doctor, coming quietly into the room, unnoticed by a dozing Lady Haleford and, since she had her back to the door, by Amabel, stood in the doorway and watched her. She wasn't quite as tidy as usual, and half obscured by sheets of wrapping paper and reels of satin ribbon. Even from the back, he considered, she looked flustered…

The old lady opened her eyes and saw him and said, 'Oliver, how nice. Amabel, I've changed my mind. Unwrap the Stilton cheese and find a box for it.'

Amabel put down the cheese and looked over her shoulder. Oliver smiled at her and she smiled back, a smile of pure delight because she was so happy to see him again.

Lady Haleford said with a touch of peevishness, 'Amabel—the cheese…'

Amabel picked it up again and clasped it to her bosom, still smiling, and the doctor crossed the room and took it from her.

'Stilton—who is it for, Aunt?' He eyed the growing pile of gaily coloured packages. 'I see you've done your Christmas shopping.'

'You'll stay for lunch?' said Lady Haleford. 'Amabel, go and tell Mrs Twitchett.' When Amabel had gone she said, 'Oliver, will you take Amabel out? A drive, or tea, or something? She has no fun and she never complains.'

'Yes, of course. I came partly to suggest that we had dinner together one evening.'

'Good. Mrs Twitchett told me that the child has bought a new dress. Because it's Christmas, she told her. Perhaps I don't pay her enough…'

'I believe she is saving her money so that she can train for some career or other.'

'She would make a good wife…' The old lady dozed off again.

It was after lunch, when Lady Haleford had been

tucked up for her afternoon nap, that the doctor asked
Amabel if she would have dinner with him one evening.
They were walking the dogs, arm-in-arm, talking easily like two old friends, comfortable with each other,
but she stopped to look up at him.

'Oh, that would be lovely. But I can't, you know. It
would mean leaving Lady Haleford for a whole evening,
and Nelly goes to her mother's house in the village after
dinner—she's got rheumatism, her mother, you know—
and that means Mrs Twitchett would be alone...'

'I think that something might be arranged if you
would leave that to me.'

'And then,' continued Amabel, 'I've only one dress.
I bought it the other day, but it's not very fashionable.
I only bought it because it's Christmas, and I...really,
it was a silly thing to do.'

'Since you are going to wear it when we go out I
don't find it in the least silly.' He spoke gently. 'Is it a
pretty dress?'

'Pale grey. Very plain. It won't look out of date for
several years.'

'It sounds just the thing for an evening out. I'll come
for you next Saturday evening—half past seven.'

They walked back then, and presently he went away,
giving her a casual nod. 'Saturday,' he reminded her,
and bent to kiss her cheek. Such a quick kiss that she
wasn't sure if she had imagined it.

She supposed that she wasn't in the least surprised to
find that Lady Haleford had no objection to her going
out with the doctor. Indeed, she seemed to find nothing
out of the ordinary in it, and when Amabel enquired

anxiously about Nelly going to her mother, she was told that an old friend of Mrs Twitchett's would be spending the evening with her.

'Go and enjoy yourself,' said that lady. 'Eat a good dinner and dance a bit.'

So when Saturday came Amabel got into the grey dress, took pains with her face and her hair and went downstairs to where the doctor was waiting. Lady Haleford had refused to go to bed early; Mrs Twitchett would help her, she had told Amabel, but Amabel was to look in on her when she got home later. 'In case I am still awake and need something.'

Amabel, the grey dress concealed by her coat, greeted the doctor gravely, pronounced herself ready, bade the old lady goodnight, bade Oscar and Cyril to be good and got into the car beside Oliver.

It was a cold clear night with a bright moon. There would be a heavy frost by morning, but now everything was silvery in the moonlight.

'We're not going far,' said the doctor. 'There's rather a nice country hotel—we can dance if we feel like it.'

He began to talk about this and that, and Amabel, who had been feeling rather shy, lost her shyness and began to enjoy herself. She couldn't think why she should have felt suddenly awkward with him; after all, he was a friend—an old friend by now...

He had chosen the hotel carefully and it was just right. The grey dress, unassuming and simple but having style, was absorbed into the quiet luxury of the restaurant.

The place was festive, without being overpoweringly

so, and the food was delicious. Amabel ate prawns and Caesar salad, grilled sole and straw potatoes and, since it was almost Christmas, mouthwatering mince pies with chantilly cream. But not all at once.

The place was full and people were dancing. When the doctor suggested that she might like to dance she got up at once. Only as they reached the dance floor she hesitated. 'It's ages since I danced,' she told him.

He smiled down at her. 'Then it's high time you did now,' he told her.

She was very light on her feet, and she hadn't forgotten how to dance. Oliver looked down onto her neat head of hair and wondered how long it would be before she discovered that she was in love with him. He was prepared to wait, but he hoped that it wouldn't be too long…!

The good food, the champagne and dancing had transformed a rather plain girl in a grey dress into someone quite different. When at length it was time to leave, Amabel, very pink in the cheeks and bright of the eye, her tongue loosened by the champagne, told him that she had never had such a lovely evening in her life before.

'York seems like a bad dream,' she told him, 'and supposing you hadn't happened to see me, what would I have done? You're my guardian angel, Oliver.'

The doctor, who had no wish to be her guardian angel but something much more interesting, said cheerfully, 'Oh, you would have fallen on your feet, Amabel, you're a sensible girl.'

And all the things she suddenly wanted to say to him shrivelled on her tongue.

'I've had too much champagne,' she told him, and talked about the pleasures of the evening until they were back at Lady Haleford's house.

He went in with her, to switch on lights and make sure all was well, but he didn't stay. She went to the door with him and thanked him once again for her lovely evening.

'I'll remember it,' she told him.

He put his arms round her then, and kissed her hard, but before she could say anything he had gone, closing the door quietly behind him.

She stood for a long time thinking about that kiss, but presently she took off her shoes and crept upstairs to her room. There, was no sound from Lady Haleford's bedroom and all was still when she peeped through the door; she undressed and prepared for bed, and was just getting into bed when she heard the gentle tinkling of the old lady's bell. So she got out of bed again and went quietly to see what was the matter.

Lady Haleford was now wide awake, and wanted an account of the evening.

'Sit down and tell me about it,' she commanded. 'Where did you go and what did you eat?'

So Amabel stifled a yawn and curled up in a chair by the bed to recount the events of the evening. Not the kiss, of course.

When she had finished Lady Haleford said smugly, 'So you had a good time. It was my suggestion, you know—that Oliver should take you out for the evening.

He's so kind, you know—always willing to do a good turn. Such a busy man, too. I'm sure he could ill spare the time.' She gave a satisfied sigh. 'Now go to bed, Amabel. We have to see to the rest of those Christmas presents tomorrow.'

So Amabel turned the pillow, offered a drink, turned the night light low and went back to her room. In her room she got into bed and closed her eyes, but she didn't go to sleep.

Her lovely evening had been a mockery, a charitable action undertaken from a sense of duty by someone whom she had thought was her friend. He was still her friend, she reminded herself, but his friendship was mixed with pity.

Not to be borne, decided Amabel, and at last fell asleep as the tears dried on her cheeks.

Lady Haleford had a good deal more to say about the evening out in the morning; Amabel had to repeat everything she had already told her and listen to the old lady's satisfied comments while she tied up the rest of the parcels.

'I told Oliver that you had bought a dress…'

Amabel cringed. Bad enough that he had consented to take her out; he probably thought that she had bought it in the hope that he might invite her.

She said quickly, 'We shall need some more paper. I'll go and buy some…'

In the shop, surrounded by the village ladies doing their weekly shopping, she felt better. She was being silly, she told herself. What did it matter what reason Oliver had had for asking her out for the evening? It had been a lovely surprise and she had enjoyed herself, and what had she expected, anyway?

She went back and tied up the rest of the presents, and recounted, once again, the previous evening's events, for the old lady protested that she had been told nothing.

'Oh, you spent five minutes with me when you came in last night, but I want to know what you talked about. You're a nice girl, Amabel, but I can't think of you as an amusing companion. Men do like to be amused, but I dare say Oliver found you pleasant enough; he can take his pick of pretty women in London.'

All of which did nothing to improve Amabel's spirits.

Not being given to self-pity, she told herself to remember that Lady Haleford was old and had been ill and didn't mean half of what she said. As for her evening out, well, that was a pleasant memory and nothing more. If she should see the doctor again she would take care to let him see that, while they were still friends, she neither expected nor wanted to be more than that.

I'll be a little cool, reflected Amabel, and in a few weeks I expect I'll be gone from here. Being a sensible girl, she fell to planning her future...

This was a waste of time, actually, for Oliver was planning it for her; she would be with his aunt for several weeks yet—time enough to think of a way in which they might see each other frequently and let her discover for herself that he was in love with her and wanted to marry her. He had friends enough; there must be one amongst them who needed a companion or something of that sort, where Cyril and Oscar would be acceptable. And where he would be able to see her as frequently as possible...

The simplest thing would be for her to stay at his house. Impossible—but he lingered over the delightful idea...

He wasn't the only one thinking about Amabel's future. Miriam, determined to marry Oliver, saw Amabel as a real threat to her plans.

She was careful to be casually friendly when she and Oliver met occasionally, and she took care not to ask him any but the vaguest questions about his days. She had tried once or twice to get information from Bates, but he professed ignorance of his employer's comings and goings. He told her stolidly that the doctor was either at his consulting room or at the hospital, and if she phoned and wanted to speak to him at the weekend Bates informed her that he was out with the dog.

Oliver, immersed in his work and thoughts of Amabel, dismissed Miriam's various invitations and suggestions that they might spend an evening together with good-mannered friendliness; he didn't believe seriously that Miriam wanted anything more than his company from time to time; she had men-friends enough.

He underestimated her, though. Miriam drove herself to Aldbury, parked the car away from the centre of the village and found her way to the church. The village shop would have been ideal ground from which to glean information, but there was the risk of meeting Amabel. Besides, people in the village might talk.

The church was old and beautiful, but she didn't

waste time on it. Someone—the vicar, she supposed—
was coming down the aisle towards her, wanting to
know if he could help her…

He was a nice elderly man, willing to talk to this
charming lady who was so interested in the village. 'Oh,
yes,' he told her, 'there are several old families living
in the village, their history going back for many years.'

'And those lovely cottages with thatched roofs—one
of them seems a good deal larger than the rest?'

'Ah, yes, that would be Lady Haleford's house. A
very old family. She has been ill and is very elderly.
She was in hospital for some time, but now I'm glad
to say she is at home again. There is a very charming young woman who is her companion. We see her
seldom, for she has little spare time, although Lady
Haleford's nephew comes to visit his aunt and I have
seen the pair of them walking the dogs. He was here recently, so I'm told, and took her out for the evening…!
How I do ramble on, but living in a small village we
tend to be interested in each other's doings. You are
touring this part of the country?'

'Yes, this is a good time of year to drive around the
countryside. I shall work my way west to the Cots-
wolds,' said Miriam, untruthfully. 'It's been delightful
talking to you, Vicar, and now I must get back to my
car and drive on.'

She shook hands and walked quickly back to her car,
watched by several ladies in the village shop, whose
sharp eyes took in every inch of her appearance.

She drove away quickly and presently pulled up on
the grass verge the better to think. At first she was too

angry to put two thoughts together. This was no passing attraction on Oliver's part; he had been seeing this girl for some time now and his interest was deep enough to cause him to seek her out. Miriam seethed quietly. She didn't love Oliver; she liked him enough to marry him and she wanted the things the marriage would bring to her: a handsome husband, money, a lovely home and the social standing his name and profession would give her.

She thumped the driving wheel in rage. Something would have to be done, but what?

Chapter 8

Quiet though the routine of Lady Haleford's household was, Christmas, so near now, was not to be ignored. Cards were delivered, gifts arrived, visitors called to spend ten minutes with the old lady, and Amabel trotted round the house arranging and rearranging the variety of pot plants they brought with them.

It was all mildly exciting, but tiring for the invalid, so that Amabel needed to use all her tact and patience, coaxing callers to leave after the briefest of visits, and even then Lady Haleford exhibited a mixture of lethargy and testiness which prompted her to get the doctor to call.

He was a rather solemn man who had looked after the old lady for years, and he now gave it as his opinion that, Christmas or no Christmas, his patient must revert to total peace and quiet.

'The occasional visitor,' he allowed, and Amabel was to use her discretion in turning away more than that.

Amabel said, 'Lady Haleford likes to know who calls. She gets upset if someone she wishes to see is asked not to visit her. I've tried that once or twice and she gets rather uptight.'

Dr Carr looked at her thoughtfully. 'Yes, well, I must leave that to your discretion, Miss Parsons. Probably to go against her wishes would do more harm than good. She sleeps well?'

'No,' said Amabel. 'Although she dozes a lot during the day.'

'But at night—she is restless? Worried...?'

'No. Just awake. She likes to talk, and sometimes I read to her.'

He looked at her as though he hadn't really seen her before.

'You get sufficient recreation, Miss Parsons?'

Amabel said that, yes, thank you, she did. Because if she didn't he might decide that she wasn't capable enough for the job and arrange for a nurse. Her insides trembled at the thought.

So Amabel met visitors as they were ushered into the hall and, unless they were very close old friends or remote members of Lady Haleford's family, persuaded them that she wasn't well enough to have a visitor, then offered notepaper and a pen in case they wanted to write a little note and plied them with coffee and one of Mrs Twitchett's mince pies.

Hard work, but it left both parties satisfied.

Though it was quite quiet in the house, the village at

its doorstep was full of life. There was a lighted Christmas tree, the village shop was a blaze of fairy lights, and carol singers—ranging from small children roaring out the first line of 'Good King Wenceslas' to the harmonious church choir—were a nightly event. And Mrs Twitchett, while making sure that Lady Haleford was served the dainty little meals she picked at, dished up festive food suitable to the season for the other three of them.

Amabel counted her blessings and tried not to think about Oliver.

Dr Fforde was going to Glastonbury to spend Christmas with his mother and the rest of his family. Two days which he could ill spare. He had satisfied himself that his patients were making progress, presented the theatre staff with sherry, his ward sister and his receptionist and the nurse at the consulting rooms with similar bottles, made sure that Bates and his wife would enjoy a good Christmas, loaded the car boot with suitable presents and, accompanied by Tiger, was ready to leave home.

He was looking forward to the long drive, and, more than that, he was looking forward to seeing Amabel, for he intended to call on his aunt on his way.

He had been working hard for the last week or so, and on top of that there had been the obligatory social events. Many of them he had enjoyed, but not all of them. He had found the dinner party given by Miriam's parents particularly tedious, but he had had no good reason to refuse the invitation—although he had been relieved to find that Miriam seemed no longer to look upon him as her future. She had been as amusing and attractive as always, but she had made no demands on his time, merely saying with apparent sincerity that he must be glad to get away from his work for a few days.

It was beginning to snow when he left, very early on the morning of Christmas Eve. Tiger, sitting very upright beside him, watched the heavy traffic. It took some time to get away from London but the doctor remained patient, thinking about Amabel, knowing that he would be seeing her in an hour or so.

The village looked charming as he drove through it and there was a small lighted Christmas tree in the cottage's drawing room window. He got out of the car, opened the door for Tiger, and saw Amabel and Cyril at the far end of the village street. Tiger, scenting friends, was already on his way to meet them. Oliver saw Amabel stop, and for a moment he thought she was going to turn round and hurry away. But she bent to greet Tiger and came towards him. He met her halfway.

There was snow powdering her woolly cap and her coat, and her face was rosy with cold. He thought she looked beautiful, though he was puzzled by her prim greeting.

He said cheerfully, 'Hello. I'm on my way to spend Christmas with the family. How is my aunt?'

'A bit tired,' she told him seriously. 'There have been a great many visitors, although she has seen only a handful of them.'

They were walking back towards the house. 'I expect you'd like to see her? She'll be finishing her breakfast.' Since he didn't speak, the silence got rather long. 'I expect you've been busy?' Annabel finally ventured.

'Yes, I'll go back on Boxing Day.' They had reached the front door when he said, 'What's the matter, Amabel?'

She said, too quickly, 'Nothing. Everything is fine.' And as she opened the door added, 'Would you mind going up to Lady Haleford? I'll dry the dogs and tidy myself.'

Mrs Twitchett came bustling into the hall then, and Amabel slipped away. Oliver wouldn't stay long and she could keep out of his way...

The dogs made themselves comfortable on either side of Oscar in front of the Aga, and when Nelly came in to say that Mr Oliver would have a cup of coffee before he went away Amabel slipped upstairs. Lady Haleford would be ready to start the slow business of dressing.

'Go away,' said the old lady as Amabel went into her room. 'Go and have coffee with Oliver. I'll dress later.' When Amabel looked reluctant, she added, 'Well, run along. Surely you want to wish him a happy Christmas?'

So Amabel went downstairs again, as slowly as possible, and into the drawing room. The dogs and Oscar had gone there with the coffee, sitting before the fire, and the doctor was sitting in one of the big wing chairs.

He got up as she went in, drew a balloon-backed chair closer to his own and invited her to pour their coffee.

'And now tell me what is wrong,' he said kindly. 'For there is something, isn't there? Surely we are friends enough for you to tell me? Something I have done, Amabel?'

She took a gulp of coffee. 'Well, yes, but it's silly of me to mind. So if it's all the same to you I'd rather not talk about it.'

He resisted the urge to scoop her out of her chair and wrap her in his arms. 'It isn't all the same to me...'

She put down her cup and saucer. 'Well, you didn't have to take me out to dinner just because Lady Haleford said that you should—I wouldn't have gone if I'd known...' She choked with sudden temper. 'Like giving a biscuit to a dog...'

Oliver bit back a laugh, not of amusement but of tenderness and relief. If that was all...

But she hadn't finished. 'And I didn't buy a dress because I hoped you would take me out.' She looked at him then. 'You are my friend, Oliver, and that is how I think of you—a friend.'

He said gently, 'I came to take you out for the evening, Amabel. Anything my aunt said didn't influence me in any way. And as for your new dress, that was something I hadn't considered. It was a pretty dress, but you look nice whatever you are wearing.' He would have liked to have said a great deal more, but it was obviously not the right moment. When she didn't speak, he said, 'Still friends, Amabel?'

'Yes—oh, yes, Oliver. I'm sorry I've been so silly.'

'We'll have another evening out after Christmas. I think that you will be here for some time yet.'

'I'm very happy here. Everyone in the village is so friendly, and really I have nothing to do.'

'You have very little time to yourself. Do you get the chance to go out—meet people—young people?'

'Well, no, but I don't mind.'

He got up to go presently. It was still snowing and he had some way to drive still. She went with him to the door, and Tiger, reluctant to leave Cyril and Oscar, pushed between them. Amabel bent to stroke him.

'Go carefully,' she said, 'and I hope that you and your family have a lovely Christmas.'

He stood looking down at her. 'Next year will be different!' He fished a small packet from a pocket. 'Happy Christmas, Amabel,' he said, and kissed her.

He didn't wait to hear her surprised thanks. She stood watching the car until it was out of sight, her mouth slightly open in surprise, clutching the little gaily wrapped box.

The delightful thought that he might come again on his way back to London sent a pleasant glow through her person.

She waited until Christmas morning before she opened the box, sitting up in bed early in the darkness. The box contained a brooch, a true lover's knot, in gold and turquoise—a dainty thing, but one she could wear with her very ordinary clothes.

She got up dressed in the grey dress and pinned the brooch onto it before getting into her coat and slipping out of the house to go to church.

It was dark and cold, and although the snow had stopped it lay thick on the ground. The church was cold too, but it smelled of evergreens and flowers, and the Christmas tree shone with its twinkling lights. There weren't many people at the service, for almost everyone would be at Matins during the morning, but as they left the church there was a pleasant flurry of cheerful talk and good wishes.

Amabel made sure that Lady Haleford was still asleep, had a quick breakfast with Mrs Twitchett and Nelly and took Cyril for his walk. The weather didn't suit his elderly bones and the walk was brief. She settled him next to Oscar by the Aga and went to bid Lady Haleford good morning.

The old lady wasn't in a festive mood. She had no wish to get out of her bed, no wish to eat her breakfast, and she said that she was too tired to look at the gifts Amabel assured her were waiting for her downstairs.

'You can read to me,' she said peevishly.

So Amabel sat down and read. *Little Women* was a soothing book, and very old-fashioned. She found the chapter describing Christmas and the simple pleasures of the four girls and their mother was a sharp contrast to the comfortable life Lady Haleford had always lived.

Presently Lady Haleford said, 'What a horrid old woman I am...'

'You're one of the nicest people I know,' said Amabel, and, quite forgetting that she was a paid companion, she got up and hugged the old lady.

So Christmas was Christmas after all, with presents being opened, and turkey and Christmas pudding and mince pies, suitably interposed between refreshing naps, and Amabel, having tucked Lady Haleford into her bed, went early to bed herself. There was nothing else to do, but that didn't matter. Oliver would be returning to London the next day, and perhaps he would come and see them again...

But he didn't. It was snowing again, and he couldn't risk a hold-up on the way back to London.

The weather stayed wintry until New Year's Day, when Amabel woke to a bright winter's sun and blue sky. It was still snowy underfoot, and as she sloshed through it with a reluctant Cyril she wondered what the New Year would bring…

As for the doctor, he hardly noticed which day of the week it was, for the New Year had brought with it the usual surge of bad chests, tired hearts and the beginnings of a flu epidemic. He left home early and came home late, and ate whatever food Bates put before him. He was tired, and often frustrated, but it was his life and his work, and presently, when things had settled down again, he would go to Amabel…

Miriam waited for a few days before phoning Oliver. He had just got home after a long day and he was tired, but that was something she hadn't considered. There was a new play, she told him, would he get tickets? 'And we could have supper afterwards. I want to hear all about Christmas…'

He didn't tell her that he was working all day and every day, and sometimes into the night as well. He said mildly, 'I'm very busy, Miriam, I can't spare the time. There is a flu epidemic…'

'Oh, is there? I didn't know. There must be plenty of junior doctors…'

'Not enough.'

She said with a flash of temper, 'Then I'll get someone who will enjoy my company.'

The doctor, reading the first of a pile of reports on his desk, said absent-mindedly, 'Yes, do. I hope you will have a pleasant evening.'

He put the phone down and then picked it up again. He wanted to hear Amabel's voice. He put it down again. Phone conversations were unsatisfactory, for either one said too much or not enough. He would go and see her just as soon as he could spare the time. He ignored the pile of work before him and sat back and thought about Amabel, in her grey dress, wearing, he hoped, the true lover's knot.

Miriam had put down the phone and sat down to think. If Oliver was busy then he wouldn't have time to go to Aldbury. It was a chance for her to go, talk to the girl, convince her that he had no interest in her, that his future and hers were as far apart as two poles. It would be helpful if she could get Amabel away from this aunt of his, but she could see no way of doing that. She would have to convince Amabel that she had become an embarrassment to him…

There was no knowing when Oliver would go to Aldbury again, and Miriam waited with impatience for the snow to clear away. On a cold bright day, armed with a bouquet of flowers purporting to come from her mother, she set out.

The church clock was striking eleven as she stopped before Lady Haleford's cottage. Nelly answered the door, listened politely to Miriam's tale of her mother's friendship with Lady Haleford and bade her come in and wait. Lady Haleford was still in her room, but she would fetch Miss Parsons down. She left Miriam in the drawing room and went away, and presently Amabel came in.

Miriam said at once, 'Oh, hello—we've met before, haven't we? I came at the wrong time. Am I more fortunate today? Mother asked me to let Lady Haleford have these flowers...'

'Lady Haleford will be coming down in a few minutes,' said Amabel, and wondered why she didn't like this visitor.

She was being friendly enough, almost gushing, and Lady Haleford, when Nelly had mentioned Miriam's name, had said, 'That young woman—very pushy. And I haven't met her mother for years.' She had added, 'But I'll come down.'

Which she did, some ten minutes later, leaving Amabel to make polite conversation that Miriam made no effort to sustain.

But with the old lady she was at her most charming, giving her the flowers with a mythical message from her mother, asking about her health with apparent concern.

The old lady, normally a lady of perfect manners, broke into her chatter. 'I am going to take a nap. Amabel, fetch your coat and take Mrs Potter-Stokes to look round the village or the church if she chooses. Mrs Twitchett will give you coffee in half an hour's time. I will say goodbye now; please thank your mother for the flowers.'

She sat back in her chair and closed her eyes, leaving Amabel to usher an affronted Miriam out of the room. In the hall Amabel said, 'Lady Haleford has been very ill and she tires easily. Would you like to see round the church?'

Miriam said no, in a snappy voice, and then, mindful of why she had come, added with a smile, 'But perhaps we could walk a little way out of the village? The country looks very pretty.'

Amabel got into her coat, tied a scarf over her head and, with Cyril on his lead, led the way past the church and into the narrow lane beyond. Being a friendly girl, with nice manners, she made small talk about the village and the people who lived in it, aware that her companion hadn't really wanted to go walking—she was wearing the wrong shoes for a start.

Annoyed though Miriam was, she saw that this was her chance—if only there was a suitable opening. She stepped into a puddle and splashed her shoe and her tights and the hem of her long coat, and saw the opening...

'Oh, dear. Just look at that. I'm afraid I'm not a country girl. It's a good thing that I live in London and always shall. I'm getting married soon, and Oliver lives and works there too...'

'Oliver?' asked Amabel in a careful voice.

'A nice name, isn't it? He's a medical man, always frightfully busy, although we manage to get quite a lot of time together. He has a lovely house; I shall love living there.'

She turned to smile at Amabel. 'He's such a dear— very kind and considerate. All his patients dote on him. And he's always ready to help any lame dog over a stile. There's some poor girl he's saved from a most miserable life—gone out of his way to find her a job. I hope she's grateful. She has no idea where he lives, of course. I mean, she isn't the kind of person one would want to become too familiar with, and it wouldn't do for her to get silly ideas into her head, would it?'

Amabel said quickly, 'I shouldn't think that would be very likely, but I'm sure she must be grateful.'

Miriam tucked a hand under Amabel's arm. 'Oh, I dare say—and if she appeals to him again for any reason I'll talk to her. I won't have him badgered; heaven knows how many he's helped without telling me. Once we're married, of course, things will be different.'

She gave Amabel a smiling nod, noting with satisfaction that the girl looked pale. 'Could we go back? I'm longing for a cup of coffee…'

Over coffee she had a great deal to say about the approaching wedding. 'Of course, Oliver and I have so many friends, and he's well known in the medical profession. I shall wear white, of course…' Miriam allowed her imagination full rein.

Amabel ordered more coffee, agreed that four bridesmaids would be very suitable, and longed for her unwelcome visitor to go. Which, presently, she did.

Lady Haleford, half dozing in her room, opened her eyes long enough to ask if the caller had gone and nodded off again, for which Amabel was thankful. She had no wish to repeat their conversation—besides, Oliver's private life was none of her business. She hadn't liked Miriam, but it had never entered her head that the woman was lying. It all made sense; Oliver had never talked about his home or his work or his friends. And why should he? Mrs Twitchett had remarked on several occasions that he had given unobtrusive help to people. 'He's a very private person,' she had told Amabel. 'Lord knows what goes on in that clever head of his.'

There was no hope of going to see Amabel for the moment; the flu epidemic had swollen to a disquieting level. The doctor treated his patients with seeming tirelessness, sleeping when he could, sustained by Mrs Bates's excellent food and Bates's dignified support. But Amabel was always at the back of his mind, and from time to time he allowed himself to think about her, living her quiet life and, he hoped, sometimes thinking about him.

Of Miriam he saw nothing; she had prudently gone to stay with friends in the country, where there was less danger of getting the flu. She phoned him, leaving nicely calculated messages to let him see that she was concerned about him, content to bide her time, pleased with herself that she had sewn the seeds of doubt in Amabel's mind. Amabel was the kind of silly little fool, she reflected, who would believe every word of what she had said. Head over heels in love with him, thought Miriam, and doesn't even know it.

But here she was wrong; Amabel, left unhappy and worried, thought about Oliver a good deal. In fact he was never out of her thoughts. She *had* believed Miriam when she had told her that she and Oliver were to marry. If Lady Haleford hadn't been particularly testy for the next few days she might have mentioned it to her, but it wasn't until two o'clock one morning, when the old lady was sitting up in her bed wide awake and feeling chatty, that she began to talk about Oliver.

'Time he settled down. I only hope he doesn't marry that Potter-Stokes woman. Can't stand her—but there's no denying that she's got looks and plenty of ambition. He'd be knighted in no time if she married him, for she knows all the right people. But he'd have a fashionable practice and turn into an embittered man. He needs to be loved...'

Amabel, curled up in a chair by the bed, wrapped in her sensible dressing gown, her hair neatly plaited, murmured soothingly, anxious that the old lady should settle down. Now was certainly not the time to tell her about Miriam's news.

Lady Haleford dozed off and Amabel was left with her thoughts. They were sad, for she agreed wholeheartedly with the old lady that Miriam would not do for Oliver. He does need someone to love him, reflected Amabel, and surprised herself by adding *me*.

Once over her surprise at the thought, she allowed herself to daydream a little. She had no idea where Oliver lived—somewhere in London—and she knew almost nothing about his work, but she would love him, and care for him, and look after his house, and there would be children...

'I fancy a drop of hot milk,' said Lady Haleford. 'And you'd better go to bed, Amabel. You looked washed out...'

Which effectively put an end to daydreams, although it didn't stop her chaotic thoughts. Waiting for the milk to heat, she decided that she had been in love with Oliver for a long time, accepting him into her life as naturally as drawing breath. But there was nothing to be done about it; Miriam had made it plain that he wouldn't welcome the prospect of seeing her again.

If he did come to see his aunt, thought Amabel, pouring the milk carefully into Lady Haleford's special mug, then she, Amabel, would keep out of his way, be coolly pleasant, let him see that she quite understood.

These elevating thoughts lasted until she was back in her own bed, where she could cry her eyes out in peace and quiet.

The thoughts stood her in good stead, for Oliver came two days later. It being a Sunday, and Lady Haleford being in a good mood, Amabel had been told that she might go to Matins, and it was on leaving the church that she saw the car outside the cottage. She stopped in the porch, trying to think of a means of escape. If she went back into the church she could go out through the side door and up the lane and stay away for as long as possible. He probably wasn't staying long…

She felt a large heavy arm on her shoulders and turned her head.

'Didn't expect me, did you?' asked the doctor cheerfully. 'I've come to lunch.'

Amabel found her voice and willed her heart to stop thumping. She said, 'Lady Haleford will be pleased to see you.'

He gave her a quick, all-seeing look. Something wasn't quite right…

'I've had orders to take you for a brisk walk before lunch. Up the lane by the church?'

Being with him, she discovered, was the height of

happiness. Her high-minded intentions could surely be delayed until he had gone again? While he was there, they didn't make sense. As long as she remembered that they were friends and nothing more.

She said, 'Where's Tiger?'

'Being spoilt in the kitchen. Wait here. I'll fetch him and Cyril.'

He was gone before she could utter, and soon back again with the dogs, tucking an arm in hers and walking her briskly past the church and up the lane. The last time she had walked along it, she reflected, Miriam had been with her.

Very conscious of the arm, she asked, 'Have you been busy?'

'Very busy. There's not been much flu here?'

'Only one or two cases.' She sought for something to talk about. 'Have you seen Lady Haleford yet? She's better—at least I think so. Once the spring is here, perhaps I could drive her out sometimes—just for an hour—and she's looking forward to going into the garden.'

'I spent a few minutes with her. Yes, she is making progress, but it's a long business. I should think you will be here for some weeks. Do you want to leave, Amabel?'

'No, no, of course not. Unless Lady Haleford would like me to go?'

'That is most unlikely. Have you thought about the future?'

'Yes, quite a lot. I—I know what I want to do. I'll go and see Aunt Thisbe and then I'll enrol at one of those places where I can train to use a computer. There's a

good one at Manchester; I saw it advertised in Lady
Haleford's paper.' She added, to make it sound more
convincing, 'I've saved my money, so I can find somewhere to live.'

The doctor, quite rightly, took this to be a spur-of-
the-moment idea, but he didn't say so.

'Very sensible. You don't wish to go home?'

'Yes. I'd like to see Mother, but she wrote to me just
after Christmas and said that my stepfather still wasn't
keen for me to pay a visit.'

'She could come here…'

'I don't think he would like that. I did suggest it.'
She added, 'Mother is very happy. I wouldn't want to
disturb that.'

They had been walking briskly and had passed the
last of the cottages in the lane. The doctor came to a
halt and turned her round to face him.

'Amabel, there is a great deal I wish to say to you…'

'No,' she said fiercely. 'Not now—not ever. I quite
understand, but I don't want to know. Oh, can't you
see that? We're friends, and I hope we always will be,
but when I leave here it's most unlikely that we shall
meet again.'

He said slowly, 'What makes you think that we shall
never meet again?'

'It wouldn't do,' said Amabel. 'And now please don't
let's talk about it any more.'

He nodded, his blue eyes suddenly cold. 'Very well.'
He turned her round. 'We had better go back, or Mrs
Twitchett will be worried about a spoilt lunch.'

He began to talk about the dogs and the weather,

and was she interested in paintings? He had been to see a rather interesting exhibition of an early Victorian artist…

His gentle flow of talk lasted until they reached the cottage again and she could escape on the pretext of seeing if the old lady needed anything before lunch. The fresh air had given her face a pleasing colour, but it still looked plain in her mirror. She flung powder onto her nose, dragged a comb through her hair and went downstairs.

Lady Haleford, delighted to have Oliver's company, asked endless questions. She knew many of the doctor's friends and demanded news of them.

'And what about you, Oliver? I know you're a busy man, but surely you must have some kind of social life?'

'Not a great deal—I've been too busy.'

'That Potter-Stokes woman called—brought flowers from her mother. Heaven knows why; I hardly know her. She tired me out in ten minutes. I sent her out for a walk with Amabel…'

'Miriam came here?' asked Oliver slowly, and looked at Amabel, sitting at the other side of the table.

She speared a morsel of chicken onto her fork and glanced at him quickly. 'She's very beautiful, isn't she? We had a pleasant walk and a cup of coffee—she couldn't stay long; she was on her way to visit someone. She thought the village was delightful. She was driving one of those little sports cars…' She stopped talking, aware that she was babbling.

She put the chicken in her mouth and chewed it. It tasted like ashes.

'Miriam is very beautiful,' agreed the doctor, staring at her, and then said to his aunt, 'I'm sure you must enjoy visitors from time to time, Aunt, but don't tire yourself.'

'I don't. Besides, Amabel may look like a mouse, but she can be a dragon in my defence. Bless the girl! I don't know what I would do without her.' After a moment she added, 'But of course she will go soon.'

'Not until you want me to,' said Amabel. 'And by then you will have become so much better that you won't need anyone.' She smiled across the table at the old lady. 'Mrs Twitchett has made your favourite pudding. Now, there is someone you would never wish to be without!'

'She has been with me for years. Oliver, your Mrs Bates is a splendid cook, is she not? And Bates? He still runs the place for you?'

'My right hand,' said the doctor. 'And as soon as you are well enough I shall drive you up to town and you can sample some of Mrs Bates's cooking.'

Lady Haleford needed her after-lunch nap.

'Stay for tea?' she begged him. 'Keep Amabel company. I'm sure you'll have plenty to talk about…'

'I'm afraid that I must get back.' He glanced at his watch. 'I'll say goodbye now.'

When Amabel came downstairs again he had gone.

Which was only to be expected, Amabel told herself, but she would have liked to have said goodbye. To have explained…

But how did one explain that, since one had fallen in love with someone already engaged to someone else, meeting again would be pointless. And she had lost a friend…

Later that day Lady Haleford, much refreshed by her nap, observed, 'A pity Oliver had to return so soon.' She darted a sharp glance at Amabel. 'You get on well together?'

'Yes,' said Amabel, and tried to think of something to add but couldn't.

'He's a good man.'

'Yes,' said Amabel again. 'Shall I unpick that knitting for you, Lady Haleford?'

The old lady gave her a thoughtful look. 'Yes, Amabel, and then we will have a game of cards. That will distract our thoughts.'

Amabel, surveying her future during a wakeful night, wondered what she should do, but as events turned out she had no need to concern herself with that.

It was several days after Oliver's visit that she had a phone call. She had just come in with Cyril, after his early-morning walk, and, since Nelly and Mrs Twitchett were both in the kitchen, she answered it from the phone in the hall.

'Is that you, Amabel?' Her stepfather's voice was agitated. 'Listen, you must come home at once. Your mother's ill—she's been in hospital and they've sent her home and there's no one to look after her.'

'What was wrong? Why didn't you let me know that she was ill?'

'It was only pneumonia. I thought they'd keep her there until she was back to normal. But here she is, in bed most of the day, and I've enough to do without nursing her as well.'

'Haven't you any help?'

'Oh, there's a woman who comes in to clean and cook. Don't tell me to hire a nurse; it's your duty to come home and care for your mother. And I don't want any excuses. You're her daughter, remember.'

'I'll come as soon as I can,' said Amabel, and took Cyril to the kitchen.

Mrs Twitchett looked at her pale face. 'Something wrong? Best tell us.'

It was a great relief to tell someone. Mrs Twitchett and Nelly heard her out.

'Have to go, won't you love?' Nelly's eye fell on Cyril and Oscar, side by side in front of the Aga. 'Will you take them with you?'

'Oh, Nelly, I can't. He wanted to kill them both; that's why I left home.' Amabel sniffed back tears. 'I'll have to take them to a kennel and a cattery.'

'No need,' Mrs Twitchett said comfortably. 'They'll stay here until you know what's what. Lady Haleford loves them both, and Nelly will see to Cyril's walks. Now, just you go and tell my lady what it's all about.'

Lady Haleford, sitting up in bed, sipping her early-morning tea and wide awake for once, said immediately, 'Of course you must go home immediately. Don't worry about Cyril and Oscar. Get your mother well again and then come back to us. Will she want you to stay at home for good?'

Amabel shook her head. 'No, I don't think so. You see, my stepfather doesn't like me.'

'Then go and pack, and arrange your journey.'

Chapter 9

The doctor had driven himself back to London, deep in thought. It was obvious that Miriam had said something to Amabel which had upset her and caused her to retire into her shell of coolness. But she hadn't sounded cool in the lane. The only way to discover the reason for this was to go and see Miriam. She had probably said something as a joke and Amabel had misunderstood her...

He had gone to see her the very next evening and found her entertaining friends. As she had come to meet him he had said, 'I want to talk to you, Miriam.'

She, looking into his bland face and cold eyes, said at once, 'Oh, impossible, Oliver—we're just about to go out for the evening.'

'You can join your friends later. It is time we had a talk, Miriam, and what better time than now?'

She pouted. 'Oh, very well.' Then she smiled enchantingly. 'I was beginning to think that you had forgotten me.'

Presently, when everyone had gone, she sat down on a sofa and patted the cushion beside her. 'My dear, this is nice—just the two of us.'

The doctor sat down in a chair opposite her.

'Miriam, I have never been your dear. We have been out together, seen each other frequently at friends' houses, visited the theatre, but I must have made it plain to you that that was the extent of our friendship.' He asked abruptly, 'What did you say to Amabel?'

Miriam's beautiful face didn't look beautiful any more. 'So that's it—you've fallen in love with that dull girl! I guessed it weeks ago, when Dolores saw you in York. Her and her silly pets. Well, anyway, I've cooked your goose. I told her you were going to marry me, that you had helped her out of kindness and the sooner she disappeared the better...'

She stopped, because Oliver's expressionless face frightened her, and then when he got to his feet said, 'Oliver, don't go. She's no wife for you; you need someone like me, who knows everyone worth knowing, entertains all the right people, dresses well.'

Oliver walked to the door. 'I need a wife who loves me and whom I love.' And he went away.

It was a pity, he reflected that his next few days were so crammed with patients, clinics and theatre lists that it was impossible for him to go and see Amabel. It was a temptation to phone her, but he knew that would be unsatisfactory. Besides, he wanted to see her face while they talked.

He drove back home and went to his study and started on the case notes piled on his desk, dismissing Amabel firmly from his thoughts.

Lady Haleford had summoned Mrs Twitchett to her bedroom and demanded to know how Amabel was to go home. 'I don't know where the girl lives. Didn't someone tell me that she came from York?'

'And so she did, my lady; she's got an aunt there. Left home when her mother brought in a stepfather who don't like her. Somewhere near Castle Cary—she'll need to get the train to the nearest station and get a taxi or a bus, if there is one.'

Mrs Twitchett hesitated. 'And, my lady, could we keep Oscar and Cyril here while she's away? Seeing that her stepfather won't have them? Going to put them down, he was, so she left home.'

'The poor child. Arrange for William down at the village garage to drive her home. I've already told her that of course the animals must stay.'

So Amabel was driven away in the village taxi, which was just as well, for the journey home otherwise would have been long and tedious and she had had no time to plan it.

It was late afternoon when William drew up with a flourish at her home.

There were lights shining from several windows, and she could see a large greenhouse at the side of the house. As they got out of the car she glimpsed another beyond it, where the orchard had been.

The front door opened under her touch and they went into the hall as she saw her stepfather come from the kitchen.

'And about time too,' he said roughly. 'Your mother's in the sitting room, waiting to be helped to bed.'

'This is William, who brought me here by taxi,' said Amabel. 'He's going back to Aldbury, but he would like a cup of tea first.'

'I've no time to make tea…'

Amabel turned to William. 'If you'll come with me to the kitchen, I'll make it. I'll just see Mother first.'

Her mother looked up as she went into the sitting room.

'There you are, Amabel. Lovely to see you again, dear, and have you here to look after me.' She lifted her face for Amabel's kiss. 'Keith is quite prepared to let bygones be bygones and let you live here…'

'Mother, I must give the taxi driver a cup of tea. I'll be back presently and we can have a talk.'

There was no sign of her stepfather. William, waiting patiently in the kitchen, said, 'Not much of a welcome home, miss.'

Amabel warmed the teapot. 'Well, it all happened rather suddenly. Do you want a sandwich?'

William went very soon, feeling all the better for the tea and sandwiches, and the tip he had accepted reluctantly, and Amabel went back to the sitting room.

'Tell me what has been wrong with you, Mother. Do you stay up all day? The doctor visits you?'

'Pneumonia, love, and I went to hospital because Keith couldn't possibly manage on his own.'

'Have you no help?'

'Oh, yes, of course. Mrs Twist has been coming each day, to see to the house and do some of the cooking, and the hospital said a nurse would come each day once I was back home. She came for a day or two, but she and Keith had an argument and he told them that you would be looking after me. Not that I need much attention. In fact he's told Mrs Twist that she need not come any more, now that you are back home.'

'My stepfather told me that there was no one to look after you, that he had no help...'

Her mother said lightly, 'Oh, well, dear, you know what men are—and it does seem absurd for him to pay for a nurse and Mrs Twist when we have you...'

'Mother, I don't think you understand. I've got a job. I came because I thought there was no one to help you. I'll stay until you are better, but you must get Mrs Twist back and have a nurse on call if it's necessary. I'd like to go back to Aldbury as soon as possible. You see, dear, Keith doesn't like me—but you're happy with him, aren't you?'

'Yes, Amabel, I am, and I can't think why you can't get on, the pair of you. But now you are here the least you can do is make me comfortable. I'm still rather an invalid, having breakfast in bed and then a quiet day here by the fire. My appetite isn't good, but you were always a good cook. Keith likes his breakfast early, so you'll have all day to see to the house.'

She added complacently, 'Keith is doing very well

already, and now he won't need to pay Mrs Twist and that nurse he can plough the money back. You'll want to unpack your things, dear. Your old room, of course. I'm not sure if the bed is made up, but you know where everything is. And when you come down we'll decide what we'll have for supper.'

Of course the bed wasn't made up; the room was chilly and unwelcoming and Amabel sat down on the bed to get her thoughts sorted out. She wouldn't stay longer than it took to get Mrs Twist back, see the doctor and arrange for a nurse to visit, whatever her stepfather said. She loved her mother, but she was aware that she wasn't really welcome, that she was just being used as a convenience by her stepfather.

She made the bed, unpacked, and went back downstairs to the kitchen. There was plenty of food in the fridge. At least she wouldn't need to go to the shops for a few days...

Her mother fancied an omelette. 'But that won't do for Keith. There's a gammon steak, and you might do some potatoes and leeks. You won't have time to make a pudding, but there's plenty of cheese and biscuits...'

'Have you been cooking, Mother?'

Her mother said fretfully, 'Well, Keith can't cook, and Mrs Twist wasn't here. Now you're home I don't need to do anything.'

The next morning Amabel went to the village to the doctor's surgery. He was a nice man, but elderly and overworked.

'You're mother is almost fit again,' he assured Amabel. 'There is no reason why she shouldn't do a little housework, as long as she rests during the day. She needs some tests done, of course, and pills, and a check-up by the practice nurse. It is a pity that her husband refuses to let her visit; he told me that you would be coming home to live and that you would see to your mother.'

'Has Mother been very ill?'

'No, no. Pneumonia is a nasty thing, but if it's dealt with promptly anyone as fit as your mother makes a quick recovery.'

'I understood from what my stepfather told me on the phone that Mother was very ill and he was without help.' She sighed. 'I came as quickly as I could, but I have a job...'

'Well, I shouldn't worry too much about that. I imagine that a few days of help from you will enable your mother to lead her usual life again. She has help, I believe?'

'My stepfather gave Mrs Twist notice...'

'Oh, dear, then you must get her back. Someone local?'

'Yes.'

'Well, it shouldn't be too difficult to persuade Mr Graham to change his mind. Once she is reinstated, you won't need to stay.'

Something which she pointed out to her stepfather later that day. 'And do please understand that I must go back to my job at the end of week. The doctor told me that Mother should be well by then. You will have to get Mrs Twist to come every day.'

'You unnatural girl.' Keith Graham's face was red with bad temper. 'It's your duty to stay here...'

'You didn't want me to stay before,' Amabel pointed out quietly. 'I'll stay for a week, so that you have time to make arrangements to find someone to help Mother.' She nodded her neat head at him. 'There was no need for me to come home. I love Mother, but you know as well as I do that you hate having me here. I can't think why you decided to ask me to come.'

'Why should I pay for a woman to come and do the housework when I've a stepdaughter I can get for nothing?'

Amabel got to her feet. If there had been something suitable to throw at him she would have thrown it, but since there wasn't she merely said, 'I shall go back at the end of the week.'

But there were several days to live through first, and although her mother consented to be more active there was a great deal to do—the cooking, fires to clean and light, coal to fetch from the shed, beds to make and the house to tidy. Her stepfather didn't lift a finger, only coming in for his meals, and when he wasn't out and about he was sitting by the fire, reading his paper.

Amabel said nothing, for eventually there was only one more day to go...

She was up early on the last morning, her bag packed, and she went down to cook the breakfast Keith demanded. He came into the kitchen as she dished up his bacon and eggs.

'Your mother's ill,' he told her. 'Not had a wink of sleep—nor me neither. You'd better go and see to her.'

'At what time is Mrs Twist coming?'

'She isn't. Haven't had time to do anything about her…'

Amabel went upstairs and found her mother in bed.

'I'm not well, Amabel. I feel awful. My chest hurts and I've got a headache. You can't leave me.'

She moaned as Amabel sat her gently against her pillows.

'I'll bring you a cup of tea, Mother, and phone the doctor.'

She went downstairs to phone and leave a message at the surgery. Her stepfather said angrily, 'No need for him. All she needs is a few days in bed. You can stay on a bit.'

'I'll stay until you get Mrs Twist back. Today, if possible.'

Her mother would eat no breakfast, so Amabel helped her to the bathroom, made the bed and tidied the room and then went back downstairs to cancel the taxi which was to have fetched her in an hour's time. She had no choice but to stay until the doctor had been and Mrs Twist was reinstated.

There was nothing much wrong with her mother, the doctor told her when he came. She was complaining about her chest, but he could find nothing wrong there, and her headache was probably due to the sleepless nights she said she was having.

He said slowly, 'She has worked herself up because you are going away. I think it would be best if you could arrange to stay for another day or two. Has Mr Graham got Mrs Twist to come in?'

'No. He told me that he had had no time. I thought I might go and see her myself. You don't think that Mother is going to be ill again?'

'As far as I can see she has recovered completely from the pneumonia, but, as I say, she has worked herself up into a state—afraid of being ill again. So if you could stay...'

'Of course I'll stay until Mother feels better.' She smiled at him. 'Thank you for coming, Doctor.'

He gave her a fatherly pat. He thought she looked a bit under the weather herself he must remember to call in again in a day or two.

Amabel unpacked her bag, assured her mother that she would stay until Mrs Twist could come, and went to see that lady...

Mrs Twist was a comfortable body with a cheerful face. She listened to Amabel in silence and then said, 'Well, I'm sorry to disoblige you, but I've got my old mum coming today for a week. Once she's gone home again I'll go each day, same as before. Staying long, are you?'

'I meant to go back to my job this morning, but Mother asked me to stay until you could arrange to come back.' She couldn't help adding, 'You will come, won't you?'

'Course I will, love. And a week goes by quick enough. Nice having your ma to chat to.'

Amabel said, yes, it was, and thought how nice that would have been. Only there was precious little time to chat, and when she did sit down for an hour to talk it was her mother who did the talking: about how good

Keith was to her, the new clothes she had bought, the holiday they intended to take before the spring brought all the extra work in the greenhouses, how happy she was... But she asked no questions of Amabel.

She said, 'I expect you've got a good job, darling. You were always an independent girl. You must tell me about it one day... I was telling you about our holiday...'

It was strange how the days seemed endless, despite the fact that she had little leisure. She had written a note to Lady Haleford, saying that she would return as soon as she could arrange help for her mother. Since her mother seemed quite well again, it was now just a question of waiting for Mrs Twist's mother to go home. Her mother, however, was disinclined to do much.

'There's no need for me to do anything,' she had said, half laughing, 'while you're here.'

'Mrs Twist does everything when she comes?'

'Oh, yes. Although I do the cooking. But you're such a good cook, love, and it gives you something to do.'

One more day, thought Amabel. She had missed Cyril and Oscar. She had missed Oliver too, but she tried not to think of him—and how could she miss someone she hardly ever saw?

Amabel had been gone for almost two weeks before the doctor felt free to take time off and go to Aldbury. His aunt greeted him with pleasure. 'But you've come to see Amabel? Well, she's not here. The child had to go home; her mother was ill. She expected to be gone for a week. Indeed, she wrote and told me she would be coming back. And then I had another letter saying that she would have to stay another week. Can't think why she didn't telephone.' She added, 'Mrs Twitchett phoned and a man answered her. Very abrupt, she said, told her that Amabel wasn't available.'

It was already late afternoon, and the doctor had a list early on the following morning, a clinic in the afternoon and private patients to see. To get into his car and go to Amabel was something he wanted to do very much, but that wasn't possible; it wouldn't be possible for two days.

He thought about phoning her, but it might make matters worse and in any case there was a great deal he could do. He went back home, sat down at his desk and picked up the phone; he could find out what was happening…

Mrs Graham's doctor was helpful. There was no reason, he said over the phone, why Amabel should stay at home. She had told him very little, but he sensed that her mother's illness had been used to get her to return there. 'If there is anything I can do?' he offered.

'No, no, thanks. I wanted to be sure that her mother really needs her.'

'There's no reason why she shouldn't walk out of the house, but there may be circumstances which prevent her doing that.'

The doctor picked up the phone and heard Miss Parsons' firm voice at the other end.

'I hoped that you might be back…' He talked at some length and finally put the phone down and went in search of Bates. After that, all he had to do was to possess his soul in patience until he could go to Amabel.

He set off early in the morning two days later, with Tiger beside him and Bates to see him on his way.

Life was going to be quite interesting, Bates thought as he went in search of his wife.

Once free of London and the suburbs, Oliver drove fast. He hoped that he had thought of everything. A lot was going to happen during the next few hours, and nothing must go wrong.

It was raining when he reached the house, and now that the apple orchard had gone the house looked bare and lonely and the greenhouses looked alien. He drove round the side of the house, got out with Tiger, opened the kitchen door and went in.

Amabel was standing at the sink, peeling potatoes. She was wearing an apron several sizes too large for her and her hair hung in a plait over one shoulder. She looked pale and tired and utterly forlorn.

This was no time for explanations; the doctor strode to the sink, removed the potato and the knife from her hands and folded his arms around her. He didn't speak, he didn't kiss her, just held her close. He was holding her when Mr Graham came in.

'Who are you?' he demanded.

Oliver gave Amabel a gentle push. 'Go and get your coat and pack your things.' Something in his voice made her disentangle herself from his embrace and look up at his quiet face. He smiled down at her. 'Run along, darling.'

She went upstairs and all she could think of then was that he had called her darling. She should have taken him into the sitting room, where her mother was… Instead she got her case from the wardrobe and began to pack it, and, that done, picked up her coat and went downstairs.

The doctor had watched her go and then turned to Mr Graham, who began in a blustering voice, 'I don't know why you're here, whoever you are—'

'I'll tell you,' said Oliver gently. 'And when I've finished perhaps you will take me to Amabel's mother.'

She looked up in surprise as they went into the sitting room.

'He's come for Amabel,' said Mr Graham, looking daggers at Oliver. 'I don't know what things are coming to when your daughter's snatched away and you so poorly, my dear.'

'Your doctor tells me that you are fully recovered, Mrs Graham, and I understand that you have adequate help in the house…'

'I'm very upset—' began Mrs Graham. Glancing at the quiet man standing there, she decided that a show of tears wouldn't help. 'After all, a daughter should take care of her mother…'

'And do the housework and the cooking?' From the look of her Amabel has been doing that, and much more besides.

'She ought to be grateful,' growled Mr Graham, 'having a home to come to.'

'Where she is expected to do the chores, cook and clean and shop?' asked Oliver coolly. 'Mr Graham, you make me tired—and extremely angry.'

'Who is going to see to things when she's gone?'

'I'm sure there is adequate help to be had in the village.' He turned away as Amabel came into the room. 'Everything is satisfactorily arranged,' he told her smoothly. 'If you will say goodbye, we will go.'

Amabel supposed that presently she would come to her senses and ask a few sensible questions, even ask for an explanation of the unexpected events taking place around her, but all she said was, 'Yes, Oliver,' in a meek voice, and went to kiss her mother and bid her stepfather a frosty goodbye.

She said tartly, 'There's a lot I could say to you, but I won't,' and she walked out of the room with Oliver. Tiger was in the kitchen, and somehow the sight of him brought her to her senses.

'Oliver—' she began.

'We'll talk as we go,' he told her comfortably, and popped her into the car, settled Tiger in the back seat and got in beside her. Presently he said in a matter-of-fact voice, 'We shall be home in time for supper. We'll stop at Aldbury and get Oscar and Cyril.'

'But where are we going?'

'Home.'

'I haven't got a home,' said Amabel wildly.

'Yes, you have.' He rested a hand on her knee for a moment. 'Darling, *our* home.'

And after that he said nothing for quite some time, which left Amabel all the time in the world to think. Chaotic thoughts which were interrupted by him saying in a matter-of-fact voice, 'Shall we stop for a meal?' and, so saying, stopping before a small pub, well back from the road, with a lane on one side of it.

It was dim and cosy inside, with a handful of people at the bar, and they had their sandwiches and coffee against a background of cheerful talk, not speaking much themselves.

When they had finished the doctor said, 'Shall we walk a little way up the lane with Tiger?'

They walked arm in arm and Amabel tried to think of something to say—then decided that there was no need; it was as though they had everything that mattered.

But not quite all, it seemed, for presently, when they stopped to look at the view over a gate, Oliver turned her round to face him.

'I love you. You must know that, my dear. I've loved you since I first saw you, although I didn't know it at once. And then you seemed so young, and anxious to make a life for yourself; I'm so much older than you...'

Amabel said fiercely, 'Rubbish. You're just the right age. I don't quite understand what has happened, but that doesn't matter...' She looked up into his face. 'You have always been there, and I can't imagine a world without you...'

He kissed her then, and the wintry little lane was no longer a lane but heaven.

In a little while they got back into the car, and Amabel, with a little gentle prompting, told Oliver of her two weeks with her mother.

'How did you know I was there?' she wanted to know, and when he had told her she said, 'Oliver, Miriam Potter-Stokes said that you were going to marry her. I know now that wasn't true, but why did she say that?' She paused. 'Did you think that you would before you met me?'

'No, my darling. I took her out once or twice, and we met often at friends' houses. But it never entered my head to want to marry her. I think that she looked upon me, as she would look upon any other man in my position, as a possible source of a comfortable life.'

'That's all right, then,' said Amabel.

She looked so radiantly happy that he said, 'My dearest, if you continue to look like that I shall have to stop and kiss you.'

An unfulfilled wish since they were on a motorway.

There was no doubt about the warmth of their welcome at Lady Haleford's cottage. They were met in the hall by Mrs Twitchett, Nelly, Oscar and Cyril, and swept into the drawing room, where Lady Haleford was sitting.

She said at once, 'Amabel, I am so happy to see you again, although I understand from Oliver that this visit is a brief one. Still, we shall see more of each other, I have no doubt. I shall miss you and Oscar and Cyril. Oliver shall bring you here whenever he has the time, but of course first of all he must take you to see his mother. You'll marry soon?'

Amabel went pink and Oliver answered for her. 'Just as soon as it can be arranged, Aunt.'

'Good. I shall come to the wedding, and so will Mrs Twitchett and Nelly. Now we will have tea...'

An hour later, once more in the car, Amabel said, 'You haven't asked me...'

He glanced at her briefly, smiling. 'Oh, but I will.

Once we are alone and quiet. I've waited a long time, dear love, but I'm not going to propose to you driving along a motorway.'

'I don't know where you live…'

'In a quiet street of Regency houses. There's a garden with a high wall, just right for Oscar and Cyril, and Bates and his wife look after me and Tiger, and now they will look after you three as well.'

'Oh—is it a big house?'

'No, no, just a nice size for a man and his wife and children to live in comfortably.'

Which gave Amabel plenty to think about, staring out of the window into the dark evening through rose-coloured spectacles, soothed by Oliver's quiet voice from time to time and the gentle fidgets of the three animals on the back seat.

She hadn't been sure of what to expect, and when she got out of the car the terrace of houses looked elegant and dignified, with handsome front doors and steps leading to their basements. But Oliver gave her time to do no more than glimpse at them. Light streamed from an open door and someone stood waiting by it.

'We're home,' said Oliver, and took her arm and tucked it under his.

She had been feeling anxious about Bates, but there was no need; he beamed at her like a kindly uncle, and Mrs Bates behind him shook her hand, her smile as wide as her husband's.

'You will wish to go straight to the drawing room, sir,' said Bates, and opened a door with a flourish.

As they went in, Aunt Thisbe came to meet them.

'Didn't expect to see me, did you, Amabel?' she asked briskly. 'But Oliver is a stickler for the conventions, and quite right too. You will have to bear with me until you are married.'

She offered a cheek to be kissed, and then again for Oliver.

'You two will want to talk, but just for a moment there is something I need to do…' he murmured.

Aunt Thisbe made for the door. 'I'll see about those animals of yours,' she said, and closed the door firmly behind her.

The doctor unbuttoned Amabel's coat, tossed it on a chair and took her in his arms. 'This is a proposal— but first, this…' He bent his head and kissed her, taking his time about it.

'Will you marry me, Amabel?' he asked her.

'Will you always kiss me like that?' she asked him.

'Always and for ever, dearest.'

'Then I'll marry you,' said Amabel, 'because I like being kissed like that. Besides, I love you.'

There was only one answer to that…

* * * * *

AN INDEPENDENT WOMAN

Chapter 1

The street, like hundreds of other streets in that part of London, was shabby but genteelly so, for the occupants of the small turn-of-the-century houses which lined it had done their best; there were clean net curtains at the windows and the paintwork was pristine, even if badly in need of a fresh coat. Even so, the street was dull under a leaden sky and slippery with the cold sleet.

The girl, Ruth, looking out of the window of one of the houses, frowned at the dreary view and said over her shoulder, 'I don't think I can bear to go on living here much longer...'

'Well, you won't have to—Thomas will get the senior registrar's post and you'll marry and be happy ever after.'

The speaker who answered, Julia, was kneeling on

the shabby carpet, pinning a paper pattern to a length of material. She was a pretty girl, with a quantity of russet hair tied back carelessly with a bootlace, a tip-tilted nose and a wide mouth. Her eyes under thick brows were grey, and as she got to her feet it was apparent that she was a big girl with a splendid figure.

She wandered over to the window to join her sister. 'A good thing that Dr Goodman hasn't got a surgery this morning; you've no need to go out.'

'The evening surgery will be packed to the doors...'

They both turned their heads as a door opened and another girl, Monica, came in. A very beautiful girl, almost as beautiful as her elder sister. For while Julia, she of the russet hair, was pretty, the other two were both lovely, with fair hair and blue eyes. Ruth was taller than Monica, and equally slender, but they shared identical good looks.

'I'm off. Though heaven knows how many children will turn up in this weather.' Monica smiled. 'But George was going to look in...'

George was the parish curate, young and enthusiastic, nice-looking in a rather crumpled way and very much in love with Monica.

They chorused goodbyes as she went away again.

'I'm going to wash my hair,' said Ruth, and Julia got down onto her knees again and picked up the scissors.

The front doorbell rang as she did so, and Ruth said from the door, 'That will be the milkman; I forgot to pay him... I'll go.'

Professor Gerard van der Maes stood on the doorstep and looked around him. He had, in an unguarded moment, offered to deliver a package from his registrar Thomas, to that young man's fiancée—something which, it seemed, it was vital she received as quickly as possible. Since the registrar was on duty, and unlikely to be free for some time, and the Professor was driving himself to a Birmingham hospital and would need to thread his way through the northern parts of London, a slight deviation from his route was of little consequence.

Now, glancing around him, he rather regretted his offer. It had taken him longer than he had expected to find the house and he found the dreary street not at all to his taste. From time to time he had listened to Thomas's diffident but glowing remarks about his fiancée, but no one had told him that she lived in such a run-down part of the city.

The girl who answered the door more than made up for the surroundings. If this was Ruth, then Thomas must indeed be a happy man.

He held out a hand. 'Van der Maes, a colleague of Thomas. He wanted you to have a parcel and I happened to be going this way.'

'Professor van der Maes.' Ruth beamed up at him. 'How kind of you.' She added, not quite truthfully, 'I was just going to make coffee…'

He followed her into the narrow hall and into the living room and Ruth said, 'Julia…'

'If it's money you want there's some in my purse…' Julia didn't look up. 'Don't stop me or I'll cut too much off.'

'It's Professor van der Maes.'

'Not the old man from across the street?' Julia

snipped carefully. 'I knew he'd break a leg one day, going outside in his slippers.'

Ruth gave the Professor an apologetic glance. 'We have a visitor, Julia.'

Julia turned round then, and looked at the pair of them standing in the doorway. Ruth, as lovely as ever, looked put out and her companion looked amused. Julia got to her feet, looking at him. Not quite her idea of a professor: immensely tall and large in his person, dark hair going grey, heavy brows above cold eyes and a nose high-bridged and patrician above a thin mouth. Better a friend than an enemy, thought Julia. Not that he looked very friendly...

She held out a hand and had it gently crushed.

'I'll make the coffee,' said Ruth, and shut the door behind her.

'Do sit down,' said Julia, being sociable.

Instead he crossed the room to stand beside her and look down at the stuff spread out on the carpet.

'It looks like a curtain,' he observed.

'It is a curtain,' said Julia snappishly. It was on the tip of her tongue to tell him that by the time she had finished with it it would be a dress suitable to wear to an annual dance which the firm she worked for gave to its employees. A not very exciting occasion, but it was to be held at one of London's well-known hotels and that, combined with the fact that it was mid-February and life was a bit dull, meant that the occasion merited an effort on her part to make the best of herself.

She remembered her manners. 'Do you know

Thomas? I suppose you're from the hospital. He's Ruth's fiancé. He's not ill or anything?'

'I know Thomas and I am at the same hospital. He is in splendid health.'

'Oh, good. But horribly overworked, I suppose?'

'Yes, indeed.' His eye fell on the curtain once more. 'You are a skilled needlewoman?'

'Only when I am desperate. What do you do at the hospital? Teach, I suppose, if you are a professor?'

'I do my best...'

'Of what? Professor of what?'

'Surgery.'

'So you're handy with a needle too!' said Julia, and before he could answer that Ruth came in with the coffee.

'Getting to know each other?' she asked cheerfully.

'Thank you for bringing the parcel, Professor. I'm sorry you won't see Monica—she runs the nursery school here. Luckily I've got the morning off from the surgery, and Julia is always here, of course. She works at home—writes verses for greetings cards.'

Ruth handed round the coffee, oblivious of Julia's heavy frown.

'How very interesting,' observed the Professor, and she gave him a quick look, suspecting that he was amused. Which he was, although nothing of it showed on his face.

Ruth asked diffidently, 'I suppose Thomas hasn't heard if he's got that senior registrar's job? I know he'd phone me, but if he's busy...'

'I think I can set your mind at rest. He should hear

some time today. He's a good man and I shall be glad to have him in my team in a senior capacity.' He smiled at Ruth. 'Does that mean that you will marry?'

She beamed at him. 'Yes, just as soon as we can find somewhere to live.' She went on chattily, 'An aunt left us this house, and we came here to live when Mother and Father died, but I think we shall all be glad when we marry and can leave it.'

'Your other sister—Monica?' encouraged the Professor gently.

'Oh, she's engaged to the local curate; he's just waiting to get a parish. And Julia's got an admirer—a junior partner in the firm she works for. So you see, we are all nicely settled.'

He glanced at Julia. She didn't look at all settled, for she was indignantly pink and looked as though she wanted to throw something. She said coldly, 'I'm sure the Professor isn't in the least interested in us, Ruth.' She picked up the coffee pot. 'More coffee, Professor?'

Her tone dared him to say yes and delay his departure.

He had a second cup, and she hated him. And she thought he would never go.

When he did, he shook hands, with the observation that the dress would be a success.

Ruth went with him to the door. When she came back she said, 'He's got a Rolls; you ought to see it.' She glanced at Julia's kneeling form. 'You were a bit rude, dear. And he's such a nice man.'

Julia snipped savagely at a length of curtain. 'I hope I never meet him again.'

'Well, I don't suppose you will. He's a bit grand for us...'

'There's nothing wrong with a rising young surgeon and a member of the clergy.' She'd almost added, 'and a junior partner in a greetings card firm,' but she didn't, for Oscar, accepted as her admirer by everyone but herself, didn't quite fit. Curiosity got the better of her.

'Why do you say he's grand?'

'He's at the very top of the tree in the medical world and he's got a Dutch title—comes from an ancient family with lots of money. Never talks about himself. Thomas says he's a very private man.'

'Huh,' said Julia. 'Probably no one's good enough for him.'

Ruth commented mildly, 'You do dislike him, don't you?'

Julia began to wield her scissors again. 'Dislike him? I don't even know him. Shall we have Welsh rarebit for lunch? I'll make some scones for tea. Monica will be ravenous when she gets home; she never has time to eat her sandwiches. And if you're going to the shops you could bring some steak and kidney and I'll make a pudding.' She added, 'Filling and cheap.'

She spoke without rancour; the three Gracey sisters, living together for the sake of economy in the poky little house a long-dead aunt had bequeathed to them, had learned to live frugally. The house might be theirs, but there were rates and taxes, gas and electricity, clothes and food to be paid for. None of them had been trained to do anything in the business world, having been left suddenly with nothing but memories of their mother and father, killed in a car accident, and a carefree life in a pleasant old house in the country with never a thought of money worries.

It had been Julia who'd got them organised, refusing to be daunted by unexpected debts, selling their home to pay off the mortgage, arguing with bank managers, solicitors, and salvaging the remnants of her father's ill-advised investments. Once in their new home, it had been she who had urged the rather shy Ruth to take the part-time job as a receptionist to the local doctor while she looked for work for herself and Monica joined the staff of the local nursery school. But Julia had had no luck until, searching through the ads in the local paper, she'd seen one from the greetings card company.

Nothing ventured, nothing gained, she had decided, and had sat down to compose a batch of verses and send them off. Much to her surprise, the firm had taken her on. It was badly paid, but it meant that she could work at home and do the housekeeping and the cooking. And they managed very well.

Ruth had met Thomas when she had gone to the hospital to collect some urgent path. lab. Results for Dr Goodman, and soon they would marry. Monica, although she liked children, had never been quite sure that she wanted to stay at home, especially in such alien surroundings, but then George had come one day to tell the children Bible stories and all ideas of going out into the glamorous world to find a job more to her liking had faded away. They would have to wait to marry, of course, until George had a parish. In the meantime she was happy.

Which left Julia, twenty-four years old, bursting with

life and energy. Because she had a happy nature she didn't allow herself to dwell on what might have been, but wrote her sentimental little verses, kept the house clean and tidy and, being clever with her needle, dressed herself in a style which, while not being the height of fashion, was a passable imitation.

It was fortunate, she supposed, that Oscar, her admirer—for he was only that at the moment, although he promised to be rather more when it was convenient for him to be so—had absolutely no taste in clothes. That horrible professor might sneer in a well-mannered way at the curtain, but Oscar wouldn't suspect. Indeed, even if he did, he would probably approve, for he was of a frugal nature when it came to spending money. He was persistent too. She had tried, over and over again, to shake him off, to suggest that she would make him a most unsuitable wife, but he refused to be shaken and, despite the countless excuses she had given, she was committed to attend the annual dance given by the greetings card firm.

Rightly, Ruth and Monica had urged her to go and enjoy herself. But neither of them had met Oscar, and she had given way because she knew that they both felt unhappy at the idea of her being left alone when they married. When she allowed herself to think about it she felt unhappy about that too.

She put away her sewing and started on the household chores, and found herself thinking about the Professor. He seemed a tiresome man, and she suspected that it would be hard to get the better of him. Probably he was horrid to his patients.

* * *

Professor van der Maes, contrary to Julia's idea, was treating the endless stream of patients attending his clinic with kindness and patience, his quiet voice reassuring, his smile encouraging. He was a tired man, for he worked too hard, but no patient had ever found him uncaring. But that was a side which he seldom showed to anyone else. The nursing staff who worked for him quickly learnt that he would stand no nonsense, that only their best efforts would suit him, and as for his students—he represented the goal they hoped to obtain one day. A good word from him was worth a dozen from anyone else, just as a quiet reprimand sent them into instant dejection. They called him the old man behind his back, and fiercely defended any criticism anyone was foolish enough to utter.

The Professor remained unmoved by other people's opinion of him, good or bad. He was an excellent surgeon and he loved his work, and he had friends who would be his for life, but he had no use for casual acquaintances. He had a social life when his work permitted, and was much sought after as a dinner party guest. Since he was unmarried, he could have taken his pick of any of the women he met. But, although he was a pleasant companion, he showed no interest in any of them. Somewhere in the world, he supposed, there was the woman he would fall in love with and want for his wife, but he was no longer young and he would probably end his days as a crusty old bachelor.

It wasn't until he was driving back to London a few days later that he thought about the three Gracey sisters. Ruth would make Thomas a good wife: a beautiful girl with her shy smile and gentle voice. He thought only fleetingly of Julia. Pretty, he supposed, but sharp-tongued, and she made no effort to be pleasant. She was the last person he imagined would spend her days writing sentimental verses for greetings cards, and what woman in her senses wore dresses made from curtains? He laughed, and forgot her.

The dance was ten days later, and, since the firm had had a good year, it was to be held at one of the more prestigious hotels. There was to be a buffet supper before everyone went to the hotel ballroom, and Ruth and Monica, anxious that Julia should enjoy herself, lent slippers and an old but still magnificent shawl which had belonged to their mother. They sent her there in a taxi—an unnecessary expense, Julia protested; the journey there would have been a lengthy one by bus but far cheaper. However, they insisted, privately of the opinion that Oscar could have come and fetched her instead of meeting her there…

The dress, despite its origin, was a success, simply made, but it fitted where it should, and unless anyone had actually seen the curtain, hanging in the spare bedroom, one would never have known…

Julia walked out of the taxi feeling quite pleased with herself, straight into the Professor's person.

He set her tidily on her feet. 'Well, well, Miss Julia Gracey. Unexpected and delightful.' He looked around him. 'You are alone?'

She bade him good evening in a choked voice. 'I am meeting someone in the hotel.'

She glanced around, looking without much hope for Oscar. There was no sign of him, of course. He had said that he would be at the hotel entrance, waiting for her. She supposed that she would have to go inside and look for him. She was not easily daunted, but the hotel's imposing entrance and the equally imposing appearance of the doorman daunted her now, and how and by what misfortune had the Professor got here? Surely he hadn't anything to do with greetings cards?

It seemed not. He said easily, 'I'm meeting friends here. We may as well go in together.' He paid the cabby and took her arm. 'Your friend will be looking for you inside?'

He was being kind, with a casual kindness it was impossible to resent. She sought frantically for something to say as the doorman opened the doors with a flourish and they joined the people in the foyer.

There was no sign of Oscar. She had been a fool to accept his invitation; she didn't even like him much.

'Let me have your shawl,' said the Professor. 'I'll let the girl have it.' And he had taken it from her and left her for a moment, returning with a ticket which he tucked into the little handbag hanging from her wrist.

She found her tongue then, 'Thank you. I'll—I'll wait here. Oscar will find me…'

'Oscar?' She mistrusted his casual voice. 'Ah, yes, of course. And if I'm not mistaken this must be he…'

She should have been glad to see him, and she might well have been if he had expressed regret at not meeting her promptly. But all he did was thump her on the shoulder and say heartily, 'Sorry old lady. I got held up; so many people wanted to have a chat.'

He looked her up and down. 'Got yourself a new dress for the occasion? Not bad, not bad at all…'

His glance fell upon the Professor, who had made no attempt to go away.

'Do I know you?'

Julia, aware of the Professor's eyes fixed on the curtain, said tartly, 'No, Oscar, you don't. This is Professor van der Maes. He knows Ruth's fiancé.'

Oscar looked uneasy under the Professor's cool gaze. 'Nice to meet you. Come along, Julia, I'll find you somewhere to sit; I've one or two important clients to talk to, but we'll be able to dance presently.'

He nodded in a condescending manner at the Professor, who took no notice but said pleasantly to Julia, 'I do hope you have a happy evening,' and, as Oscar turned away rudely to speak to a passing couple, 'but I doubt it.' He looked amused. 'I can't say that I agree with Oscar about your dress, but then I know it's a curtain, don't I?'

He was sorry the moment he had said it; for a moment she had the look of a small girl who had been slapped for no reason at all. But only for a moment. Julia stared up into his handsome face. 'Go away, Professor. I don't like you and I hope I never see you again.'

She had spoken quietly but she looked daggers at him. She turned her back then, surprised at how upset she felt. After all, she hadn't liked him the first time, and she couldn't care less if he jeered at the dress or liked it. If Oscar liked it, that was all that mattered, she told herself, not believing a word of it. But presently, when Oscar had finished his conversation, she went with him to the hotel ballroom, to be sat on one of the little gilt chairs and told to wait awhile until he had the leisure to dance with her.

A not very promising prospect—but quickly lightened by a number of men who, seeing a pretty girl sitting by herself, danced her off in rapid succession. Which served Oscar right by the time he found himself ready to partner her.

'Some of these modern dances are not dignified,' he told her severely, propelling her round the ballroom with correct stiffness. 'You would have done better to have sat quietly until I was free to come to you.'

'But I like to dance, Oscar.'

'Dancing in moderation is splendid exercise,' said Oscar, at his stuffiest.

They came to a dignified halt as the music stopped. Julia spoke her thoughts out loud. 'Do you want to marry me, Oscar?' she asked.

He looked at her with astonishment and displeasure.

'My dear Julia, what a very—very…' he sought for the right word '…unwomanly remark to make. I must only hope it was a slight aberration of the tongue.'

'It wasn't anything to do with my tongue; it was a thought in my head.' She looked at him. 'You haven't answered me, Oscar?'

'I have no intention of doing so. I am shocked, Julia. Perhaps you should retire to the ladies' room and compose yourself.'

'You sound like someone in a Victorian novel,' she told him. 'But, yes, I think that would be best.'

The ballroom was at the back of the hotel; it took her a few moments to find the cloakroom where the Professor had left her wrap. She would have to take a bus, she hadn't enough money for a taxi, but it wasn't late and there were plenty of people about. She wrapped the vast mohair shawl she and her sisters shared for evening occasions round her and crossed the foyer, comfortably full of people. And halfway to the door the Professor, apparently appearing from thin air, put a hand on her arm.

'Not leaving already?' he wanted to know. 'It's barely an hour since you arrived.'

She had to stop, his hand, resting so lightly on her arm, nevertheless reminding her of a ball and chain. She said politely, 'Yes, I'm leaving, Professor.' She looked at his hand. 'Goodbye.'

He took no notice; neither did he remove his hand.

'You're upset; you have the look of someone about to explode. I'll take you home.'

'No, thank you. I'm quite capable of getting myself home.'

For answer he tucked her hand under his elbow. 'Your Oscar will come looking for you,' he said mildly.

'He's not my Oscar…'

'Ah, I can't say that I'm surprised. Now, come along. This is indeed a splendid excuse for me to leave with you—a pompous dinner with endless speeches to which I have been bidden.'

He had propelled her gently past the doorman, out

into the chilly night and, after towing her along gently, popped her into his car, parked nearby.

Getting in beside her, he asked, 'Are you going to cry?'

'Certainly not. And I have no wish to be here in your car. You are being high-handed, Professor.' She sniffed. 'I'm not a child.'

He looked at her, smiling a little. 'No, I had realised that. Are you hungry?'

She was taken by surprise. 'Yes...'

'Splendid. And, since you are not going to cry and I'm hungry too, we will go and eat somewhere.'

'No,' said Julia.

'My dear girl, be sensible. It's the logical thing to do.'

He started the car. 'Let us bury the hatchet for an hour or so. You are free to dislike me the moment I see you to your front door.'

She was hungry, so the prospect of a meal was tempting. She said, 'Well, all right, but not anywhere grand— the curtain...'

He said quietly, 'I'm sorry I said that. You look very nice and it was unforgivable of me. We will go somewhere you won't need to be uneasy.'

He sounded kind and her spirits lifted. Perhaps he wasn't so bad... He spoilt it by adding, 'Is your entire wardrobe made up of curtains?' He glanced at her. 'You must be a very talented young lady.'

She was on the point of making a fiery answer when the thought of a meal crossed her mind. She had no idea why he had asked her out and she didn't care; she would choose all the most expensive things on the menu...

He took her to Wilton's, spoke quietly to the maître d', and followed her to one of the booths, so that any fears concerning her dress were instantly put at rest.

'Now, what shall we have?' asked the Professor, well aware of her relief that the booth sheltered her nicely from the other diners. 'I can recommend the cheese soufflé, and the sole Meunière is excellent.' When she agreed he ordered from the waitress and turned his attention to the sommelier and the wine list. Which gave Julia a chance to study the menu. She need not have bothered to choose the most expensive food; everything was expensive.

When it came it was delicious, and cooked by a master hand. She thought fleetingly of Oscar, and applied herself to her dinner, and, being nicely brought up, made polite conversation the while. The Professor replied suitably, amused at that and wondering what had possessed him to take her to dinner. He went out seldom, and when he did his companion would be one of his numerous acquaintances: elegant young women, dressed impeccably, bone-thin and fussing delicately about what they could and couldn't eat.

Julia, on the other hand, ate everything she was offered with an unselfconscious pleasure, and capped the sole with sherry trifle and drank the wine he had ordered. And that loosed her tongue, for presently, over coffee, she asked, 'If you are Dutch, why do you live in England?'

'I only do so for part of the time. My home is in Holland and I work there as well. I shall be going back there in a few weeks' time for a month or so.'

'How very unsettling,' observed Julia. 'But I suppose you are able to pick and choose if you are a Professor?'

'I suppose I can,' he agreed mildly. 'What are you going to do about Oscar?'

'I dare say he won't find me a suitable wife for a junior partner...'

'And will that break your heart?'

'No. He sort of grew on me, if you see what I mean.'

He said smoothly, 'Ah—you have a more romantic outlook, perhaps?'

She took a sip of coffee. 'It's almost midnight. Would you take me home, please?'

Not one of the women he had taken out to dinner had ever suggested that it was getting late and they wished to go home. On the contrary. The Professor stifled a laugh, assured her that they would go at once, and signed the bill. On the journey through London's streets he discussed the weather, the pleasures of the English countryside and the prospect of a fine summer.

The street was quiet and only barely lit. He got out and opened the car door for her, before taking the door key from her. He opened the door and gave her back the key.

Julia cast around in her mind for something gracious to say. 'Thank you for my dinner,' she said finally, and, since that didn't sound in the least gracious, added, 'I enjoyed the dinner very much and the restaurant was—was very elegant. It was a very pleasant evening...'

She didn't like his smile in the dimly lit hallway. 'Don't try too hard, Julia,' he told her. 'Goodnight.'

He pushed her gently into the hall and closed the door soundlessly behind her.

'I hate him,' said Julia, and took off her shoes, flung the shawl onto the floor and crept upstairs to her bed. She had intended to lie awake and consider how much she disliked him, but she went to sleep at once.

The Professor took himself off home, to his elegant Chelsea house, locked the Rolls in the mews garage behind it, and let himself into his home. There was a wall-light casting a gentle light on the side table in the hall and he picked up the handful of letters on it as he went to his study.

This was a small, comfortably furnished room, with rows of bookshelves, a massive desk, a chair behind it and two smaller ones each side of the small fireplace. Under the window was a table with a computer and a pile of papers and books. He ignored it and put the letters on his desk before going out of the room again and along the hall, through the baize door at the end and down the steps to the kitchen, where he poured himself coffee from the pot on the Aga and acknowledged the sleepy greetings from two small dogs.

They got out of the basket they shared and sat beside him while he drank his coffee: two small creatures with heavily whiskered faces, short legs and long, thin rat-like tails. The Professor had found them, abandoned, terrified and starving, some six months earlier. It was apparent that they weren't going to grow any larger or handsomer, but they had become members of his household and his devoted companions. He saw them back into their basket, with the promise of a walk in the morning, and went back to his study. There were some notes he needed to write up before he went to bed.

He sat down and pulled the papers towards him and then sat back in his chair, thinking about the evening. What had possessed him to take Julia out to dinner? he wondered. A nice enough girl, no doubt, but with a sharp tongue and making no attempt to hide the fact that she didn't like him. The unknown Oscar was possibly to be pitied. He smiled suddenly. She had enjoyed her dinner, and he doubted whether Oscar rose much above soup of the day and a baked potato. He acknowledged that this was an unfair thought; Oscar might even now be searching fruitlessly for Julia.

When Julia went down to breakfast in the morning, Ruth and Monica were already at the kitchen table, and without wasting time they began to fire questions at her.

'Did you dance? Was it a splendid hotel? What did you eat? Did Oscar propose? Did he bring you home?'

Julia lifted the teapot. 'I danced three and a half times, and the hotel was magnificent.'

She shook cornflakes into a bowl. She didn't like them, but, according to the TV ad, the girl who ate them had a wand-like figure—a state to which she hoped in time to subdue her own generous curves. She said, 'I didn't eat at the hotel.' She took a sip of tea. 'Oscar didn't propose. I don't think he ever will now. And he didn't bring me home.'

'Julia, you didn't come home alone?'

'No, Professor van der Maes drove me back.'

She finished the cornflakes and put bread in the toaster.

'Start at the beginning and don't leave anything out,' said Ruth. 'What on earth was the Professor doing there? He doesn't write verses, does he?'

'No. Though I'm sure he is very handy with a needle.'

Her sisters exchanged glances. 'Why did you dance half a dance?' asked Ruth.

Julia said through a mouthful of toast, 'Oscar was annoyed because I hadn't stayed on my chair to wait for him, so I asked him if he wanted to marry me.'

'Julia, how could you…?'

'He told me to go to the ladies' room and compose myself, so I found my shawl and left, and the Professor was at the entrance. He said he was hungry and asked me if I was, and when I said yes, he took me to Wilton's.'

'Wilton's?' chorused her sisters, and then added, 'The dress…?'

'It was all right. We sat in a booth. It was a nice dinner. And then, when I asked him to bring me home, he did.'

Two pairs of astonished blue eyes stared at her. 'What about Oscar?'

'He was shocked.'

'And the Professor? Whatever did he say?'

'He said he wasn't surprised that Oscar wasn't mine. You will both be late for work…'

'But why should the Professor take you out to dinner?' asked Ruth.

'He said he was hungry.'

'You can be very tiresome sometimes, Julia,' said Monica severely.

When they had gone Julia set about the household chores and then, those done, she made coffee and a cheese sandwich and sat down to write verses. Perhaps Oscar would be able to get her the sack, but on the other hand her verses sold well. The senior partners might not agree. For it wasn't the kind of work many people would want to do and it was badly paid. She polished off a dozen verses, fed Muffin, the family cat, and peeled the potatoes for supper. Oscar, she reflected, wouldn't bother her again.

Chapter 2

Oscar came four days later. Julia was making pastry for a steak pie and she went impatiently to the front door when its knocker was thumped. Oscar was on the doorstep. 'I wish to talk to you, Julia.'

'Come in, then,' said Julia briskly. 'I'm making pastry and don't want it to spoil.'

She ushered him into the house, told him to leave his coat in the hall, and then went back into the kitchen and plunged her hands into the bowl.

'Do sit down,' she invited him, and, when he looked askance at Muffin the household cat, sitting in the old Windsor chair by the stove, added, 'Take a chair at the table. It's warm here. Anyway, I haven't lighted the fire in the sitting room yet.'

She bent over her pastry, and presently he said stuff-ily, 'You can at least leave that and listen to what I have to say, Julia.'

She put the dough on the floured board and held a rolling pin.

'I'm so sorry, Oscar, but I really can't leave it. I am listening, though.'

He settled himself into his chair. 'I have given a good deal of thought to your regrettable behaviour at the dance, Julia. I can but suppose that the excitement of the occasion and the opulence of your surroundings had caused you to become so—so unlike yourself. After due consideration I have decided that I shall overlook that…'

Julia laid her pastry neatly over the meat and tidied the edges with a knife. 'Don't do that,' she begged him. 'I wasn't in the least excited, only annoyed to be stuck on a chair in a corner—and left to find my own way in, too.'

'I have a position to uphold in the firm,' said Oscar. And when she didn't answer he asked, 'Who was that man you were talking to? Really, Julia, it is most unsuitable. I trust you found your way home? There is a good bus service?'

Julia was cutting pastry leaves to decorate her pie. She said, 'I had dinner at Wilton's and was driven home afterwards.'

Oscar sought for words and, finding none, got to his feet. 'There is nothing more to be said, Julia. I came here prepared to forgive you, but I see now that I have allowed my tolerance to be swept aside by your frivolity.'

Julia dusted her floury hands over the bowl and

began to clear up the table. Listening to Oscar was like reading a book written a hundred years ago. He didn't belong in this century and, being a kind-hearted girl, she felt sorry for him.

'I'm not at all suitable for you, Oscar,' she told him gently.

He said nastily, 'Indeed you are not, Julia. You have misled me...'

She was cross again. 'I didn't know we had got to that stage. Anyway, what you need isn't a wife, it's a doormat. And do go, Oscar, before I hit you with this rolling pin.'

He got to his feet. 'I must remind you that your future with the firm is in jeopardy, Julia. I have some influence...'

Which was just what she could have expected from him, she supposed. They went into the hall and he got into his coat. She opened the door and ushered him out, wished him goodbye, and closed the door before he had a chance to say more.

She told her sisters when they came home, and Monica said, 'He might have made a good steady husband, but he sounds a bit out of date.'

'I don't think I want a steady husband,' said Julia, and for a moment she thought about the Professor. She had no idea why she should have done that; she didn't even like him...

So, during the next few days she waited expectantly for a letter from the greetings card firm, but when one did come it contained a cheque for her last batch of verses and a request for her to concentrate on wedding cards—June was the bridal month and they needed to get the cards to the printers in good time…

'Reprieved,' said Julia, before she cashed the cheque and paid the gas bill.

It was difficult to write about June roses and wedded bliss in blustery March. But she wrote her little verses and thought how nice it would be to marry on a bright summer's morning, wearing all the right clothes and with the right bridegroom.

A week later Thomas came one evening. He had got the job as senior registrar and, what was more, had now been offered one of the small houses the hospital rented out to their staff. There was no reason why he and Ruth shouldn't marry as soon as possible. The place was furnished, and it was a bit poky, but once he had some money saved they could find something better.

'And the best of it is I'm working for Professor van der Maes.' His nice face was alight with the prospect. 'You won't mind a quiet wedding?' he asked Ruth anxiously.

Ruth would have married him in a cellar wearing a sack. 'We'll get George to arrange everything. And it will be quiet anyway; there's only us. Your mother and father will come?'

Julia went to the kitchen to make coffee and sandwiches and took Monica with her. 'We'll give them half an hour. Monica, have you any money? Ruth must have some clothes…'

They sat together at the table, doing sums. 'There aren't any big bills due,' said Julia. 'If we're very careful and we use the emergency money we could just manage.'

Thomas was to take up his new job in three weeks' time: the best of reasons why he and Ruth should marry, move into their new home and have a few days together first. Which meant a special licence and no time at all to buy clothes and make preparations for a quiet wedding. Julia and Monica gave Ruth all the money they could lay hands on and then set about planning the wedding day. There would be only a handful of guests: Dr Goodman and his wife, George, and the vicar who would take the service, Thomas's parents and the best man.

They got out the best china and polished the tea spoons, and Julia went into the kitchen and leafed through her cookery books.

It was a scramble, but by the time the wedding day dawned Ruth had a dress and jacket in a pale blue, with a fetching hat, handbag, gloves and shoes, and the nucleus of a new wardrobe suitable for a senior registrar's wife. Julia had assembled an elegant buffet for after the ceremony, and Monica had gone to the market and bought daffodils, so that when they reached the church—a red-brick mid-Victorian building, sadly lacking in beauty—its rather bleak interior glowed with colour.

Monica had gone on ahead, leaving Julia to make the last finishing touches to the table, which took longer than she had expected. She had to hurry to the church just as Dr Goodman came for Ruth.

She arrived there a bit flushed, her russet hair glowing under her little green felt hat—Ruth's hat, really, but it went well with her green jacket and skirt, which had been altered and cleaned and altered again and clung to, since they were suitable for serious occasions.

Julia sniffed appreciatively at the fresh scent of the daffodils and started down the aisle to the back views of Thomas and his best man and the sprinkling of people in the pews. It was a long aisle, and she was halfway up when she saw the Professor sitting beside Mrs Goodman. They appeared to be on the best of terms and she shot past their pew without looking at them. His appearance was unexpected, but she supposed that Thomas, now a senior member of the team, merited his presence.

When Ruth came, Julia concentrated on the ceremony, but the Professor's image most annoyingly got between her and the beautiful words of the simple service. There was no need for him to be there. He and Thomas might be on the best of terms professionally, but they surely had different social lives? Did the medical profession enjoy a social life? she wondered, then brought her attention back sharply to Thomas and Ruth, exchanging their vows. They would be happy, she reflected, watching them walk back down the aisle. They were both so sure of their love. She wondered what it must feel like to be so certain.

After the first photos had been taken Julia slipped away, so as to get home before anyone else and make sure that everything was just so.

She was putting the tiny sausage rolls in the oven to warm when Ruth and Thomas arrived, closely followed by everyone else, and presently the best man came into the kitchen to get a corkscrew.

'Not that I think we'll need it,' he told her cheerfully. 'The Prof bought half a dozen bottles of champagne with him. Now that's what I call a wedding gift of the right sort. Can I help?'

'Get everyone drinking. I'll be along with these sausage rolls in a minute or two.'

She had them nicely arranged on a dish when the Professor came into the kitchen. He had a bottle and a glass in one hand.

He said, 'A most happy occasion. Your vicar has had two glasses already.'

He poured the champagne and handed her a glass. 'Thirsty work, heating up sausage rolls.'

She had to laugh. Such light-hearted talk didn't sound like him at all, and for a moment she liked him.

She took her glass and said, 'We can't toast them yet, can we? But it is a happy day.' And, since she was thirsty and excited, she drank deeply.

The Professor had an unexpected feeling of tenderness towards her; she might have a sharp tongue and not like him, but her naïve treatment of a glass of Moet et Chandon Brut Imperial he found touching.

She emptied the glass and said, 'That was nice.'

He agreed gravely. 'A splendid drink for such an occasion,' and he refilled her glass, observing prudently, 'I'll take the tray in for you.'

The champagne was having an effect upon her empty insides. She gave him a wide smile. 'The best man— what's his name, Peter?—said he'd be back…'

'He will be refilling glasses.' The Professor picked

up the tray, opened the door and ushered her out of the kitchen.

Julia swanned around, light-headed and lighthearted. It was marvellous what a couple of glasses of champagne did to one. She ate a sausage roll, drank another glass of champagne, handed round the sandwiches and would have had another glass of champagne if the Professor hadn't taken the glass from her.

'They're going to cut the cake,' he told her, 'and then we'll toast the happy couple.' Only then did he hand her back her glass.

After Ruth and Thomas had driven away, and everyone else was going home, she realised that the Professor had gone too, taking the best man with him.

'He asked me to say goodbye,' said Monica as the pair of them sat at the kitchen table, their shoes off, drinking strong tea. 'He took the best man with him, said he was rather pressed for time.'

Julia, still pleasantly muzzy from the champagne, wondered why it was that the best man had had the time to say goodbye to her. If he'd gone with the Professor, then surely the Professor could have found the time to do the same? She would think about that when her head was a little clearer.

Life had to be reorganised now that Ruth had left home; they missed her share of the housekeeping, but by dint of economising they managed very well.

Until, a few weeks later, Monica came into the house like a whirlwind, calling to Julia to come quickly; she had news.

George had been offered a parish; a small rural town in the West country. 'Miles from anywhere,' said Monica, glowing with happiness, 'but thriving. Not more than a large village, I suppose, but very scattered. He's to go there this week and see if he likes it.'

'And if he does?'

'He'll go there in two weeks' time. I'll go with him, of course. We can get married by special licence first.' Then she danced round the room. 'Oh, Julia, isn't it all marvellous? I'm so happy…!'

It wasn't until later, after they had toasted the future in a bottle of wine from the supermarket, that Monica said worriedly, 'Julia, what about you? What will you do? You'll never be able to manage…'

Julia had had time to have an answer ready. She said cheerfully, 'I shall take in lodgers until we decide what to do about this house. You and Ruth will probably like to sell it, and I think that is a good thing.'

'But you?' persisted Monica.

'I shall go to dressmaking classes and then set up on my own. I shall like that.'

'You don't think Oscar will come back? If he really loved you…?'

'But he didn't, and I wouldn't go near him with a bargepole—whatever that means.'

'But you'll marry…?'

'Oh, I expect so. And think how pleased my husband will be to have a wife who makes her own clothes.'

Julia poured the last of the wine into their glasses. 'Now tell me your plans…'

She listened to her sister's excited voice, making suitable comments from time to time, making suggestions, and all the while refusing to give way to the feeling of panic. So silly, she told herself sternly; she had a roof over her head for the time being, and she was perfectly able to reorganise her life. She wouldn't be lonely; she would have lodgers and Muffin...

'You'll marry from here?' she asked.

'Yes, but very quietly. We'll go straight to the parish after the wedding. There'll be just us and Ruth—and Thomas, if he can get away. No wedding breakfast or anything.' Monica laughed. 'I always wanted a big wedding, you know—white chiffon and a veil and bridesmaids—but none of that matters. It'll have to be early in the morning.'

Monica's lovely face glowed with happiness, and Julia said, 'Aren't you dying to hear what the vicarage is like? And the little town? You'll be a marvellous vicar's wife.'

'Yes, I think I shall,' said Monica complacently.

Presently she said uncertainly, 'Are you sure you'll be all right, Julia? There has always been the three of us...'

'Of course I'll be fine—and how super that I'll be able to visit you. Once I get started I can get a little car...'

Which was daydreaming with a vengeance, but served to pacify Monica.

After that events crowded upon each other at a great rate. George found his new appointment very much to his liking; moreover, he had been accepted by the church wardens and those of the parish whom he had met with every sign of satisfaction. The vicarage was

large and old-fashioned, but there was a lovely garden…
He was indeed to take up his appointment in two weeks'
time, which gave them just that time to arrange their
wedding—a very quiet one, quieter even than Ruth's
and Thomas's, for they were to marry in the early morning and drive straight down to their new home.

Julia, helping Monica to pack, had little time to think
about anything else, but was relieved that the girl who
was to take over Monica's job had rented a room with
her: a good omen for the future, she told her sisters
cheerfully. Trudie seemed a nice girl, too, quiet and
studious, and it would be nice to have someone else
in the house, and nicer still to have the rent money…

She would have to find another lodger, thought Julia,
waving goodbye to George's elderly car and the newly
married pair. If she could let two rooms she would
be able to manage if she added the rent to the small
amounts she got from the greetings card firm. Later on,
she quite understood, Ruth and Monica would want to
sell the house, and with her own share she would start
some kind of a career…

She went back into the empty house; Trudie would
be moving in on the following morning and she must
make sure that her room was as welcoming as possible.
As soon as she had a second lodger and things were running smoothly, she would pay a visit to Ruth.

A week went by. It was disappointing that there had
been no replies to her advertisement; she would have to
try again in a week or so, and put cards in the windows
of the row of rather seedy shops a few streets away. In
the meantime she would double her output of verses.

Trudie had settled in nicely, coming and going quietly, letting herself in and out with the key Julia had given her. Another one like her would be ideal, reflected Julia, picking up the post from the doormat.

There was a letter from the greetings card firm and she opened it quickly; there would be a cheque inside. There was, but there was a letter too. The firm was changing its policy: in future they would deal only with cards of a humorous nature since that was what the market demanded. It was with regret that they would no longer be able to accept her work. If she had a batch ready to send then they would accept it, but nothing further.

Julia read the letter again, just to make sure, and then went into the kitchen, made a pot of tea and sat down to drink it. It was a blow; the money the firm paid her was very little but it had been a small, steady income. Its loss would be felt. She did some sums on the back of the envelope and felt the beginnings of a headache. It was possible that Oscar was behind it… She read the letter once again; they would accept one last batch. Good, she would send as many verses as she could think up. She got pencil and paper and set to work. Just let me say on this lovely day…she began, and by lunchtime had more than doubled her output.

She typed them all out on her old portable and took them to the post. It would have been satisfying to have torn up the letter and put it in an envelope and sent it back, but another cheque would be satisfying too.

The cheque came a few days later, but still no new lodger. Which, as it turned out, was a good thing…

Thomas phoned. Ruth was in bed with flu, could

she possibly help out for a day or two? Not to stay, of course, but an hour or two each day until Ruth was on her feet. There was a bus, he added hopefully.

It meant two buses; she would have to change halfway. The hospital wasn't all that far away, but was awkward to get to.

Julia glanced at the clock. 'I'll be there about lunchtime. I must tell Trudie, my lodger. I'll stay until the evening if that's OK.'

'Bless you,' said Thomas. 'I should be free about five o'clock.'

Trudie, summoned from a horde of toddlers, was helpful. She would see to Muffin, go back at lunchtime and make sure that everything was all right, and she wasn't going out that evening anyway. Julia hurried to the main street and caught a bus.

The house was close to the hospital, one of a neat row in which the luckier of the medical staff lived. The door key, Thomas had warned her, was under the pot of flowers by the back door, and Julia let herself in, calling out as she did so.

It was a very small house. She put her bag down in the narrow hall and went up the stairs at its end, guided by the sound of Ruth's voice.

She was propped up in bed, her lovely face only slightly dimmed by a red nose and puffy eyes. She said thickly, 'Julia, you darling. You don't mind coming? I feel so awful, and Thomas has to be in Theatre all day. I'll be better tomorrow...'

'You'll stay there until Thomas says that you can get up,' said Julia, 'and of course I don't mind coming. In fact it makes a nice change. Now, how about a wash and a clean nightie, and then a morsel of something to eat?'

'I hope you don't catch the flu,' said Ruth later, drinking tea and looking better already, drowsy now in her freshly made bed, her golden hair, though rather lank, it must be admitted, neatly brushed. All the same, thought Julia, she looked far from well.

'Has the doctor been?' she asked.

'Yes, Dr Soames, one of the medical consultants. Someone is coming with some pills...'

Thomas brought them during his lunch hour. He couldn't stop, his lunch 'hour' being a figure of speech. A cup of coffee and a sandwich was the norm on this day, when Professor van der Maes was operating, but he lingered with Ruth as long as he could, thanked Julia profusely and assured her that he would be back by five o'clock. 'I'll be on call,' he told her, 'but only until midnight.'

'Would you like me to keep popping in for a few days, until Ruth is feeling better?'

'Would you? I hate leaving her.'

He went then, and Julia went down to the little kitchen, made another hot drink for Ruth and boiled herself an egg. Tomorrow she would bring some fruit and a new loaf. Bread and butter, cut very thin, was something most invalids would eat.

It was almost six o'clock when Thomas returned, bringing the Professor with him. The Professor spent a few minutes with Ruth, assured Thomas that she was looking better, and wandered into the kitchen, where Julia was laying a tray of suitable nourishment for Ruth.

'Get your coat,' he told her. 'I'll drive you home.' Julia thumped a saucepan of milk onto the stove. 'Thank you, but I'll get a bus when I'm ready.'

Not so much as a hello or even a good evening, thought Julia pettishly.

His smile mocked her. 'Thomas is here now. Two's company, three's none.'

'Thomas will want his supper.'

Thomas breezed into the kitchen. 'I'm a first-rate cook. We're going to have a picnic upstairs. You go home, Julia. You've been a godsend, and we're so grateful. You will come tomorrow?'

'Yes,' said Julia, and without looking at either of the men went and got her coat, said goodnight to her sister and went downstairs again.

The two men were in the hall and Thomas backed into the open kitchen door to make room for her, but even then the Professor took up almost all the space. He opened the door and she squeezed past him into the street. Thomas came too, beaming at them both, just as though he was seeing them off for an evening out.

The Professor had nothing to say. He sat relaxed behind the wheel, and if he felt impatience at the heavy traffic he didn't show it. Watching the crowded pavements and the packed buses edging their way along the streets, Julia suddenly felt ashamed at her ingratitude.

'This is very kind of you,' she began. 'It would have taken me ages to get home.'

He said coolly, 'I shan't be going out of my way. I'm going to the children's hospital not five minutes' drive away from your home.'

A remark which hardly encouraged her to carry on the conversation.

He had nothing more to say then, but when he stopped before her house he got out, opened the car door for her and stood waiting while she unlocked the house door, dismissing her thanks with a laconic, 'I have already said it was no trouble. Goodnight, Julia.'

She stood in the open door as he got into the car and drove off.

'And that's the last time I'll accept a lift from you,' she said to the empty street. 'I can't think why you bothered, but I suppose Thomas was there and you had no choice.' She slammed the door. 'Horrid man.'

But she was aware of a kind of sadness; she was sure that he wasn't a horrid man, only where she was concerned. For some reason she annoyed him...

She got her supper, fed Muffin, and went to warn Trudie that she would be going to Ruth for the next few days. 'No one phoned about a room, I suppose?' she asked.

'Not a soul. Probably in a day or two you'll have any number of callers.'

But there was no one.

For the next few days Julia went to and fro while Ruth slowly improved. Of the Professor there was no sign, although her sister told her that he had come frequently to see her. Dr Soames came too, and told her that she was much better. 'Though I look a hag,' said Ruth.

'A beautiful hag,' said Julia bracingly, 'and tomorrow you're going to crawl downstairs for a couple of hours.'

Ruth brightened. 'Tom can get the supper and we'll

have it round the fire, and I dare say Gerard will come for an hour…'

'Gerard?'

'The Professor. I simply couldn't go on calling him Professor, even though he seems a bit staid and stand-offish, doesn't he? But he's not in the least, and he's only thirty-six. He ought to be married, he nearly was a year ago, but he's not interested in girls. Not to marry, any-way. He's got lots of friends, but they're just friends.'

'You surprise me…'

Ruth gave her a thoughtful look. 'You don't like him?'

'I don't know him well enough to know if I like or dislike him.'

Ruth gave her a sharp look. 'I'm feeling so much better; I'm sure I could manage. You've been an angel, coming each day, but you must be longing to be let off the hook.'

'There's nothing to keep me at home. Trudie looks after herself and keeps an eye on Muffin. And if you can put up with me for another few days I think it might be a good idea.'

'Oh, darling, would you really come? Just for a cou-ple more days. I do feel so much better, but not quite me yet…'

'Of course I'll come. And we'll see how you are in two days' time.'

After those two days Julia had to admit that Ruth was quite able to cope without any help from her. It was all very well for her to spend the day there while Ruth was in bed, but now that she was up—still rather wan—Julia felt that Ruth and Tom would much rather be on their own.

The moment she arrived the next morning she told Ruth briskly, 'This is my last day; you don't need me any more...'

Ruth was sitting at the table in the tiny kitchen, chopping vegetables. She looked up, laughing. 'Oh, but I do. Sit down and I'll tell you.'

Julia took a bite of carrot. 'You want me to make curtains for the bathroom? I told you everyone could see in if they tried hard enough.'

'Curtains, pooh! Dr Soames says I need a little holiday, and Thomas says so too. He wants you to go with me. Do say you can. You haven't got another lodger yet, and Trudie could look after Muffin.'

'You're going to Monica's?' It would be lovely to go away from the dull little house and duller street. 'Yes, of course I'll come.'

'You will? You really won't mind? Thomas won't let me go alone...' She added quickly, 'And we're not going to Monica. We're going to Holland.'

Before Julia could speak, she added, 'Gerard has a little cottage near a lake. There's no one there, only his housekeeper. He says it's very quiet there, and the country's pretty and just what I need. Thomas wants me to go. He's got a couple of days due to him and he'll drive us there.'

'There won't be anyone else there? Only us?'

'Yes, you and I. Tom will stay one night and come and fetch us back—he won't know exactly when, but it will be a week or two. You're not having second thoughts?'

Which was exactly what Julia was having, but one look at her sister's still pale face sent them flying; Ruth needed to get away from London and a week in the country would get her back onto her feet again. Although early summer so far had been chilly and wet, there was always the chance that it would become warm and sunny. She said again, 'Of course I'll love to come. I'll fix things up with Trudie. When are we to go?'

'Well, Thomas can get Saturday and Sunday off—that's in three days' time. We shan't need many clothes, so you'll only need to bring a case—and I've enough money for both of us.'

'Oh, I've plenty of money,' said Julia, with such an air of conviction that she believed it herself.

'You have? Well, I suppose you have more time to work for the greetings card people now, and of course there's the rent from Trudie…'

Which was swallowed up almost before Julia had put it into her purse. But Ruth didn't have to know that, and she certainly wasn't going to tell anyone that she no longer had a market for her little verses. There would be another lodger soon, she told herself bracingly and she would find a part-time job; in the meantime she would enjoy her holiday.

The nagging thought that it was the Professor who had been the means of her having one rankled all the way home. For some reason she hated to be beholden to him.

She felt better about that when she came to the conclusion that he didn't know that she would be going; beyond offering the use of his house, he wouldn't be concerned with the details.

The Professor, phoning instructions to his house-keeper in Holland, was very well aware that she would be going with Ruth; he had himself suggested it, with just the right amount of casualness. He wasn't sure why he had done so but he suspected that he had wanted her to feel beholden to him.

He was an aloof man by nature, and an unhappy love affair had left him with a poor opinion of women. There were exceptions: his own family, his devoted house-keeper, his elderly nanny, the nursing staff who worked for him, life-long friends, wives of men he had known for years. He had added Ruth to the list, so in love with her Thomas—and so different from her sharp-tongued sister. And yet—there was something about Julia…

No need to take a lot of clothes, Ruth had said. Julia foraged through her wardrobe and found a leaf-brown tweed jacket, so old that it was almost fashionable once again. There was a pleated skirt which went quite well with it, a handful of tops and a jersey dress. It was, after all, getting warmer each day. As it was country they would go walking, she supposed, so that meant comfort-able shoes. She could travel in the new pair she had had for the weddings. She added undies, a scarf and a thin dressing gown, and then sat down to count her money. And that didn't take long! There would be a week's rent from Trudie to add, and when she got back there would be another lot waiting for her. She went in search of her lodger and enlisted her help.

Trudie was a quiet, unassuming girl, saving to get married, good-natured and trustworthy. She willingly agreed to look after Muffin and make sure that the house was locked up at night.

'You could do with a holiday. No doubt when you get back you'll have a house full of lodgers and not a moment to yourself.'

A prospect which should have pleased Julia but somehow didn't.

Three days later Thomas and Ruth came to fetch her. They were to go by the catamaran from Harwich, a fast sea route which would get them to their destination during the afternoon. Julia, who had received only a garbled version of where they were going, spent a great part of their journey studying a map—a large, detailed one which the Professor had thoughtfully provided.

Somewhere south of Amsterdam and not too far from Hilversum. And there were any number of lakes and no large towns until one reached Utrecht.

Ruth said over her shoulder, 'It's really country, Julia. Gerard says we don't need to go near a town unless we want to, although it's such a small country there are lots of rural areas with only tiny villages.'

It didn't seem very rural when they landed at the Hoek and took to the motorway, for small towns followed each other in quick succession, but then Thomas turned into a minor road and Julia saw the Holland she had always pictured. Wide landscapes, villages encircling churches much too large for them, farms with vast barns and water meadows where cows wandered. And the further they drove the more remote it became. The land was flat, but now there were small copses and glimpses of water. Julia looked around her and sighed with pleasure. Maybe there were large towns nearby, and main roads, but here there was an age-old peace and quiet.

Ruth, who had been chattering excitedly, had fallen silent and Thomas said, 'See that church spire beyond those trees? Unless I've read the map wrongly, we're here...'

Chapter 3

When they reached the trees Thomas turned into a narrow brick lane between them which opened almost at once into a scattered circle of houses grouped around the church. Any of the houses would do, thought Julia, for they were really all cottages, some larger than others, all with pristine paintwork, their little windows sparkling. But Thomas encircled the church and went along a narrow lane, leading away from the road.

'Hope I'm right,' he said. 'The Prof said it was easy to find, but of course he lives here! Five hundred yards past the church on the right-hand side…'

They all chorused, 'There it is,' a moment later. It was another cottage, but a good deal larger than those in the village, with a wide gate and a short drive leading to the front door.

It had a red-tiled roof, white walls and small windows arranged precisely on either side of its solid door, and it was set in a garden glowing with flowers, all crammed together in a glorious mass of colour. Julia, standing by the car, rotated slowly, taking it all in. She hadn't been sure what kind of a house the Professor would have—something dignified and austerely perfect, she had supposed, because that would have reflected him. But this little cottage—and not so little now that she had had a good look—was definitely cosy, its prettiness fit to grace the most sentimental of greetings cards. She tried to imagine him in his impeccable grey suiting, mowing the lawn…!

The door had been opened and a short, stout lady surged to meet them.

She was talking before she reached them. 'There you are—come on in. You must want a cup of tea, and I made some scones.'

She shook hands all round, beaming at them. 'Mrs Beckett, the housekeeper, and delighted to welcome you. Such a nice day you've had for travelling, and it's to be hoped that we'll get some fine weather. A bit of sun and fresh air will soon put you back on your feet, Mrs Scott.'

She had urged them indoors as she spoke. 'Now, just you make yourselves comfortable for a minute while I fetch the tea tray, then you can see your rooms. A pity Mr Scott can't stay longer, but there, you're a busy man like Mr Gerard. Always on the go, he is, pops in to see me whenever he can, bless him. He's so good to his old nanny.'

She paused for breath, said, 'Tea', and trotted out of the room.

Thomas sat Ruth down in one of the small armchairs and went to look out of the window. Ruth said, 'Oh, darling, isn't this heavenly? I'm going to love it here, only I'm going to miss you.'

Thomas went and sat beside her, and Julia wandered round inspecting the room. It was low-ceilinged, with rugs on the wooden floor, comfortable chairs and small tables scattered around a fireplace with a wood stove flanked by bookshelves bulging with books. Julia heaved a sigh of contentment and turned round as Mrs Beckett came in with the tea tray.

They were taken round the cottage presently—first to the kitchen, with its flagstone floor and scrubbed table and old-fashioned dresser, its rows of saucepans on either side of the Aga and comfortable Windsor chairs on either side of it. And on each chair a cat.

'Portly and Lofty,' said Mrs Beckett. 'Keep me company, they do. Mr Gerard brought them here years ago—kittens they were then; he'd found them.'

She led the way out of the kitchen. 'There's a cloakroom here, and that door is his study, and there's a garden room…'

Upstairs there were several bedrooms, and two bathrooms luxurious enough to grace the finest of houses.

'He does himself proud,' murmured Julia, leaning out of the window of the room which was to be hers.

They strolled round the garden presently, and then Julia went to her room again on the pretext of unpacking, but really so that Thomas and Ruth could be together. And later, after a delicious meal of asparagus, lamb cutlets, new potatoes and baby carrots, followed by caramel custard and all washed down by a crisp white wine, she excused herself from taking an evening stroll with the other two on the plea of tiredness. Not that she was in the least tired. She slept soundly, waking early to lie in bed examining the room.

It wasn't large, but whoever had chosen the furniture had known exactly what was right for it: there was a mahogany bed with a rose-patterned quilt and a plump pink eiderdown, pale rugs on the polished floor, a small dressing table under the window and a crinoline chair beside a small table. There were flowers on the table in a Delft bowl.

Like a fairy tale, decided Julia, and got up to lean out of the window.

Mrs Beckett's voice begging her to get back into bed and not catch cold sent her back under the eiderdown to drink the tea offered her.

Breakfast would be in half an hour, said Mrs Beckett, sounding just as an old-fashioned nanny would sound. 'Porridge and scrambled eggs, for I can see that Mrs Scott needs feeding up.' Her small twinkling eyes took in Julia's splendid shape. 'Women should look like women,' observed Mrs Beckett.

I shall get fat, thought Julia, buttering her third piece of toast. Not that it mattered. Now, if she were married to someone like Thomas she would go on a diet; men, so the TV advertisements proclaimed with such certainty, liked girls with wand-like shapes...

Declaring that she wanted postcards, she took herself

off to the village and didn't get back until lunchtime. Thomas was to leave shortly and Ruth did most of the talking: clean shirts, and mind to remember to change his socks, and to wind the kitchen clock, and she hoped that she had stocked the fridge with enough food...

'I'll be back in just over a week, darling,' said Thomas.

When he had gone Mrs Beckett sent them to the village again, to buy rolls and croissants for breakfast, and they strolled back while Ruth speculated as to Thomas's progress. Julia put in a sympathetic word here and there and ate one of the rolls, still warm from the bakery.

'You'll get fat,' said Ruth.

'Who cares?' The strong wish that someone would care kept her silent; it would be very nice if someone—someone who didn't even like her very much, like the Professor—would actually look at her and care enough to discourage her from eating rolls warm from the oven.

There was no reason why she should think of him, she told herself. It was because she was staying at his home, and it was difficult to forget that. I don't like him anyway, she reminded herself.

Between them, she and Mrs Beckett set about getting Ruth quite well again. It was surprising what a few days of good food, temptingly cooked, walks in the surrounding countryside and sound sleep did for her. After five days Ruth satisfied her two companions; she was now pink-cheeked and bright-eyed and, although she missed Thomas, she was willing to join in any plans Julia might suggest.

Another four or five days, thought Julia, getting up early because it was such a lovely morning, and we shall be going home again. But she wouldn't spoil the day by thinking about that. She skipped downstairs and out of the front door.

The Professor was sitting on the low stone wall beside the door. He didn't look like the Professor; the elderly trousers and a turtle-necked sweater had wiped years off him. He said, 'Hello, Julia,' and smiled.

She stood staring, and then said, 'How did you get here? It's not eight o'clock yet.' A sudden thought struck her. 'Is Thomas ill? Is something wrong?'

'So many questions and you haven't even wished me good morning. Thomas is in the best of health; nothing is wrong. I came to make sure that you were both comfortable here.'

'Comfortable? It's heaven! How did you get here?'

'I flew.'

'You flew? But how? I mean, do planes fly so early in the morning?'

'I have my own plane.'

'Your own plane?'

'This conversation is getting repetitive, Julia.'

'Yes, well, I'm surprised. Are you going to stay?'

'Don't worry, only for an hour or so.'

'And you'll fly back? You mean to say you've come just for an hour or so?' The Professor smiled, and she hopped onto the wall beside him. 'When we got here I was surprised—it didn't seem your kind of home. But now you're in slacks and a sweater I can see that it is. I just couldn't picture you in grey worsted and gold cufflinks being here…'

He didn't allow his amusement to show. 'You make me feel middle-aged.'

'Oh, no. Ruth told me that you're thirty-six or so, but you're remote, indifferent…' She paused to look at him. He was smiling again, but this time it was a nasty smile which sent her to her feet. 'I'll tell Ruth you're here.'

Indoors, flying up the stairs, her cheeks burning, she wondered what on earth had possessed her to talk to him like that. It was because he had seemed different, she supposed, but he wasn't, only his clothes. He was still a man she didn't like. She would make some excuse to go to the village after breakfast and stay there until he had gone again.

When, at the end of the meal, she stated her intentions, he told her carelessly to enjoy her walk, while Ruth said, 'Get me some more cards if you go to the shop, Julia.'

Mrs Beckett observed, 'You'd best say goodbye to Mr Gerard; he'll be gone before you get back.'

So Julia wished him goodbye, and he got up and opened the door for her—a courtesy which she was convinced was as false as his friendly, 'Goodbye, Julia.'

She spent a long time in the village—buying things she didn't need, going the long way back, loitering through the garden—for he might still be there.

He wasn't. 'How kind of him to come and make sure we were all right,' said Ruth. 'And he's arranging things so that Thomas can spend the night here before we go back next week. I've loved being here, but I do miss Tom…'

She glanced at Julia. 'You haven't been bored? We

haven't gone anywhere or done anything or met anyone…'

Julia was replaiting her tawny hair. A pity she hadn't put it up properly with pins that morning; a pigtail over one shoulder lacked dignity.

'I've loved every minute of it,' Well, this morning was something best forgotten. It was obvious that the Professor had no intention of being friendly—something which she found upsetting and that considering she didn't like him in the least, was puzzling. All the same, just for a little while she had enjoyed sitting there on the wall beside him.

It had turned warm, warm enough to sit in the garden or potter around watching things grow. She would have liked to have weeded and raked and pulled the rhubarb and grubbed up radishes and lettuce from the kitchen garden at the back of the house, but the dour old man in charge wouldn't allow that. Whatever the language, it was obvious he objected strongly to anyone so much as laying a finger on a blade of grass.

Thomas phoned each day. The Professor had arrived back safely, he told Ruth, and had gone straight to his late-afternoon clinic. News which Julia received without comment and an inward astonishment at the man's energy.

The week passed too quickly. Thomas would come on Saturday morning, so they must be ready to leave soon after breakfast. Julia, packing her few things, looked round her charming room with real regret; she was going to miss the comfort and unobtrusive luxury of the cottage, and still more she would miss Mrs Beckett's company. She was a contented soul, only wanting everyone else to be contented—the kind of person one could confide in, reflected Julia, who had, in truth, told her a good deal about her hopes and plans. And quite unwittingly revealed her uncertainty as to the future.

Mrs Beckett had listened with real sympathy and some sound advice. It wouldn't be needed, of course; if ever two people were made for each other they were Julia and Mr Gerard. Of course, they hadn't discovered that yet, but time would tell, reflected Mrs Beckett comfortably.

The sun shone on Saturday morning, and the garden had never looked so lovely. Julia, dressed and ready to leave, had gone into the garden to wish it goodbye. Ruth was in the kitchen with Mrs Beckett, but Julia didn't want to wish her goodbye until the very last minute. She strolled round, sniffing at the flowers and shrubs, and, coming upon a patch of white violets, got down on her knees to enjoy their scent.

'My mother planted those,' said the Professor from behind her.

Julia shot to her feet in shock and whirled round. 'Why are you here again?' she demanded.

'This is my home,' he said mildly.

Julia went red. 'I'm sorry, that was rude, but you took me by surprise.'

When he didn't speak she added, 'Have you come to stay? We are so grateful to you for inviting us to stay here. We've had a glorious time. You must be very happy living here; the garden is so beautiful too.'

'What a polite little speech.' The faint mockery in

his voice brought the colour back into her cheeks once more. 'I'm glad that you have enjoyed your stay. Are you ready to leave? Mrs Beckett will have coffee waiting for us.'

She went into the house with him, not speaking, and Ruth came running to meet them.

'Julia, isn't it wonderful? Thomas can stay until tomorrow. We're going to fly back—we shall have a whole day together.' She put a hand on the Professor's sleeve. 'You've been so kind…'

'Thomas is due a couple of days off, and this has given me a good excuse to arrange things to suit all of us. I'm only sorry I can't stay longer.'

He took the mug of coffee Mrs Beckett offered him. 'I'll see Julia safely home.'

She was swallowing hot coffee…choked, and had to suffer the indignity of having her back patted and being mopped up. Then she said frostily, 'Is this something I should know about?'

Ruth laughed. 'Oh, didn't the Professor tell you? He's driving you back.' Before Julia could utter, he said, 'We need to leave in five minutes or so. I've patients to see later on today.'

Julia said childishly, 'But you've only just got here. I'm sure you must want to stay.'

'Indeed I do. As it is, I can't. So, if you would do whatever you still need to do, we'll be on our way.'

They were all looking at her and smiling; the Professor's smile was brief and amused and he turned away to stroll to the window and study the garden. She fetched her jacket, and was kissed and hugged and escorted to the Rolls with exclamations of delight at her good fortune at having such a comfortable journey.

Ruth poked her head through the window. 'I'll phone you when we get back. Trudie will be there, won't she? You won't be alone?'

'Who is Trudie?' asked the Professor as she settled back after a last wave.

'My lodger. Which way are you going back?'

'From Calais by hovercraft. That should get us back by the late afternoon.'

She must make an effort to be an agreeable companion—probably he didn't want her company anymore than she wanted his. 'A long drive,' she observed, striving for an easy friendliness.

It was at once doused by his casual, 'Yes—doze off if you want to, and you have no need to make polite small talk.'

Rude words bubbled and died on her lips; she couldn't utter them; he was giving her a lift, and she depended on him until she was back on her own doorstep. She sat silently seething, staring out at the countryside. But once they had reached the motorway there wasn't a great deal to look at, only the blue and white signposts at regular intervals. She watched them flash past.

'Why are we going to Amsterdam?' she wanted to know. 'You said we were going to Calais; you ought to be going south.'

He answered her in a patient voice which set her teeth on edge. 'We are going to Amsterdam because I need to. From there we will continue on our way to Calais. Don't worry, we are in plenty of time to catch the ferry.'

'I'm not worried.' Since there was nothing more to be said, she lapsed once more into silence.

But once they reached the city and had driven through its suburbs and reached the heart of it she forgot to be quiet. The old streets were lovely, the houses lining them much as they had been three hundred years earlier. 'Look at that canal,' she begged him, 'and those dear little bridges—and there's a barge simply loaded with flowers—and I can hear bells ringing…'

'Carillons. The barge is moored close to the street so that people can buy the flowers if they wish. There are bridges everywhere connecting up the streets. We are going over the one you see ahead of us.'

The street on the other side of it was narrow, brick-built and lined with large gabled houses on one side and a narrow canal on the other side.

Halfway down it the Professor stopped the car, got out and opened her door.

'Would you rather I stayed in the car?' asked Julia. 'Perhaps…'

He opened the car door wider. 'Come along, I haven't time to waste.'

She got out huffily then, and went wordlessly with him up the double steps to the solid front door with its ornate transom. She was hating every minute of it, she told herself, while admitting to a longing to see inside the house. Friends of his, she wondered, or some kind of business to do with his work?

The rather bent elderly man who opened the door broke into voluble Dutch at the sight of them, which was of no help at all. It was obvious that he knew the

Professor, and that the Professor held him in some regard, for he had clapped him gently on the back as they went in and addressed him at some length.

She allowed her gaze to wander around their surroundings and felt a surge of pleasure. They were in a long narrow hall with doors on either side and at its end a curving staircase. The walls were panelled, and it was all rather dark, but it was sombrely rich, she told herself, with a brass chandelier, undoubtedly old, a black and white tiled floor strewn with rugs of colours faded with age and a console table upon which someone had set a porcelain bowl of flowers.

The Professor's voice recalled her to her surroundings. 'This is Wim. He looks after the house and everyone in it.' When she offered a hand it was gently shaken and she was made welcome in his thin reedy voice.

The penny dropped then. 'This is your house?' said Julia.

'Yes. My home. We will have coffee and then I must ask you to excuse me while I deal with one or two matters. We must leave in half an hour or so.'

Wim was going ahead of them to open a door, into a long narrow room, panelled, like the hall, and furnished with comfortable chairs grouped round a vast fireplace. Its walls were lined with cabinets, a great long-case clock and a walnut bureau bookcase. There were small tables too, bearing gently shaded lamps, their glow enough, with the firelight, to bathe the room in soft light. And the room had an occupant, for a large dog came bounding to meet them, large and woolly with fearsome teeth.

'It's all right; he's only smiling,' said the Professor, bracing himself to receive the delighted onslaught of the devoted beast.

'This is Jason, he's a Bouvier, a splendid chap who will guard those he loves with his life. Offer him a fist.'

Julia liked dogs, but she tried not to see the teeth as she did as she was told—to have her hand gently licked while small yellow eyes studied her face from under a tangle of hair. She said, 'I'm Julia,' and patted the woolly head.

'You must miss him,' she said, and sat down in the chair the Professor was offering.

'Yes, but I plan to spend more time here than in England. In the meantime, I snatch a few moments whenever I can.'

A casual remark which left her feeling vaguely disquiet.

Wim came in with coffee, and presently the Professor excused himself on the grounds of phone calls to make.

'We must leave in fifteen minutes. Wim will show you where you can tidy yourself.'

He went away, Jason at his heels, and Julia was left to finish her coffee before going slowly round the room, inspecting its treasures. She supposed that it was the drawing room, but there were several other doors in the hall. It was a large house; if all its rooms were as splendidly furnished as this one then the Professor must live in some style.

'Ancestors going back for ever and ever,' said Julia, addressing a portrait of a forbidding gentleman in a wig, 'and loaded with money.'

She became aware of a wet tongue on her hand. Jason was standing silently beside her. She turned quickly; the Professor would have heard her... But apparently he hadn't; he was across the room, looking out of a window. She sighed with relief and said quickly, 'You want to go? If I could ask Wim...?'

'By the staircase. The door on the right. Don't be long.'

He sounded much the same as usual: polite, detached, faintly amused. She joined him after a few minutes with the polite remark that she hoped she hadn't kept him waiting, bade goodbye to Wim and was swept out to the car without any further delay. Jason, standing in the hall, had rumbled goodbye when she had bent to stroke him, and on impulse she had bent down and thrown her arms around his neck and hugged him.

'You mustn't mind,' she'd said softly. 'He'll be back soon.'

She had turned away then, not wanting to see the parting between master and dog.

The Professor drove through the city and onto the motorway, giving her little opportunity to look around her. She sat silently beside him, sensing that he didn't wish to talk. No doubt he had a great many important matters to think about. She settled down to watch the countryside. He was driving fast and she was enjoying the speed; it was a pity that the motorway bypassed the villages and towns, but there was plenty to hold her attention and she kept a sharp eye open for road signs— a map would have been handy...

'There's a map in the pocket beside you,' said the Professor. Was he a thought-reader or did he want to keep her occupied so that there was no need to talk? The latter, she decided, and opened the map.

South to Utrecht, on to Dordrecht and then Breda, where they stopped at a roadside café just outside the town. As they went in he said, 'Fifteen minutes. Coffee and a Kaas broodje?'

Julia had spied a door at the back of the cafe with Dames written above it in large letters. 'Anything,' she told him as she sped away.

The Professor got up and pulled out a chair for her when she returned to the table. The coffee was already there, so were the cheese rolls. Obviously this wasn't to be a social meal; they ate fast and silently and were away again with her mouth still full.

'Sorry to rush you,' said the Professor laconically.

To which she replied, 'Not at all, Professor.'

To tell the truth she was enjoying herself.

They bypassed Antwerp, took the road to Gent, bypassed Lille and flew on to Calais.

'Just nicely in time,' observed the Professor, going aboard the hovercraft with two minutes to spare.

He settled her at a small table by a window and said, 'Run along and do your hair; I'll order tea.'

It was early for tea, but the sight of the tea tray and a plate of scones gladdened her heart. The Professor, watching her pour second cups, thought how pretty she looked and how uncomplainingly she had sat beside him. The seat beside him might have been empty. Upon reflection he was glad that it hadn't been. A pity they couldn't like each other...!

They talked during the crossing, careful to talk about

mundane things, and when he suggested that she might like to have a brief nap before they landed she closed her eyes at once, thinking that it was a polite way of ending their conversation. She wouldn't sleep, she told herself, but if she shut her eyes she wouldn't need to look at him…

A gentle tap on her shoulder woke her. 'Ten minutes before we land,' the Professor told her. 'Run along before there's a queue.' He paused. 'And your hair's coming down.'

How was it, thought Julia, that her hair being untidy and going to the loo should seem so normal and unembarrassing between two people who didn't even like each other? She remembered with a shudder Oscar's coy references to powdering her nose, and the disapproving frown if she needed to stick a pin back into her hairdo.

There was no time to pursue the thought; they were going through Dover and speeding along the motorway to London without loss of time.

Saturday, she thought. She would have to race to the shops and get some food for the weekend. The idea of a cold house and an empty fridge didn't appeal, but of course a man wouldn't think of such things. No doubt, she reflected peevishly, the Professor would go to wherever he lived when he had seen his patients and have a splendid meal set before him. She peeped at his calm profile; he appeared unhurried and relaxed but he certainly hadn't dallied on the way…

As they slowed through London's sprawling suburbs she began her rehearsed thank-you speech. 'It was very kind of you to give me a lift,' she began. 'I'm very grateful. I hope it hasn't held you up at all, me being with you. If you want to drop me off at a bus stop or the Underground…'

'You live very close to the hospital; it will be easier to take you to your house. Stopping anywhere here will hold me up.'

So much for trying to be helpful. She held her tongue until he stopped before her door. The house looked forlorn, as did the whole street, but she said brightly, 'How nice to be home—and so quickly.'

A remark which needed no comment as he got out of the car, took her case from the boot, the key from her hand, opened the door and ushered her into the narrow hall.

'Don't wait—' and that was a silly thing to say '—and thank you again.'

'A pleasure. Goodbye, Julia.'

He drove away without a backward glance.

'He's a detestable man,' said Julia fiercely, standing on her doorstep. 'I hope I never meet him again. Rushing me back home just because he was in a hurry. Well, I hope he's late for whatever it is.' She added rather wildly, 'I hope it's a beautiful woman who will make him grovel!'

He would never grovel, of course, and she didn't mean a word of it, but it made her feel better.

She went indoors then, and into the kitchen to be greeted by Muffin, and a moment later by Trudie, coming downstairs to meet her.

'I knew you'd be back. The man who brought the box said you'd be here some time today.'

Julia went to fill the kettle. 'Box? What box?'

'It's from some super shop in Jermyn Street. It's on the table.'

They went to look at it together. It was a superior kind of box, very neatly packed under its lid; tea and coffee, sugar, milk, a bottle of wine, croissants, eggs, cold chicken in a plastic box, a salad in another plastic box, orange juice, smoked salmon…

Julia unpacked it slowly. 'There must be a mistake.'

Trudie shook her head. 'I asked to make sure. The delivery man said there was no mistake. A Professor van der Maes had ordered it by telephone late yesterday evening to be delivered this afternoon.'

'Oh, my goodness. He never said a word. He gave me a lift back so that my sister's husband could stay in Holland for a day. We had to hurry to get to Calais and we only stopped once on the way. He had to get back by the late afternoon.'

'Well, it's a gorgeous hamper,' said Trudie cheerfully.

'It's coals of fire,' said Julia.

'Well, I'm going out this evening,' Trudie went on. 'You'll be all right?'

'Me? I'm fine, and thank you for keeping an eye on Muffin and the house. No one called about a room?'

'No. You had a good time?'

'It was heaven. I'll tell you some time.'

Presently, alone in the house, she unpacked, fed Muffin and got her supper. The contents of the box might be coals of fire, but they made splendid eating.

Presently, in bed, she lay awake composing a letter to the Professor. Fulsome thanks would annoy him, considering the coolness between them, all the same he would need to be thanked. She slept at last, only to wake from time to time muttering snatches of suitable phrases.

The letter, when it was at last written, was exactly right. Neatly phrased, politely grateful—and it would have served as a model letter for a Victorian maiden to have written. The Professor read it and roared with laughter.

The house, after the charming little cottage, was something Julia would have to get used to. Ruth, back home, had phoned her, bubbling over with the day she had spent with Tom and happy to be back in her little house.

Julia had assured her that she was fine, that there was the prospect of a lodger and that the garden was looking very pretty. None of which was true. She didn't feel fine. For some reason she felt depressed.

And I'll soon deal with that, Julia told herself, and went off to the newsagent's to put a To Let sign in his window, and then back to mow the small square of grass in the garden.

There were two applicants for the room the next day. A foxy faced middle-aged man who smelled strongly of beer and wanted to cook his meals in the kitchen, and a youngish woman, skilfully made up, with an opulent bosom and very high heels, who said coyly that she was expecting to get married and would Julia have any objection to her boyfriend calling from time to time?

She told them that the room was already let and watched them go with regret. The rent money would have been useful...

Something would turn up, she told herself, and in the meantime she got a temporary job delivering the local directory. It was dull business, for the neighbouring streets all looked alike, as did the houses, but she enlivened the tedium of it by memories of the cottage, and at the end of the week there was a little money in her pocket and she had written in reply to six vaguely wanting help with houses and small children—something she could surely do without any kind of training. And it wouldn't be for long, she told herself. If she could let a room—two rooms at a pinch—she could sleep in the box room.

She went to Ruth's for lunch on Sunday, and Thomas came over from the hospital for an hour or two. After the meal Ruth said, 'While you're here, Julia, would you look at that little chair I was going to cover? It's in the other bedroom and I've tried to do it, but it doesn't look right. You're so good at that kind of thing.'

So Julia went up the little stairs and into the second bedroom, which was small and unfurnished save for suitcases, a bookcase which was too large to go anywhere and the chair. It was a pretty little chair, and Ruth had pinned the velvet onto it in a haphazard fashion. Julia got down on the floor, undid it all to cut and fit, pinned and tacked, and sat back on her heels to study her work. It would do, but Ruth wanted a frill, she thought.

She was on the stairs when she heard Ruth's voice.

The sitting room door was open and the house was small, with thin walls.

'Oh, Thomas, I can't ask Julia. Where would she go? But it would be wonderful. We'd have the money to start buying our own house, and Monica and George need central heating and a new bathroom—the house would sell for enough money for that?'

'Oh, yes, darling. Split three ways you would each get a very useful sum. But we mustn't think about it. If Julia marries you could suggest it then, but not before.'

Julia crept back into the room, closed the door quietly and sat down on the chair. Of course she had thought of it before, but had put it out of her mind. How could she have been so stupid? There was nothing remarkable about the house, but it had three bedrooms, and although the street was shabby it was quiet, and those who lived in it were law-abiding—striving to keep so. Moreover, there were buses and the Underground into the City. It would fetch a fair price—Ruth and Thomas could get a house of their own; Monica could have her central heating. As for herself…a small flat somewhere, and the money to take a course in something or other. She could think about that later. She would have to wait for a few days and then broach the subject…

Steps on the stairs sent her onto her knees, fussing with the frill.

Ruth put her head round the door. 'You had the door shut. You didn't hear me?'

'No. Were you calling? Look, do you want a frill? I think it would be too much.' She got to her feet. 'Has Thomas gone back? I'll come down, shall I?'

Chapter 4

The opportunity to do something about the house came sooner than she had expected. Monica phoned to ask abut their stay in Holland, and when that subject had been exhausted she talked at length about George and the house and the village. 'I'm so happy, Julia…'

It seemed to be the right moment. Julia knew exactly what to say; she had rehearsed it carefully and now she made her suggestion with just the right amount of eagerness. 'I can't think why I haven't thought of it before. I haven't said anything to Ruth yet. Do you think it's a good idea? It's only an idea, anyway…'

She could hear the excitement in Monica's voice. 'But what about you?'

'I'd get a small flat and take a course in dressmaking. You know how I love making clothes.'

'Would we get enough from the house for all of us?'

'Yes, but perhaps Ruth wouldn't like the idea…'

'I'll talk to her and find out. Is this what you really want, Julia?'

'Oh, yes. Just think, I wouldn't have to depend on lodgers. I'd be free—have a holiday when I wanted to, come and go as I pleased and work at something I enjoy doing.'

She rang off presently, knowing that she had convinced Monica. Now she must wait and see what Ruth would decide, and let the news come from Monica.

She didn't have long to wait, Ruth phoned that evening. 'Monica rang and told me you'd suggested selling the house. But, Julia, what about you?'

So Julia repeated her carefully thought out words and added, 'Do you like the idea? It's only an idea…'

'You really want to? You'd be happier somewhere else? There would be enough money for you to feel secure?'

'I don't feel secure now,' said Julia. 'I need three lodgers to keep this house going and so far I've only got one; I didn't tell you that I got the sack from the greetings card people—but then I expected that; Oscar, you know. I could train as a dressmaker, live in a small flat…'

'Oh, my dear, I didn't know. I think it's a marvellous idea.' Ruth paused. 'As a matter of fact, Thomas and I have seen a house near the hospital—in a cul-de-sac, and so quiet. It's for sale…'

'You see,' said Julia bracingly. 'It's the hand of fate!'

Of course there was a good deal to discuss during

the next few days. Julia, striking while the iron was hot, had the house valued, and the price the agent suggested clinched the matter. He had people on his books waiting for just such a house to come on the market. Ruth and Thomas, inspecting the house they so wanted to buy, had no doubts.

'A pity the Prof is away,' Thomas observed. 'By the time he gets back we'll probably have moved.'

'Will he be in Edinburgh much longer?'

'No, a few days more, but he's going straight to Vienna to give lectures and then a week or two in Holland.'

'He'll have a nice surprise. Oh, Thomas, I do hope the house sells quickly.'

Something Monica hoped too, with her writing desk awash with central heating brochures and magnificent bathroom catalogues.

As for Julia, unaware that the Professor was away, she went to see the solicitor who held the deeds of the house, bullied the house agent in the nicest possible way, explained everything to Trudie and hoped that the hand of fate she had been so sure about would point a finger at her. Now that they were selling the house she wanted to be gone quickly, to start a new life. That she woke in the night to worry about that was something she did her best to ignore.

The house sold within a week. Moreover, it was a cash sale, and the new owner wanted to move in as soon as Julia could move out. Monica and Ruth came, and, helped by a cheerfully co-operative Trudie, they all set to work to pack up the house.

It wasn't just the packing up. There was the furniture—what was left after they had each decided what they wanted to keep and, since Trudie hoped to marry soon, she had had her share—and then the removal men, the gas, the electricity, the telephone, the milkman—an unending stream of things which needed her attention.

With three days left before the new owners took over Julia found herself in an almost empty house. Trudie had moved in with the other teacher at the kindergarten, George had driven up in a borrowed van and taken the furniture Monica had chosen, and the local odd-job man had collected the tables and chairs and beds which Ruth wanted for her new home. Which left Julia with a bed, a number of suitcases, a box of books, the kitchen table and two chairs. The fridge and cooker had been sold with the house, so meals were no problem although lack of comfort was. Ruth had wanted her to go and stay with them, but to leave the house empty was risky. And it was only for two nights.

Tomorrow, thought Julia, getting into bed with Muffin for company, she would go in search of a room to rent. She knew what she was going to do: find a small flat in a quiet street in a better neighbourhood. Islington would be nice, if she could find something to suit her purse. Perhaps a basement flat with a bit of garden at the back—or Finsbury—somewhere not too far from Ruth and Thomas. She wished that she had someone to advise her.

The Professor's face flashed before her closed eyes and she said out loud, 'What nonsense. He's not even in the country, and in any case he hasn't the least interest.'

Ruth had said that he was away, and that they hadn't

told him that they were moving. 'We're going to surprise him,' said Ruth happily. 'He'll be back soon.'

'Not before I've gone,' reflected Julia now. 'Disagreeable man.'

She went in search of a room the next day and returned home disappointed. She had been to several likely addresses, but most of them had proved to be top-floor attics which wouldn't do at all for Muffin. One or two had been grubby, and the only one which would have done at a pinch she'd been denied. 'Not cats!' the lady of the house had said. 'Nasty, dirty creatures.'

'We'll try again tomorrow,' she told Muffin, inspecting the fridge for their suppers.

She was just finishing breakfast the next morning when there was a thump on the door. And when she went to open it there was the Professor.

She was aware of delight at seeing him, and that was something she would have to think about later on. For now she stared up at him wordlessly. His 'Good morning, Julia,' was coolly friendly.

Since he stood there, obviously expecting to be asked in, she said, 'Oh, do come in—has something happened to Ruth or Thomas?' She shut the door behind him with something of a snap. 'It's very early...'

'This has nothing to do with Ruth or Thomas. I wished to talk to you.'

He stood in the hall, looking around him at the empty place. 'Is there somewhere...?'

She led the way to the kitchen, angry that he should see its poverty stricken appearance: the milk bottle on

the table, a loaf of bread beside it, her mug and plate
with a slice of bread and butter half eaten…

'Do sit down,' she begged him in a voice of a polite hostess who must entertain an unwelcome guest,
and when he had taken the other chair at the table she
asked, 'Would you like a cup of tea? There's still some
in the pot.'

His mouth twitched. 'Yes, please,' he responded as
his eye fell on the loaf.

'Would you like some bread and butter?' she asked.

'Breakfast is always such a pleasant meal,' he observed, before he cut a slice and buttered it.

'There's no need to be sarcastic,' said Julia. 'Why
have you come?'

'It must be obvious to you that this is not a social
visit. Unfortunately it is the only time of day when I'm
free…'

She interrupted him. 'Ruth said you weren't in England.'

'I got back yesterday evening. Tell me, Julia, have
you any plans for your immediate future?'

'Why do you want to know?'

'If you will answer my question I will tell you.'

'I can't see why you should ask, but since you have, no.'

'You have somewhere to go tomorrow? A flat or
rooms?'

'No. I intend to find something this morning.' She
frowned. 'I don't see that it's any of your business—
and we're not even friends…' She blushed scarlet the
moment she had said it and mumbled, 'Well, you know
what I mean.'

'I hardly think that friendship has anything to do with it, and it is my business in so far that I am asking for your help.'

'Me? Help you?'

'If you would refrain from interrupting, I will explain.'

He drank his tea and looked at her. She was untidy, for she had done some last-minute packing; her hair was in a plait over one shoulder, she had a shiny nose, and was wearing a cotton top faded from many washings. But she looked quite beautiful, he thought. Her sisters were beautiful too, but Julia was full of life, impulsive, refusing to admit that life wasn't quite what she had hoped for. She had a sharp tongue, and a temper too…

He said gently, 'Indeed you could help me if you would consider it. You haven't forgotten Mrs Beckett? I have been with her for a day or two. She is ill—pneumonia—and in hospital. It is a viral infection and she isn't so young. Would you consider going over to Holland and minding the cottage while she is away, and then staying for a while when she gets back until she is quite well and I can arrange some sort of help for her?'

It was so unexpected that she could only gape at him.

'Go to Holland?' said Julia at length. 'But does Mrs Beckett want me—and how long would I be there?'

'Mrs Beckett will be very happy to see you again,' said the Professor smoothly. 'I cannot say for certain how long your stay might be. But she will be in hospital for at least two weeks, and when she returns home she will need a good deal of cosseting.'

'She is in hospital now?'

'Yes, in Leiden. A colleague of mine is the consultant physician there. I have arranged for someone to look after her cats and the cottage but it is a temporary arrangement. I want someone with no other commitments so that I can be sure that both Mrs Beckett and the cats and cottage are in the hands of a person who is willing to remain until she is quite fit.'

'But why me?'

He ignored that. 'I am aware that this may interfere with whatever plans you have made. You would, of course, receive a salary and any expenses.'

'Well, I haven't any real plans. I mean none that can't be put off for a few weeks. There is no reason why I shouldn't go. When do you want me to be there?'

It was impossible to tell whether he was pleased or not. 'Within the next day or so. I will arrange for you to fly over. You will be met and taken to the cottage. You will be kept informed as to Mrs Beckett's condition and taken to visit her if you wish.'

He got up and she, perforce, got up too. His goodbye was brief and he had gone before the dozen questions tumbling around in her head could be uttered.

She had been glad to see him, she couldn't deny that, and not having to decide about her future for another few weeks was a relief she didn't admit to. It was while she was going through her scanty wardrobe that she started to wonder how he had known that she was leaving the house. Had he been back in England earlier and had Ruth told him? Surely he hadn't made up his mind to ask her in the space of a few hours?

It wasn't until she was getting her lunch that her eye fell upon Muffin…

The phone hadn't been transferred yet, thank heaven; moreover, she was put through to the Professor at once.

'Muffin,' she began without preamble. 'I can't go to Holland—Ruth's far too busy moving house and he'll pine in the cattery.'

'No problem. My housekeeper in London will be delighted to look after him. I have arranged for you to fly over tomorrow afternoon. I will come for you at midday and we can leave Muffin with her as we go.'

And he had hung up without giving her a chance to say anything.

She addressed Muffin. 'I've been a fool. I have allowed Professor van der Maes to make use of me. I must be losing my wits.' Although, she reflected presently, it would be delightful to stay in that cottage again, and it would give her time to decide exactly what she intended to do next.

She was ready for him when he came; the new owners were moving in later that afternoon, everything was signed and sealed, the money was in Ruth's care, and her share would be waiting for her when she got back. In the meantime she had enough of her own to keep her going. The Professor had mentioned a salary, but probably it had just been a passing thought.

He greeted her in a businesslike manner and stowed Muffin on the back seat, her case in the boot and herself beside him without more ado. She didn't look back as he drove away. She and her sisters had lived in the house but it had never been home to any of them.

She sat without speaking as he drove through the busy streets. Presently he said, 'I shall have to drive straight to Heathrow.'

He had shown no signs of impatience at the slow progress they were making, but a glance at the clock told her that at the rate they were going they would never get to the airport on time. All she said was, 'Muffin?'

'I will take the cat to my house as soon as I have seen you on to the plane. I promise you that I will see that he is in safe hands.' He gave her a quick look. 'Trust me, Julia.'

'Yes,' said Julia, knowing that she meant it.

She was the last to board the plane; there had barely been time to bid Muffin goodbye before she was hurried away, told that she would be met at Schipol and would she telephone him that evening?

'The phone number is in the envelope with your ticket. Goodbye, Julia.'

Schipol was overflowing with people; Julia stood for a moment, wishing wholeheartedly that she hadn't come, then a short, thickset man, bearing her name on a placard he was holding before him, came to a halt in front of her.

'Miss Gracey? Sent by Professor van der Maes? I am Piet, to drive you to his house.' His English was strongly accented but fluent.

Julia held out a hand. 'How do you do? Is it a long drive?'

'No, I drive fast.' He picked up her case and led the way through the crowds, out to the car, which was an elderly Mercedes. Its appearance, she quickly discovered, was deceptive; it was capable of a fine turn of speed which, coupled with Piet's obvious wish to be a racing driver, took them at a hair-raising speed to the cottage.

As she got out Piet told her that he would call for her in the morning and take her to see Mrs Beckett at Leiden. He took her case into the cottage, gave her a broad grin and was gone.

There was someone in the cottage, waiting for her: a small woman with an old-fashioned hairdo, wearing a severe black dress. She smiled a welcome and broke into voluble speech, unfortunately in Dutch.

Julia smiled in return, offered a hand and mustered her few words of that language.

The woman was amused. 'I go. I come at morning, early.' She thought for a moment. 'Work, cook.'

'All day?'

'Mornings. Professor van der Maes tell.'

'I should hope so. How like a man,' said Julia crossly and her companion smiled and nodded. 'Nice man. Food ready. *Dag.*'

She trotted off in the direction of the village and Julia closed the door and found Mrs Beckett's cats staring at her.

'Well, at least I can talk to you,' said Julia, and at that moment the phone rang.

'You had a good journey?' enquired the Professor. 'Mevrouw Steen was at the cottage?'

'Is that who she is? Why are you ringing me? You told me that I was to phone you this evening.'

'I thought that you might be anxious about Muffin. Why are you cross?'

'I am not cross.' She sounded peevish. 'I am in an empty house with two cats, I want a cup of tea, and *Mevrouw*'s English is as basic as my Dutch.'

'An excellent opportunity for you to improve your knowledge of the language.'

'I have no wish to do so,' said Julia haughtily. 'Is there anything you wanted to say to me? Because if there isn't I'm going to put the kettle on...'

He took no notice. 'Piet will take you to see Mrs Beckett tomorrow morning. Arrange with her or the doctor when you wish to visit her and let him know. Piet will drive you wherever you should wish to go and do any odd jobs or errands for you.'

She said stiffly, 'Thank you. Is Muffin all right?'

'Settled down very nicely. I hope you will do the same, Julia.' With which he rang off.

'Rude man,' said Julia.

She had every intention of wallowing in self-pity as she went into the kitchen, but the sight of the tea tray standing ready on the kitchen table made her hesitate. There wasn't only a pretty teacup and saucer and plate on it, matching the teapot, sugar bowl and milk jug, but also a plate of buttered scones and a little dish of jam, and when she opened the fridge door while the kettle boiled she found salmon, ready to eat, and salad and a bowl of potato straws. Moreover, there were strawberries and cream and a bottle of white wine.

She made the tea, carried the tray through to the sitting room and wondered uneasily if she had been a bit too off-hand with the Professor...

Her bedroom welcomed her: flowers on the dressing table, a pile of books and magazines on the bedside table, a carafe of water and a tin of biscuits, and in the bathroom towels and soaps and a delicious selection of oils for the bath. Somebody had been very thoughtful about her well-being, she reflected, going downstairs and taking the bottle of wine from the fridge. She didn't feel lonely or hard-done-by any more; it was as though she had been warmly welcomed even if there had been no one there to do that.

Presently she ate her supper, drank the rest of her glass of wine, fed the cats and, accompanied by them both, went upstairs to lie in the bath and then get into bed. Her two companions settled each side of her and she hoped that Muffin was being as well cared for. She would be all right, she decided sleepily; the Professor had said that he would look after her…

She woke to a splendid morning; hanging out of the window, she looked down at the garden, which was a riot of colour, and beyond it to the flat, peaceful countryside… She showered and dressed and skipped downstairs, intent on breakfast. She had fed the cats and was eating her boiled egg when Mevrouw Steen arrived.

She greeted Julia with a cheerful *'Dag'* and then added, 'Piet comes; I stay.'

So Julia gobbled down the rest of her breakfast, found her handbag, got into Piet's car and was driven to Leiden—a trip she would have enjoyed if she hadn't been so scared of the speed at which Piet drove. But he was a splendid driver, and of course the road ahead of them was flat as far as the eye could see. He put her down at the hospital, rather shaken and glad to feel solid ground beneath her feet. He would return in an hour, he told her, and wait until she came. She was not to hurry.

Mrs Beckett, looking half her normal size, was propped up against her pillows with an oxygen mask clamped over her nose. But she smiled and nodded to Julia and waved a languid hand.

'Don't talk,' said Julia urgently. 'I'm going to sit here and tell you all the news!'

Mrs Beckett listened, nodding from time to time, then asked, 'Portly and Lofty—how are they?'

'Both in splendid health; they slept on my bed. You don't mind?'

Mrs Beckett smiled. 'I'm glad. Mr Gerard has been to see me. He'll come again; he's so good to me.'

'He's organised everything,' Julia assured her. 'As soon as you're well again you are coming home, and I'll stay until you are perfectly fit.'

'You'll want to go home,' whispered Mrs Beckett. 'To your own home.'

'I haven't got one. We've sold it. I'll find somewhere to live when I get back. It's lovely being here again. The cottage looks lovely and I'll look after everything.' She bent and kissed the pale cheek. 'I'm going now. I shall phone every day and come and see you again in a day or two. You are going to get well quickly; the Professor told me so.'

Which wasn't true, but a lie in a good cause…

'If he said so, then I shall.'

It was a relief but no surprise to find that the doctor she asked to see spoke English as good as hers. Mrs

Beckett was making good progress, he assured her. She had been seriously ill—pneumonia in the elderly was not to be treated lightly—but she had responded well to treatment.

'You are a friend of Professor van der Maes?'

It would save a lot of explanations if she agreed…

'May I come at any time? Not every day, perhaps, but I will phone each morning and you will let me know at once if it's necessary.'

'Of course.'

He walked with her to the entrance, where Piet was waiting, and watched her getting into the car. A delightfully pretty girl, he reflected. Gerard had told him that she was a sensible young woman, very well able to look after herself and deal with any situation which might arise. And of course Gerard would come at once in an emergency…

After that first day Julia slipped into a gentle pattern of days. Visiting Mrs Beckett, even beginning to enjoy Piet's breakneck driving, cherishing Portly and Lofty, filling the cottage with flowers because she knew that Mrs Beckett would like that, weeding and tending the flowerbeds when the gardener allowed, practising her sparse Dutch on Mevrouw Steen and each evening listening eagerly for the phone to ring. The Professor never had much to say but his voice was reassuring.

She had been there for several days when he said, 'The question of your salary. I have arranged for my bank to send it to you each week in guilders.'

'I don't need any money,' said Julia.

'Money is something which everyone needs from

time to time,' said the Professor, and hung up before she could utter another word.

When the postman brought it she sat at the kitchen table and counted it. There seemed to be a great deal, even when she did careful mental sums and changed it into pounds. 'For a month, I suppose,' she said and, feeling rich, went to the village and bought postcards, stamps and chocolate.

The following week the same amount arrived, so that evening when he phoned she pointed out to him that there had been a mistake; she already had her salary.

'Did I not make myself clear? Each week you will receive your money from my bank...'

'But it's too much.'

'I must beg you not to argue. When are you going to see Mrs Beckett?'

'Tomorrow, in the morning. Why?'

'If you will give me time to speak, I will tell you. She is so much better she will probably be able to come home within the next few days. She will need to convalesce in a leisurely fashion. I rely upon you to see that she does.'

'I'll take the greatest care of her. How will she come home? Shall I go with Piet and fetch her?'

'I will tell you in due course. In the meantime you will see her doctor tomorrow.'

'Very well.' Then she added, 'Don't you ever say goodbye?'

'Not to you, Julia.' And he hung up!

Mrs Beckett was sitting in a chair by her bed when Julia got to the hospital. She looked weary and far too pale, but Julia was pleased to see that she was taking an interest in life once more.

'I'm coming home soon,' she told Julia. 'I've missed it so…' Her eyes filled with tears.

'Won't it be fun? Lofty and Portly will be so glad to see you…the garden looks lovely, and so many people have asked me how you are. You have so many friends. They'll want to come and see you, but the doctor says you must be a bit quiet for a little longer.'

'I know. Mr Gerard told me. I'm to do what you say just for a time; he's promised that everything will be just as it always was.'

'Well, of course it will. And I promise you that I won't make you do anything that you don't want to do.'

She hugged Mrs Beckett because she looked so small and frail.

'If the weather is warm and fine, you shall sit in the garden and tell me what to do.'

Four days later Julia was awakened by a thunderous knocking on the door.

'Mrs Beckett—something's happened,' she told the cats as she tore down the stairs, tugging on her dressing gown as she went, her feet bare.

The Professor was on the doorstep.

'I didn't use my key; I didn't want to disturb you…'

'But you have disturbed me. You've given me the fright of my life—I thought something had happened to Mrs Beckett. And why are you here?'

'If I might come in?' he asked meekly. 'This is my home!'

He sounded meek, but he gave her a mocking smile as she stood aside to let him pass.

'Oh, well—sorry,' said Julia. 'You could have phoned.'

He agreed blandly; he hadn't known until the very last minute that he could snatch twenty-four hours away from his work; too late to warn her of his intention.

'Tea? Breakfast?' Julia went ahead of him into the kitchen and turned to look at him. It was then she saw how tired he was…

'You've had no sleep. How did you come? When do you have to go back?'

'Tonight. I've come to bring Mrs Beckett home.'

'You'll have a cup of tea, then go and sleep for an hour or so while I get breakfast. What time do you plan to go to Leiden?'

'Shortly after midday.'

She had the kettle on, was setting out mugs, sugar and milk. 'Mevrouw Steen won't be here before eight o'clock.' She got the loaf and butter and cut him a generous slice. 'What a good thing I made the beds up yesterday…'

He sat at the table, watching her. Her hair was all over the place, her dressing gown had come untied, her feet were bare. She was, he decided, just what a man would want to see after a sleepless and tiring night.

Julia, far too busy to bother about appearances, put his tea before him, cut him more bread and butter and poured herself a mug. 'There's plenty of hot water,' she told him. 'Did you bring the car?'

'Yes. I'll have a shower and a nap. Breakfast about nine o'clock?'

It was barely seven. 'Yes, would you like it in bed?'

He choked back a laugh. 'The last time I had breakfast in bed I was nine years old, suffering from the mumps.'

When she looked at him, he added, 'That was twenty-seven years ago.'

He smiled, and the smile made her suddenly aware of the flyaway dressing gown and no slippers. She said briskly, 'I will call you at nine o'clock.'

He went away then, and she saw to the cats, put everything ready for breakfast and went quietly upstairs. The bathroom door was open but the three bedroom doors were closed. She had a shower, dressed, then made her bed and went downstairs again. Just in time to say *dag* to Mevrouw Steen.

There was no need to tell her that the Professor was there; the car was before the door. Mevrouw Steen broke into voluble talk, smiling widely.

'Mrs Beckett is coming home today.' Julia thought for a moment and added in Dutch, 'This afternoon.'

Mevrouw Steen nodded. 'I clean house…'

She trotted off, but not before Julia had warned her not to go upstairs until the Professor was awake. 'No sleep,' she told her in her fractured Dutch. 'Driving all night.'

Mevrouw made sympathetic clucking noises, went into the sitting room and shut the door on the sound of the Hoover.

Julia began to get breakfast. Bacon and eggs, tomatoes, mushrooms, fried bread. There was no lack of food in the house. Toast and marmalade to follow, and tea or coffee. And while she was busy she considered lunch. Salad, and there was ham in the fridge, and in the evening before he went back she would cook him a meal. A Spanish omelette, potatoes in their jackets and a salad—a bread and butter pudding, perhaps, or a sponge pudding with custard...

The bacon was sizzling in the pan and it was nearly nine o'clock. Time to rouse him...

He came into the kitchen through the door leading to the garden.

'You're up,' said Julia, and frowned because that had been a silly thing to say.

'I wanted to have a quick look at the garden. Something smells delicious.'

He looked as though he had slept all night—shaved and immaculately turned out. Of course he would have clothes here, thought Julia, and, suddenly conscious that she had been staring at him, she blushed.

The Professor studied the blush with interest and decided that it made her even prettier than she already was.

'Can't I help?' He sounded casual.

'If you would make the toast?'

Mevrouw Steen came in then. She had a great deal to say and it was frustrating, for Julia only understood one word in a dozen. The dear soul paused for breath presently and Julia offered her a mug of coffee and she trotted off with it. She would go upstairs, she said, and clean.

'A good soul,' said the Professor as he speared a mushroom. 'When you leave here I must find some kind of help for Mrs Beckett. Mevrouw Steen's a splendid worker but she doesn't like responsibility.'

Julia looked down at her plate. 'I expect you would like me to go once Mrs Beckett is settled here.'

'Now, why should you think that? Mrs Beckett is going to need you for another three weeks at least. You wish to go home?'

'No, no. I love it here,' she burst out. 'I don't know how you can bear to live anywhere else. Well, I dare say that's not true, for you have your lovely house in Amsterdam.'

'You liked that too?'

'My goodness me, indeed I did.'

'Then we must find time to go there again.' He added casually, 'I am planning to do rather more work over here—go over to Scotland from time to time when necessary.'

'You mean you won't live in London?' The thought filled her with a dismay she couldn't understand.

The Professor watched her face. 'From time to time,' he repeated gently. 'I'm going down to the village to see Piet. Shall we have lunch before we go to Leiden?'

'We? Wouldn't it be better if I stayed here and had everything ready—tea—and the cats waiting.' She looked at him. 'A welcome, if you see what I mean.'

He agreed readily, and presently she watched him walking along the lane. Even from the back he looked full of energy—a man who had had a good night's sleep and with not a care in the world.

Chapter 5

The Professor didn't come back until she was putting lunch on the table. 'Well,' said Julia to Portly, sitting beside her while she made a salad, 'I'm sure if he doesn't want my company I couldn't care less. After all, I'm only a kind of housekeeper.'

She wallowed in a comforting self-pity for a few minutes, and then forgot about it as the Professor came into the kitchen.

'Piet will come each day,' he told her without preamble. 'He'll do anything you want him to do and if you wish to leave the place he will stay with Mrs Beckett and Mevrouw Steen.'

'Thank you, but I'm happy to stay here. Will Mrs Beckett be able to sit outside for a while each day?'

'Dr de Groot—you saw him at Leiden—will come

and see her in a day or so and let you know what he wants done.'

'I see. When will you go back?'

'Anxious for me to be gone, Julia?' He sounded amused. 'I'm going back this evening.'

'But you've only just got here. You've had no sleep; you'll be dead on your feet.'

'I'm going back from Harwich on the night ferry. I'll sleep then.'

He drove away after lunch and she tidied up, put the tea things ready and went up to her room. She wasn't a vain girl, but she had the sudden urge to make the most of herself. It would have to be the same blue denim skirt, because she hadn't another, but there was a newly washed and ironed cotton blouse, and she wasted a good deal of time trying out various ways of doing her hair, only to tug out the pins and bundle it up on the top of her head. 'He won't notice anyway,' she told Lofty, watching her from the bed.

Of course he noticed, the moment he got out of the car and saw her waiting on the porch. He lifted Mrs Beckett out of the car and carried her into the cottage, and as he passed Julia he observed, 'I like the hair. Is it in my honour?'

She went pink, going ahead of him to open the sitting room door as he bore his housekeeper in and settled her in the chair Julia had put ready. Mrs Beckett said in a wispy voice, 'My dear, how well you look—such lovely pink cheeks. I do hope I'm not going to be too much of a nuisance.'

Julia gave her a gentle hug. 'What nonsense. I love

being here and I shall love looking after you. I'm going to get the tea; you must be dying for a cup.'

She got herself out of the room and Mrs Beckett settled back in her chair and nodded her head. 'A dear girl, don't you agree, Mr Gerard?'

He grinned at her. 'Don't fish, Nanny. When we've had tea you're going to bed, and mind you do exactly what Julia tells you. I must give her all the details of your treatment before I go.'

Tea was quickly over, which was a good thing for Julia could think of very little to say. The Professor made gentle small talk, addressing her from time to time and staring at her in a way which both annoyed and disturbed her. His remark about her hair had shaken her calm—perhaps she should have taken more pains with it.

He'll be gone in a few hours, thought Julia, and for some reason her spirits sank.

Getting Mrs Beckett to bed took time. There were her things to unpack and put away and frequent pauses while she discussed the hospital and her illness. When Julia finally went downstairs she found the Professor in the kitchen.

'I must leave in just over an hour,' he told her. 'Come here and listen carefully to what I have to say.'

'You must have a meal before you go. You can still tell me while I'm cooking it.'

She had her nose in the fridge. 'A bacon omelette? Asparagus? New potatoes?'

'Excellent. If you are as handy with the frying pan as you are with the needle I am indeed a lucky man.'

'You have no reason to be sarcastic…'

'What do you intend to do when you get back to London, Julia?'

'Be a dressmaker. Only I must be taught properly first.'

'And where will you live?'

'Oh, somewhere…'

Since he didn't answer, and the silence got a bit lengthy, she added, 'Ruth and Thomas have found such a nice house; I expect you've seen it. And of course Monica and George have a lovely old vicarage…'

'And you, Julia—do you not wish for a home and a husband and children, or is the fashioning of garments the acme of your ambition?'

'I don't like you when you talk like this,' said Julia fiercely. 'Never mind me, and much you care anyway, just tell me what I must do to get Mrs Beckett on her feet again.'

He didn't speak for a moment, but looked at her with lifted eyebrows, and when he did speak he was Professor van der Maes, giving courteous instructions to a patient's attendant.

She listened carefully while she beat eggs and chopped bacon and mushrooms, and when he had finished said, 'Thank you, that's all quite clear, but please write her medicines down so that I can be quite sure.'

'And here is Dr de Groot's phone number. Don't hesitate to ring him if you feel the necessity.'

She set the potatoes to cook. 'Will you come again to see Mrs Beckett?'

'If it's possible. I have complete faith in de Groot.

As for yourself, I think that Mrs Beckett will be fully recovered in three weeks. I shall arrange for suitable help before you return.' He wandered to the door. 'Will you let me know when my supper is ready? I'm going to sit with Nanny.'

It's my own silly fault, reflected Julia. Why can't we be friends? And why did he want me to come here if he dislikes me so much? Once I leave here I won't see him again; I'll find somewhere miles away.

Somewhere where—hopefully—she could make a living, find friends, perhaps meet a man who would want her for his wife. There must be any number of men around not in the least like Oscar, or, for that matter, the Professor. There was no one like him, she added...

She laid a place for him at the table, tossed the potatoes in butter and mint and had the pan hot ready for the omelette. She could hear the murmur of voices as she went into the hall when she called him and he came at once.

'There are strawberries and cream,' she told him, 'and I've made coffee.'

'Thank you. I've said goodbye to Nanny; she's a bit tearful, so I think a glass of claret might do her good before her supper. And you too, of course.'

He didn't talk much as he ate, and presently he went and got his bag.

She said awkwardly, 'I hope you have a safe journey and won't be too tired.' She had gone to the door with him. 'I promise I'll take good care of Mrs Beckett.'

He stood looking down at her. 'I'm sure of that. Look after yourself, Julia.'

He got into the car and drove away and she stood in the porch staring down the now empty lane. She felt empty too.

There were letters from Monica and Ruth in the morning; it was nice to know that selling the house had brought them so much happiness. And Monica wanted her to go and stay after she'd spent time at Ruth's, which solved the problem as to where she would go next. Somehow the future had seemed vague and far off, but the Professor had mentioned three weeks. In that time she must make up her mind what she intended to do.

Mrs Beckett was a model patient and, like a trusting child, did everything asked of her without question. Julia cooked her small tasty meals, helped her with the slow, tiring business of dressing and undressing, and after a few days led her carefully downstairs to sit and watch the TV or chat. Talking was something she enjoyed, and Julia was soon in possession of the Professor's family history.

Old family, said Mrs Beckett, wealthy and respected. 'His father was a surgeon, you know. Retired now. His mother's a sweet lady. He has brothers and sisters too. A brother in Canada and two sisters in New Zealand. All married. His parents are visiting them and will be away for some months.'

'They live in Amsterdam?'

'No. No, dear. In den Haag. Mr Gerard took over the Amsterdam house when he came of age. Lovely old house too, but he needs a wife to run it…'

'I should have thought that the Professor would

have had no difficulty in finding someone; he's rich and good-looking and well known in his profession.'

Mrs Beckett peered over her specs. 'Yes, dear, but Mr Gerard will never marry unless he finds his dream girl—he told me that a long time ago.' Before Julia could pursue the subject she added, 'I fancy a cup of tea. Make it in the brown pot, dear, it tastes so much better.'

It was in one of the numerous magazines Mrs Beckett had sent from England that Julia, idly leafing through its pages, saw the advertisement.

Skilful needlewomen were required to help in the repair of old fabrics and upholstery at a stately home in the north of England. Small salary and accommodation on the estate property. References would be required and full details as to the applicant's skill. Interviews would be held in London in one month's time.

Just what I'm looking for, reflected Julia, and miles away from London. Although why that should be so vital a need was something she didn't enlarge upon, even to herself. That evening she sat down and wrote a letter...

The weather was delightful and Mrs Beckett, spending quiet hours in the garden with Lofty and Portly in close attendance, began to look like her former plump self. As for Julia, cooking tasty meals, washing and ironing, pottering around the garden, she found life was a pleasure which she would have liked to continue for ever.

Mevrouw Steen and Piet smoothed her path, and if they found her Dutch inadequate and frequently laughable, they were too kind to say so. She had little time to herself, though, for Mrs Beckett liked to have company and was sometimes fretful at having to sit quietly and watch activity which she would normally have enjoyed herself. But as the days passed and she began to take up her normal life again Julia gradually handed over to her. In another week she would be back to her normal state of health.

The thought of leaving depressed Julia, although she told herself that it was time she went back to England and got on with her own life. After all she had money now, and soon she could decide what she wanted to do...

A problem solved for her for one morning, when a letter arrived for her. If she cared to present herself at a certain London hotel on a day three weeks from now, she would be interviewed with the possibility of being employed at the stately home. She should bring with her two references and a sample of her needlework. She would be good enough to acknowledge the letter...

Which she did, without saying anything to Mrs Beckett, trusting to luck that she wold be free by then. That done, she expressed a wish to do some embroidery. 'So that I can sit with you and not feel guilty while you knit,' she explained, and wished that she could take Mrs Beckett into her confidence.

Mrs Beckett was enthusiastic: there was a box in the attic, full of bits and pieces. Julia could rummage around and take whatever she fancied.

She found the ideal thing: a piece of patterned damask and a bundle of silks. She set to work, embroidering the pattern in a variety of stitches and various colours, and Mrs Beckett, examining it, declared that it was a lovely piece of embroidery.

'What a clever girl you are,' she observed. 'It's almost professional.' And she smiled so fondly at Julia that she almost told her of her plans. But she couldn't, of course, otherwise Mrs Beckett might feel that she was anxious to be gone—which thought was followed by another: if she told her companion what she hoped to do, the Professor might come to hear of it, and it seemed of the utmost importance that he should be unaware of her plans for the future.

He came a few days later, coming unhurriedly into the garden where they were having tea. Mrs Beckett saw him first.

'Mr Gerard—what a sight for sore eyes. And just in time for tea!'

He bent to kiss her. 'You're well again, Nanny. You look splendid…'

He nodded to Julia, half smiling. 'Julia has done a splendid job.'

'I'll get a cup and saucer and more tea,'she said, and took herself off indoors. So she was to go, and quite soon. And was he staying? Because if he was she would have to make a room ready and reorganise supper. She put the kettle on and warmed a teapot, found a cup and saucer and plate and a tray to put them on, and picked up a knife to cut the cake on the table.

It was taken from her and the Professor cut an enormous slice and began to eat it.

'Are you hungry?'

'For a home made cake? Always—don't you know that the way to a man's heart is through his stomach?'

She spooned tea into the pot. 'Are you staying?' Her voice sounded wooden in her own ears. Why, oh, why did she feel so awkward with him?

'For supper. I flew over; Piet will drive me back to the airfield later. I wanted to see how Nanny was getting on. She's fit again, but I have asked Dr de Groot to come tomorrow and give her a check-up. If he agrees with me, I'll be over in a few days with a nice middle-aged woman who will take over from you. You will be glad to go home, Julia?'

He had eaten the cake so she cut him another slice. 'Oh, yes, although I've been happy here, but Mrs Beckett wants to get back to her normal life. This lady who is coming—does Mrs Beckett know her?'

'Yes. She used to work for my mother. They were good friends and she will stay for as long as Nanny wants her to. I have told her and she's delighted.'

He picked up the tray and Julia followed him, the rest of the cake on a plate. She hoped that he would have time to tell her how Thomas and Ruth were and, more importantly, how she was to get back home. 'Home,' she muttered to herself. 'I haven't got a home…'

There was no talk of the return as they had tea, and it was Mrs Beckett who did most of the talking.

'I have never felt better,' she assured the Professor. 'This dear girl has looked after me as though she were my own daughter—all the delicious food she has cooked for me—I have grown quite plump.' She chuckled. 'Julia says she has grown fat, but I tell her that she is just right—I like a woman to have a shape...'

Julia went pink and looked away, but not before the Professor had caught her eye. 'You take the words out of my mouth, Nanny.'

Julia found his smile so disquieting that she jumped to her feet, declaring that she must see what there was for supper, and nipped smartly into the cottage. Safe in the kitchen, she shut the door, muttering to herself, and poked her head into the fridge, glad that she had something as prosaic as supper to take her mind off that smile.

She had made watercress soup earlier that day; there would be just enough for the three of them if she served it carefully. She had intended omelettes for the two of them, but now she took lamb chops from the fridge, scrubbed new potatoes, baby carrots and added to the broad beans. These on the Aga, she turned her attention to a pudding. Egg custards with plenty of cream...

That dealt with, she laid the table in the dining room. She and Mrs Beckett ate their meals in the kitchen, but for this evening Julia set the table as Mrs Beckett liked it, with flowers and a starched tablecloth, polished silver and the best glasses. It looked nice when she had finished it and it had been a good excuse to stay in the cottage. She went back to the kitchen, inspected the chops, and the Professor asked from the door. 'Can we talk now, or shall it be after supper?'

'Well, everything will be ready in ten minutes.'

'Ample time. You will want to know how you are to return home; it will take only a few minutes to tell you.'

So much for wanting the pleasure of her company, thought Julia, and clashed the saucepan lids with unnecessary noise.

She said, 'Well?' in an icy voice, and didn't look at him.

'If everything is as I hope it will be, I will come on Saturday—that's three days away. I shall bring with me Miss Thrisp, who has been here before and is already in possession of the facts of Nanny's illness. I want to leave after lunch. I shall have the car and we will go back by ferry.'

'Very well.' She added, 'Thank you.'

'Where will you go?'

'I'm staying with Ruth and Thomas for a while, and then Monica's asked me.'

'And after that?'

When she didn't answer he said carelessly, 'Oh, that isn't any of my business, is it? If supper's ready I'll pour us some sherry. When does Nanny have her glass of red wine?'

'With supper. Piet brought a case of claret; we've had some of that.'

'Good. I'll fetch Nanny in and bring you your sherry.'

Julia gave the potatoes a prod. 'Thank you.'

He came back presently with the sherry and put it on the table. 'You're as cross as two sticks,' he observed cheerfully. 'Was it because I admired your shape?'

Julia, her back to him, tossed back the sherry. 'Certainly not. I hope I'm not so childish...'

'Not childish, Julia, but very much a woman. Give me those dishes; I'll carry them to the table.'

It must be the sherry, decided Julia, making her feel peculiar. And she had every intention of forgetting what the Professor had said, or rather the manner in which he had said it. Had he been poking fun at her? Trying to annoy her? She found that hard to believe; he wasn't that kind of a man.

He left soon after their meal, thanking her pleasantly for his supper. He might annoy her but she had to admit that he had lovely manners. When he had gone she cleared away and settled Mrs Beckett in her chair, then sat and listened to that lady's reminiscences of the van der Maes family and the Professor in particular. 'Always knew what he wanted to do, yet he found the time to backpack round the world, spent his holidays working for them poor starving children in Africa, and a year or so ago he went with a team to Bosnia. Not a word to anyone, mind you.'

Mrs Beckett settled herself more comfortably in her chair. 'You'd never think it to look at him, would you? And he don't lack for social life, either. Could have married half a dozen times, and when I remind him—respectful, of course—that it is time he settled down with a wife and had children, all he says is he hasn't found his dream girl. Although goodness knows it wasn't lack of trying on the part of various young ladies.'

She peered at Julia over her specs. 'I dare say you've wondered about him, Julia?'

A truthful girl, Julia pondered her reply. 'Well, a bit, sometimes. But you see, Mrs Beckett, we don't know each other very well. Circumstances brought us together, but once I've left here I dare say I shan't see him again. You see, I have nothing to do with hospitals, and I don't know anyone he might know.'

'Such a pretty girl. I can't believe that you haven't had a boyfriend.'

'Well, hardly that…' She told her about Oscar then, and Mrs Beckett nodded her head when Julia explained why she had run away from the hotel. 'Quite right too, nasty man. How fortunate that Mr Gerard happened to be there.'

'Yes, he was very kind and helpful. Now, I'm going to get your hot milk and see you to your bed; it's been a busy day.'

'Yes, but a most interesting one,' said Mrs Beckett thoughtfully.

Lying cosily in her bed presently, Mrs Beckett reflected that the pair of them were ideally suited. It was to be hoped that they would discover that for themselves as soon as possible, though it seemed likely that Mr Gerard had already done that…

Ruth phoned in the morning. It would be lovely to have Julia to stay, and she was to make herself at home for as long as she wanted to. Thomas was busy at the hospital, but they could go shopping and there was such a lot of talking to do. 'And then Monica wants you to go and stay with them, so don't hurry to get yourself settled. I'm not sure when you'll arrive exactly, but I'll be home waiting for you.'

Julia should have felt happy and content that her future was arranging itself so pleasantly. First Ruth, then Monica, and then, if she was lucky, the job at the stately home.

'I'm free as air,' said Julia, and wished that she weren't.

Three days had never gone so fast. Julia and Mevrouw Steen got a room ready for Miss Thrisp, and while Mevrouw Steen polished and Hoovered Julia did the flowers, stocked the fridge with the food Piet went to buy for her and then did her own packing. That didn't take long, for she had had no chance to buy anything other than small necessities from the village. She would buy clothes when she got home; the money she had been sent each week was almost untouched. She allowed her mind to dwell on the pleasant prospect of buying the kind of clothes she hankered after. No more curtains, she promised herself. She would gather together an elegant wardrobe. It was a pity that the Professor would never see her in it...

There had been no word from him, but she hadn't expected it. Dr de Groot had seen Mrs Beckett, pronounced himself satisfied, observed that Julia had taken good care of his patient and gone again. Presumably the Professor didn't think it necessary to add to that.

She was up early, anxious to have everything just so before he and Miss Thrisp came; she organised fresh flowers, salad and cold meat in the fridge, strawberries and cream, plus a selection of cheeses; Miss Thrisp might not want to spend time in the kitchen after her journey. Julia had coffee ready too, and some of the little almond biscuits Mrs Beckett had shown her how to bake. As for that lady, Julia had made sure that she looked her best, sitting now in the sitting room, a good breakfast inside her, her hair just so...

Julia went to do her own hair then. There was too much of it, she thought impatiently, tugging it viciously. Perhaps she would have it cut really short. It was the fashion, and it would be nice to be fashionable.

The Rolls stopped without a whisper of sound and the Professor got out and opened the car door for Miss Thrisp. Julia, who had conjured up several mental pictures of her, was pleased to see that she was exactly as anyone with a name like that would look, being tall, and thin, with a long face and a long thin nose, very dark eyes and a mouth which would stand no nonsense. But her smile was warm and friendly, and Julia thought that, despite the nose, she was rather nice. Well, she would be, she reflected, ushering the pair of them into the cottage, otherwise the Professor wouldn't have allowed her near Nanny.

And why should I be so sure of that? she wondered.

She left them in the sitting room after their brief introduction and a casual nod from the Professor, and went to the kitchen to fetch the coffee. She dawdled over that to give them time to exchange their first greetings, and presently, when she took the tray in, she found the two ladies sitting side by side, both happily talking their heads off. The Professor had gone to the open window and was looking at his garden.

He turned to face her as she put the tray down.

'We shall leave directly after lunch,' he told her. 'You're ready?'

She wondered what he would say if she said that no, she wasn't; he so clearly expected her to be waiting, case in hand.

She said, 'Yes. At what time do you want lunch?'

'Noon. So that there is ample time for goodbyes.'

She said tartly, 'Will you come and sit down for your coffee?' Once everyone had coffee and biscuits, she sat down herself and joined in the ladies' conversation.

Miss Thrisp was shown to her room, then went to the kitchen with Julia to make sure she knew where everything was. Before she went back to the sitting room she put a bony hand on Julia's arm. 'You've taken such good care of Mrs Beckett; I couldn't have done better myself. I'd have come the moment the Professor told me she was needing someone, but I was getting over a nasty attack of flu myself and I was real bothered as to what would happen. But he was right, you're worth your weight in gold—he never makes mistakes about people. You look exactly as he described you.'

It would have been nice to have known just what that was, thought Julia.

Lunch was a cheerful meal, but they didn't linger over it. Julia helped Miss Thrisp clear the table and then, obedient to the Professor's look, fetched her case and made her goodbyes.

Mrs Beckett was inclined to be tearful. 'But of course you'll come again?' she asked hopefully, and Julia mumbled that perhaps she would, if and when she had got settled.

'You must get Mr Gerard to bring you over for a weekend.'

Julia mumbled again, shook Miss Thrisp's bony hand, and got into the car, to turn and wave to the two ladies and the cats as they drove away.

The Professor had had little to say, but he had been pleasant in a remote kind of way and there were several things that she wanted to know.

'Where does the ferry leave from and at what time?'

'The catamaran—it leaves tomorrow around two o'clock, and gets to Harwich in the early evening.'

'Tomorrow? You mean today?'

'I mean tomorrow. We are spending the night in Amsterdam.'

She sat up very straight. 'You may be Professor, but I'm going back today.'

'Why are you making a fuss? A few hours more or less can't make a difference to your plans, but it is a matter of urgency that I stay until tomorrow.'

'I should have been told; I could have made other arrangements. I have no wish to stay in Amsterdam. And where am I to go, pray?'

'To my house, of course. Where else? And don't worry; I shan't be there. Wim and my housekeeper will take care of you.'

'Why won't you be there?' she asked sharply.

'I shall be at the hospital, operating early this evening, and I shall be there all night until I judge my patient to be in a stable condition. I hope that satisfies you?'

She felt mean. 'I'm sorry I snapped, but if you'd told me that when I first asked I wouldn't have said anything more about it.'

He didn't answer, and she added cautiously, 'Won't you be too tired to travel tomorrow?'

His 'no' discouraged her from saying another word.

But presently she asked, 'Why do we quarrel?'

'I never quarrel, and nor, I think, do you. We strike sparks off each other, Julia.' He turned his head briefly and smiled at her. 'And that's as good a beginning as any.'

She was about to ask him what he meant, but then thought better of it, and they stayed silent as they neared Amsterdam, but it was a friendly silence.

The quiet street by the canal seemed remote from the bustling streets of the city, the old houses silent under the trees which bordered it.

It's like coming home, reflected Julia as Wim opened the door to them and greeted her as though he had known her all his life.

The Professor spoke to him quietly and he nodded and went away, to return with a solidly built elderly woman who listened to what the Professor had to say, smiled at Julia and beckoned her to follow.

'This is Getske, my housekeeper,' the Professor said.

'Go with her; she will show you to your room. We have time for tea before I have to go.'

Julia followed the housekeeper along the hall and up the staircase at its end. It opened onto a circular gallery with passages leading off it and any number of doors. Getske opened a door and stood aside for her to go into the room beyond. It wasn't a large room but was instantly welcoming, with its canopied bed, the dressing table to one side, a small upholstered chair with a table beside it under the long window and a soft carpet underfoot. Through a door in the far wall there was a bathroom, and leading from it a wardrobe fit to house more clothes than Julia would ever buy.

Alone, she prowled round, picking things up and putting them down again. Then, remembering that the Professor might want to leave, she tidied her person, stuck a few more pins in her hair, dabbed powder on her nose and went back downstairs.

He was waiting with well-concealed impatience in a little room leading from the hall. Really, the house was a rabbit warren, she thought, but a very luxurious one and very much to her taste.

Tea had been laid out on a small table between two chairs. The Professor got up from one as she went in and Jason pranced to meet her.

'He will keep you company this evening.' The Professor drew up a chair for her. 'Will you be Mother?'

She sat down and picked up the silver teapot. She would miss this elegance, she reflected. It was something she had become accustomed to during the last few weeks. The thought saddened her.

The Professor had his tea, ate a slice of cake and got up to go.

'I'll see you tomorrow morning,' he told her. 'Wim will take you round the house if you would like that—ask for anything you want.'

He was standing in front of her, looking down at her upturned face.

'Oh, I should like that; it's a lovely old house.' She smiled at him, and he bent down and kissed her. It was a gentle kiss, so why did it arouse such strong feelings in her person? she wondered, watching the door close behind his vast back.

Wim's English was as sparse as her Dutch, but they contrived to understand each other well enough. He had been with the Professor's family, he told her, for fifty years or more, and they and the house were his life. With Jason at their heels, they went from room to room, taking their time, while he pointed out the plasterwork ceilings, the heavy brocade curtains at the tall windows, the bow-fronted display cabinets filled with porcelain and silver, the exquisite marquetry on a long-case clock. Julia looked at it all with delight, wishing that the Professor was there too, so that she could tell him what a splendid home he had.

The house was surprisingly large, with rooms opening from one to another until the final one opened onto a long narrow garden. Tomorrow, she promised herself, she would explore the garden early in the morning, before the Professor got home.

Wim took her upstairs then, waiting patiently while she poked her nose round each door on each landing, until they reached the final narrow staircase to the attic. When Wim smiled and nodded she took a look, then climbed up to the small door and opened it. The attic was long and narrow, with small windows at each end and a steeply sloping roof. It wasn't empty, containing odds and ends of furniture, rolled up rugs, a row of ice skates hanging from hooks on the wall and a baby's cradle. In one corner there was a stack of framed pictures and old photographs. She bent to look and picked up the top one. A boy, a quite small boy. She didn't need to read the date and name on it. She put it down again, feeling as though she had pried into the Professor's private life. He was smiling in the photo and his smile hadn't changed...

She had dinner in the same small room where they had had tea: watercress soup, duckling in an orange sauce and *pofferjes* light as air and smothered with cream. There was a light white wine, and coffee to follow, and a beaming Wim to serve her.

It was a reward for looking after Mrs Beckett, she supposed; he had paid her wages, but he could hardly tip her...

She offered a morsel of the little sugary biscuit which had come with the coffee to Jason and allowed herself to daydream. But presently she sat up. She had allowed her thoughts to run away with her just because the Professor had kissed her.

'I shall go to bed,' she told Jason, and did so.

She was awake after a dreamless sleep when a stolid young girl brought her tea. She showered and dressed and went down to the hall and found Wim. Breakfast would be in half an hour he told her; the Professor wasn't home.

So she went into the garden and walked with Jason up and down its narrow paths in the morning sun. It was full of old-fashioned flowers, with a circular rose bed and flowering shrubs against the brick wall at its end. She could have stayed there, sitting on the rustic seat, surrounded by honeysuckle and wisteria, but breakfast waited.

The Professor was standing by the window of the

room leading to the garden. His good morning was pleasantly friendly, his enquiry as to whether she had had a good night uttered in the tones of a thoughtful host. He was immaculately dressed and one would have supposed that he had enjoyed a good night's sleep too, but Julia saw the tired lines in his face.

'Have you had any sleep?'

'Enough,' he told her, and smiled so that she remembered the little boy in the photo.

I must forget that, she told herself, and went with him to eat her breakfast. They ate in silence for a time until she asked, 'Was it successful? The operation? Or would you rather not talk about it?'

He didn't answer at once, and she said quickly, 'All right, you don't have to tell me. I'm not being curious, you know.'

He loaded butter onto toast. 'It was entirely successful. And I don't mind you asking, Julia.' He stared at her across the table. 'I think that I would have been disappointed if you had not done so.' He passed his coffee cup. 'A mutual interest is to be desired.'

'Oh, is it?' said Julia, bewildered. She had a feeling that things were moving too fast for her to understand, but she was aware of a pleasant excitement. And they had the rest of the day together.

Chapter 6

Julia's pleasant speculations about the morning were quickly cut short.

'We shall need to leave here after an early lunch,' said the Professor. 'I shall go back to the hospital presently, and I'll take Jason with me and give him a run. Perhaps you want to explore or go to the shops? I would be easier in my mind if you stayed here...'

She said brightly, 'I shall sit in the garden. I can do all the shopping I want when I get home.'

So he went away with Jason and she went into the garden again and sat down with the newspapers Wim had handed to her. She could so easily have gone with him, she thought; perhaps waited in the car while he was at the hospital, and then gone with him and Jason. He was deliberately avoiding her...

'I couldn't care less!' said Julia, and picked up the *Daily Telegraph* and read it from front to back page. She was none the wiser when she had. She tried the *Haagsche Post* next—she might as well improve her Dutch while she could—although it was a complete waste of time. She was puzzling out the small ads when the Professor joined her.

He said affably, 'Oh, splendid, you're improving your Dutch.'

'I have very little Dutch to improve,' said Julia coldly. 'I hope your patient is improving.'

He sat down beside her with Jason squeezed between them.

'Yes, I think he has a very good chance. I've left him in good hands.'

'Was he someone important?' She turned to look at him. 'Did they send for you specially?'

'Yes, and yes. Will you be sorry to leave Holland?'

'Oh, yes, although I've not seen anything of it. I'm sorry to leave the cottage and this splendid house, but they'll be lovely memories.'

'You would like to come back some time?'

'Perhaps.' She put an arm round Jason's woolly shoulders and he licked her hand gently. 'Jason is going to miss you.'

'Yes, and I shall miss him, but I shall be here again very shortly and he is used to my coming and going.'

He glanced at his watch. 'We had better have our lunch.'

The day which had seemed to stretch before her for hours of delight had telescoped into an all too short day.

The Professor might not like her, but that couldn't prevent her from enjoying his company. She supposed that she didn't like him either, but she was no longer quite sure about that. Of course, there was still the journey back to London...

Which was disappointing, in so far that the Professor, while thoughtful for her well-being, made only the most casual conversation, giving her no opportunity to get to know him better. On board, he excused himself smiling and began to study a case full of papers—first, however, making sure that she had something to read and a tray of tea.

She leafed through the magazines and wondered what he was thinking about.

She would have been astonished to know it was herself. Usually so sure of himself, the Professor found himself uncertain. That he had fallen in love with Julia and wanted her for his wife he now freely admitted, but she had shown no preference for his company; he thought that she liked him a good deal more than she was prepared to admit, but he wasn't prepared to rush her. Once back in London, he would have the opportunity to see her frequently. In the meantime, it was only by maintaining a casual disinterested manner that he was able to keep his hands off her...

They discussed the weather, the countryside and the state of the roads as he drove back to London. All safe subjects which lasted them nicely until he drew up before Thomas's and Ruth's new home.

They were warmly welcomed but the Professor didn't stay. He had a brief smiling chat with Ruth, observed that he would see Thomas at the hospital in the morning, and got back into the Rolls, brushing aside Julia's careful little speech of thanks.

He couldn't have been pleasanter, she thought, or more remote.

Mrs Potts, his housekeeper, and the two dogs were waiting for him. His housekeeper was middle-aged, brisk and devoted to him, and as for Wilf and Robbie, their welcome was estatic.

He took the car round to the mews at the back of the house, promised to be back for his dinner and took the little dogs for a run. The streets were quiet; London on a summer's evening could be delightful. He thought about the cottage—he would have to ring Nanny when he got back—and he wondered if Julia was thinking of it too. She had loved the house in Amsterdam; she would fit so easily into his life...

Despite his casual goodbye, Julia had expected to see him again while she was staying with Ruth, but, beyond saying that he was working too hard, Thomas had nothing to say about him. Ruth wondered from time to time why he hadn't come to see them or at least phoned, but Julia's monosyllabic replies led her to a rather thoughtful silence. Julia looked splendid: full of fresh air, nicely tanned, apparently well pleased with life—and yet there was something wrong...

Ruth entered into the plans Julia had for an entire new wardrobe, and when she wasn't there phoned Monica. 'She looks marvellous, but there is something wrong. Do you suppose she met someone in Holland? She's coming to stay with you—try and find out.'

Getting ready for bed, Ruth asked Thomas, 'Has Gerard said anything about Julia?'

'Only that she has been a splendid help with Mrs Beckett. He's off to Glasgow tomorrow. He'll be gone for a couple of days.' Thomas gave her a sharp look. 'Why did you ask?'

'Oh, nothing, darling. They don't get on, do they?'

Thomas got into bed. 'Don't they? It isn't something I'd ask him—or Julia, for that matter.'

There were still ten days before her interview for the job. Beyond telling Ruth vaguely that she had heard of something, Julia had said nothing; instead she and Ruth went shopping.

With money in her purse Julia ignored the High Street chain stores and poked around boutiques, and, egged on by her sister, spent a good deal more than she had intended to. But the results were worth it; she bought well-cut jersey dresses, elegant tops and skirts, dresses for summer and a silk dress suitable for the evening. She thought that she might never wear it, that it would probably hang in the cupboard forgotten and regretted, but there was always the chance that she might need it—supposing the Professor should ask her to dine with him one evening?

It was highly unlikely—and even if he asked her she might refuse…

There were undies to buy too, shoes, a raincoat, a short jacket, a sensible outfit to wear if she got that job…

Afterwards she went to stay with Monica and George. She had a long weekend in which to explore their home and the village and listen to George preaching a splendid sermon. He had a good congregation too, said Monica proudly and she herself ran the Mothers' Union and Sunday School. Village life suited her, and now there was money to see to the plumbing and refurbish the vicarage. There was so much to see and talk about that no one noticed that Julia had almost nothing to say about her stay in Holland once she had given a brief account of it—and an even briefer reference to the Professor.

Back with Ruth, she dressed in one of the jersey dresses and, for once very neat about the head, went to her appointment. It was to be held in one of the smaller hotels and, urged by the porter to take the first door on the left of the foyer, Julia did so. There were five or six other women there, all armed as she was with specimens of their handiwork. They paused in their talk to stare at her, answer her good morning with nods and then resume their chatting. There was one older woman who had smiled at her, but others were young, smartly dressed and discreetly made up. Julia decided that she had very little chance against their self-assurance. Probably they had all been to a needlework school and had diplomas and marvellous references.

They were called in, one after the other, and came out looking pleased with themselves. The older woman went in, looking anxious, and when she came out she said nothing, only smiled again as Julia opened the door in her turn.

There were three women sitting behind a table. They greeted her pleasantly, told her to sit down, and the one in the middle, middle-aged and looking how one would imagine a strict schoolteacher would look, asked her why she wanted the job.

This was unexpected; there was no time to prepare a speech. Julia said, 'I want to get away from London,' and then wished that she hadn't said it, so she added, 'And I like needlework and sewing and making things out of things.'

The three women looked at each other. 'Will you show us your work?'

So she unwrapped the tapestry, its pattern picked out with the silks Mrs Beckett had given her, and spread it out on the table and sat down again. It was passed from one hand to the other, looked at through magnifying glasses and held up to the light. She was asked which stitches she had used and why she had chosen to embroider the tapestry.

'I hadn't anything else. I was in the country with no shops for miles. So I used what I found in the attic.'

'You understand that this is temporary employment? A week's notice on either side. Tedious work, repairing very old curtains. Quite long hours and the remuneration is small. Bed and board is free, of course. We are prepared to employ you on those terms.'

Julia didn't give herself time to think. She said, 'Thank you; I should like the job.'

'It will be confirmed by letter and you will be given

directions as to how to reach the estate. You will need to go to Carlisle and then to Haltwhistle, where you will be met. Are you free to travel within the next day or so?'

'Yes, I can be ready in two days' time.'

Back in the waiting room, she found the older woman still there.

She said hesitantly, 'I waited. I thought they might take you. I've got a job there.'

'You have? I'm glad—so have I. Perhaps we could travel up together. Do you know that part of the world?'

'I was born near the estate. I came to London with my husband. He died and I wanted to go back home.'

'I'm sorry about your husband. I just wanted to get away from London.'

They were standing on the pavement outside the hotel. 'Do you have a phone number? Perhaps we could meet at the station?'

The woman nodded. 'My name's Woodstock—Jenny. It would be nice to travel together.'

It wasn't difficult to convince Ruth that the job was something which was exactly what she had hoped for. 'And,' she pointed out, 'it isn't a permanent one; I expect that once the repairs are made we shan't be needed. And while I'm there I can decide where I want to live and what I want to do.'

Ruth said, 'Yes, dear,' in an uncertain way. Something was wrong. Perhaps Julia *had* met someone in Holland? She was about to ask when Julia said casually, 'Ruth, don't let the Professor know where I am. Don't look like that. It's just that he has this way of turning up with some offer of a job or something…'

It sounded pretty feeble but Ruth, thinking her own thoughts, said at once, 'I won't say a word. It sounds rather fun, this job. It's a long way away, of course, but probably it will be a lovely old house full of treasures and you'll meet lots of people.'

The day before she was due to leave the Professor came. Ruth had gone to the hairdresser and Julia was in the kitchen getting lunch when he knocked on the door. She had opened it expecting the postman, and the sight of the Professor standing there, smiling a little, did things to her breath. She had wanted to see him just once more, for after she had gone from London she had every intention of forgetting him. On the other hand she would have liked to have gone away before he found out that she was no longer at Ruth's.

She said now, 'Oh, hello. Did you want Ruth? She's out…'

'I came to see you.'

There was nothing for it but to ask him in. 'I'm getting lunch,' she told him, and led the way to the kitchen. It would be easier to calm down if she had something to do. And why should she need to calm down? she wondered.

'You're glad to be back?' he asked.

She whisked eggs in a bowl and didn't look at him. 'Yes, yes, I am.'

'Will you have dinner with me tomorrow evening, Julia?'

It was so unexpected that she put the bowl of eggs

down with something of a thump on the table. 'Tomorrow? No—no, thank you.'

She looked at him then, wishing with her whole heart that she wasn't going miles away, knowing suddenly that she loved him and that the thought of not seeing him again was unbearable.

She said carefully, 'I'm sorry, I can't… I wasn't going to tell you—I'm going away—tomorrow morning.'

Something in his quiet face made her add, 'I've got a most interesting job. I want to get away from London…'

'You were not going to tell me?' His voice was as quiet as his face.

'No—no, I wasn't.' She had spoken too loudly, and now added recklessly, 'Why should I?'

'Indeed, why should you?' He smiled gently. 'I hope that you will be very happy.'

'Of course I shall be happy,' said Julia in a cross voice, wishing that he would go so that she might burst into tears in peace.

Which was exactly what he did do, blandly wishing her goodbye, telling her cheerfully that he would see himself out.

She wept into the eggs then, and, since she couldn't see to do anything for a moment, sat down and buried her face in Muffin's furry body. Muffin, who loved her in his own cat fashion, bore with the damp fur and Julia's incoherent mutterings, but it was a relief when she settled him back in his chair. Feline instinct warned him that she was unhappy, that she was probably going away. But she would be back, and in the meantime he was quite comfortable with Ruth. He settled down for a nap and Julia went and washed her face, and then went back to the eggs.

Ruth, back home again, took a quick look at Julia. 'You don't have to go, dear. You know you can stay here as long as you like, and if you want to get away from London, Monica would love to have you.'

She went to the fridge and poured two glasses of white wine. 'Is that a soufflé? It looks delicious...'

Presently Julia said, 'The Professor came. I told him I was going away but he doesn't know where I'm going. Don't tell him, Ruth.'

'Of course not, love.' Ruth was brisk. 'Did he want to know?'

'No,' said Julia bleakly. She added, 'He didn't even say goodbye.'

Ruth forebore from pointing out that he was a man who never said anything he didn't mean. She began to talk instead about the morrow's journey.

Jenny Woodstock was at the station in the morning, mildly excited and happy at the thought of going back to her home. She talked in her quiet way about it during their journey and Julia was thankful for that, for it kept her own thoughts at bay. And she was glad to have someone with her who knew her way about once they reached Carlisle and, finally, Haltwhistle.

Even then their journey wasn't over. There was a middle-aged man, stocky, with a Land Rover waiting for them, and they drove for what seemed like hours through the wide countryside until he turned into a wide gateway and onto a long drive. They could see their destination now, an imposing mansion with a few trees around it. Even on a summer's day it looked bleak, but as they neared it Julia could see that it was lived in and that there were cars parked to one side of the house and people going in and out of the great entrance.

Mrs Woodstock enlightened her. 'They're open to the public twice a week.'

And the driver said over his shoulder, 'I'll drive you round to one of the side doors. The housekeeper will settle you in.'

A surly man, thought Julia. She hoped that the house-keeper would be more friendly.

Her hopes were realised. Mrs Bates was large and stout, with twinkling eyes and a wide smile. She offered tea and then led them out of the house and across a wide courtyard. 'Most of the sewing ladies come from the village,' she explained. 'I've put you here, Mrs Wood-stock.' She opened a door in one of the outbuildings. 'It's a nice little room and there's a bathroom and a gas ring and so on, so's you can be cosy.' She looked at Julia. 'If you'll wait here, Miss…'

She was back in a few minutes. 'You're over here, up these steps.' She observed, 'The place is used for stor-age but you won't be disturbed.'

She surged up the steps and unlocked the door at the top, and Julia followed her. The room was quite large, with a low ceiling and a wide window. It was comfort-ably furnished—a divan bed, a table and two chairs, an easy chair and bookshelves. There was another door leading to a shower room and an alcove with a gas ring and cupboards.

'You'll eat over in the house but I'll see you have tea and milk so that you can have a drink in your own room. You'll be wanted in half an hour or so. Will you come back to me and I'll take you?'

Left alone, Julia took another look around her; it was nice to have a room of her own, away from the house, and once she had unpacked and put her small posses sions round the place it would look more like home. She tidied herself and then went in search of Jenny.

Jenny was delighted. 'It's like a hotel,' she observed happily, 'and I'm only a few miles from where I was born.'

They followed the housekeeper through endless corridors until they reached a small staircase tucked away in a narrow passage. They climbed to the second floor before they were finally ushered into a vast attic with overhead lighting and a row of windows overlooking the front of the house. The severe woman who had interviewed them was waiting and they spent the next hour or so being led along the long tables where the repair work was being done. A cup of tea would have been nice, reflected Julia, being shown the wall tapestry she would be working on.

There wasn't much of the afternoon left. The half-dozen women around her began to pack up presently, and thankfully she and Jenny were shown the way to a room on the ground floor where tea was waiting. It was more than tea; there were eggs and ham, several kinds of bread, butter, pots of jam, a splendid cake and a great pot of tea. Julia, eating with a splendid appetite, wondered if this was the last meal of the day, for it was almost six o'clock.

As they got up from the table one of the women said in a friendly voice, 'You're new, aren't you? There's sandwiches and hot drinks about eight o'clock. Some of us live in the village but two of us live here in the house.'

It was going to be all right, Julia decided, going sleepily to her bed later that evening. Everyone was friendly, she had a pleasant room, good, wholesome food and she would be working at something she enjoyed doing. Nevertheless she cried herself to sleep, and her last thoughts were of Gerard. He would forget her, of course. Probably by the time she got back to London he would have gone back to Holland and got married into the bargain.

The Professor went about his work in his usual calm manner. For the moment there was nothing to be done; first he had to find out where Julia had gone. It was some days before he saw Ruth and enquired casually as to whether she had heard from Julia. And Ruth blushed because she was longing to tell him where Julia was, but a promise was a promise…

'She's very happy…'

'Splendid. What kind of a job is it?'

There would be no harm in telling him that. 'Repairing old tapestries.'

'And where is she?'

Ruth blushed again. 'She asked me not to tell you and I promised.'

'Then I won't bother you. I hope she will settle down and enjoy life. How fortunate that she heard of something so soon after coming back.'

'Oh, it wasn't sudden; she told me she'd applied for the job while she was still in Holland with Mrs Beckett—she saw it advertised in a magazine.'

Now he had one or two clues. He said casually, 'And how are Monica and George getting on? Will you be visiting them now that you're nicely settled in here?'

So Ruth told him all about the new bathrooms and the central heating in the vicarage, pleased that she had given nothing away about Julia.

It was the following day before the Professor had the leisure to phone Mrs Beckett. He listened patiently to her detailed account of her progress and when she paused for breath he asked, 'Nanny, which magazines do you read?'

'Now there's a funny question,' observed Mrs Beckett. 'English ones, of course, they get sent each week.' She named them and added, 'Why do you want to know, Mr Gerard?'

'Do any of them advertise jobs?'

'Not all of them. The *Lady* does—pages and pages of them.'

'Nanny, have you heard from Julia?'

Mrs Beckett looked out of the window and smiled. 'Well, yes, bless the dear child. Sent me a long letter but forgot the address. Got a lovely job, she says, embroidering and suchlike. The post mark was Carlisle. Seems a long way from home, but I dare say she was visiting friends.'

His 'Probably' was non-committal, and she put down the phone with another smile. The path of true love never did run smooth, she informed a rather surprised Miss Thrisp.

True enough. But that wasn't going to deter the Professor from his own particular path. His secretary was bidden to obtain back copies of the *Lady* and he searched the advertisements until he found what he sought…

Life was very different for Julia now. The work was interesting and she enjoyed it; the other women were friendly and they were well looked after. There was a vast park to walk in when she had finished work in the evening, and an estate Land Rover took the staff to the village or Haltwhistle when they were free. All the same, she was lonely. It was a splendid job, she told herself. The country around was vast and lonely and very much to her liking, and although she didn't regret leaving London it was impossible to forget Gerard. She consoled herself with the thought that he would have forgotten her by now, but that couldn't stop her loving him.

She took to getting up early and walking in the park before breakfast. It was peaceful there: birds singing, distant sounds coming from the Home Farm, subdued noise from the great house waking to another day. It was such a vast place that she had only seen a little of it, and nothing of its owners.

She had been there for almost two weeks when a particularly splendid morning got her out of bed earlier than usual. She showered and dressed and drank her early-morning tea and let herself out of her room. There was no one about and she crossed the courtyard and went into the parkland beyond. Part of it was wooded, and there was a lake which dribbled into a small stream, and on such a morning it was a delight to the eye.

She wandered along and presently sat down on a tree stump, allowing her thoughts to wander too. She supposed that sooner or later she would go back to London, find herself a small flat and put her talents to good use. At least she would have a reference, and there were museums and art galleries and private houses who would employ her. And, although she might never see the Professor, she would be near him...

A cheerful 'Good morning'got her to her feet. A man was coming towards her, a young man with a pleasant rugged face. There were two dogs with him who crowded round her, tails wagging.

'You'll be one of the needle women,' said the man cheerfully. 'I heard Mother saying that there were one or two new ladies.' He held out a hand. 'Menton— Colin Menton.'

Julia smiled at him, warmed by his friendliness. 'Gracey,' she said in her turn. 'Julia. How do you do?'

They shook hands and he asked, 'Where are you from?'

'London.'

'You're a long way from home. Do you like it here? It is really rather different.'

'I didn't live in a very nice part of London; this seems like heaven.'

'It is.' They were strolling back towards the house. 'But it's not to everyone's taste—too quiet.'

'That's why it's heaven.' They had reached the court
yard. 'I must go.'

'Nice meeting you. Perhaps we shall see each other
again. Do you go walking each morning?'

'Well, yes.'

'Then we'll meet again.'

She thought about him while she stitched patiently.
It had been pleasant to talk to someone of her own age;
the other needlewomen were really friendly, and she
got on well with them, but they were twice her age and
Jenny went to her home when she was free. Julia explored when she was free. Haltwhistle was near enough
for her half-day expeditions. It was a small market town
with a fine church, and she sent picture postcards to
Ruth and Monica, quite forgetting that they might be
shown to the Professor.

One day she got a lift to the small village of Green-
head. The road running through it was close to the
Roman Wall and she walked for miles until she found
a side road which took her back to Haltwhistle and
eventually back to the estate. It was a long walk and
she enjoyed every minute of it. She didn't feel lonely
in the country and she had her thoughts of Gerard to
keep her company.

She had done the right thing, she told herself; she
had no intention of mooning after a man who hardly
noticed her. Once or twice she had thought they could
have been friends, but that had been a flash in the pan.
And anyway there was always the possibility that Gerard would have gone back to Holland.

The thought of never seeing him again was unbearable, but she would have to learn to bear it and it would surely be easier as time passed. There was always the chance that they might meet… She would stay at the estate for as long as there was work for her, and then she would have to decide her future and what better place in which to do it than this remote countryside?

She wrote cheerful letters to Ruth and Monica, though both of them were mystified as to why she shouldn't want anyone to know where she was. But since she seemed so happy and content with the job, and they were both fully occupied with their own lives, they didn't pursue the matter further. Perhaps if the Professor had mentioned her on one of his infrequent visits they might have given it more thought…

A few days later Julia met Colin Menton again. The day's work was finished and she was crossing the courtyard to go to her room. It was late afternoon and still warm. She would go for a walk before supper and then write letters.

He met her halfway. 'Hello, finished work for the day? I don't suppose you feel like a walk? I'm going to the other end of the park to see if the trees we planted are doing well.' He smiled at her. 'Do say yes.'

Julia laughed. 'Well, all right, yes.'

The park was vast, merging now and again into fields of rough grass. Close to the house the gardens had been skilfully laid out, and there was a lake bordered by trees, but presently they followed a path into the trees on the edge of the park. It was pleasant walking and they found plenty to talk about. He begged her to call him Colin and told her that he'd been spending a month or two at his home before taking up a post abroad as an agricultural adviser. 'I shall be getting married before we go,' he confided.

Julia sensed a wish to talk about his fiancée. 'Is she pretty?' she asked.

The rest of their walk was taken up with a detailed description of his fiancée's perfections, and as they neared the house again he said awkwardly, 'Have I been boring you? Only I do like to talk about her.'

'Well, of course you do. She sounds a perfect dear, as well as being so pretty. I'm sure you'll both be very happy. How much longer will you be here?'

'Ten days. We're being married from her home in Wiltshire. We didn't want a big wedding, but you know what mothers are.'

They were standing in the courtyard. 'I enjoyed our walk. I suppose you wouldn't like to drive over to Hexham? I have to see someone there but it shouldn't take too long. There is a splendid abbey there that you might like to visit if you're interested.'

'I should like that. I get two half-days in the week—Tuesday and Thursday, both in the morning.'

'Next Tuesday? It's no distance—fifteen miles or so. If we left around nine o'clock we could have coffee before I see this fellow. You can look round and visit the abbey and I'll meet you for lunch.'

'I have to be back at work by two o'clock.'

'Easily done. We can lunch early.'

Julia agreed; the prospect of an outing was inviting and there might be time to do some shopping.

Jenny, working beside her on the worn tapestry they

were patiently repairing, gave her a quick glance as they started to stitch.

'How are you getting on?' she wanted to know. 'This is a grand job. If we ever get our time off together you must come home with me. You've no idea how marvellous it is to be back with the family. You look perky. Have you made any friends?'

Julia nodded. 'And I walk miles—I love walking and the country is beautiful. I met Mr Menton one morning. He's offered me a lift to Hexham—I'd like to see the abbey and do some shopping.'

'Young Mr Menton? He's nice—getting married soon, did you know?'

'Yes, he told me about his fiancée and the job he's going to. He's leaving very shortly. Will the family go to the wedding? What happens here if they do? Will we still be open to the public?'

'I shouldn't think so. We'll be told, I suppose.' Jenny gave Julia an enquiring look. 'It's likely that there will be enough work for us until early next year. There are the curtains in the drawing room to mend and that wall tapestry in the hall. It'll be cold here after London. Will you stay?'

'Why not? Unless I have a good reason to go back to London. I have two married sisters; they might have babies or need me for something or other.'

She spoke cheerfully but, much though she liked her surroundings, the prospect of being there for almost another six months was daunting. After all she had money now, enough to get a mortgage on a small flat—not necessarily in London—and find work. She choked back dismay at the prospect. She was letting herself drift; she who had never been faint-hearted in her life before.

That evening she borrowed an atlas. She mustn't be too far away from Ruth and Monica, but far away enough from London and Gerard. She made a list of likely towns and went to bed feeling that she had at last begun to organise her future.

And on Tuesday afternoon, bending over her stitching, she went over the trip to Hexham. It had been a success. She and Colin had fallen into an easy friendship and there had never been a lack of something to talk about during the short drive. They had had coffee before parting, and she had spent a happy morning looking round the abbey and then looking at the shops, buying some books and other small items on a list she had made. They had met at a pleasant old pub and had an early lunch before driving back. It had been a pleasant morning and she would miss his cheerful face and casual friendliness. He was leaving on Thursday, and she had said that she would say goodbye to him before she set off on a walk before starting work that afternoon.

He was to leave early, but she had breakfast before she went out to the yard. He had already said goodbye to his family and his car, an Aston Martin, was there, with him in the driving seat.

Julia lent over to shake his hand. 'Go carefully, and have a lovely wedding.'

'Oh, we will. I'm glad we met, Julia. I hope you will have a lovely wedding to some lucky chap one day.' He kissed her cheek just as the Professor drove the Rolls into the yard.

Chapter 7

Julia straightened up with a laugh—and saw the Professor's car. The wild rush of delight at the sight of him turned at once to a mixture of panic and bad temper. Panic because he might have bad news of her sisters, and temper because she was wearing an old skirt and a cotton top, suitable for a walk in the country but not for meeting him of all people.

She waved in answer to Colin's wave, and watched the Professor get out of his car and come towards her. She would have liked to have run to meet him, but something in his leisurely approach stopped her. Yet when he reached her his, 'Hello, Julia,' was uttered in the mildest of voices.

She asked breathlessly, 'How did you know I was here?' She frowned. 'I asked Ruth…'

'Who told me nothing. But rest assured that I am quite capable of finding you if I wish to do so.'

'So why did you?'

'There would be no point in telling you that at the moment. I'm glad to see that you have found friends. Or should I say a friend.' His voice was silky.

'Colin?' She wanted to shake his calm. 'Oh, yes, we've had some pleasant walks. He is the son of the house.' She added, without much truth, 'We've seen quite a lot of the surrounding country—Hadrian's Wall...'

When he didn't speak she asked uneasily, 'Do you have friends in this part of the world?'

'Colleagues at the hospital in Carlisle.'

'Oh, you're doing something there?'

He didn't answer, only asked, 'When do you work?'

'From nine in the morning until five o'clock. We get breaks for meals and two half-days.' She added defiantly, 'I'm loving it.'

'And is this a half-day?'

She said yes so reluctantly that he smiled.

'Then perhaps you will spend it with me? We could drive to Hadrian's Wall and have a walk and an early lunch. When must you start work?'

'Two o'clock.'

'An hour or two in the fresh air and a brisk walk will do you good.'

'I go walking each morning...'

He said smoothly, 'Ah, yes, but now that you will be walking alone it is never as inviting, is it? Go and do something to your hair. I'll wait here. Ten minutes?'

'I haven't said I would come...'

He smiled and her heart turned over. 'But you will!'

She went to her room then and got into a cotton jersey dress, and did her hair again and made up her face nicely, all the while telling herself that she was mad to be doing it. On the other hand, he would soon be gone again, back to London. Surely an hour or so in his company wouldn't make any difference to her resolve not to see him again. She wondered briefly how he had discovered where she was... She didn't waste time thinking about it; half-days were precious, and every minute of them had to be enjoyed. She hurried back to the yard and found the Professor leaning against his car, talking to Jenny, on her way to start her morning's work.

'Lucky you,' she called cheerfully. 'Don't forget the time, though in your shoes I would.'

Julia tried not to see the wink which accompanied the remark.

The Professor stowed her into the Rolls and drove away, embarking at the same time on a casual conversation which put her instantly at ease. She reflected that this unexpected meeting should have bothered her, but it hadn't. It seemed the most natural thing in the world that Gerard should have appeared out of the blue, as it were, and that they should be spending the morning together as if they were old friends. But, of course, it wasn't that at all; he had felt the need of company and had an hour or so to spare.

The Professor glanced at her puzzled face and smiled to himself. Just for once Julia had lost her tongue.

He took her to Brampton, not many miles away, gave

her coffee at the hotel there, parked the car, booked a table for lunch and marched her off briskly. Hadrian's Wall was no distance, and when they reached it they walked beside it. It was quiet and the countryside was empty; the road was nearby but there was little traffic, and it was cool enough to make walking a pleasure. And they talked.

It was surprising how easy it was to talk to him, thought Julia, discussing her future, her doubts and problems until at a certain moment she stopped abruptly. She was a fool, telling him all this; he wouldn't be in the least interested. He might even be bored.

'Do you know this part of the world?' she wanted to know.

'Not well enough.' He had seen her sudden reluctance to talk about herself and so slipped easily into a casual discussion of the country around them. Presently she was lulled into the idea that he hadn't been listening, had shown no sign of interest. She had been a fool, telling him of her plans when she had made up her mind not to see him again. She supposed that being in love made one foolish...

Back at the hotel they had lunch in a delightful restaurant, its windows overlooking a well-kept garden. The place was half full and the service friendly. Julia, hungry after their walk, made a splendid meal. The food was well cooked and plentiful on the estate, but the food set before her now was something of a treat: game soup, a meal in itself, roast beef with Yorkshire pudding to dream of, roasted parsnips, crisp and golden brown, and a crême brulée which melted in the mouth.

'I'm not going to offer you wine,' said the Professor, 'or you'll droop over your curtains!' So they drank tonic water.

He drove her back afterwards, making casual small talk, and back in the court yard, when she would have uttered her carefully rehearsed thank-you speech, he said abruptly, 'I'm glad you enjoyed the morning. You must get Colin to take you again while the weather is good.'

Julia could think of nothing to say but, 'Yes', and watched him drive away while all she wanted to say crowded her tongue unuttered. Perhaps it was just as well, she thought unhappily. For a short time she had thought that perhaps he had sought her out because he had wanted to see her again, but that wasn't so; he had had a morning to spare and had used it to make sure that she was all right so that he could tell Ruth. It was a lowering thought...

The Professor drove himself back to London deep in thought. Julia had been glad to see him, he had seen the look on her face, but had the delight been at the sight of him or because he was someone from home? And this man, this young man, reflected Gerard, deeply aware that at thirty-six he could no longer be considered young. Though a man of no conceit, he was aware that he could make her fall in love with him—but he had no intention of doing that; she must learn to love him of her own free will. That they were meant for each other was something he never doubted.

He didn't think that she was happy; she liked her

work and the surroundings in which she lived but she was sad about something. There was nothing he could do for the moment only have patience.

He phoned Ruth when he got back and gave her a reassuring account of Julia.

'I suppose he went to the Carlisle hospital,' she told Thomas, 'and discovered where she was.'

And Thomas, who knew better, agreed with her.

A week or two went by. The weather was unusually warm and dry, even in the north of the country, and sitting for long hours stitching was tiring. Julia, taking her solitary early morning walks, made plans for the future and then discarded them. There was a rumour that once the tapestry they were working on was finished they would be asked to work at the town-house the family owned in London. The local women wouldn't go, but Jenny and she might be offered work there. That wouldn't do. Forgetting Gerard was harder than she had thought it would be. And how could she forget him when she loved him? The only thing to do was to go away, as far as possible…

She wrote cheerful letters to Ruth and Monica and scanned their replies for a mention of the Professor, but it was as though he had never existed.

It was some time after four o'clock in the afternoon when the fire broke out. A sightseer, disregarding the 'No Smoking' notices, had lighted a cigarette and tossed the still burning match to one side. It had fallen onto the curtains shrouding the state dining room windows. Dry as dust, and fragile with age, they had smouldered unnoticed for some minutes and then suddenly burst into flames which had swept across the room and into an adjoining salon. From there it leapt from wall-panelling to tapestries, to chairs and tables, through the wide archway and into the music room beyond...

It was a large, rambling mansion, and there was no one in that wing when the fire started. By the time the alarm was raised it had spread, burning the telephone cable and the fire alarm which connected it to the police station at Haltwhistle.

There was a certain amount of panic and great confusion, so that no one remembered that up on the fourth floor, under the roof, there were seven women, stitching...

Sounds from outside the house were muted in the attics; cars and coaches arriving with visitors were sounds so frequent that they were disregarded, as were the voices. The windows at the front of the house were kept shut on open days, since fumes from the cars might harm the delicate materials they were working upon, but that afternoon Julia's ear caught another sound: voices raised in alarm—more than alarm, terror: And seconds later she smelled the smoke. She went to a window and looked out and saw one wing of the house in flames, people getting into cars and buses and a confused mass of those who didn't know what to do...

By then the other women had left their work and joined her at the window.

'We'd better make haste and get out.' One of the women from the village, older than the rest, spoke urgently. 'We're quite safe if we go down the back stairs.' And indeed the fire was reassuringly distant from them.

But when they reached the second landing it was to find the staircase below already alight.

So far there had been no panic, they weren't women to do that, but now the sight of the smoke and the flames creeping around the staircase on the floor below shattered their calm. Someone screamed.

'The garden door at the back of the house—there's a small staircase…'

Someone told the screamer to be quiet, in a voice rendered hoarse by anger and fright, and they ran through the main part of the house along corridors and passages Julia had never seen before and found the staircase. It was still intact, but the floor below was well alight.

Julia caught one of the older women by the arm. 'If we go back to the attics we can break the windows—there's a narrow parapet, isn't there? Someone will see us; there will be a fire escape…'

The woman nodded. 'We're going back,' she shouted above the panicky voices. 'They'll get us off the roof.'

They went back the way they had come, and although there was a smell of burning and wisps of smoke and a great deal of noise the fire was out of sight. And once back in the attics they set about breaking the glass in the windows at the front of the house, shouting for help as they did so.

The fire had spread to the centre of the house by now, and there were a great many people running to and fro, but the noise of the fire carried away the voices of the women in the attic and no one saw them.

It was Julia who picked up a stool and hurled it over the parapet, and within seconds they were all tossing anything they could carry into the sweep below. And now they could see upturned faces, waving arms, people running and the heartening sight of the first of the fire engines belting up the drive. The third floor was alight now and the hoses were turned on to it. If the fire could be halted there, thought Julia, we'd have a good chance of getting out. She said so, loudly, and the little band of terrified women took heart.

It was five minutes—the longest five minutes of her life, reflected Julia later—before the fire rescue team arrived, and another five minutes saw the first of them being edged over the parapet and into the arms of the fireman perched on the end of the fire escape. In unspoken consent, the women who had children were the first to be rescued, then the two elderly ladies who were married to estate workers, and lastly Jenny and Julia.

And Julia, waiting alone in a blur of held-back terror, allowed herself to scream—for there was no one to hear above the roar of the flames below. She felt better once she had screamed; she had nothing to be frightened about now, the firemen would be back for her in a few minutes. Only she wished with her whole heart that Gerard was there beside her telling her not to worry...

The attic was filling with smoke when she was helped over the parapet.

The Professor was home early. He went to his study with Wilf and Robbie, closely followed by Mrs Potts and the tea tray, and sat down at his desk. He had a good deal of paperwork to do, and notes for a lecture to write. He drank his tea, gave his dogs the biscuits and turned to the pile of papers on his desk. But before picking up his pen, he turned on the radio.

Just in time for a news flash that an estate in the north of England was on fire. No casualties had been reported so far, said the voice, but it was feared that there might be people trapped in the house.

The Professor's instinct was to leap from his chair into his car and drive north within seconds. Instead he picked up the phone and dialled the hospital; Thomas was still on duty. He didn't waste words. 'I'm flying up within half an hour,' he told Thomas. 'Tell Ruth that I will bring Julia back here.'

'You're sure it's where Julia is?'

'They gave the name on the radio.'

The rush hour hadn't started. The Professor, as good as his word, left his house within minutes, outwardly calm, and made for the airport. He concentrated on flying, firmly keeping other thoughts at bay.

Almost at his journey's end, after picking up a hire car, he could see the glow of the fire ahead of him, and shortly after he turned into the drive leading to the house. He was stopped before he was halfway there.

'Sorry, sir, you can't go any further. Can I help?'

'Indeed you can. My future wife works here. She would have been on the top floor. I've come to take her back home.'

At the officer's look of enquiry, he said, 'London. I've flown up. I'm a surgeon at one of the hospitals there.'

'Then you'd best find her. There's a rare old muddle checking everyone's out of the building, and quite a few have been taken off to hospital for a check-up or been taken home—local folk.' He nodded at the Professor. 'I'll phone through.'

The Professor drove on, parked the hire car and got out. The sweep in front of the house was crowded with people: firemen, police, estate workers and people from the village. The officer he spoke to was helpful; everyone had been got out and had been sent home, if they lived in the village, or into hospital at Carlisle… It was an elderly man standing near them who interrupted.

'Not all of 'em,' he said. 'There's one of the sewing ladies over at my place with the missus. Not from hereabouts, she isn't, and got nowhere to go.' He added, 'I'm the head gardener here.'

He glanced at the Professor. 'You'd best go and take a look. It's the end cottage, on its own.' He waved an arm. Tell the missus I sent you.'

The Professor thanked him and made his way through the throng, holding down his impatience and anxiety with a firm hand. When he reached the cottage he paused for a moment as an elderly woman came to the door. She was a sensible woman, who listened to his quick explanation and told him to go into the kitchen. 'If it's a girl called Julia, it's her,' she told him softly. 'She's not hurt, but she was the last to be rescued and it's shook her up badly.'

He thanked her quietly and pushed open the kitchen door. Julia was sitting in a chair by the old-fashioned stove, and when she looked up at him the Professor forgot that he was tired, hungry and thirsty. He would have flown ten times the distance he had to see that look on her face.

He spoke quickly, because he could see that she was struggling with tears.

'It's all right, my dear. We'll go home just as soon as I've let someone know that you are in safe hands.' He smiled down at her with the kindliness of an old family friend or elder brother.

She found her voice. 'Gerard, oh, Gerard. I've been so terrified and I didn't know what to do—and then you came…'

She gave him a lop-sided, watery small smile, and perhaps it was as well that the gardener's wife came in then.

'You could do with a cup of tea. You'll just have to see the police—the one who got the others sorted out is in that car with the blue light.' She turned to Julia. 'You do know this gentleman, miss?'

Julia nodded. 'Oh, yes, we're…' She stopped and added, 'He knows my family too; he'll take me home.'

'Then I'll boil the kettle, sir, and you come back as soon as you can. I dare say you've got a way to go.'

The Professor only smiled and went away, and Julia said, 'London.'

'You mean to say he's come up from London?'

'No, no. He sometimes comes to Carlisle, to the hospital—he's a surgeon.'

'Well, that's good fortune indeed. Here's your tea. Drink it hot; you're still all of a shake.'

Which was true enough. She had drunk half of it when the Professor came back. He drank his own tea,

thanked the gardener's wife and walked Julia to the
car. He had an arm around her and she was glad of it,
for her legs felt like jelly. When they reached the car,
he picked her up and popped her in, and fetched a rug
from the boot and wrapped her in it. And all this with
the air of an elder brother...

The car was warm and comfortable and she closed
her eyes, only opening them when a police officer put
his head through the open window.

'You're Miss Julia Gracey? I'm just checking that
everything is OK.'

She managed a smile. 'Yes, that's me, and this is
Professor van der Maes, who is a friend of my family.'

He nodded. 'There'll be someone round to see you
at home, just to make sure that you are fit and well—
get the record straight.' He grinned at her. 'You had a
lucky escape, miss.' He turned to the Professor. 'Safe
journey, sir.'

Gerard got into the hire car and drove back down
the drive and on to the road. They would have to stop
on the way to the airport. He was tired and hungry, and
Julia, even if she slept, would need a break and food. He
glanced sideways at her, cocooned in the rug.

'We should be back in a couple of hours. We will
stop on the way for a hot drink and something to eat.
Are you all right?'

He sounded reassuringly normal. 'Yes, thank you.
Oh, Gerard, how fortunate that you were here—I mean,
at the hospital in Carlisle.' When he didn't answer she
said, 'You were there, weren't you? I mean, how else
could you have come so quickly?'

'I heard the news when I got home...'

She peered at him over the rug. 'You came all the way from London?' Her voice was an unbelieving squeak.

'Yes. Now go to sleep, Julia.'

And, while she was still feeling indignant about that, she did.

The Professor looked at Julia's sleeping face. She was pale and smelled of smoke and her hair was in a tangle, but she was here, beside him, safe and sound. He kissed her grubby cheek and drove on.

At a service station he woke her gently. 'I'll get us tea and something to eat,' he told her. 'But first I'll walk you to the facilities.'

Julia, feeling better, was soon shovelled back into the car and told to stay awake.

The tea was hot and sweet and there were sandwiches, cut thick and filled with corned beef. They ate and drank in comfortable silence, the quiet dark around them.

Later, halfway through their short flight, Julia said, 'Would you mind if I went to sleep again for a little while? I'm tired.'

He had expected that, and had already tucked a rug round her. He held his own tiredness at bay while he considered plans and discarded them. Once Julia had recovered from her fright and shock she would probably disappear again; the last thing he wanted was for her to feel beholden to him.

In London, he had to stop once more. 'I'm going to be sick,' said Julia, suddenly awake. He stopped, hauled her briskly out of the car and held her while she heaved and choked and then burst into tears. He mopped her face, popped her back into the car, tucked her up once more and gave her a handful of paper tissues. 'You'll feel better now, try and rest again.'

She closed her eyes but she didn't sleep. She thought about him. He had been quick and gentle and matter-of-fact and impersonal, and she sensed a professional remoteness. And why should it be otherwise? she reflected sadly. The only times they met hadn't been because they had wanted to but by force of circumstances. *Why* had he come all the way from London? She was too sleepy to think about that, but just as she was dozing off she muttered, 'Ruth would have been worried—and he likes her and Thomas.'

The Professor smiled to himself. It was as good a reason as any.

It was late when he stopped before his house. He had phoned before they had left the estate and asked Mrs Potts to get a room ready for Julia. 'And go to bed,' he had told her, 'for we shall be back after midnight.'

Julia was awake again. He got out of the car and, with an arm round her, opened his front door. There was a wall lamp alight and as they went in Mrs Potts, cosily wrapped in a woolly dressing gown, came down the staircase.

'There you are,' she observed, 'and tired to death, I'll be bound, sir. Now, just you go to the kitchen and eat and drink what's there while I take miss upstairs. She'll have a nice warm bath and bed, and a glass of warm milk.' She nodded her head. 'And you'll go to bed too, sir.'

The Professor smiled at her. 'You're an angel, Mrs Potts. Have you had any sleep yourself?'

'Bless you, sir, I went to bed early, seeing as how things were.'

He picked up Julia and carried her upstairs and laid her on the bed in a small bedroom.

'Don't go,' said Julia, clutching his arm. 'I haven't thanked you.' She sounded meek and tearful, and later she would feel ashamed of herself for being so silly.

'We will talk in the morning,' said the Professor bracingly, and went away. Next she heard Mrs Potts's soft voice. 'Now, we'll have these clothes off you. You just sit there while I help you. Then a nice bath, and I'll wash your hair, and then bed and a good sound sleep. The Professor's going to bed too and you can both have a nice chat in the morning.'

So Julia was bathed and shampooed, and all the while Mrs Potts talked in a soothing voice and finally tucked her up in bed and told her to go to sleep. Which she did.

She woke to hear dogs barking and the muted sounds of a household getting ready for the day and, reassured, went back to sleep.

It was mid-morning when she sat up in bed, feeling perfectly well again, and found Mrs Potts standing by the bed with a breakfast tray.

'Oh, I could have got up for breakfast,' said Julia. 'I've given you so much trouble already and I feel fine...'

Mrs Potts arranged the tray on a bed table. 'Now

just eat your breakfast, Miss Gracey. Your sister will be here with some clothes for you presently.'

'Ruth? How did she know that I was here?'

'Why, the Professor phoned her before he went to the hospital this morning. She's to stay for lunch.'

'Lunch? What's the time, Mrs Potts?'

'A little after ten o'clock.'

'The Professor said he'd see me in the morning. He's still here?'

'Lor' bless you, miss, he's been gone these past two hours.' Mrs Potts shook her head. 'There's no stopping him. A couple of hours' sleep and he's off again. I'm to tell you he'll see you some time.'

Julia drank her tea and swallowed tears with it. 'Yes, of course. I've given him a lot of trouble. I'll go back with my sister after lunch. Is there somewhere I could write him a note?'

'I'll have pen and paper ready for you,' promised Mrs Potts, and left Julia to finish a breakfast which tasted of sawdust. He had gone to a great deal of trouble to rescue her, but now that was accomplished he would forget her—a momentary nuisance in his ordered life.

'But I'm not going to cry about it,' said Julia, and ate the breakfast she no longer wanted, then got up and showered. Wrapped in a voluminous dressing gown produced by Mrs Potts, she went downstairs, where she was shown into a small, cosily furnished room. There was a small writing desk with paper and pen set ready for her.

'Your sister will be here presently,' said Mrs Potts comfortably, and left her to write her note.

Not an easy thing to do, Julia discovered. She had to

make several attempts before she was satisfied, but she hoped that her warm thanks coupled with the assumption that she was unlikely to see him—his work—her intention to leave London as soon as possible—would strike the right note. She had just sealed the envelope when Ruth arrived, bringing clothes and agog to hear exactly what had happened.

When Julia had finished telling her everything she said, 'I didn't know anything about it until Gerard phoned Thomas to say that he had found you and that you were safe…'

Julia said slowly, 'I thought he had come because you were worried about me?'

'No, no. Thomas told me that Gerard phoned him around half past four—he'd heard a newsflash about the fire. He was on the point of leaving.'

She saw the look on Julia's face and said quickly, 'You'll stay with us, of course, love, until you decide what you want to do.'

Julia said slowly, 'Would you mind if I went to Monica for a while?'

'No, of course not. It will be quiet there; you will have time to think.'

Something Julia didn't want to do, for she would only think of Gerard, who had rescued her and left a laconic message that he would see her some time. Well, that was something she could deal with. If she went to Monica he could forget her, something he must be wanting to do, only fate seemed intent on throwing her in his path.

They had their lunch, thanked Mrs Potts for her kindness and took a taxi to Ruth's home. Thomas was at the hospital and Julia seized the opportunity to phone Monica and invite herself to stay. 'Just for a week. I won't be in the way, but it would be nice to have a few days while I make up my mind what I'll do.'

'Come for as long as you like,' said Monica largely. 'No one will bother you. It must have been horrible, Julia, and so far away. You must have been glad to see Gerard.'

'Yes,' said Julia. 'I was. He's been very kind…'

'More than kind,' said Monica dryly. 'Come when you like, Julia; there's a room ready for you. The nearest station is Cullompton. George will meet you with the car.'

Thomas came home presently. He was glad to see her, and wanted to know about the fire—and never mentioned Gerard. She said in a carefully casual voice, 'I haven't seen Gerard since we got back here. I hope he wasn't too tired…'

'Gerard's never tired,' said Thomas. 'He's done a day's work and he's dining out this evening with the widow of one of his patients who has been angling for him for some time.'

Well, thought Julia peevishly, I don't need to waste any concern on the man. I hope she catches him and leads him a simply horrible life. She smiled brilliantly at her brother-in-law and wished she could go and shut herself somewhere dark and lonely and cry her heart out.

And Ruth made it worse by observing that Olivia Travis was one of the most beautiful women she had ever met. 'If I were a man I'd fall in love with her the moment I saw her.'

Thomas grunted, which could have meant anything.

Julia stayed for three days at Ruth's. She had to buy clothes and be interviewed by someone from the police, who assured her that they merely wished to be sure that she was quite unharmed and safe with her family. And each morning when she woke she wondered if she would see the Professor. But he didn't come. Nor did Thomas speak of him. She told herself that she was glad. He could at least have acknowledged her note, though. Perhaps he hadn't read it. His secretary might have put it with the junk mail and all the invitations which he didn't wish to accept.

On the third day she made arrangements to go to Monica. Ruth asked worriedly, 'Will you stay for a while, love? Come back here when you want to.'

'I'm being a worry for them,' Julia told herself as she got ready for bed. 'I must find something somewhere and settle down.'

Perhaps in some small town in the West Country. A small flat—she could rent one—or a shop. She had money enough; there was no reason why she shouldn't make a pleasant life for herself. She might even marry...

Out of the question, of course. She loved Gerard and no one else would do.

Up until the very last minute, until the train was leaving the station, she had the forlorn hope that she would see Gerard. But there was no sign of him. He'd be in Holland, thought Julia despairingly, and then, as the train swept past the suburbs and through green fields and trees, That's it, she told herself. You're going to forget him just as he's forgotten you. You're wasting your life hankering after a person who doesn't care a straw for you.

After which heartening speech she picked up the magazine she had bought and began to read it. It was full of artfully posed teenagers wearing what looked like fancy dress costumes, and they were all painfully bony, with sharp elbows and jutting collarbones. Julia felt fat and almost middle-aged just looking at them. She handed the magazine over to a young woman who had been peering at it from the opposite seat and then looked out of the window. The country looked lovely and she felt a sudden surge of interest in the future.

You never know what's round the corner, thought Julia.

Chapter 8

George, driving Julia away from Cullompton station, didn't bother her with questions. He thought that she looked tired and, despite her bright chatter, unhappy. He would leave the questions to Monica, he decided.

Monica was waiting for them with a string of questions and they had a cheerful lunch together.

'I'll take you over the house again, now that we've had the alterations done,' said Monica. 'It's far too large for us, of course, but we love it. And now we've got central heating and the plumbing works, it's easy to run.'

They had gone to Julia's bedroom after lunch and Monica was sitting on the bed while Julia unpacked.

'Is Ruth all right? And Thomas? And have you seen the Professor since you got back? What a man—going all that way to fetch you home. I expect he must have seen how worried Ruth was, but it was a noble thing to do, especially as you don't like each other much.'

Julia had her head in a drawer. 'Yes, it was. I haven't seen him since, though, but I didn't expect to.'

'Ruth told me that there's a beautiful woman lurking!'

'Yes.' Julia emerged rather red in the face. 'I had a present for you, but of course I lost it in the fire. Perhaps we could find something to take its place. This really is a lovely old house, isn't it? Ruth's house is nice, too…'

Monica said concernedly, 'But you haven't a home, love. We do worry about you.'

Julia closed her case and put it tidily under the bed. 'Well, don't. I know exactly what I want to do. Leave London, for a start, and settle in a town between the two of you. I'll rent a flat to start with, and then find a small shop with living space. I shall sell everything to do with needlework and knitting and embroidery. While I'm here, if you don't mind, I shall take a look at some of the small towns round and about. I can hire a car. I know I haven't driven for years but I can't have forgotten how.'

Monica said suddenly, 'Do you ever wish that you'd married Oscar?'

Julia laughed. 'Monica, you must be joking! I'm happy as I am. "Footloose and fancy-free"—isn't that what someone or other wrote?'

Monica laughed too, and didn't believe a word of it.

It was delightful living in the country. The village was a large one with a widespread parish, and Monica and George made her more than welcome, but after a few days she declared her intention of exploring the surrounding countryside with an eye to the future.

Honiton seemed as good a place to start as any. A small market town straddling the main road from London to the West, it was famous for its lace-making and antiques shops, but she discarded it reluctantly. It was too near Monica and too far from Ruth. It needed to be somewhere between her sisters and far enough away from both of them so as not to encroach on their lives. She pored over maps and guidebooks and, sitting one morning with Monica in the garden asked, 'Where's Stourhead?'

'North of Yeovil. Not on a main road but easy to get at. It's a lovely place; we went there a month or so ago. Heavenly gardens and a Palladian house full of treasures.'

'There's an ad in your local newspaper. Guides for the house and people to repair and refurbish the furniture and the hangings. I know I want to start up on my own, but it looks rather inviting.'

She could see Monica's look of uncertainty and knew what she was thinking: that she was wasting time, drifting from one job to another, that she should settle down and make a secure future for herself—that was if she didn't marry, and that didn't seem likely.

Monica said worriedly, 'Yes, that might be a good idea. While you were there you might scout around and find a suitable shop in one of the small towns not too far away. There's Sherborne—the most likely, I should think. Yeovil is nearby, too, but that's quite large—too large for the kind of shop you're thinking of, I imagine. There's Warminster and there's Gillingham and Shaftesbury, but I'm not sure if you could make much of a living with the kind of shop you're thinking of. I'd opt for Sherborne...'

So Julia went to Sherborne and liked what she saw there. It was an abbey town with a well-known public school and the right kind of shops. For the first time since she had returned from the north she felt enthusiastic about her future. She supposed that all this time she had been hoping that she would see Gerard again, that he might even discover that he liked her... But that wasn't going to be the case. Once and for all she would forget him.

Quite sure now that she knew what she wanted to do, she wasted no time. A visit to the town's estate agents left her with a handful of possible shops to buy or lease. She would strike while the iron was hot, she decided, viewing the future through rose-coloured spectacles. And phoned Monica to tell her that she was going to stay the night in Sherborne and inspect what was on offer.

'You haven't got anything with you,' Monica reminded her, so she went out and bought a cheap nightie and a toothbrush and booked in at a quiet hotel five minutes' walk from the town centre. It was already late afternoon, but it was a small town and she had no trouble finding the handful of addresses. The first three were no use at all, tucked away down side streets, but the fourth had possibilities; it was close to the abbey and the main shopping street, tucked in between an antiquarian book shop and a picture gallery. Its window was small, but it was in a good state of repair and the paintwork was fresh. She peered through the glass door. The shop was small too, with a tiny counter and a door behind it. The leaflet claimed that there were living quarters too.

She reached the estate agents as they were about to close and arranged to inspect the shop in the morning.

Momentarily inflated with a strong sense of purpose, she took herself off then to the hotel, had a splendid dinner and slept soundly.

The shop was small but it had possibilities. There was a little room behind it and a kitchen beyond that, and upstairs there was a bedroom and a shower and a toilet. She could, she decided, make it home without too much expense. And she could rent it on a year's lease which meant that she wouldn't need to dig too deep into her capital.

She said that she would rent it subject to a surveyor's report. 'I'll need a solicitor,' she said, 'and I'd like to take possession as soon as possible.'

She went back to Monica's that afternoon, her head full of plans and ideas. She would stay in Sherborne, get the place fit to live in, buy her stock and move in at her leisure.

Monica, told the news, nodded her head in approval. 'If that is what you want,' she said cautiously. 'I've no doubt you'll make a success of it, and you're bound to make friends—if that is what you want?'

Julia assured her that it was. Which wasn't quite true, of course. What she wanted was for Gerard to fall in love with her, marry her and live with her happily ever after, but, since that was something which wasn't going to happen, she must turn herself into a successful businesswoman.

'You'll probably meet a nice man,' said Monica.

There was no point in telling her that she already had.

'I'll have to go back to London to see the solicitor and the bank. May I stay here for a few more days while the agent gets organised at Sherborne? I'll have to sign papers and so on.'

'Stay as long as you like, love. You know you'll always be welcome here. You're not far away, and if you get a car... Could you afford that?'

'I think so. A small second-hand one.'

Several days later she went back to London and told herself that she felt relief to hear that the Professor was in Holland.

The solicitor was helpful in a cautious way; he hoped that she had thought about the drawbacks as well as the advantages of setting up a small business.

'A young lady on her own,' he said, shaking a grey head. He hadn't moved with the times, but she liked him for his fatherly concern. And the bank manager was cautious too. He would have liked her to have invested her money in something safe, so that she would have had a small steady income, and possibly lived with one or other of her sisters...

While she had been working on the estate she had picked up quite a lot of information about the wholesale firms which had supplied the materials for the work there, and it had given her some idea as to how to contact them; she intended to sell tapestries, knitting wools, embroidery silks and patterns as well as canvases and embroidery frames and anything else needful to the serious embroiderer. She would also knit herself, and sell what she knitted. She wouldn't allow herself any doubts; she had always been able to cope and this was a challenge...

She was in Ruth's sitting room, and making yet another list, when the Professor opened the door and walked in.

She sat back and gaped at him, unable to think of anything to say.

'Close your mouth, my dear,' said the Professor. 'Why are you so surprised?'

'I thought you were in Holland.' Mingled with the delight of seeing him again was annoyance that he had sneaked in on her without warning.

He sat down and stretched out his legs, the picture of ease. 'So you're about to become a businesswoman? No doubt you will be very successful, make lots of money and fulfil whatever dreams you have...'

'Don't be sarcastic,' said Julia waspishly. 'And it's none of your business.'

'You're cross. Are you not pleased to see me? I thought that we might have dinner together this evening. We could talk over old times?'

She eyed him carefully. To spend an evening with him would be a dream come true, but on the other hand she had promised herself that she would forget him. The Professor, watching her face, said in just the right offhand manner, 'I'm going back to Holland and you are leaving London.'

In that case, reflected Julia, there would be no harm done, would there? He was making it clear that they weren't likely to see each other again.

'All right. Though I'm sure we won't find anything to talk about.'

'No? The cottage? My home in Amsterdam? Mrs Beckett? I think we may be able to sustain some kind of conversation!' He got to his feet. 'I'll call for you at half past seven.'

'Shall I dress up?'

It was the kind of remark to make him fall in love with her all over again. One moment so haughty and the next as uncertain as a schoolgirl.

He said gently, 'Something short and pretty. We'll go to Claridge's.'

The moment he had gone she ran up to her room. There was a dress which might do. She hadn't meant to buy it but it had been so pretty: amber chiffon over a silk slip, plain, high-necked, and long-sleeved and elegant. She had bought it because it had seemed to her to stand for all the pretty clothes she had never been able to buy. Well, she would wear it—and even if she never wore it again it would be worth every penny of the money she had squandered on it.

Thomas and Ruth came in together and Julia said at once with a heightened colour, 'I've done the veg for supper and made a fruit pie. You won't mind if I go out? Gerard has asked me to dinner.'

Ruth gave Thomas an 'I told you so' look, and said, 'Oh, nice. Where's he taking you?'

'Claridge's.'

Ruth was on the point of saying, Lucky girl, but changed her mind. Having fallen in love with Thomas, just as he had fallen in love with her, without any doubts or complications, she found it hard to understand why two sensible people like the Professor and her sister could be so slow in discovering that they were meant for each other. She caught Thomas's eye and said instead, 'You could wear that amber chiffon dress...'

Studying herself in the dress later, Julia wondered if she would ever wear the dress again. She knew no one in Sherborne. It would take time to make friends, and they might not be the kind to take her anywhere as splendid as Claridge's. She would make the most of her evening, she promised herself.

She was glad that she was wearing the dress when the Professor came for her. In his sober, beautifully tailored suits he looked the epitome of the well-dressed man, but in a dinner jacket he looked magnificent.

He was standing in the hall talking to Thomas when she went down, but he turned and looked at her as she came down the stairs. 'Very pretty,' he observed, which left her doubtful as to whether he was referring to the dress or her person. She wrapped herself in the paisley shawl—the family heirloom she shared with her sisters—and bade him hello. She assured Ruth that she wouldn't be late back and went out to the car with him. She hoped that they would have the lovely time Ruth had wished them...

The streets were fairly free of traffic but their way took them through the heart of the city. Julia, mindful of good manners, made small talk from time to time, but since he replied in monosyllables she said coolly, 'You don't like me to talk?'

He glanced briefly at her. 'Why should you think that? You are determined to think the worst of me, Julia.'

Suddenly contrite, she said, 'I don't—really, I don't. You've helped me so often, even if you haven't meant to. I mean, circumstances...' She stopped. 'I've made a mess of saying that. I'm sorry. I would like us to part friends.'

'A most laudable notion. I hope that at last you are trying to overcome your initial dislike of me.'

Before she could think of an answer to that he had stopped before Claridge's entrance. And, after that, serious talk, even if she had wanted it, wasn't easy. She left the shawl in the hands of the haughty lady in charge of the cloakroom, rather deflated by the disparaging glance it was given, but her spirits were uplifted by the warm appreciation in Gerard's eyes when she joined him.

They didn't dine immediately but had their drinks in a magnificent room where a small orchestra played gentle background music. The surroundings were of a kind to make even the most uncertain girl feel cherished and beautiful, so that by the time they were seated at a table Julia felt both. Moreover, she was sitting opposite the man she loved, even if it was for the very last time. Nothing must spoil this, their final meeting...

She might be head over heels in love, but it hadn't

spoiled her appetite. They had watercress soup, Dover
Sole with lemon grass and tiny sautéed potatoes, and a
lemon tart that was out of this world—and two glasses
of champagne which gave her eyes a sparkle and her
tongue a ready liveliness. She had, for the moment,
quite forgotten that this was their last meeting...

The Professor, under no illusions as to that, led their
talk from one thing to the other. He saw now that when
Julia forgot that she didn't like him she was entirely
happy in his company, so it was just a question of patience. He had no intention of forcing her hand, so he
would let her have her shop for a while, and once the
first flush of independence had worn off, she would turn
to him. She was a darling, he reflected, but pig-headed,
liable to be contrary. She must find out for herself...

So they had a delightful evening together, and it
wasn't until they got back to Ruth's that Julia remembered that this really was their final meeting. All her
good resolutions came tumbling back into her head, so
that she said stiffly, 'Thank you for a lovely evening;
I enjoyed it. I hope you will...' She began again. 'I expect you're glad to be going back to Holland. Please give
my love to Mrs Beckett when you see her.' She couldn't
help adding, 'Will you come back to England at all?'

'From time to time.' Indeed, he was going to Holland for a short time only, for consultations and hospital commitments there, but he had no intention of
telling her that.

He got out of the car and helped her out and stood,
her hand in his, looking down at her. 'A delightful evening, Julia, thank you for coming.'

She would never know what made her ask then, 'Are you going to get married?' She would have given a great deal to have unsaid her words, but they were spoken now, weren't they? And what did it matter, anyway?

The Professor studied her pink embarrassed face. He said evenly, 'Yes, that is my intention.' Idle curiosity? he wondered. Or could it be more than that?

Julia recovered herself. 'Well, I hope you'll be very happy,' she told him.

'And you, Julia?'

'Oh, I can't wait to do something I've wanted to do for so long…'

'And what is that?'

'Be independent.' How easy it was to tell fibs, she reflected, when one was desperate.

'Ah, yes, of course. I must wish you every success.' He bent his head and kissed her then. A kiss to drive all thoughts of independence out of her head. But he didn't wait for that. He pushed her gently through the door and closed it behind her, and she stood in the hall, listening to the gentle purring of the Rolls as he drove away.

She wasn't going to cry, she told herself, creeping silently to her room to hang up the pretty dress she supposed she would never wear again before getting into bed to weep silently all over Muffin, who had crept up with her. He was Ruth's cat now, but he had a strong affection for Julia and bore patiently with her snuffles and sighs.

Thomas had already left for the hospital by the time she got down to breakfast. Ruth took one look at her face and turned her back to make the toast.

'Did you have a lovely evening? We didn't hear you come in. Was the food good? I suppose it was all rather grand?'

'Well, it was, but you didn't notice it, if you see what I mean. It's a beautiful restaurant and the food was marvellous. It was a lovely evening.'

A remark which Ruth took with a pinch of salt, although she said nothing.

'Monica phoned yesterday evening. I'm to tell you that you're to go there if there is any kind of hitch at Sherborne. You have got everything fixed up?'

'Yes, I'll stay at a bed and breakfast place while I get the shop ready and buy some furniture. That ought not to take too long.'

She had been to a wholesaler and ordered her stock, packed her bags once more and there was nothing to keep her in London. And the Professor had gone back to Holland. The sooner she started her new life the better.

It was raining and chilly when she reached Sherborne, and she was glad that the estate agent had been kind enough to recommend a place where she could stay. She had arranged to go there for a week, but probably it would be longer than that...

The house was in the centre of the town, one of a row of stone-built cottages of a fair size, and when the taxi stopped before its door Julia thought how cosy it looked. But the lady who answered the door didn't look cosy; she was immaculately dressed, not a hair out of place, a no longer youthful face carefully made up. Mrs Legge-Boulter welcomed Julia with chilly courtesy and within five minutes had made it clear that only most unfortunate circumstances had forced her to take in guests.

'It is not at all what I've been used to,' she observed, 'but beggars cannot be choosers, can they?' She laughed, but since she didn't look in the least amused Julia murmured in a non-committal manner as she was led upstairs to her room.

'I serve breakfast at half past eight,' said Mrs Legge-Boulter, 'and my guests are expected to be out of the house by ten o'clock. You may return after six o'clock. At the moment you are the only guest, so you may use the bathroom between nine and ten o'clock in the evening.'

'You don't offer evening meals?' said Julia hopefully.

Her landlady looked affronted. 'My dear Miss Gracey, you can have no idea of the work entailed in providing a room and breakfast for my guests. I am totally exhausted at the end of my day.'

Left alone, Julia examined her room. It was furnished with everything necessary for a bedroom, but the colour scheme was a beige and brown mixture unrelieved by ornaments or pictures. A place to sleep, decided Julia, and hoped that breakfast would be substantial. The sooner she could move into her little shop the better.

She unpacked her things and, since it was mid-afternoon, went into the town. She had tea and then went to take another look at her future home. Tomorrow she would see the estate agent and ask if he would let her have the key. She had signed the papers and paid over the money for the lease and the first month's rent.

She sat over tea, making a list of all the things which had to be done, and then she wandered round the shops, looking for second-hand furniture and the mundane household equipment she would need. She earmarked several items, and then went in search of somewhere she could get her supper.

She found a small café near the abbey, serving light meals until eight o'clock, and she sat over a mushroom omelette and French fries and a pot of coffee until closing time and then returned to Mrs Legge-Boulter's house.

That lady opened the door to her with a thin smile, a request that she should wipe her feet and a reminder that breakfast was at half past eight. 'I must ask you to be punctual; I have my day to organise.'

Not only her day, reflected Julia, mounting the stairs, but the day of any unfortunate soul lodging with her. She had a bath and, mindful of the notice on the door, cleaned it and went to bed. She had a good deal to think about; the next few days were going to be fully occupied. But when she finally closed her eyes she allowed herself to think of Gerard. Even though she never intended to see him again, there was no reason why she shouldn't dream a little of what might have been...

She was tired, so that she slept well, and when she woke her only thoughts were concerned with getting down to breakfast. It was a frugal meal, served by Mrs Legge-Boulter with disdain, as though offering a boiled egg and two slices of toast was an affront to her social status. A miserable meal, decided Julia, gobbling everything in sight and shocking her landlady by asking for more hot water. The tea was already weak...

She left the house before ten o'clock, saw the estate agent, got the shop key and, fortified by coffee and a bun, let herself into what was now, for the moment, her property.

Not a great deal needed doing, she decided. A carpenter for the shop fittings, carpeting for the living room, and a good clean everywhere. So she went to the shops and returned presently with a bucket, broom, dusters and cleaning materials and set to. She paused for lunch and then went in search of a carpenter and a carpet shop.

It took a good deal of the afternoon but she found a carpenter who would come in the morning and also someone who would come and measure the floors. She went back to the café for a meal and then made her way back to Mrs Legge-Boulter's house, where she received the same tepid welcome as before. Really, thought Julia, lying in a hot bath and eating potato crisps, one wondered why her landlady chose to have lodgers when she obviously disliked them so much.

Breakfast was a boiled egg again. At least I shall get slim, thought Julia, and wondered if Gerard might like her better if she wasn't so curvy. A stupid thought, she told herself; he didn't like her whatever shape she was. She might be deeply in love, but it had made no difference to her appetite; she was still hungry when she left the house, and went along to the shop armed with a bag of currant buns, still warm from the oven at the bakers. Munching them, she went round the little place again, quite clear in her head as to what needed doing, so that by the time the carpenter arrived no time was lost. The floors measured, she took herself off to choose carpets, persuading everyone that everything had to be done as quickly as possible. A good morning's work, she decided, eating a splendid lunch in a friendly pub.

Buying a sewing machine and material for curtains took up her afternoon; tomorrow she would get them made and go in search of furniture. Hopefully she would be able to move in by the end of a week...

She had been busy all day, so that it had been fairly easy to forget Gerard. But now, back in her unwelcoming room, she forgot all about the shop and thought only of him. It wouldn't do, she told herself, sitting up in bed making yet another list. The sooner she got the shop open and had her hands full, the better. All the same, before she slept, in her mind's eye she roamed through the house in Amsterdam, remembering its ageold beauty and the endless quiet. She supposed that she would never forget them. She allowed herself a moment to wonder what Gerard was doing before she slept.

He was sitting in his magnificent drawing room and his mother was sitting opposite him, drinking after-dinner coffee by the small fire, for the evenings were cool.

Mevrouw van der Maes was a tall, imposing woman, elegantly dressed, not showing her age save for her white hair, worn in a French pleat. She had good looks still, and bright blue eyes. She sipped her coffee.

'This is delightful, Gerard; I see you so seldom. That

can't be helped, I know. Den Haag is only half an hour's drive away, but that's too far if you've had a long day at the hospital. But I wish I saw more of you.'

'I'm thinking of cutting down on my work in England—not the London hospital but some of the provincial ones.'

'That means that you will make your home base here?' his mother asked, and added, 'You are thinking of getting married at last?'

He smiled. 'I've taken my time, haven't I? But, yes, that is my intention.'

'Do I know her? Oh, my dear, I shall be so happy...'

'An English girl; you may remember I mentioned her coming over here to look after Mrs Beckett?'

'And Nanny loved her, as I'm sure I shall. You will bring her to see me?'

'In a while, I hope.'

Something in his voice made her ask, 'She knows that you want to marry her?'

'No. When we first met it was hardly on the best of terms, and she has been at great pains to let me know that she is indifferent to me. At times she has allowed me to think that she likes me at least, but I think that has been due to circumstances...'

Mevrouw van der Maes asked quietly, 'You have told her that you love her?'

'No, and I've been careful not to show my feelings.'

His mother sighed silently. She loved Gerard deeply, and she was proud of him, his brilliant career, his good looks, his complete lack of pride in his success—and yet despite all those he was behaving like an uncertain youth in love for the first time. Men are so tiresome at times, reflected Mevrouw van der Maes.

There were a great many questions she wanted to ask him, but they must wait. When he had anything to tell her he would do so. Instead she began to talk about family matters.

The Professor, in Holland for a number of consultations, lectures and meetings with colleagues, found time to visit Mrs Beckett. He found her quite her old self again.

'Well, now,' said Nanny, offering a cheek for his kiss, 'how nice to see you, Mr Gerard. Miss Thrisp has been away for a week and I'm ripe for a gossip.'

So he told her all the news and gossip he knew that she enjoyed.

'And what's this I hear about Julia? She writes to me, bless her, but never a word about herself until this very day.' Mrs Beckett got out her specs. 'I had a letter this morning. Dear knows what the girl is doing—opening a shop, if you please. Full of plans, as bright as a button—and such nonsense. Why, she should be getting herself a husband instead of setting up on her own...'

The Professor asked casually, 'And where is this shop to be?'

'Sherborne—that's a small town in Dorset.' She took the letter from a pocket and re-read it. 'She's going to sell wools and embroidery and suchlike, and do a bit of dressmaking if there's a chance.'

Nanny turned the page. 'Here's a bit I missed. What does it say?'

She read it and looked worriedly at the Professor.

'She says not to tell anyone where she is—and now I've told you, Mr Gerard.'

He said placidly, 'Don't worry, Nanny, I won't tell a soul. I'm glad she still writes to you and that she appears to have such a bright future.'

'Future?' said Mrs Beckett pettishly. 'Nonsense. A lovely girl like her, selling wool to old ladies...' She added, 'And I thought you were taken with her...'

She looked at him, sitting at his ease, Jason at his feet, and saw his grin. And then she smiled herself while thoughts crowded into her elderly head: a wedding, babies and small children coming to stay with old Nanny.

But all she said was, 'Well, you've taken your time, Mr Gerard.'

Chapter 9

Spurred on by Julia, the carpenter made shelves and did some small repairs while two men laid a carpet in the living room; two more came to install a small gas stove and a gas fire. The little place was wired for a telephone and she had been promised that she would be connected as soon as possible. Everything was going smoothly, she thought with satisfaction, and took herself off to buy furniture.

She has already found a second-hand furniture shop down a small street, and she spent almost an hour there, searching out a nice small round table and two straight-backed chairs, a bookcase and a rather battered oak stand to hold a table lamp. She chose a chest of drawers too, and an old-fashioned mirror to go with it, and another little table which would do for a bedside stand with a lamp. Pleased with her purchases, she went back into the main street and bought a small easy chair. It cost rather more than she had expected, as did the padded stool for the bedroom and the bed, but she reminded herself that she could afford it.

She stopped for lunch presently, and then went in search of bed linen, towels and tablecloths, pots and pans, cutlery and all the small odds and ends which make up a home. She was tired by the evening, but she was getting everything done so far without a hitch; she slept like a proverbial log in her unwelcoming room and went downstairs in the morning to eat the inevitable egg, her head full of what still had to be done.

The little shop was ready to receive its contents; the first consignment of wool arrived that afternoon and she spent a long time arranging it on the shelves the carpenter had made. And some of the furniture had been delivered.

She saw Mrs Legge-Boulter, who, told that Julia would be leaving the next day, said with an unkind little titter, 'Well, I hope you won't regret opening a shop. I'm sure there isn't much call for wools and embroidery and so on, and that's not in the best shopping area.'

Julia, tired and to tell the truth a bit frightened of the future, said airily, 'I dare say I shall make more of a success of it than you with your bed and breakfast trade.'

To which Mrs Legge-Boulter took thin-lipped exception. 'Not a *trade*, Miss Gracey,' she explained coldly. 'A perfectly genteel way in which gentlefolk may add to their income.'

'Well, you're not adding much, are you?' observed

Julia tartly. 'You'd do much better to put a few flowers in the rooms and offer some bacon for breakfast.'

She took herself off to bed and spent the next hour feeling ashamed of herself. She would apologise in the morning.

Which she did, for she was a kind-hearted girl even if her temper was a little out of hand at times. Her landlady ignored the apology, reminded her that she must be out of the house by ten o'clock and offered a boiled egg, not quite cold and rock-solid, and toast burnt at the edges.

There was no sign of her when Julia left the house. She had presented the bill at breakfast, waited while Julia paid, and then gone out of the room without a word.

A bad start to the day, thought Julia, although it had its funny side too. Only there was no one to laugh with her about it—the Professor for preference...

But once in the little room behind the shop she felt better. The odds and ends of furniture and the cheerful carpet and curtains made it quite cosy. She went into the tiny kitchen and arranged her few saucepans on the wall shelf and put the kettle on for a cup of coffee. There was no room for a table, only a worktop over the two small cupboards. Later, she promised herself, she would give the walls a coat of cheerful paint. She went through the shower room and loo and opened the back door. The patch of garden outside was neglected but the fences were sound and there was plenty of room for a wash-line.

The day went quickly; by the time she had made her

bed and unpacked her things it was noon. She stocked her cupboard after lunch, made a cup of tea and sat by the gas fire drinking it. Tomorrow she would arrange the window, and then she would open the shop.

She phoned Ruth and Monica in the morning, after a sound night's sleep in her new bed, and warned them that until she had the phone connected they weren't to worry if she didn't ring for a day or two. The nearest phone box wasn't far away, but it would mean locking up the shop to go to it and she didn't want to miss the chance of a customer.

The window looked attractive, she thought: a small display of knitting wools, embroidery silks and patterns, tapestry for canvas work, a little pyramid of coloured sewing thread… She sat behind the counter and watched people passing. Some stopped to look in but no one came into the shop. 'Well,' said Julia, 'I didn't expect anyone on the first day.'

Ruth and Monica had sent cards of good wishes, and Mrs Beckett had sent her a letter. The Professor, apprised of the opening date by Nanny, had restrained himself from rushing out and ordering six dozen red roses.

Julia had her first customer on the following day; an elderly woman came in and, after deliberation, bought a reel of sewing thread.

Her first customer and hopefully the start of many more.

Julia closed her little shop for the day and had tea and crumpets round the fire. The days were drawing in and the evenings were chilly; the housewives of Sherborne would be thinking of quiet evenings with their knitting or embroidery...

She hadn't expected instant success, but as the days went by with a mere trickle of customers her initial euphoria gave way to doubts which she did her best to keep at bay. Perhaps the ladies of Sherborne didn't knit? Perhaps they needed a little encouragement? She dressed the little window in a different fashion, with half-finished knitting arranged with careful careless-ness in the corner, an almost complete tapestry oppo-site, and between them a basket filled with everything a knitter or needlewoman might need. And that brought customers—not many, not nearly enough!—but it was early days yet, she told herself.

Monica and George drove over to see her, and she led them round the shop and house, assuring them that everything was fine and that she was happier than she had been for years.

'So why does she look like that?' demanded Monica of her George as they drove back home. 'As though her world has come to an end? Oh, I know she was laugh-ing and talking nineteen to the dozen, but that's not like her.' She frowned. 'Do you suppose...?'

George said, 'I agree that she isn't happy, but since she was at such pains to conceal that from us I feel that we should respect that.'

'She's in love,' said Monica, to which George said nothing. He was fond of his sister-in-law but she was a fiercely independent young woman. Any efforts to alter that, he considered, weren't for him or her sisters.

Monica, on the phone to Ruth, voiced her concern.

'And George says we mustn't interfere,' she added, with which Ruth agreed.

She wouldn't interfere, but she might drop a hint. She couldn't help but notice that whenever she saw the Professor he never once mentioned Julia. Ruth, sharing Mevrouw van der Maes' opinion that the best of men could be tiresome at times, bided her time.

A senior consultant at the hospital was retiring and she and Thomas had been invited to attend his farewell party—a sober affair, with sherry and morsels of this and that handed round on trays. Once the speeches had been made there was ample opportunity to mingle and chat. It took a little while to get the Professor to herself, and she wasted no time.

One or two remarks about the retiring consultant, a brief enquiry as to when Gerard would be going to Holland again, and then Ruth came to the point in what she hoped was a roundabout manner.

'So you're going to Holland…?'

She glanced up at him. He loomed over her, the picture of ease and she added, 'I expect you will go to your dear little cottage. That was a lovely holiday; Julia loved it too. She's quite settled, you know.'

'Sherborne is a charming little town, I'm told. I hear she has set up shop.'

Ruth gaped at him. 'You know? Who told you? She made us promise not to tell…'

He smiled down at her worried face. 'I thought that might be the case. It wasn't too difficult to discover where she was living.'

'Why do you want to know? I mean, you're not—that

is, I didn't think that you liked each other much, even though you were always there when she needed someone.' She touched his sleeve. 'I'm sorry—I shouldn't have said anything. Only she's my sister and I love her very much.'

Two dignified members of the hospital committee were about to join them. 'So do I,' said the Professor gravely, and he turned to greet them.

She had no chance to speak to him again, and when a few days later she asked Thomas in a purposely vague manner if he had gone to Holland, Thomas answered just as vaguely that he was still at the hospital. 'Catching up on his work,' he added, but didn't mention that his chief was busy because he was planning a few days off.

Monica, at the other end of the phone, agreed that there was nothing to be done. 'Julia can be as stubborn as a mule; if she got even a hint of all this she'd shut the shop and disappear. And as for Gerard, he'll sort everything out in his own good time. When you think about it, it's inevitable, isn't it? Only they've been at cross purposes ever since they met, haven't they? And they are so obviously suited to each other...'

A week later, on a fine, bright and chilly morning, the Professor bade Mrs Potts goodbye and, with Wilf and Robbie curled up in the back of the car, drove away from London going west.

Julia, totting up the week's takings, had to admit that business was slow. There had been several customers but none of them had bought more than a skein of wool or some embroidery silks. Even her simple arithmetic told her that she was running at a loss… And she had been open for three weeks now.

She rearranged the window display and added a notice that garments could be knitted, telling herself that it might be several months before she was established, then she made herself a cup of coffee, determined not to be downhearted.

She was rewarded not half an hour later by a customer who bought three ounces of wool and some knitting needles, and she was followed by a cross-looking woman who wanted a knitting pattern. She spent a long time sifting through the little pile Julia offered her, choosing with as much care as someone spending hundreds of pounds on a purchase. She still hadn't made up her mind when the shop door opened again and the Professor walked in.

Julia gave a gasp and the woman looked round and then back at the patterns. None of them, she told Julia, were what she wanted. She would do better if she went to a larger shop. And she swept out of the door.

The Professor eased his bulk from the door to the counter, his head bowed to prevent it coming in contact with the ceiling, and the little place was all at once overcrowded.

He said blandly, 'I hope that the rest of your customers are more profitable than that one!'

Julia glared at him. Her heart had turned over and leapt into her throat and she had only just managed to get it back where it belonged. She supposed that being in love made one feel giddy. But she was cross too; walking in like that without so much as a 'hello'—and if he hadn't then the woman might have bought something.

He leaned on the counter, disarranging the pile of patterns.

He said, 'You ran away...'

'I did no such thing. I have always wanted to own a shop and be independent...'

He leaned over the counter, opened the till drawer and looked at the handful of small change in it. 'Well,' he observed genially. 'You own a shop, but are you independent? Is that today's takings?'

It was a temptation to fib, but somehow she couldn't lie to him even if it was about something trivial. She said, 'The week's.'

He closed the drawer. 'It's a lovely day; will you have lunch with me?' And when she hesitated he asked, 'Have you ever been to Stourhead? There's a splendid lake there, with ducks and magnificent trees and all the peace in the world.'

He smiled slowly. 'Just for an hour or two? You must close for lunch; an extra hour won't make too much difference.'

'Well, it would be nice, but I must be back for the afternoon.'

She came from behind the counter and turned 'Open' to 'Closed' on the door, and asked, with her back to him, 'Are you on holiday?'

'Yes, for a day or two.'

'You aren't going to Holland?'

'Yes, but not immediately.'

She said, 'I won't be long—I must get a jacket.'

She opened the door to the living room. 'If you'll wait here…'

She left him there and went up to her room, found a jacket and sensible shoes, poked at her hair and added lipstick and went downstairs. She was out of her mind, she told herself, seeing him sitting in the armchair, looking as though he belonged there. She wondered why he had come and how he had known where she was. Perhaps he intended to tell her that he was going back to Holland for good, to marry and live in his lovely old house in Amsterdam.

Doubtless she would be told over their lunch.

He had parked the car at the end of the little street and she was surprised and pleased to see Wilf and Robbie side by side in the back of the Rolls.

The Professor popped her into the car and got in beside her.

'We'll go to Stourhead; these two need a good walk.' He drove out of the town carrying on the kind of conversation which needed no deep thought and few replies. Their way took them through a quiet countryside with few villages and only the small town of Wincanton halfway. It was a bright day, and autumn had coloured the trees and hedges. The approach to the estate, with tantalising glimpses of its magnificent trees and shrubs over the high stone wall bordering the narrow road, was like a great tunnel, opening into a narrow lane leading to the gates.

There was a pub on one side, and a house or two on the other, and Gerard turned into the car park by the pub.

'We can lunch here. Shall we have coffee and then take the dogs for a walk? There's plenty of time.'

'Yes, please, I'd like that. Will Wilf and Robbie be allowed inside?' She looked down at the two whiskered faces and said, 'I never imagined that you would have dogs like these two.' And then went red because she had spoken her thoughts out loud and they had sounded rude.

He smiled a little. 'Neither did I; sometimes things happen whether one wants them or not. I wouldn't part with them now for a small fortune.'

They were walking to the pub entrance. 'And they're company for Mrs Potts when you're in Holland. Will you take them with you when you leave England?'

'They will go where I go,' he told her, and opened the pub door.

There was no one in the bar, but the cheerful man who was stacking glasses wished them good day and had no objection to Wilf and Robbie—and certainly, he told them cheerfully, they could have coffee.

I shouldn't be here, reflected Julia. I ought not to have come. But she knew that nothing would have stopped her; she felt as though she had left her mundane life behind and had gone through a door into a world where there was no one but Gerard. And this really is the last time, she told herself, forgetting how many times she had already said that.

The Professor, watching her thoughts showing so clearly on her face, had his own thoughts, but all he said was, 'Shall we go? If we walk all round the lake it will take an hour or so.'

There was a church by the pub, small and old, and while Gerard got their tickets from the kiosk at the gate she wandered up the path between the ancient tombstones and peered through its open door. It was beautiful inside, quiet with the quietness of centuries, and there were flowers everywhere. Presently she felt the weight of Gerard's arm on her shoulders and they stood together without speaking, then turned and went down the path together.

The dogs were waiting patiently, so they each took a lead and started along the path round the lake, not hurrying; there was too much to see—towering trees, bushes and shrubs, ducks on the water and, hidden away from the path, Grecian temples and presently a waterfall, and a wooden bridge under which there were shoals of small fish. They didn't talk much, but every now and then Julia clutched Gerard's arm to point out something she wanted him to see.

There weren't many people there and it was quiet save for the birds. They found the grotto presently, at the bottom of narrow steps, and then walked the short distance back to the gates.

There were a few people in the pub now, but they found a table in a window and Wilf and Robbie, refreshed with water and a biscuit, curled up at their feet while they ate a Ploughman's lunch and emptied a pot of coffee. And Julia, munching warm bread and cheese, didn't think of the past or the future, only the happy present.

She looked up and caught his eye. 'I feel happy,' she told him seriously, a remark which brought a gleam to his eye.

He drove her back to Sherborne presently, talking easily about their walk, and discussing what they had seen. When they got to the shop, he got out and unlocked the door for her, listened to her thanks, assured her that he had enjoyed himself as much as she had and then bade her a cheerful goodbye.

She watched him drive away and went through the shop and sat down in the living room. She wanted very much to have a good cry, but a customer might come. No one came. She locked the door at half past five and made herself a pot of tea. She wasn't hungry, and the memory of the Ploughman's lunch, eaten so contentedly in the Professor's company, would serve for her supper.

Of course she didn't sleep; she lay awake thinking of him driving back to London. He had had a free day and, having discovered where she was, had made her the purpose of a drive into the country. He had wished her goodbye in a most casual manner; now he had seen for himself where she was he would lose all interest— if he'd had any in the first place. But he had been kind to her on several occasions; perhaps he felt under an obligation to Thomas…

She dropped off to sleep at last and woke with a start. The shop doorbell was ringing—the postman must be getting impatient. She got into her dressing gown and slippers and hurried to the door, not stopping to pull up the blind.

Wilf and Robbie trotted in, and hard on their heels was the Professor. He shut the door behind him, turned the key in the lock and then stood for a moment, looking down at her sleepy face and tangled mane of hair.

He had had a sleepless night too, but there was no sign of that in his quiet face.

He gathered her into his arms. 'Tell me truly,' he begged. 'Are you happy here?'

She shook her head against his chest.

'Then would you consider marrying me? I have waited patiently for you to make a career for yourself, for it seemed to me that that was what you wanted more than anything else. But there is a limit to a man's patience and I am at the end of mine. But you have only to say, Go away, and I will go.'

Julia sniffed back tears as she mumbled, 'Don't go. Please don't go.' And then, 'You shouldn't be here; its seven o'clock in the morning. And if you love me, why didn't you say so? And I don't want to be independent. Only there wasn't anything else and I thought you didn't like me.'

'My darling,' said the Professor soothingly. 'Let us get one thing straight. I fell in love with you when we first met, although perhaps I didn't realise that at once. I have never stopped loving you and I never shall.'

'Really?' She looked up into his face and smiled at what she saw there.

'Really,' said the Professor, and bent to kiss her.

It was quite a while before she went upstairs to dress, leaving Gerard to put the kettle on and let the dogs into the little back garden. Her head was a jumble of thoughts: they would marry just as soon as possible; she would go back to London with him that morning; she was not to worry about the shop, he would deal with that; they would live in his lovely old house in Amsterdam. But none of these were important. The one thought which filled her head was that he loved her. She bundled up her hair, dashed powder on her nose and ran downstairs to tell him once again that she loved him too.

* * * * *

*After escaping her abusive ex, Cassie Zetticci is
thankful for a job and a safe place to stay at the
Gallant Lake Resort. Nick West makes her nervous
with his restless energy, but when he starts teaching her
self-defense, Cassie begins to see a future that involves
roots and community. But can Nick let go of his own
difficult past to give Cassie the freedom she needs?*

Read on for a sneak preview of
A Man You Can Trust,
*the first book—and Harlequin Special Edition debut!—
in Jo McNally's new miniseries, Gallant Lake Stories.*

"Why are you armed with pepper spray? Did something
happen to you?"

She didn't look up.

"Yes. Something happened."

"Here?"

She shook her head, her body trembling so badly
she didn't trust her voice. The only sound was Nick's
wheezing breath. He finally cleared his throat.

"Okay. Something happened." His voice was gravelly
from the pepper spray, but it was calmer than it had been
a few minutes ago. "And you wanted to protect yourself.
That's smart. But you need to do it right. I'll teach you."

Her head snapped up. He was doing his best to look at her, even though his left eye was still closed.

"What are you talking about?"

"I'll teach you self-defense, Cassie. The kind that actually works."

"Are you talking karate or something? I thought the pepper spray…"

"It's a tool, but you need more than that. If some guy's amped up on drugs, he'll just be temporarily blinded and really ticked off." He picked up the pepper spray canister from the grass at her side. "This stuff will spray up to ten feet away. You never should have let me get so close before using it."

"I didn't know that."

"Exactly." He grimaced and swore again. "I need to get home and dunk my face in a bowl full of ice water." He stood and reached a hand down to help her up. She hesitated, then took it.

Don't miss
A Man You Can Trust *by Jo McNally,*
available September 2019 wherever
Harlequin® Special Edition books and ebooks are sold.

www.Harlequin.com

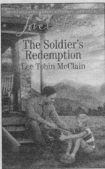
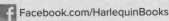
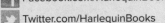

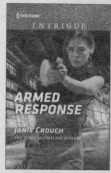

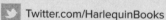
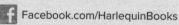

Looking for inspiration in tales
of hope, faith and heartfelt romance?

Check out **Love Inspired**® and
Love Inspired® **Suspense** books!

New books available every month!

Love Harlequin romance?

DISCOVER.

Be the first to find out about promotions, news and exclusive content!

Facebook.com/HarlequinBooks

Twitter.com/HarlequinBooks

Instagram.com/HarlequinBooks

Pinterest.com/HarlequinBooks

ReaderService.com

EXPLORE.

Sign up for the Harlequin e-newsletter and download a free book from any series at **TryHarlequin.com.**

CONNECT.

Join our Harlequin community to share your thoughts and connect with other romance readers!
Facebook.com/groups/HarlequinConnection

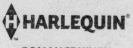

HARLEQUIN®

ROMANCE WHEN YOU NEED IT